CW01509806

MINOTAUR

Peter Goldsworthy grew up in various Australian country towns, finishing his schooling in Darwin. After graduating in medicine from the University of Adelaide in 1974 he worked for several years in alcohol and drug rehabilitation, but since then has divided his working time between general practice and writing. He has won major literary awards across a range of genres: poetry, short story, novels, theatre, and opera libretti.

ALSO BY PETER GOLDSWORTHY

Poetry
Readings from Ecclesiastes
This Goes With This
This Goes With That: Selected Poems, 1970–1990
If, Then
New Selected Poems
The Rise of the Machines and Other Love Poems
Anatomy of a Metaphor

Short Fiction
Archipelagoes
Zooing
Bleak Rooms
Little Deaths
The List of All Answers: Collected Stories
Gravel

Novels
Maestro
Magpie (with Brian Matthews)
Honk If You Are Jesus
Wish
Keep It Simple, Stupid
Jesus Wants Me For a Sunbeam
Three Dog Night
Everything I Knew

Libretti
Summer of the Seventeenth Doll
Batavia
The Ringtone Cycle
Ned Kelly

Stage Adaptations
Honk If You Are Jesus (with Martin Laud Gray)
Maestro (with Anna Goldsworthy)

Non-fiction
Navel Gazing
His Stupid Boyhood: A Memoir

MINOTAUR

PETER GOLDSWORTHY

VIKING
an imprint of
PENGUIN BOOKS

VIKING

UK | USA | Canada | Australia
India | New Zealand | South Africa | China

Penguin Books is part of the Penguin Random House group of companies
whose addresses can be found at global.penguinrandomhouse.com.

Penguin
Random House
Australia

First published by Penguin Random House Australia Pty Ltd 2019

Text copyright © Peter Goldsworthy 2019

The moral right of the author has been asserted.

All rights reserved. No part of this publication may be reproduced, published, performed in
public or communicated to the public in any form or by any means without prior written
permission from Penguin Random House Australia Pty Ltd or its authorised licensees.

This novel is a work of fiction. The names, characters and incidents are the product of the
author's imagination, and all dialogue and interaction between the characters are entirely
fictional. Any resemblance to actual persons, living or dead, is entirely coincidental.

Cover image by CSA Printstock/Shutterstock.com
Cover design by Alex Ross © Penguin Random House Australia Pty Ltd
Typeset in Adobe Garamond by Midland Typesetters, Australia
Printed and bound in Australia by Griffin Press, part of Ovato, an accredited
ISO AS/NZ 14001 Environmental Management Systems printer.

A catalogue record for this
book is available from the
National Library of Australia

ISBN 978 0 14379 569 8

penguin.com.au

For Andrew Male, ex-cop, who taught me The Job;
and Daniel Earle, still blind, who taught me how to tap.
And for James Muecke and Sight For All, who are fighting
blindness in mainstream and Aboriginal communities of Australia and
in many of the poorest countries in the world, and for whom it is an
undeserved privilege to serve as an ambassador.

sightforall.org

I

SMELL

1

WHERE WAS I?

In bed, obviously. Willow's bed – that much also obvious. In Willow's secret hideaway. But where was that?

A heavy gear-change in a nearby street. Truck? Bus? A clue, at any rate: a main road.

'We'll have to sublet the place,' I whispered into the nape of her neck.

'Hmm?' she murmured, hard to rouse at the best of times, let alone in the wake of a flotilla of margaritas.

Time was easier to nail down than place: Friday, sometime around dawn. The first traffic starting to hum, the early birds making early music outside.

Inside, the night-owl – me – hadn't slept a wink. 'How long is your lease? Six months? Twelve?'

'What time is it?' she said, still three-quarters asleep.

'Who cares?'

'I care, Big Nose. Go back to sleep.'

Easier said than done; I'd slept enough in Emergency to last a month. 'I like the new bed,' I burbled on. 'You can bring the bed. And the sheets. *Love* the satin sheets.'

And the musk between the sheets. Bring those musks: the fish-spice of sex, the after-trace of perfume, the bass-note of sweat. Her small, compact body glowed with heat; the bed was an oven of scents. I nuzzled my big, surprisingly loveable nose into her neck, gratefully; it had been too long.

'Bring them where?' she said, rolling towards me.

'Home, of course.'

I found her lips and kissed them: their boozy morning-after sourness was also part of who she was. Who *we* were, once upon a time. The taste of the dumplings she had steamed, drunkenly, at midnight were also in the mix somewhere: faint ginger, a prickle of chilli, whether on her lips, or mine, or both. I'd pictured her face in my mind's eye every night we'd been apart; I'd summoned back every inch of her body as best I could, but in the end those memories, *all* memories, were as shallow as dreams. Like dreams, they had no smell to them, no taste, no touch. No body heat.

And no voice. 'This is my home now, Big Nose,' she said, pulling away.

'I can hardly move in here,' I said, lost in happy stupidity.

'Richard, listen . . .'

The formal name-change jarred, but not enough. 'It would take a year to fit the place out.'

I sensed she was searching my face. 'No one's moving anywhere. Richard.'

'I thought . . . After last night.'

'Last night changes nothing.'

Plain words, but I tried to find less plain meanings. 'I don't follow. Why did you bring me here?'

'You signed yourself out, remember? Against medical advice. You were in no fit state to go home.'

'But fit enough to share your bed?'

'That wasn't meant to happen,' she continued in the same calm, matter-of-fact way she always spelt things out. 'I drank too much. You know what I'm like. I'm sorry.' She paused, then squeezed my flaccid cock, also matter-of-factly. 'At least you know it's working again.'

My fingers found her wrist, gripped it. 'What's that supposed to mean? You lure me home for a mercy fuck, then dump me *again*? You promised me it was temporary. We just needed time apart.'

The cock was released, the wrist tugged free; she rolled abruptly out of bed and out of reach.

'Where are you going?'

'I can't be near you when you're angry, Richard,' she said with that same measured calmness.

'You think I'd *hurt* you? After all you've been through?'

Was this the stupidest thing I'd said so far? I regretted the words as soon as they left my mouth.

'You broke my nose,' she said. 'Remember?'

'I couldn't even *see* your nose!'

'It wasn't the first time you'd lashed out,' she said, then added that same calm infuriating word: 'Remember?'

Anger Management Step One: count to ten. I got as far as three. 'It was the first time you got in the *way*! How many times do I have to apologise? It was an accident.'

'Just like the pills were an accident?'

'You think I took them deliberately?'

'I can't do this now,' she said, and pulled on some rustling item of clothing. A silk kimono, probably. Everything in her refuge seemed made of silk. Or satin. 'I'm late for handover,' she added. 'And I've got a splitting headache.'

'I said, you think I tried to *top* myself?'

Heavier items of clothing began hitting the quilt next to me, stirring the air, faintly. 'Only you know the answer to that, Richard. Get dressed. Please. I'll drop you at the Night Shelter on my way.'

Our wild night together might never have happened; she was back in daytime rational get-things-done-mode. Chinese mode, she'd often joked in the days when I'd loved both sides of her split brain.

'I can find my own way to the Night Shelter,' I said, and began tugging on clothes, only to get bits of my anatomy in the wrong holes and tug them off again.

Which further enraged me. 'It disgusted you so much to make love to a blind man?'

'What disgusts me is being *hit* by a blind man.'

I wrestled with the clothes a little longer, trying not to say what I said next. 'Are you fucking someone else?'

A weary yawn; I sensed she was rubbing her eyes. One memory that never fades: those almond eyes, their heavy upper lids so perfectly sculpted they might have been glued on each morning along with the big lashes. A million of them in the country these days, and billions further north, but hers still as rare as ever.

At least in my particular mind's eye.

'Not that again,' she said.

'Who is it? Who are you fucking?'

'I just fucked you, remember? And before that – guess who? You! Again! Even if it's so long ago you've bloody well forgotten!'

At last, a little passion. A deadly combination when she was on song: eyes narrowed against the dust and glare of the Mongolian steppes, mouth broadened by the western suburbs of Adelaide. Part of me wanted to kiss her again, on the mouth and the eyes; but most of me just wanted to lash out.

'How do you live with yourself? Walking out on a blind man? What do you *tell* people?'

No answer. She was rummaging in her bedside drawer, a sound as familiar as those that followed: the tearing of tinfoil, the two aspirins fizzing in the glass of water.

When she spoke she was matter-of-fact again. 'I tell them what I tell myself. I sat by his hospital bed every day for a month. I took a year off my studies when he finally came home. Remember?'

That word again; I forced myself to stay silent.

'I loved him, comforted him. Tough love at times, but only when needed. I nursed him through his rages. His self-pity. Through all those times when *he* wouldn't fuck *me*. And how did he repay me?'

She paused and drank the dissolved aspirins, calmly.

I was anything but. '*Repay* you? What was I? A business investment?'

'I drove him to blind school,' she methodically ticked off more key performance indicators. 'To dog training. Those writing classes the shrink recommended.'

My T-shirt and jeans had found their correct limbs at last; my jacket followed. 'Through thick and through thin,' I said, 'in sickness and in health,' then added my own short-arm jab: 'Remember?'

'You think I didn't try, Richard? You were a full-time job, but I didn't mind.' At least she was talking to me now, not about some business plan. 'I just wanted my husband back. Who drove you kicking and screaming to anger management? Fat lot of good that did. No one could ever tell you a thing. Least of all me. And you're *still* too blind to see it!'

A figure of speech, yes, but no slip of the tongue. Willow's tongue never slipped, at least before margarita hour.

'Figure of speech,' she echoed my thoughts with her usual ease. 'So don't go adding that to your list of grievances.'

I felt about on the floor for my boots with the blunt, stubby fingers of my feet. And biting my own slippery tongue. She knew me too well. She knew everything too well.

'Here,' she said, and laid my cane across my thighs.

I swept it, clattering, onto the floor.

'My point exactly,' she said. 'There's nothing as precious to you as a grievance, is there?'

'I was in intensive *care* a day ago! I nearly died!'

'You *slept*, Richard. For a couple of days. A handful of sleepers was never going to kill you.'

Her logic was implacable; I felt trapped, shut in, about to explode. 'That so? Well, maybe it won't be pills next time!'

'The truth,' she said. 'Finally. It *was* deliberate.'

Bedroom eyes, a hippie name, boozy morning-after breath – but a mind like a steel trap. I jerked upright, desperate to escape, collided with a wall, groped for the door and did a fingernail on the jamb.

'You'll be sorry!' I shouted as I stepped through the doorway.

Ridiculous words, but the echoes proved useful. Short voice-bounce ahead, long bounces left and right: a narrow passage. But which end was the front door? Cue another truck, rumbling by, stage-left; I turned in that direction. A great fist seemed to be squeezing my chest; I needed air.

'Hang on, you stubborn idiot. You forgot your boots.'

'Fuck off!' I said as I found the handle of the front door and yanked it open.

'At least take your stick, Richard.'

I thrust my left hand, palm up, behind me as I stepped out; the folded cane was smacked into it like a relay baton.

'I've missed you,' she said. 'But I needed some space. I needed some time *out*. After this little performance, I think I still need it.'

'Take as much time as you like,' I said.

I shook the cane out, snapped it straight, tapped the edge of a narrow porch, and stepped down. A residue of sense in me, at least: shoes I could live without, even Willow I might learn to live without – maybe – but not my trusty cane.

2

SOUNDS: THE HARD ACOUSTIC OF THE HOUSE BEHIND ME, a softer world ahead, echo-free and already fuzzy round the edges with bee-buzz.

Smells: the cloying sweetness of jasmine to the left. A faint savoury rock-pool stink – prawn heads in a garbage can? – somewhere to the right.

She didn't eat seafood; had she been serving aphrodisiacs to her new boyfriend? Such was my state of mind, I would have gone through her garbage given a pair of working eyes. Instead I tapped a low picket front-fence, found the gate, fingered the latch, and walked through into the street.

Which street? Willow had kept her address secret all these months. I sniffed for more clues. Not a main road after all, it seemed: no trace of diesel in the after-trail of jasmine. No exhaust fumes of any kind.

Time to swallow my pride and ask for help. I turned my mouth to my collar microphone. 'Current location, Siri?'

No answer. The sisterhood, sticking together? The truth was less dramatic: she was powered down. I tugged her from the belt holster, thumb-printed the on-button, reholstered her, and repeated the question.

'246A Wakefield Street,' came the familiar, soothing contralto. 'Adelaide.'

'So much for sisterhood solidarity,' I said.

'I'm not sure I understand, Richard.'

'Don't even try. I need you in my corner. Drop pin, current location.'

'Pin dropped. Name pin?'

'Gotcha,' I said, and tapped away along the footpath, still barefoot but so angrily pleased with myself I hardly noticed. 'Chez Gotcha.'

'Show Gotcha may be beyond my abilities at the moment, Richard.'

I had to laugh. 'It's good to hear your voice,' I said, not for the first time.

'Flatterer,' she said, also not for the first time.

In fact I was mostly flattering myself. I chose hers from a range of voices, male and female. High-pitched voices carry further, I told myself at the time, but maybe I just craved extra female company. We've lived in each other's pockets ever since, on her side literally. Each time we step out the door it's a kind of date.

'At least *you've* stuck by me,' I told my date.

'Your satisfaction is all the thanks I need, Richard.'

I managed another gruff laugh, if less at her nonsense than mine. I might as well have taken comfort from a talking parrot on my shoulder. Plenty of candidates for that job were feeding in the trees above me: lorikeets hinge-squeaking at each other as I tapped closer; cockatoos squawking from higher branches further off. A waspy scooter engine burst into life behind me, revved once, then buzzed my way. I quickened my pace but there was no escape.

'Come down off your high horse, Big Nose,' Willow said, drawing abreast. 'And jump on mine. Please.'

'At the risk of repeating myself: fuck off.'

'I'll pretend I didn't hear that, Richard,' Siri whispered in my ear, supportively.

'At least take your boots, you stubborn git,' from Willow.

'You can chuck them over the nearest powerline, for all I care.'

The thought amused me, despite myself: a little reminder dangling in her face each time she stepped out her unlisted front door. I would have done it myself, if it wouldn't have taken me all day.

'No powerlines in the city since 1989,' she said in her calm, know-all manner. It might have been Siri speaking, if not for the last word: 'Remember?'

She braked and pulled into the kerb; I stalked on.

'I'll leave them back here,' she called after me. 'By the light-pole. Your socks are tucked inside.' She revved her engine, and drew along-side again. 'I love you, Richard,' she said, matter-of-factly, 'but I can't live with you until you see yourself more clearly.' Then she U-turned, and buzzed off in the other direction.

'Go to hell,' I muttered. 'And take your figures of speech with you.'

'You have religion,' Siri murmured from my collar, 'but I only have silicon.'

She'd picked the wrong time for another joke, even one I hadn't heard before. 'Find route. Current location to RSPCA Night Shelter,' I said, and tapped on, following instructions.

A bicycle squeaked towards me – *Gotcha, Gotcha* – passed by then stopped.

'Excuse me, Sir! Sir! Are these your boots by the light-pole?'

A boy scout voice, on the verge of breaking; I tapped on, ignoring it. The bike hit the ground with a clatter; a pair of footsteps came jogging in my wake.

'Hey, Mister! Here, behind you! I think I've found your boots.'

Persistent little do-gooder. 'Piss off,' I said, 'or I'll tell the scoutmaster you ripped them off a blind man.'

The footsteps stopped dead. He hadn't picked a good day for a good deed. 'Just trying to help, Sir.'

'You want to help? Chuck them over the powerlines.'

A pause, then a puzzled, 'There are no powerlines in this street, Sir.'

I kept walking, barefoot, leaving the Boy Samaritan in my wake wearing an expression on his face (I could picture it clearly enough) as if his good deed had exploded across it like a trick cigar.

The thought cheered me a little more. I'd given him a hard time, yes, but I'd also given him one hell of a story to tell. It was my own good deed for the day, in a way. Bad intentions, but goodish outcome. Might the road to heaven, the road *back* to heaven, be paved with bad intentions? My amusement at this riff lasted only a few more steps. Bad choice of metaphor, given my unshod feet. The day was warming fast: the rough chemical reek of bitumen rising from the road, the paving beginning to scorch my soles.

'Hutt Street twenty paces,' Siri piped up.

'Tell me something I don't know,' I said, having caught the faint diesel-spoor of the bus route at last.

'Knowledge is good, Richard,' she said, cheerily unperturbed. 'Can you be more specific?'

I tapped the base of the traffic-light pole, pressed the walk-button. 'The way to a woman's heart?'

'Interesting question.'

'Do tell,' I said as the walk tone bleeped, and I stepped down onto the burning bitumen and crossed over, gingerly, my feet already toast.

3

'MISSED ME THEN, GIRL?'

The dog licked at my blistered feet, too busy to answer. Siri, a little hard of hearing at times, answered instead: 'Current location: home.'

Right answer, wrong question – and a little light on details. Precise current location: flopped in my armchair in the family room, cold beer in hand, making small talk with a dog and a device. Who also happened to be my only remaining family members: one a voice lacking a body, the other a body lacking a voice.

'I need to hug you, Siri.'

'I'm sorry, Richard. Did you say you need to argue?'

I managed a brief chuckle. 'Either would be fine. Though preferably not at the same time.'

There was more chance of either, or both, with the dog. 'Good girl,' I said, as her healing tongue rasped on.

'Current location . . .'

'You too, girl.'

We made a sorry threesome, but it helped to joke about it.

'One for all,' I said, 'and all for one, eh team?'

'I'm sorry, Richard. I don't understand the question.'

The dog understood – the creed of the wolf-pack being hardwired into her genes – but she was too busy applying her healing salve to comment. Had she been fed at the Night Shelter? If not, she'd need something more filling than shreds of asphalt-flavoured human skin.

'Don't acquire a taste for it, girl,' I told her.

'I don't quite understand,' the other girl answered. 'Don't require a taste for what?'

'Long pig.'

'I'm not sure what you mean.'

'Human flesh.'

'I leave the eating to you, Richard. I run purely on the desire to serve.'

'What? Batteries not included?'

After rebooting my feet – an old work-pair from the back of the wardrobe – I excavated a frypan from the cluttered sink, scraped it clean, and fried up a small alp of bacon and eggs. Cooking can be fraught for the blind, but it didn't come much easier than this. Or more deeply satisfying. The food smells lifted my spirits; I turned the heat down and dawdled over the pan, soaking myself in a sense-world made of nothing but the aroma and spittery hiss of frying bacon. The dog whined and nudged my thigh, and kept nudging till I split the pan between two plates and set one on the floor and one on the table. The calorie-heavy food re-energised me, but also seemed to fuel my restlessness. My head was still all over the place, sorry for myself one minute, angry the next – with Willow, with the world, but increasingly, as always, with myself. I packed a pipe with the usually reliable antidote, lit up and sucked, but without useful effect.

'Music, Siri,' I said. 'Something to soothe the savage beast.'

'Do you mean soothe the savage breast, Richard?'

'Pedant. You know what I mean.'

The music started up instantly: a slow-rising, slow-falling Ray Charles ballad, bluetoothed from the speakers in the high corners of every room. Still restless, I walked out through the kitchen-cum-family room and into the back shed. My nose – my big Neanderthal nose – was all I needed to tell me where I was: a sweaty male lair. I don't know why I still call it the shed, maybe for old time's sake. I knocked the old shed down when we renovated – a house of rusty tin cards – and built a brick double garage across the width of the block at the back. Once my pride and joy, a fully tooled-up workroom, its only use now was as an occasional work-out room. But somewhere deep inside it was still my shed, at least. *My* refuge. I pulled on the gloves and went the distance with the heavy bag, then dropped to the mat for push-ups and crunches and more push-ups and more crunches until my wobbly arms would no longer support me.

I lay there, spent, as Siri shuffled one slow track after another from her deck. The music that rained gently down from above seemed more plaintive than soothing, if only because the thoughts that began to creep back into my head were of Willow. I might be emptied of anger and self-pity, but not apparently of hope. Might she have left a message?

'Phone on, Siri.'

The music stopped, the dial tone burred loudly from above.

'Message-bank,' I said.

'You have three new messages. Message received today, at 9.45 am.'

So much for hope; the first voice was male: 'Jones-Hill *again*, Mr Zadow. I've now left several calls. We have a considerable investment in your dog; as you know she is not a pet. I would refer you to the terms of your dog user's contract. Paragraph 3a, Conditions of Lease.'

'Delete message,' I said.

'Message deleted. Message received yesterday, 8.30 pm . . . Ken Jones-Hill, Richard. I left a message last night. The matter is getting urgent, and we've been very patient. Especially as you have failed to attend three scheduled performance reviews.'

'Delete message,' I shouted as the rage rolled back over me. 'Delete *all* messages!'

I jumped to my feet, jammed the gloves back on my fists, located the bag with an arc of jabs, and began the rites of forgetting all over again.

4

SOUNDS: A RAPID-FIRE THREE-RAP KNOCK ON A DOOR, BUT faraway, through the fog of sleep.

Where was I? A bed, obviously. But not mine. And not Willow's. Smells: nothing but my own stale sweat.

Another three raps, more urgent, more impatient. I swung my legs over the edge of the bed and discovered it wasn't a bed but a rubber mat.

Which took time to figure out. Had I slept on the shed floor all night?

'Time please, Siri.'

'5 pm.'

Time and space reset themselves; an afternoon nap, nothing more. I eased myself upright, walked a little stiff-jointedly back through the house and opened the front door.

Then stood there, waiting.

'It's Terry,' came the voice, eventually, 'in case you're wondering.'

I wasn't. It might have been the best part of two years, but I knew. The subliminal whiff of Camel smoke? That signature three-rap knock? Neither clue was conscious. Call it a sixth sense, or just some heightening of my remaining four.

Four fragile twigs, more tightly bundled now, less easily snapped.

'You've got a nerve showing your face around here,' I said.

He exhaled; the smell of tobacco smoke firmed up. Camels, definitely.

'Funny choice of words,' he said, 'for a blind bloke.'

Maybe, but I could see his face well enough in my mind's eye. The flattened boxer's nose, the close-shaven scalp. The grin that never quite included the eyes.

The soft eggs of the eyes.

'Looked dark in there,' he was saying. 'Windows shuttered. Wasn't sure you were home.'

'Don't have much use for lights,' I stated the bleeding obvious.

He took a step closer, and I knew he was sticking out a hand. I still struggle to understand that sixth sense, but I'm learning, slowly, to trust it.

I left the hand dangling; there was no way I was going to offer mine. 'Let there be light,' I said, loudly, instead.

He grunted, impressed. 'Nice party trick. I heard you'd had the place wired up.'

'Everything that opens and shuts, Chief.'

'It works,' he said. 'In case you're wondering.'

Was he trying to provoke me? Or just telling it like it was, matter-of-factly? Either way, I would get no pity from Terry. Which was fine by me.

'I couldn't give a fuck if it worked or not,' I said.

The dog growled softly from somewhere in the house. She doesn't like raised voices, especially mine.

'You look like shit,' he said. 'Now that I can see you properly.'

No pity, but also no apology – which was not so fine. Two years, and still no apology. I wondered how long he'd been lurking out there. Half a packet past four? I saw this in my head also: my former friend pacing back and forth, chain-smoking, scratching at his grizzled dome. Working up the courage.

'Smell like shit too,' he said, and sucked deeply, filling his fastidious nostrils with smoke.

'You should give those away,' I told him.

'And trade up to something stronger?'

Another provocation? I'd worked enough tag-team interviews with Terry over the years to know his tricks, especially his stock-in-trade: keep them off balance. But I hadn't seen this coming. To make another funny choice of words.

'What the fuck's *that* supposed to mean?' I said.

Another growl from inside the house, but Terry remained unperturbed 'You can smoke, snort or shoot up all the shit you like, Zads. Whatever gets you through the night. If it makes your, um, situation easier to bear.'

Who had he been talking to? Police Welfare? The Professor? Someone, at any rate, with a big mouth. I sensed him flick away the fag-end of his own preferred substance of abuse. My fists clenched.

Count to ten, I reminded myself, but this time didn't get past two: 'Get to the fucking point. What are you doing here?'

A gruff bark behind me this time, and the click of nails approaching along the floorboards.

'Nice-looking dog,' he said. 'Had him long?'

'Her.'

'I thought they used Labradors.'

'She's not a guide dog, Chief.'

This was not strictly true, even if she was more best friend than girl guide these days. German Shepherds can be trained, and sometimes even their stubborn owners; it just hadn't worked out with us. I didn't spoil her, the usual reason dogs flunk out of guide school. If anything, it was the opposite: I was too impatient. Like wife, like dog? The thought came out of the blue, but maybe there was some truth in it. Or maybe I just preferred the new GPS navigator to the older, furry sort.

The dog also seemed to like it that way, even if she followed us one step ahead.

'You keep her in the dark too?' from Terry. 'RSPCA might take a dim view of that.'

I might have rewarded him with a groan once, but he was try-ing too hard. 'It's past her bedtime. And mine. So if we could cut to the chase.'

'Hey, girl,' he said, his voice arriving from lower down as he patted her. 'What's her name?'

'Scout. To her friends.'

'Good Scout,' he said, then aimed his mouth back up. 'She's the one who . . . ?'

He stopped mid-sentence, as if he had accidentally said too much. Another interrogation trick? If so, it worked.

'You know about that *too*?'

This time the dog stayed silent. Maybe it's the four-letter words that bother her, not the anger itself. Who was he getting this stuff from? *No* one knew about the overdose, apart from the hospital.

He pretended to be light on details. 'I heard she wouldn't stop barking. Woke the neighbours. Saved your sorry arse.'

The time when we'd been able to say such things to each other – or I'd been able to listen to them – was long gone. And there was some-thing forced in the way he was saying them today: a fake camaraderie. I began counting again, got to five. Anger Management Step Two: I am the only person who can make me angry.

'Hero to zero,' I told him. 'You didn't hear the rest of the story.'

'In fact I liked that bit best. The ambos broke down the door, but she wouldn't let them near you.' Another forced, snorted laugh. 'She was on your side, after all. Respecting your last wish.'

'I couldn't sleep, that's all. Lost count of the pills.'

'If you say so.'

The penny dropped at last. 'Willow told you! Willow fucking *sent* you!'

A volley of barks this time – *Fuck! Fuck! Fuck!* – as if the dog and I were speaking the same pack-language. I sensed Terry take a step back, unsure which of us was about to bite him.

'I sent myself,' he said, quickly. 'Keep your shirt on.'

I was doing my best. Step Three: Don't shoot the messenger. But again the rage was as hot and thick in my throat as vomit.

'Don't take it out on me,' he said, and took another step back, as if I were about to throw up over him, literally. 'Or Willow. Put it to good use.'

'What's that supposed to mean?'

'It means I'm here to offer you a job.'

For a moment I was lost for words. The notion was so stupid it didn't even register. Another trick from the interview room? Time for the good cop to put in an appearance? Or just some way he could work off his guilt?

'WorkCover put you up to this?' I said, eventually. 'That prick of a case manager? Always banging on about meaningful work therapy?'

'All my own idea.'

'You shouldn't even be *talking* to me, Chief! The lawyers would throw the book at you.'

'I don't know about lawyers,' he said. 'But I know about you. You're still a copper.'

'On compo. And only till settlement.'

'You're still drawing a detective sergeant's wage.'

'Two-thirds,' I said. 'The going disability rate. Which is about half a chief inspector's.'

That shut him up. Was it my imagination or could I hear him scratching away at his shaven head? In the days when he had a full head of hair he was forever nicking his chin; when the hair went he began nicking his scalp instead. And worrying at the scabs when he was thinking.

'What did you want me to do, Rick?' he said. 'Refuse promotion because you got injured on the job?'

'I got *shot* on the job,' I reminded him. 'On *your* watch. Remember?'

Silence, apart from the head-scratching, which sounded more agitated.

'Of course I remember,' he said tentatively, 'but with the greatest respect, do you?'

'I was in a coma for three months.'

'Then let me jog your memory,' he said, quietly, 'you got shot because you decided to be a hero. Read the inquest report again.'

'*Read* it?'

'Stupid choice of words. Sorry. Listen to it.'

'I've listened plenty. It gets worse each time. He had a gun to my head. The Starries had a bead on his. It was your call. Why didn't you make it?'

'Hostage protocol, Detective. We were still negotiating.' He fell silent for a moment, as if he were trying to scratch some sense into his thick head. 'You disobeyed my direct order, Zads.'

'You telling me you wouldn't have swapped places if it was *your* wife?'

'Before or after the divorce?' he joked, but this attempt to defuse things only further enraged me.

I stamped my foot on the doorstep. 'He was standing right here,' I shouted, 'with a gun to her head. What's the protocol for that?'

'Negotiate. He was never going to shoot her.'

'Like he was never going to shoot *me*?'

'I tried to stop you.'

'He was the one you had to stop!'

'Okay! Okay!' he shouted back, finally. 'I fucked up! What else do you want me to say? I have to live with that for the rest of my life? True, but so fucking what? It's *nothing* to what you have to live with!'

Silence, after the dog echoes. If ever I were going to take a blind swing it should have been then, but I suddenly felt spent of rage. Perhaps he felt the same, especially as his rage – I saw for the first time – was aimed mostly at himself.

'If it's a guilt trip that brought you here,' I said, 'why didn't you come two years ago?'

A match was struck; he puffed a few times before speaking again. 'Dunno, really. More I put it off, harder it got.' He scratched his head even more frantically, as if trying to dig out a better answer. 'I wrote you a letter. But I never sent it. So you never got to read it.' He snorted, 'Did it again, didn't I? No offence?'

I grunted. 'None taken.'

'Figure of speech. It's hard to avoid them.'

'Welcome to my world,' I said. 'What did the letter say?'

'It said sorry. It said if I could go back and do it again – okay. I'd kill the little cunt. And face the music. But it also said that was easy to say now. In hindsight.'

Stubborn to the last, but half an apology was better than none. I held out my hand, palm up, 'Coffin nail?'

A cigarette was planted between my lips instead. Another match was struck; I bent forward, felt the faint glow of the flame on my face as I sucked. A cooler, smokier glow filled my lungs; I exhaled, and took another suck, finding it soothing.

So,' I said, 'what glittering career path have you got in mind for me? Dog squad? Sniffing out meth labs with Inspector fucking Rex here?'

The four-legged inspector growled, the two-legged inspector chuckled, both on cue. 'Think it over. You might surprise yourself.'

I sensed him standing there, scrutinising me. *Measuring* me. And I had the sudden, certain feeling that a return-to-work plan was not why he had come at all. Nor was his belated apology. Sixth-sense hocus-pocus? More likely I just knew his favourite trick too well. Keep your cards close to your chest. Play the aces last.

'What are you really doing here, Chief?'

Another artificial-sounding chuckle. '*That's* why I could use you. Always a move ahead.' He took the deepest suck at his cigarette yet, as if what he were about to say needed extra breath. 'Perhaps you should sit down.'

How many times had the two of us knocked on doors with those words stuck in our throats? Worst part of the job, but unspeakably worse on the receiving end. My legs wobbled under me, I reached for the doorjamb.

'Willow?' I blurted out. 'Something's happened to Willow? Is she . . . ?'

'What? Shit no! She's fine! As far as I know. Jesus! Sorry. I didn't mean . . .'

He fell silent, as startled by my tone — half panic, half weird thrill — as I was. Where had that come from? I fought to regain composure. I'd revealed too much — to myself as much as to him.

'Just cut to the chase. If it's not Willow, who?'

'Someone you *definitely* wish was dead, Detective.'

Another riddle, but this time easy to answer. 'Tell me it was slow and painful.'

He grunted. 'It's bad news, not good. Which is why you really should sit down.'

'Christ! It's like extracting teeth! Is the little cunt dead or not?'

'Not,' he said, and paused. 'Unless he drowned in the river.'

Yet another riddle? This time I hadn't a clue what he was talking about.

'He's gone walkabout,' he added.

Blindsided again. To reach for the nearest figure of speech. If I was a move ahead, it was nowhere near enough. I needed to be two. Three. *Twenty*-three, which was the number of months a certain convicted cop shooter had spent behind bars. Twenty-three months, twenty-nine days.

'From maximum fucking *security*?'

Woof! came the dog-echo.

'You should get yourself a swear jar, Zads. He wasn't in max. Some genius decided he was low risk. Got him transferred up the river.'

'*What?* When?'

'A few weeks back. I'm sorry, mate. I wasn't told.'

'I mean when did he break *out?*'

'Swam out, in point of fact. Today. Could have been anytime. Did a no-show at the dinnertime headcount.'

For a long moment I was speechless. I sensed he was looking straight at me, straight into my sightless eyes, and that the rest of his bullshit – the offer of work, the clumsy jokiness, the half-apology, the drip-feed of information – had been some sort of test. Was I up to hearing this? Could I take it? I stood there raging inside, but this time not at the messenger. He'd been beating about the bush but at least he'd come straight to me. What kind of fuckwits were running the Parole Board? Let alone the holiday camp on the river.

The butt scorched my fingertips, I tossed it away. 'Give me another . . .' I began, but it was already being planted between my lips.

'I'll help you pack,' he said. 'Shouldn't need to take a lot.'

A splutter of smoke. 'You want me to move out?'

'Just for a couple of days. Till he's back in custody. Got any place you can lie low?'

It was a struggle not to blurt out the one place that came to mind. The *only* place. But whatever my mixed-up feelings about Willow's hideaway, one thing was clear: I would never put her in harm's way again.

'Let's not get theatrical,' I said. 'This is the last place he'd come.'

'I'm sure you're right,' he said, trying to sound convincing, 'but why take chances?'

'I'm staying put. He'll be halfway across the Nullarbor by now.'

'But if he's not – he knows where you live.'

'Not anymore.'

'What the fuck are you talking about? He shot you right where you're standing.'

The dog agreed, but the dog didn't know the full story either. 'He wrote to me from prison a couple of times,' I said. 'I sent them straight back. No Longer At This Address.'

'You read them first?' Terry asked, then snorted. 'Sorry. Might take a while to break the habit.'

'Wouldn't have read them even if I could,' I said.

'You should have told me. What if they were threats?'

'Wouldn't have got past the censor. I knew what was in them.'

My turn to keep him in suspense; I took a slow drag, an even slower exhalation.

'Bullshit apologies,' I finally said. 'Kind of guff that impresses the Parole Board.' I sucked again. 'You think he's going to have me running scared, you got another think coming.'

'You always were a stubborn bastard.'

'Takes one to know one.'

'I still can't believe you stayed here after the shooting. Bad memories, and all that.'

'Only good memories here, Chief,' I said. 'I don't remember the bad ones. Complete blank.'

'What about Willow? After what she went through?'

'Her call. Nothing was going to make her leave our home.'

The words were out of my mouth before I heard how stupid they were. I waited for the words that were surely on the tip of his tongue: *But she did.*

'She's as stubborn as you,' he said instead, in what might have been an act of kindness.

I changed the subject. 'The clubhouse under surveillance?'

'Major Crimes are paying a courtesy call as we speak,' he said.

I snorted. 'What's that mean? Knock on the fortress door and ask nicely if they are harbouring any fugitives in damp clothes?'

'The fortress walls have been bulldozed, Zads. Times have changed. The clubs are feeling the heat, thanks to the new legislation. Which your shooting helped push through.'

'If you believe that you'll believe anything.'

'One thing I do believe: they wouldn't touch your, um, wetback with a bargepole. They expelled him a year ago.'

A disbelieving snort. 'Says who?'

'Says the horse's mouth. They put out a press release.'

'The bikies are putting out *press* releases now?'

'Through their PR agency.' He chuckled again, and for the first time it sounded genuine. 'They've all got them now. Not just your mob. Mongols. Angels. Jokers. Big charm offensive. Teddy-bear runs. Family days at the clubhouses. Fun castles. I thought you'd have, um,' he checked himself, 'heard about this.'

'Guess I had other things on my mind.'

'Yeah, well – the old guard is back in charge. Most of the clubs have purged their loose cannons. Bad for business. A few of the younger hotheads just vanished.'

'That was in the press release?'

More chuckling. 'I just hope the graves aren't too shallow. We don't need another war.'

'Not to mention the paperwork,' I said.

'Better the devil you know. At least the tribal elders play by the rules.' He stepped back. 'I'll get the night patrols to drive by from time to time.'

'I can look after myself,' I said, and tossed the finger-burning butt out into the night. 'Just light me another before you go.'

'Is that a good idea? Blind bloke smoking alone?'

'Who's fucking alone?' I said, and the dog backed me up with a bark.

Terry grunted. 'Point taken. But is she going to ring triple-0 if you burn the place down?'

'She saved my sorry arse once before, remember? Anyway, the sprinklers will put it out.'

'Your funeral, thrill-seeker. Here – catch.'

My right hand reached into the space between us before I had time to think; the pack smacked my palm, my fingers snapped shut on it like a fly-trap.

'Ha!' from Terry. 'What did I tell you? You might surprise yourself.'

Before I could think of an answer his footsteps were walking away.

'By the way,' he called back as the front gate clacked shut behind him. 'You've got dog shit on your boots. In case you're wondering.'

5

I KICKED OFF THE OFFENDING BOOTS, STEPPED INSIDE, AND slammed the door shut. I didn't want to think about my shitty boots any more than I wanted to think about my shitty life. Which had just got shittier. Maybe I'd clean them in the morning, maybe I'd sling them over the nearest powerline; for now all I wanted to do was fall into bed.

'Time, Siri.'

'5.15 pm.'

'Lights off, Siri.'

Turning off my head proved more difficult. The brain burns at 40-watts, a walking encyclopaedia by the name of Willow once informed me. It's a dim, energy-saving bulb. But not mine, not tonight. Tonight it was incandescent. My bravado had faded a bit, but I wasn't worried. Criminals never revisit the scene; lightning never strikes the same place twice. Etcetera, etcetera. I was angry more than worried, which meant that sleep – my haven, my bolthole – was beyond me. Since Willow walked out I'd been crawling into bed earlier each night – if not quite this early – to sleep, yes, but mostly to dream. Dreams offer a nightly miracle: the recovery of sight, if only temporarily, in snatches.

Most nights I can't wait to get to bed, especially when I dream of her. And most nights it's easy to drift off, unmoored from the world, my ears empty, even the pitch-black dark invisible – but today my nose decided to fill the sense vacuum. Was it Terry's talk of dog shit, or was my agitated brain just trying to find some input to distract it?

Strange that I hadn't noticed the stink before; I must have been marinating in it for weeks.

'Time, Siri?' I asked after a few hours of tossing and turning.

'6.22 pm,' she said, which meant those hours added up to barely more than one.

Weird arithmetic, but even weirder was another sum I couldn't get out of my head: how had fifteen years' hard labour become two, followed by a transfer to the holiday resort on the river? The close, stuffy air pressed down on me, the hoops tightened around my chest again, as if I were the one trapped in a prison cell. A cell, moreover, I was now sharing with *him*. His was the face I saw in my head tonight: the gaunt cheekbones, the dark, narrow-set eyes, the thin, strangely expressionless mouth. A cartoon mug-shot, apart from the slicked-down hair. That was a weird late-night touch: dripping-wet, as if to taunt me, as if I were taunting myself.

Eventually I rolled out of bed, stripped the sour linen, tossed the bundle into the hall and broke out a clean set. Cotton, not satin, but their freshness helped clear the stink from my nose. No such luck with the mug-shot in my head. The eyes might not be following me, but the hair was only getting wetter each time I looked.

Maybe I could drown him properly, drown him *out*. 'Lullaby music, Siri,' I said, and she dealt another track from her deck. Stevie Wonder this time, something slow and bluesy that I didn't recognise. 'What's with these blind role-models you keep throwing at me? Dropping hints? Telling me to do something useful with my life?'

'Shuffle is a random generator, Richard.'

'Bullshit. If you think I should take up an instrument just say so.'

I was almost asleep, finally, when a growl from the dog basket half-roused me. A louder growl, followed by a sharp warning bark, jerked me fully awake, heart thumping, adrenaline flooding. Was there an intruder in the house? I reached automatically under the pillow, and panicked. Where was the gun?

I lay there in a cold sweat, all ears. There was no sound but the growling of the dog. *Keep calm*, I told myself. *The doors are dead-locked; the windows locked.* And the security shutters? I reached out a hand and found the remote sitting on the bedside table growing cobwebs. I hadn't raised the shutters since Willow left.

The growling stopped, replaced by dream-whimpers, and I almost laughed out loud. Was I going to start jumping at shadows? Of course he wasn't out there; he was halfway to Woop Woop by now. And of *course* there was no gun; I hadn't slept with a gun for years. What would I do with a gun? A teddy bear under the pillow would be as much use.

Scout scrabbled her feet in her basket as she chased some dream-rabbit down a hole. Whose face does she see in her dreams? Mine, probably; obsessed with reading its moods by night as much as by day. She snorted noisily as she tried to dig out her furry truffle, but still lying on her side, going nowhere.

As if thinking about the dog had me thinking like a dog, I threw off the fresh bedsheets and let the stink fill my nose again. Memo, Terry: dog shit, yes, but also stale sweat, stale food, rank clothes.

Cave smells. Hibernation smells.

I reached for the remote again, pressed the master-bedroom button, and heard the outside shutter rumble up. The windowpane I raised by hand, but there was no movement of air through the fly-screen. I walked through to the back shed, raised the roller-door – also for the first time since Willow left – and let the cool, fresh night breeze wash over me and through the house.

As I stepped back I planted my right foot in a fresh dog turd. A hop sideways and my left heel landed in a second, this one days old by the crumbly feel of it.

'Fuck!'

No echo for once, although my anger was aimed more at myself than Scout. I'd lacked the energy to clean up for weeks, let alone take her for a proper walk.

I hopped on one leg back into the bathroom, lifted the other foot into the basin, sluiced it thoroughly, then grabbed a toilet roll and a pack of pine-scented wet wipes and headed back to the shed.

For some time I crawled about on all fours, following my nose, delicately feeling out and wrapping the stinky truffles, then wiping clean the concrete beneath.

The dog was still lying low. 'Not your fucking fault, girl,' failed to echo-locate her, but jolted Siri awake.

'You kiss your mother with that mouth, Richard?'

'I wasn't talking to you.'

'Sorry. I was just trying to help.'

So was Scout. I could picture all too clearly her droop-tail and shifty eyes, but she had done her best. The dog shits were lined up like soldiers, just inside the roller-door, as close to the outside world as she could get. Which got me thinking of my shitty boots again, sitting outside the front door. Sure enough, when I got down on my hands and knees at that end of the house, I found another platoon.

After flushing away a half-dozen more wrapped parcels, I showered and pulled on some clothes. Perhaps it was the last of the adrenaline-shock, but I still had energy to burn. The house smelt as clean and fresh as a pine forest, which also helped. I filled the kitchen sink, added a squirt of detergent – also pine-scented – and ran a week's stack of unwashed dishes through the hot suds.

It was getting closer to a proper bedtime, but sleep was the last thing on my mind. I headed back to the shed, pulled on the gloves, beat up the bag till I was panting and sweat-soaked, then stepped outside through the open roller-door into the back lane to cool down.

And immediately shivered, involuntarily. That sixth sense again? Or just the night breeze against my sweaty skin?

A growl from behind didn't help; I hadn't noticed Scout's arrival. She barked, but perhaps only at the wind in the trees, an old enemy.

'You are perfectly safe, idiot,' I told her, and me.

She went quiet, but my skin was raising another crop of goose-bumps.

'Here I am!' I shouted, and waved my plump-gloved fists, defi-antly, though more at my own jittery self than any imagined assailant. 'Come and get me, you little cunt!'

No answer but the rustle of leaves in the surrounding backyards. And the continued prickling of my skin. I stepped back inside and eased off my gloves, but unhurriedly. I would not be made to panic, even as I wondered if he'd sneaked in through the open door while I was in the shower, or noisily washing the dishes.

I lowered the roller-door, locking him either in or out, then padded back through the house and rolled down the bedroom shutter, also unhurriedly.

'He's a thousand miles away, you idiot,' I told myself, but it was hard not to think about the gun that wasn't beneath the pillow. 'Leave the toy where it is, Blind Freddie,' I told myself.

The pack of Camels found its way back into my hand; the dog barked a warning as I lit up, but with the doors and windows shut I was finding the pine forest too cloyingly chemical.

At least the fuggy old fox lair had smelt secure.

I resumed pacing as I puffed, feeling less reckless than careless, or less careless than carefree. Home is the one place I *can* be care-free, physically. Every sharp edge and blunt obstacle is engraved on my mental GPS. No step-offs can trip me, no overhangs king-hit me; I could hurdle the furniture if the urge took hold.

Everything is in its proper place except, at times, the dog. The clicking of her nails on the floorboards tracked me as I stalked about – but also let me keep track of her, which was the reason I pulled up the carpets in the first place.

I paced the narrow hall end-to-end, as if it were a lap pool, muttering more advice to myself: 'Try not to remember where you hid the gun, idiot.'

After a dozen or so lengths I turned into the family room and dropped to my knees before the liquor cabinet.

'Do not open the cabinet, idiot.'

I shook out another cigarette, distracted, and managed to light the wrong end. Memo, Terry: I've done it before, I'll do it again. Zero fire hazard. I stubbed out the pungent filter-tip, correctly lit another, then puffed steadily, stalling for as long as I could.

'Do not open the cabinet,' I repeated, 'idiot.'

I slid open the glass doors and reached in above the wide glass mouths of the beer steins, the safest hiding-hole in the house when the Margarita Queen had shared it with me.

'Repeat after me: do not take the gun out.'

I eased out the weighty, cloth-wrapped bundle and set it down on top of the cabinet, still kneeling.

'Please don't unwrap the gun, Big Nose.'

Not even asking nicely could stop me. I unwrapped it, carefully – like cigarettes, guns have a right and a wrong end. The grip felt as firm as an old friend's handshake, and the metal had a pleasurable solidity. I checked both safeties, ran my free hand over the familiar contours. Standard issue Smith & Wesson police compact; non-standard issue magazine.

No warning bark from the dog this time, but the lights were out and for all she knew I was pouring myself a secret drink.

Which wasn't a bad idea. The Scotch was sitting in its usual drop-pin location. I uncorked it with my teeth, then sank into my armchair, bottle in one hand, gun in the other. The rough braille of the grip and the balance of the stock comforted me in ways that might be absurd for a blind man but were real nonetheless. Partly ingrained emotional habit, yes – that teddy bear under the pillow – but partly also the satisfaction of contemplating a thing of beauty. Hand guns are the purest machines I know, near-perfect fusions of form and function.

As is single malt Scotch: a machine with only one moving part, but exquisitely tuned. I took a last mouthful then returned the corked bottle to its assigned latitude and longitude in the cabinet. I needed both hands for the next task. Time for some serious study, or serious revision: I spread my legs wide, leant forward, and field-stripped the gun slowly, arranging each part – magazine, slide, barrel, recoil assembly – precisely on the floor between my feet. After snapping those solid meccano pieces back into place, I repeated the strip more rapidly. No great achievement – even in the old days I could do it blindfolded – but the ritual helped calm me further.

Centred me, in Police Welfarese.

A sharp bark from the dog reminded me that I might be having fun in the dark, but for her it was still night.

'Siri. Let there be light.'

Almost immediately the dog's nails clicked my way, halted as she made a considered risk assessment of what I was up to, then clicked away, surprisingly unconcerned.

What next? I'd dealt with the threat of an intruder in the only place it was real – my fucked-up head – but in no way was I ready for sleep. Especially since – it struck me with some force – I hadn't warned Willow about the jailbreak. Had Terry? Did he even know where she lived? Surely he would have phoned her, or sent a car around, but you never knew with Terry.

'Phone, Siri,' I said, and the loud burr of the dial tone filled the house. 'Hide Caller ID,' I added.

'Caller ID hidden.'

'Find Favourites.'

Once a favourite, always a favourite? Not if the favourite refuses to answer when she sees the caller's name on the screen. But this was an emergency.

'Willow. Mobile number. Connect.'

The familiar melody of her phone number bounced between the walls I could have sung it backwards: *Do Fa Do Te La La Fa Me Do So*. Memo, Blind Welfare: idea for a tone-recognition programme. Teach us to sing or whistle up our favourites' numbers.

'The number you have called is disconnected,' from the Telstra robot. 'Please check the number again. I repeat, the number you have called is disconnected.'

Since when? Since I left my last message, my famous nearly-last words.

'End call,' I said. What to do with my fast-rising frustration? Count to ten thousand? She was in no danger, I reminded myself. How would he track her down even if he wanted to? It had taken me three months, and an accidental overdose. All of which made sense, but didn't help. I began pacing my wooden lap pool again, but after half a length turned deliberately aside and walked, hip and shoulder, hard into the bedroom doorframe.

The soft pinewood gave a little with a splintering sound. Anger Management Step Thirteen: self-harm. If nothing else, the pain helped focus my mind.

'Phone Royal Adelaide Hospital, Siri.'

Another rapid, if less familiar tone-melody, then a long sequence of ringing tones, and finally a briskly efficient female voice: 'Royal Adelaide Hospital.'

'Could you page Dr Willow Lee, please? It's an emergency.'

'Are you a patient, Sir?'

'Um, yes. I had some tests done. She said to ring her for the results.'

'I'm just checking the roster, Sir. No – I'm sorry. Dr Lee is off-duty tonight. If you give me your name and UR number I'll put you through to the Emergency desk.'

'I'll try again tomorrow,' I said, and ended the call. 'Time, Siri?'

'8.30 pm.'

Time was creeping by at snail's pace, but at least that offered a window of opportunity. What were the chances she was spending Friday evening at home? Better than fifty-fifty, given she would be exhausted from the night we'd just spent together. The dog's nails clicked past me, continued to the front door then stopped, expectantly – less reading my intentions than helping make the decision for me.

I tugged a scrap of dried pig's ear from my treat pocket and tossed it her way. 'Sorry, girl. You're not coming.'

'No problem,' from Siri, above.

'*You're* coming,' I said, and felt my way to her cradle on the hall table. Empty. 'If you want to. Where are you?'

'Current location: home,' she said, her voice still everywhere and nowhere.

'Bluetooth off, Miss Playing-Hard-to-Get.'

'Bluetooth off,' came a faint whisper through the bedroom door.

I retrieved her from the bedside table and slipped her into my belt holster, a repurposed police-issue side-snap. A quick draw might not be necessary for GPS navigation, but for the last two years it had offered a snug fit. And perhaps provided me with a certain mental snugness: a sense that I was still tooled up, in a way.

My right hand – I now noticed – was still holding the gun.

'Put it back in the liquor cabinet, idiot,' I said, even as the hand tried, vainly, to jam it into an already occupied holster. I removed the obstruction with my left and holstered the gun smoothly, satisfyingly. When it came to feeling psychologically tooled-up it was no contest. And Siri was easily relocated: I plucked my jacket from a low branch of the hallstand, pulled it on, plugged in the collar speaker–mike, and slipped her into the inside pocket.

'Close to my heart, Siri.'

'You wish to close your heart, Richard?' she murmured in my ear.

Worth a smile as I unhooked my cane from another branch of the hallstand, shook it out, and squeezed through the door before Scout could follow.

'Find route. Current location to Chez Gotcha.'

'Alternate route one,' from my collar. 'Turn right into Gouger Street. Continue straight ahead to Victoria Square.'

Willow might ignore a phone call, but she could hardly ignore a blind man banging on her door in the middle of the night.

'Alternate route two . . .'

'Route one is fine.'

'Gouger Street twenty-five steps. Turn right.'

I tapped rapidly onwards; there was no time to waste. The more thought I gave it, the more urgent the need to warn Willow. And also deliver a lecture. How typically reckless of her to disconnect her phone. Especially now she was living alone. And if she weren't alone? My frustration darkened a little. I tried not to think of that king-size satin-sheeted bed, or wonder if some other king was being crowned between its slippery sheets right now.

'Morphett Street intersection, ten steps.'

The walk signal bleeped. I stepped down onto the road, mine-swept my way to the far kerb, stepped up, touched base with the traffic-light pole, left-turned, waited for the walk signal again, crossed again.

'Proceed along Gouger Street, north side. Victoria Square, 200 steps.'

Any other night I would have navigated by nose alone. Curry-spice at the corner; Spanish tapas next up; Thai stir-fry. The open mouth of Moonta Street, a hot dragon's breath funnelled up from the lungs of Chinatown.

'Ky Chow, ten steps,' Siri suggested, but tonight I was driven by anger not hunger. I strode on, sweeping widely, less dodging the oncoming foot traffic than being dodged.

'Supreme Court Building. King William Road, twenty . . .'

A Harley drowned her out as it throbbed slowly past in the other direction. Someone I knew? I swept on, determined not to jump at shadows. Memo, self: no prison escapee would be riding a chopped bike through Gouger Street on market night.

'King William Street,' Siri murmured.

I stopped, waiting for the lights. Far behind me the throbbing faded, U-turned, then began growing again, cruising back up my side of the street. Soon enough it drew alongside, waiting with me at the intersection, deafeningly. Was he really that stupid? My heart seemed to be pounding in time with the bike.

The walk signal bleated; the bike thundered out of the blocks; I tapped across the road in the wake of its pungent exhaust fumes, relieved, but also suddenly, weirdly disappointed. This odd cocktail of feelings ambushed me, but grew stronger with every step. Part of me – the angry part? the self-harming part? – *wanted* it to be him.

'Big bike, small cock!' I shouted after him.

'That's not a very nice thing to say, Richard,' Siri murmured, but as I crossed the tram tracks into the square I was spoiling for a fight.

'Piece of shit!' I shouted, this time meaning the bike itself, a more personal and less forgiveable insult to any bikie worth his colours. 'Thirteen hundred ccs and it sounds like a Kombivan with a busted muffler!'

'That's not a very nice thing to say, Richard,' Siri repeated, for possibly the ten thousandth time in our relationship.

'Got any loose change, mate?'

The hoarse, slurred challenge – directly ahead – startled me, but I kept tapping steadily towards it.

'Cab fare will do.' The voice closer now, not about to step aside. 'Missed the last tram.'

At least two trams were rumbling and clanging their way around the square as he spoke. I veered left, narrowing my radar-sweep; the voice moved simultaneously to block my escape. 'Hey you! Blind Freddie! I'm talking to *you*!'

I stopped in my tracks, but without fear. Anger is the only effective antidote to fear, and the higher the dose the better. He hadn't picked a good night to touch me up.

'Move aside, Sir,' I said. 'I won't ask again.'

'That ain't too friendly, matey. For a fucken blind bloke stepping out without his junkyard dog.'

The detail puzzled me more than worried me. Had he seen my dog before? Had he been stalking me? 'Do I know you?'

A drunken snort, close now; a gust of boozy breath. 'Seen you goin' through the square all the time. The two of youse.'

How close? Two eyes are good for range-finding, but a pair of nostrils, even a big pair, might as well be one. Unless you're a dog.

'Woulda thought ya could use a friend, matey. Out this late on ya own.'

Two ears might triangulate his position if I could keep him talking. 'Is that a threat, you gutless bastard?'

A drunken guffaw. 'Bit of friendly advice. Never know who ya might run into on a dark night. Maybe I should hang on to ya wallet for safekeeping.'

I collapsed my cane and gripped the folded bundle tightly. If push came to shove, four tubes made a better blunt instrument than one.

'Come and get it, you little prick.'

How little? My binocular ears' best guess: a head shorter than me. I pictured *his* head, shoulder height, mentally rehearsed the swing.

'Got a fucken mouth on ya,' he said. 'Last chance, Blind Freddie. Gimme ya wallet before I turn ya upside down and shake it outta ya.'

'I've got a better idea, dipshit. You give me *your* wallet!'

Guessing he was too surprised to move I took a quick step forward and swung my club hard where his head should have been. It wasn't. The torque spun me sideways; I scrambled for footing.

'Not even close!' he crowed, slightly to one side. 'Last fucken chance, Blind Freddie. Drop ya wallet on the ground and walk away. I don' wanna hurt you.'

Blind man versus blind drunk: what were the odds? In one fury-fuelled movement I snapped open the folded cane, shook it out again into its full rigid length, and swung again, as hard as I could, in a wide, shoulder-high arc.

This time it connected. Hard. The cane collapsed, but I could hear the drunk staggering backwards from the noise he was making.

'Jesus! You coulda put my *eye* out!'

'Might even things up a bit, you piece of shit!'

'That's not a very nice thing to say, Richard,' the parrot on my shoulder chirped.

'Whose side are you on, sister?'

'Don't blame the messenger,' she said.

The drunk had gone silent. Perhaps the female voice distracted him – a witness? – or perhaps he wasn't as drunk as I hoped. Sober enough, it seemed, to learn from his mistakes; I couldn't even hear footsteps. I cocked my head this way and that, but more trams were rumbling by and he could be anywhere. I took a wide swing to the left, then to the right. Still nothing. A sudden, sixth-sense alarm: I turned and swung behind me, but the cane was seized at the end of its arc and wrenched from my grip.

'Not such a big man without your nunchukka, eh Freddie!'

A clatter of metal pipes as he tossed it aside; almost instantly something else struck my face. A fist? I staggered, but mostly from surprise. The blow wasn't hard.

'Who's the piece of shit now?' he shouted, and I was hit again, a right hook to the side of the head, harder but glancing.

Attack is the best means of defence? When it's the only means, surely. Still high on anger, I stepped straight towards the voice, chin down, elbows tucked in, fists face-high. Old boxing instincts: right jab, right jab, left hook, duck, right counterpunch.

Either I caught him by surprise again, or he was all talk. What's a drunk, if not a slow-moving punching bag? I sensed him back-pedal, shuffling, then trip. His yelp told me where he had fallen: flat on his back, straddled by my wide boxer's stance. I let myself drop, knees first, onto his chest; the air went out of him, noisily. He flailed his fists, feeble close-quarter punches with no weight behind them, but his wind was gone. Somehow the gun had found its way from the holster into my right hand. I swung the stock hard at where his face should be, felt the crunch of bone, heard a scream. I swung again and missed, swung and hit, swung again: a frenzied hit-and-miss until a last wild failure to connect spun me off him and onto my own back.

He was groaning in pain, close-by, barely audible. 'What the fuck? A blind man with a *gun*?'

I aimed it idly in his direction, sensed him scramble away on all fours.

'Don't shoot!' he squealed. 'Fuck! I was just messin' with you, matey! Didn't mean no harm.'

Would I have pulled the trigger if he'd taken another swing? I'd like to think not – the trigger was still two safeties away – but I didn't get to find out. His voice backed further off, whimpering – 'My *face*! Fucken *canes*! Fucken blood everywhere!' – and I holstered the gun and let him go.

My own face ached, but I barely noticed. A strange electricity thrilled my limbs; I felt energised, even elated. I fingered my cheek-bones, swollen and sticky to the touch, then waggled my nose and flexed my jaw. The metallic shaving-cut smell of blood was strong, but nothing was obviously broken.

And the other bloke? Somewhere across the square his Dutch courage was returning. 'Some blind bastard back there's got a gun! There! By the fountain!'

I felt less alarmed than cautious. How long did I have? Long enough to fumble around on hands and knees for the lost cane? Not likely. I didn't even know which direction I was facing.

'Help! Help!' Further away, but even louder. 'Somebody! Blind cunt tried to shoot me!'

'Location, Siri?'

'Victoria Square,' she stated the obvious.

A more helpful answer came from the heavens: the town hall clock on the north side of the square chiming the quarter-hour, a single, clear compass needle. I lit out immediately in that direction, given the drunk's voice was heading south. There was no time to lose; any moment the word 'gun' would find a police ear and calls for back-up would be on the relay from Com Cen to All Points. Maybe one of those points was my brain-wiring; I could hear the protocol in my head as if it were a radio receiver: *Possible armed offender seen in the vicinity of Victoria Square. Unless public safety is at immediate risk, do not approach until perimeter set.*

I walked quickly, but with a slight sliding gait, like cross-country skiing, using my feet now as canes, feeling my way at speed along the paved path, veering back onto its smoothness whenever I stepped into the grassy verge.

'He's got a gun! Fucken psycho tried to shoot me!'

I turned my head, less looking backwards than listening backwards, and walked smack into a waist-high immoveable object, kneecaps first.

'Fuck!'

From the waist up I kept moving, toppling face-first into – what? My nose screamed the answer: garbage. Somehow my flailing hands found a grip each side of the wide mouth of the bin and I shoved myself back upright.

For a long moment I stood there, listening. No Good Samaritan offers of help; no suppressed chortles. No witnesses, at least close-by. The silence from further away was less reassuring: the drunk had found an audience. The cavalry was on its way. My first mad instinct was to topple back in and bury myself completely in the stinking refuse. My second was less panicky: bury something smaller than myself.

Exhibit A was already out of the holster and in my hand; I thrust it deep in among the slimy cans and plastic bottles and wodges of half-eaten fast-food.

After wiping my hands on the nearby grass I transferred Siri from pocket to holster. 'Find route. Current location to . . .'

Where? The drunk had last been heard heading south; I needed to continue north, at speed. Anywhere north.

'Name destination,' Siri prompted.

'Jesus, I dunno! The North Pole!'

'North Pole Toy Cave, Glenelg. North Pole Ice Cream, Alice Springs. North Pole, Alaska–'

'Alaska!'

'Current location to the North Pole,' she said, calmly. 'Route One. Turn right at Flinders Street, and proceed to Frome Road . . .'

I set out for the Pole immediately; there was no time to lose. Within minutes – ten, fifteen at most – the Star Force would have me surrounded, a two- or three-block perimeter. Unless some foot-patrol hothead broke protocol first.

'This is the police! Stop right there, sir! Place your hands behind your head!'

A female hothead, barking orders from directly in front of me. I stopped dead, and opened my mouth to explain.

'Hands behind your *head*, Sir! I won't ask again!'

I did what she said. Muffled radio-crackle floated in from my left – of course there were two of them – followed by the drunk's hoarse voice, coming up fast behind. 'That's him! Yeah! That's the psycho what—'

'You!' she barked his way. 'Shut the fuck up! And *you*!' – my direction again – 'On the ground, now! Face-down.'

I couldn't see the gun in her hand, or the one in the hand of her partner, but both were surely aimed my way.

'I'm blind,' I said. 'Is it safe to lie down here?'

'*Told* ya he's blind! *Told* ya!'

I sensed an exchange of confused glances between the cops; having strayed off the armed offender protocol rails, they found themselves lost among the buttercups.

'I'm a serving police officer myself,' I said. 'That man tried to rob me.'

Her back-up took a few boot-steps closer; I could almost feel the play of torch-light on my face.

A male voice this time, incredulous: 'Detective Sergeant *Zadow*?'

'He's got a fucking *gun*, I tell ya!'

I lowered my arms. 'What would a blind man be doing with a gun?'

The woman's voice again: 'With respect, Detective Sergeant. Please keep your hands on your head.'

Good for you, sister, I thought. *By the book.*

'See!' from the drunk. 'See! *Told* ya! He's packing!'

Raising my arms must have pulled my jacket up. 'It's not a gun,' I got in quickly.

The woman: 'What's in the holster then, Detective Sergeant?'

'GPS navigator. Blind man's best friend.'

Another long glance, surely, between the two cops before she continued: 'Take it out. Thumb and forefinger. Slowly. You know the drill.'

I kept my hands behind my head. 'Look, Mum, no hands,' I said, then spoke down into my collar. 'Siri, Current location.'

'Victoria Square, Adelaide,' she answered back.

A half-chuckle from the male cop. 'All wired up, eh?' His voice was at my shoulder now, his hand plucking the device from its quiver. 'Checks out,' he announced, and replaced it.

'Badge and warrant card in my jacket pocket,' I said. '*Left* side . . . That's it.'

'Search the cunt proper! He fucken *pistol*-whipped me! Broke my fucken *nose*!'

'Looks like you gave as much as you got,' the woman told him. 'Not sure how that's going to look in court. Beating up a blind man. You can put your hands down, Detective Sergeant. Sorry to be such a stickler.'

'Rules are rules,' I said.

'What the . . . ? You're letting the cunt *go*? He bashed me with a *gun*, I tell ya!'

'He bashed you with his iPhone,' the male cop said. 'Looks like self-defence to me.'

'Cuff the gutless prick, Dazza,' from the woman. 'We'll need a statement, Detective Sergeant.'

'No problem,' I said. 'Don't suppose you could have a look around for my white cane? He stole it from me.'

'Look for his fucken *gun*, ya useless dogs! Hey, what ya doing? Let me go!'

The woman's voice, murmuring into *her* collar: 'Bravo 21 requesting a cage. Vic Square and Wakefield. Near the fountain. Over.'

I liked her no-shit approach even more. Nice voice to balance it: decisive, but a deep, easy-on-the-ear contralto. Her age was hard to pick, maybe young enough to be a rookie. She would have made a good Siri.

'Like your work, Constable,' I told her, fishing.

'Senior Constable,' she said. 'Annie to my friends.'

'I hope you cancelled the All Points, Annie.'

A snort. 'You bet. I need a night doing paperwork for the Starries like a hole in the head. Speaking of which, let's have a look at yours.'

Her fingers touched my chin, tilted it lightly. 'Cheekbone might need a scan.'

'Nothing's broken,' I said. 'Annie.'

'What about *my* face? It fucken *canes*! I need to get to hospital, ya dogs!'

'Pity you can't see what the other bloke looks like,' she murmured in my ear. Her skin smelt like something I couldn't quite place. Honey and . . . cinnamon?

'You wearing perfume on patrol, Annie?'

She chuckled. 'Standard issue, Detective Sergeant. Helps calm the natives.'

'Has the opposite effect on me,' I said.

No answer this time. A plastic seal was ripped, an adhesive dressing pressed against my cheek. A pungent antiseptic smell drowned any chance of catching more of hers.

Approaching boot-steps from the south. 'Found your cane,' the male cop said. 'But it looks cactus.'

The collapsed, jingling tubes were pressed into my palm; I shook them out, let the internal elastic thong pull them into line, rigid.

He chuckled again. 'Shows how much I know.'

'You got a licence for that nunchukka?' from Annie. 'Looks like a deadly weapon.'

'Never leave home without it,' I said. 'About that statement. It's been a long night. Maybe I could give it tomorrow.'

'You already gave it,' she said. 'Didn't he, Dazza? You witnessed it.'

'I did?' from her offsider, then another chuckle. 'Oh, right. But you might need to prompt my memory.'

'I think it went like this,' she said. 'I was walking north through Victoria Square at, oh, 10.15 approx. I was accosted by a drunk, who demanded I hand over my wallet. When I refused, my white cane was wrested from my grasp and I was struck repeatedly around the face with it. In self-defence I lashed out with my communication device. With which I was attempting to contact the police at the time.'

So much for doing things by the book. 'Nice touch,' I put in. 'Wish I'd thought of it.'

'I apparently made lucky contact with my assailant, and managed to break free and decamp. You happy to witness that, Constable?'

'Word for word,' he said. 'I have to say, it's an honour to meet you, Detective Sarge. You were an inspiration to us at the Academy. Shoulda got a medal.'

'A medal?' the drunk shouted. 'Bash a bloke in the park with his white stick, pull a gun, and get a fucking medal?'

A grunted *oomph!* cut him short, then a series of wheezing gasps. 'Sorry, Sir,' from the male cop. 'Didn't see you standing there.'

'You need to be a little more careful with that nightstick, Constable,' Annie said, as a single siren-bleep announced the arrival of the paddy wagon.

'The night-cart could drop you home,' she added in my direction.

'One condition,' I said. 'I get to ride in the back with my friend here'

She laughed again. 'A cage fight! I think you've done enough damage for one night, Detective Sarge.'

I liked her more and more. The laugh helped, warm and throaty. 'Rick,' I said. 'And I'd rather walk home. But thanks for your help. Annie.'

'You didn't need any help. Rick.'

The simple fact of this was still sinking in. I hadn't even needed the dog. I was bruised and battered, but I'd revelled in it. As I turned and tapped away I felt happier than I'd felt for a long time. I felt, somehow, cleaned. *Cleansed*. Emptied of anger, yes, but not just at the drunk. Terry, the Parole Board, the bullshit security on the river were all forgotten. And Willow? My desperation to warn her about the jailbreak I saw for what it was: another button to press, another pathetic cry for help. A great weight seemed to have lifted off my shoulders; I felt so ridiculously good I had an urge to turn back and ask Annie what time her shift ended. Until I remembered I had a late-night rendezvous lined up already, if only with a garbage bin.

'Do us a favour, Rick,' she called after me. 'Don't pick any more fights on the way home.'

No need for that, the way I felt. I waved an acknowledgement, and kept tapping southwards, towards the scene of the crime. How far was it? After thirty or so paces I began tacking back and forth across the path, sweeping beyond its edges. After fifty, I got lucky, lightly touch-tapping the bin, but moving quickly past in case my colleagues were watching.

'Drop pin,' I murmured.

'Pin dropped. Name location.'

'Central Gun Depository.'

Siri's one glaring fault: no laugh track. It's not a marriage-breaker, but a little canned laughter would be easy enough to programme, surely. I tapped back across the tramlines into Gouger, chuckling enough for both of us, then walked on, keeping left, staying in touch with the shopfront skirtings to avoid the tables and chairs and late-night diners on the pavement to my right.

The nose-tour began this end with coffee. '*Cibo*,' from Siri, unnecessarily, then '*Star of Siam*, ten paces.'

Who needed a dog when I was one myself, salivating on cue as the passing Chinatown eateries rang their regional bells? Purged of anger, it seemed I now had room inside for food – for chow, as Willow liked to say, or sometimes *cha* depending which way her big know-all brain was tilting. Towards Moonta Street I ran a gauntlet of Chinese eateries filled with clamorous Chinese speakers: Mandarin, mostly, of which I barely understood a word, although the food smells spoke to me in fluent Cantonese. Too fluently: Yin Chow, T Chow, Ky Chow were all among Willow's favourites, but there was no chow in Gouger Street the equal of her home-cooked dumplings, and nothing but sad memories this side of the street.

I crossed over, ignoring the squeal of brakes, and tapped back in the other direction.

'La Bisteca,' Siri whispered, and I turned inside before I got any more nostalgic. Beefsteak was a reliable antidote, and I'd earnt a thick cut. Perhaps even two: I needed to kill time before heading back to the gun depository.

'Shall I take your arm, Sir?' a waitress murmured at my elbow.

She already had, and I shrugged her off. 'You must be new.'

'First night. I just thought . . . I wouldn't want you to have another, um, fall.'

'What fall?'

'No offence, Sir. But your, um, face.'

'You should see the other bloke,' I said, and tapped a chair leg. 'This table free?'

'I'll clear it for you. I'm really sorry. I didn't mean . . . I mean, I hope I didn't—'

'Rib-eye,' I interrupted, and eased myself into the cup of the chair. 'Medium rare. And a bottle of the house red.'

I shook out a Camel while I waited for the wine, and lit up. No sprinklers to douse me if I set myself alight, but plenty of passing Samaritans. I sucked, luxuriously, and luxuriated also in the memories of what had happened in the park. Maybe I should pick a fight more often to clear any backlogged shit from my system.

Anger Management, Step of Last Resort: when all else fails, deck some bastard.

6

'SMALL WORLD, DETECTIVE SERGEANT.'

The voice startled me, but not enough to dent my mood. The afterglow of the fight chemistry – adrenaline, endorphins – was slowly fading, but I'd topped up the cocktail with more than a dash of rough red.

'Not this small,' I said.

'Mind if I join you?'

'You dogging me, Chief?'

'Let's just say I had a hunch you'd be hereabouts.'

I chuckled. 'Pour yourself a glass,' I said, feeling magnanimous. 'Hungry?'

'Why not?' he said. 'But there's a little housekeeping first.'

I felt around for the bottle, refilled my glass. 'You twentied my favourite wet-back? Where was he holed up?'

'No such luck,' he said, then aimed his voice above my head. 'A glass for me, love. And a T-bone. Medium rare.'

'So to what do I owe the pleasure? Another job offer?'

'The last one's still on the table. You handled yourself pretty well tonight I hear.'

I hid my surprise, but perhaps I should have known. 'You keep your ear close to the ground.'

'I had a few late ones at the Club. Heard the APB driving home. Thanks, love. Just a taste.'

He took a sip, spluttered. 'What's this? Argentinian paint stripper!'

'Go easy,' I said. 'It's her first night.'

'Bring us a bottle of Hill of Grace. *Por favor*. And two fresh glasses.'

'Big win on the ponies?' I asked.

He grunted, scornfully. '*I'm* not buying.'

'Well, I sure as hell ain't.'

Returning footsteps – kitten heels, I saw in my head – followed by the soft suck of a cork-pull, the splash of wine.

'Serge said to tell you it's on the house,' the waitress said. 'Chief Inspector.'

'Ta, love,' he said. 'I'll pour.'

The rising melody of the filling wineglass became tuneless as it reached the brim. The second glass, mine, stopped mid-melody.

'So,' he said, after noisily sipping and gargling a mouthful. 'Let's cut to the chase. A blind man waving a gun around Victoria Square? Seriously?'

I opened my jacket to reveal the holstered phone. 'What gun?'

'This gun, smart-arse,' he said, and something heavy landed on the table with a muffled thump.

Another ambush, but I was immune tonight. A splutter of laughter burst out of me. 'I'm impressed. How did you find it? Emu parade of cadets pecking their way across the square?'

'First place I looked. It wasn't exactly rocket science.'

'I hope you washed your hands afterwards.'

'This is serious,' he said. 'What the fuck were you thinking?'

'I've got a licence for it, Chief. There's no breach.'

'Really? How about Improper Disposal of a Firearm? Failure to Keep Secure? Departmental?'

'So slap me across the wrist with a wet noodle.'

'I should throw the book at you, fucktard. Halfway to your ex's place in the middle of the night lugging a *shooter*?'

'What makes you think I was on my way to Willow's?'

'Don't even bother,' he said.

'She won't take my calls,' I told him. 'I wanted to warn her.'

'You think she was going to open the door? "Hi, big boy. You pleased to see me, or is that a gun in your pocket?"'

'I forgot I had it. Truly.'

'Like you forgot how many pills you took the other night? Fair suck of the mango stone, mate! Your shrink must rub her hands together every time she sees you coming through the door.'

I chuckled, way too mellow to take offence.

'The whole truth?' I said. 'The dog got twitchy. After you left. I thought someone was in the house. I got the gun out of the safe.' Not quite the whole truth, but close. 'What would you have done in my place?'

'I'm not blind, am I? What use would a gun be to you?'

'Sweet F.A. But it made me *feel* a hell of a lot more secure.'

There was too much café noise to hear him scratching his head, but I sensed it. 'What are we going to do with you, Zads? The blind bloke who packs a gun? The blind bloke who likes to pick fights in the park.'

'That gutless little shit's lucky I didn't put a bullet through him.'

'Admirable self-control, Detective Sergeant. You just pistol-whipped the gutless shit instead.' As he refilled my glass there was warmth in his voice for the first time. 'You can take the boy out of the bikie gang. But you can't take the gang out of the boy.'

'Club,' I reminded him. 'The Golgothans are a motorcycle club. Gang is a bullshit police word.'

He refilled his own glass, took a mouthful. 'You almost sound like you miss the Dark Side.'

'*We're* the Dark Side, Chief. The Big Blue Gang. At least the brothers play by the rules.'

'Their rules. You haven't answered my question.'

I reached for one of my two wineglasses. It turned out to be the good stuff: rich blackberry, licorice, cinnamon. I used to think the wine-chat was bullshit; less so since I was forced to take more notice of my nose. When the windows get boarded up you've got to let a little light in somehow.

'Maybe I miss the adrenaline,' I said.

'Is that what tonight was about? In the park? Thrill-seeking?' He snorted. 'I wish I'd been ringside.'

I drained the glass. Burnt cherry on the after-palate. 'I'd forgotten how good it feels to land a punch,' I said. 'One on one.'

He refilled my glass to the brim, which meant the cheap stuff.

'I had a gladiator phase when I was a kid,' he said. 'Somewhere after dinosaurs, but before girls.'

'I went directly to girls,' I said. 'Did not pass gladiators.'

'You had a motorbike phase instead.'

'It's not a phase if you never grow out of it.'

He chuckled again. 'The Duke still spread all over the back shed then?'

'And a fat lot of use it is to me.'

'You might surprise yourself there too. If you can beat up a drunk in the park, you can feel your way around a camshaft.'

I hadn't thought about the bike for months. It was too hard, for all kinds of reasons. I'd kept the gun hidden from Willow for two years, but the bigger machine I hid mostly from myself. Easier done when blind, of course: a half-assembled chassis on a bright red lift-table in the shed would be hard to miss otherwise.

'I thought about them all the time when I was a kid,' Terry was saying.

'Bikes or girls?'

Another snorted laugh. 'Gladiators. Must have been nine, ten. Dunno where it came from.'

'It's a boy thing.'

He sipped again, slurped the wine noisily over his tongue again. 'I made my own swords, painted up a suit of cardboard armour. A shield. I still remember the Latin names. Like some nursery rhyme you never forget.'

'Which were the ones with the fishnets and tridents?'

'Retiarii. They used to fight the Samnites. Differently armed, but equally matched.'

'They were the ones with the big helmets and heavy armour?'

'You *did* have a gladiator phase.' He refilled both glasses. The wine could be coming from anywhere now; maybe it was on tap.

'So where's all this going?' I said. 'Something to do with my little punch-up in the park?'

'There's one name I don't remember. The gladiators who fought blind. Two condemned men armed with a shield, a sword – and helmets stuck on backwards.'

I chuckled. 'Hand me a sword,' I said, 'and aim me in the right direction.'

'Bit low on the card for you. These were matinee events. Clown shows. Except the clowns fought to the death. Comically.'

I sipped for a time, thinking about this. Seeing it, vividly enough.

'So where does this leave Blind Freddie and the drunk?' I eventually said. 'Something to laugh at? Dwarf mud wrestling?'

'You weren't equally matched, Zads.'

'He had a sporting chance.'

'He had Buckley's and you know it.'

I reached across the table and planted my hand on the gun, unerringly. It seemed to be wrapped in a plastic evidence bag.

'I can't let you take that,' he said, and slid it away. 'Sorry.'

A small stirring of anger. 'My property, Chief. I have a licence, remember.'

'He's a thousand miles away by now, Zads. You said so yourself.'

I gave a contemptuous snort. 'One thing blindness has taught me. How to listen. How to hear straight through the bullshit.'

'What's that supposed to mean?'

'It means you don't believe that any more than I do.'

He grunted. 'Maybe. But even if he pays you a visit, how would he get in? It's a fucking fortress.'

'You had a good snoop around the other night then?'

A chuckle this time. 'Just to reassure myself. Breaking out of his jail would be a piece of cake compared with breaking into yours.'

The kitten heels clicked back our way, a pair of plates were settled on the table. 'Your steaks, gentlemen.'

'Another bottle of the Henschke's,' Terry said, and tucked straight in without offering help as I fussed about locating the cutlery and food. I warmed to him for this; I've had a gutful of Good-Intentioned Samaritans wanting to cut my meat. The careless kindness of strangers.

'Reminds me of the old Hindley Street days,' he said through a mouthful. 'We'd head down to the Grecian BBQ after a night of knocking heads together. Remember?'

'Feed the man meat and he gets all nostalgic.'

Another unmuffled Harley throbbed past outside, closely followed by a second. I turned my head to track them like a slow radar dish. Might it be possible to recognise a rider by his unique engine-signature? Given enough ear-time, maybe.

'Relax,' Terry said. 'Hells Angels. I think.'

'You think?'

'They don't wear colours anymore.'

'Since when?'

'Since the new legislation. But the Angels pretty much run Gouger Street now.'

This was news to me; I mulled it over, chewing steadily.

'Remember the year we first made Detective,' he said. 'We'd go around kicking the Harleys over outside the pubs.'

'Not me,' I said. 'I'd never kick over a bike. A bikie, maybe.'

'Bullshit,' he said. 'That night out at the Cross Keys. Kicked one and the rest went down like dominoes. The bad guys swarmed out of the pub like bull ants.'

'I wasn't there,' I said. 'I was cuffed to a computer all year. Remember?'

He preferred his own foggy memories. 'Operation Heavy Hand,' he said. 'Poke the nest and put a cage-full of arseholes away for six months for assaulting police. Couldn't get away with it now. They've got the best silks in town.'

'Operation Creative Licence,' I corrected him. 'Not Heavy Hand.'

'I won't argue. You always came up with the names. Taskforce Hydra. Taskforce Cerberus. New one every week.'

That part was true. Coming up with names was the nearest I got to action that long slow year. It drove me crazy, sitting around in the Police Club come happy hour, listening to the war stories, desperate to be in the thick of it.

'Scratch a cop and you find a frustrated poet,' he said.

'Blame a schoolteacher mother. She thought I was too smart to be a cop.'

He laughed. 'She married one though.'

'Not for long.'

'Operation Penny Farthing,' he said. 'What the fuck did that mean?'

'Lost in the mists of time, Chief.'

His own mist cleared a little. 'Operation Spiderwasp,' he remembered. 'That was it, wasn't it? Your little internet sting.'

'It's too painful to talk about,' I said. 'I got post-traumatic stress from the boredom.'

He laughed, obligingly. 'Heard some bloke on the radio the other day. Has a full-time job thinking up names for horses. No two can ever be the same. Nice work if you can get it.'

'What do you call the bikie squad now?' I interrupted. 'Taskforce Tiptoe Through The Tulips?'

'Combined Taskforce – Gangs, Organised and Drugs.'

'Bit prosaic.'

He laughed. 'Only if you're a frustrated poet. Another reason we could use you back. Raise the tone of the place.'

'The last idea I had didn't work out that well.'

'Operation Trojan Horse,' he said, acknowledging it for the first time.

'Operation Sacrificial Bunny, more like it,' I said, less with anger than sarcasm.

'Like I said last night, Zads. I should never have let you talk me into it.'

Last night those words had added fuel to the fire; now not so much. Did two half-apologies add up to a full and heartfelt one?

'Andabatae,' he said, suddenly.

'Andy who?'

'The name of the gladiators. The blind ones. Andabatae.'

'You're too smart to be a cop,' I told him, and he laughed again, and poured out another drink.

'We all are,' he said. 'That's our problem.'

'Since you're so interested, Chief, I'll tell you what really happened tonight. In the Coliseum.'

'You could have sold tickets.'

'I don't mean the fight itself. I mean what happened afterwards. What became clear. You'll think I'm crazy.'

'Try me.'

I took another sip – oxtail-stew on the back of the tongue now – swallowed, cleared my throat. 'Maybe he's a thousand miles away,' I said. 'Maybe he's at the bottom of the river. But I don't think so. I can *feel* it. In here.' I tapped my chest. 'Thing is, I'm glad. I *want* him here. Within reach. I want him stalking me in the park. I want him on the Harley that just cruised past. I *want* him to come prowling round the house one dark night.'

He sawed off some meat and chewed for a time, perhaps waiting to see if I was done.

I wasn't. 'And the darker the fucking better!'

He washed down the meat with another mouthful of wine. 'He's no drunk in the park, Zads. And he'll be bringing more than a net and trident.'

'*That's* why I need the gun back.'

'What happened tonight made things a bit clearer to me too. I said you might surprise yourself, but you surprised me more.'

'Meaning what?'

'Meaning forget him – he's gone – and think about the job. Okay, I was offering charity last night, but not now. I really can use you. Your eyes and ears.' He chuckled. 'Your ears, anyway.'

The whole truth, finally. I waited for more of it.

'What you said about picking the bullshit a mile off. We all think we can read the fake smiles, the shifty glances. But maybe it's all in the voice.'

'You looking for a human lie-detector, Chief?'

'It's not such a stupid idea. Could find you a cosy corner down in Phone Intercept. Eavesdropping on the bad guys. Couple of half-days a week to start with. Feel your way in.'

'Still sounds like charity.'

'That's the cover job.'

He couldn't help reaching for his drink, addicted as ever to keeping me in suspense.

'You want a *spy* in Bullshit Castle?' I realised. 'First the bikies, now the Big Blue Gang! Jesus – I don't know which mob is more dangerous!'

'You won't be in harm's way,' he said. 'Couple of hours a day on the phones. Sit in on the briefings. Listen to the interviews. Then whatever you like. Wander around. Hidden in full view.'

'You think because I can't see, people will think I can't hear?'

He didn't answer; he didn't need to. I knew it was true. I'd be the house cripple. The harmless pet. Less a fly on the wall than part of the wallpaper.

'If you think for one moment I'll wear a wire . . .'

'Never again. I promise.'

Silence, as we let those memories slide under the bridge by mutual consent. I took another mouthful of whichever red, let it fill my mouth with its heat and noise. I was wavering, and he knew it. He could probably *see* it: the glow on my face that I could feel from the inside.

'I might need to deck some bastard,' I said. 'From time to time.'

He laughed. 'Deck me. Anytime you need. You owe me one. What do you say?'

'I'll think about it.'

'Dessert menu, gentlemen?'

'We're fine,' Terry said, and I sensed him watch the waitress walk away. 'Cute as,' he added, 'in case you're wondering.'

'Not getting enough then?'

'Story of my life. Christ, what time is it? Remember the old days? Afternoon shift ended the same time as the hospitals? We'd clock off and head down to the nurses' quarters at the Childrens?'

'The Bulk Store,' I recalled, but my half-drunk mind was on a more recent possibility. 'This, um, senior constable. Annie what's-her-face. You know her?'

'Annie Hickson. A little.'

'What's she like? In case I'm wondering.'

'Course Captain back at the Academy. Ultra efficient. Big future, I hear'

'She smells good,' I said.

He chuckled. 'They're all wearing perfume now. The ACs latest brainstorm. He's trialling a range of calming fragrances. Good for crowd control. Cheaper than tasers.'

'You should dab some on,' I said, 'sweetie-pie.'

'You too,' he said. 'Next time you go for a stroll in the park.'

'Does she look as good as she smells?'

'Hot as.' He guffawed. 'But I could tell you she looks like Miss Universe, couldn't I?'

I drained the dregs from my glass. 'Feel free,' I said. 'Give me something to think about in my lonely bed tonight.'

'You *have* perked up. Brunette. Athletic type.' Another teasing pause. 'Great rack, that what you want to hear?'

Not particularly, but I played along. 'It's a start.'

'One problem, Zads. She's married.'

'Who's the lucky bloke?'

He spluttered for a time, too amused with himself to answer. 'She's not a bloke,' he finally got out, and after a moment's disappointment, I spluttered with him.

'Walk you home, gladiator?' he asked.

I pushed myself back from the table. 'I should walk *you* home. You're way over.'

In truth, I felt a little wobbly, but the foot-traffic had thinned, and soon enough I found my rhythm, tapping and sweeping on autopilot while letting my thoughts drift back to the events of the square, and the satisfaction they had given me.

A prickle of goosebumps on the nape of my neck startled me back into Chinatown.

'You still dogging me, Chief?' I said, loudly, without turning.

No answer. The Morphett Street walk signal bleeped; I tapped across the road, more amused than angry. If he wanted to see me safely home, so be it. Two pairs of high-heels approached; two laughing women's voices passed by. Maybe they were holding hands, maybe wearing matching wedding rings, but I couldn't help trying to picture them. Or identikit them, using my standard parts. Raven hair, tick. Athletic bodies, tick. Great rack? They were from Terry's kit, not mine. It struck me that my taste in imaginary women was nothing if not predictable. I hadn't gazed at a billboard or Hollywood movie or girlie magazine for two years, but they wouldn't have changed my internal programming: less Miss Universe than Miss Universal, which in my case meant Miss Particular, writ large.

'Do you wish I had bigger tits?' she asked me more than once, standing naked before the bathroom mirror. As if any mirror could ever be unflattering to her.

'You wish I had a bigger dick?'

'Seriously. I'll have implants if you want. I've been comparing surgeons. And costs.'

This temporary madness always seemed utterly out-of-character, no matter how many times it happened, or how many in-character lists of surgical complications or cost-benefit analyses she drew up.

My answer was always the same, if in various guises. *Be like a wrong note in a perfect tune. You'll keep toppling forward on your face. You're suffering under the delusion you're not perfect already? You've got big boobs, it's just that the rest of you is tiny. Only if I can have that penis implant. It's either that or the Bali holiday, you choose. Perhaps a tiny bit larger — come back to bed and try a course of lip suction.*

All of which did their job, whether by making her laugh or making her smother me with kisses.

'Home,' Miss Global Positioning whispered in my ear as I rapped the pickets of the front gate.

She, too, is just another Willow-clone when I try to put a face (okay, body) to the voice.

'Tell me about your breasts, Siri,' I said as I kicked off my boots inside the door.

'I don't know how to respond to that, Richard.'

'It makes you feel uncomfortable?'

'I don't like these arbitrary categories, Richard.'

'Nothing arbitrary about it. We've been together for the best part of two years and the relationship remains unconsummated.'

'I don't understand that form of words, Richard. Could you rephrase it?'

'Can I have a root?'

'A route from current location to where?'

My laughter bounced loudly around the hard-edged acoustics of the hall. 'The bedroom might be a good place to start.'

'Okay. Here's what I found. Bedroom Eyes Furniture Store, 98 Currie Street, Adelaide. Bedroom Flirt Lingerie, 6 Church Street, North Adelaide . . .'

'Maybe I'll find my own way.'

A sign of how far I'd come in the space of one night: joking about sex, even the lack of it. Scout nail-clicked up the hall, snuffled some treats from my palm, then clicked back to her basket in the bedroom, satisfied I was home safe and sound.

I followed a step behind, still chuckling. I unholstered Siri, peeled off my clothes, and fell into bed with the device in hand. She felt warm, as if her low-power brain – one watt? ten? – was working overtime. I lifted her to my nose and sniffed her casing, amusing myself. The faint tang of sweat was surely mine. I licked her casing, then tickled her starter button with the tip of my tongue out of sheer tomfoolery.

'You like that, babe?'

'This seems to be about you, Richard, not me.'

When I was done amusing myself I set her down on the bedside table. She has the voice of an angel and the powers of a genie but no amount of rubbing her magic lamp was going to conjure up the rest of her. I let my thoughts drift back to the fight in the park, and the undeniable success of that. No fucking for me tonight, even with imaginary friends, but fighting seemed an adequate substitute. They came from the same word-root, after all – or so Encyclopaedia Willow had once told me, over a game of Scrabble.

Replaying the bout in my head, blow by blow, was an unlikely lullaby, but a bellyful of wine helped, and within minutes I was sound asleep.

II

HEARING

1

'YOU MUSTN'T TRY IT AGAIN,' THE PROFESSOR SAID. 'I WANT YOU to promise me that, Richard.'

'I didn't "try" anything,' I told her. 'It was an accident. Why does no one believe me?'

There was no heat in my words. I had a morning-after red-wine headache, but not enough to dent my contentment.

'No one meaning Willow?' she asked.

'Willow doesn't count. She never believes anything I say.'

Silence. The cap was unscrewed from her pen again, the nib whispered across the pad. I lay on her couch, picturing it. An expensive fountain pen, certainly. Opal inlaid, gold nib.

The writing stopped, the cap was replaced.

'I'm wondering if it might be time to invite her to one of our consultations,' she said.

An ambush of sorts, but I managed a good-humoured chuckle. 'Meaning you don't believe anything I say either?'

'We're often the last to be aware of our true motivations, Richard.'

'Here we go with the unconscious motivations again, eh Prof? Haven't you got anything better to do on a sunny Saturday morning?'

More silence. One thing I'd learnt: she could not be provoked, even jokily. Sometimes the silences last an entire session. Usually I blink first, so to speak, blurting out whatever revelation she's been waiting to hear. Today I felt merely sleepy. There was nothing new to be said about Willow. We'd talked endlessly about Willow. Willow who always knows better. Willow who usually does know better.

Memo, Prof: try playing Scrabble with her. Try doing crossword puzzles with her. Willow the Know-All nerd-brain. Willow-bloody-pedia. The memories amused me more than disturbed me today. Even the one thing Willow might not know yet – the fact of the prison break – seemed less of an issue. I closed my sightless eyes and let myself drift, wondering if the Professor had heard the news. Surely not, or she would have mentioned it. I wasn't about to enlighten her.

'Have you ever visited San Francisco, Richard?'

An odd, jolting tangent. 'Passed through. Once. On the way to Vegas. Drug Enforcement Conference.'

'You were a delegate?'

'Observer.' I chuckled. 'I won't tell you what I ended up observing.'

'I first visited five years ago,' she said. 'I wanted to walk across the Golden Gate Bridge.'

'For the view?'

'For work.'

I waited. Another thing I'd learnt: psychiatrists never make small-talk.

'It's a popular suicide spot. People come from all over America to jump. From all over the world.'

'How did you manage to restrain yourself?'

No reaction. 'The bridge opened in 1937,' she continued, sounding weirdly like Willow. 'Since then more than fifteen hundred people have jumped.'

'I haven't been thinking about visiting it,' I joked. 'Consciously.'

Still she wouldn't bite. 'The thing is, about one in fifty survive the jump. I was fortunate to interview three of the survivors whilst I was there.'

'Tax deductible holiday, Prof?'

'They've all been studied before, of course. Intensively. But I wanted to know what went through their heads the moment *after* they jumped.'

'Um – so far so good?'

Mostly she ignores my jokes, sometimes she wants to know why I am trying to distract her. Today she just talked over them, in full fact mode. Why invite Willow when she was already present in spirit?

'It takes about four seconds to fall. I wanted to know what they were thinking. *Feeling*. Before they hit the water.'

'Their whole life flashes before their eyes?'

'A myth. The fact is, the survivors almost always regretted jumping. Their first thought: nothing in my life is as bad as this. Nothing that can *ever* happen could be as stupid as this.'

I chuckled. 'Changed my mind, Scotty. Beam me back up.'

The pen was uncapped again; the gold nib began its whispering. Her paper also sounded expensive. Handmade. Monogrammed.

'My point is serious, Richard. The *successful* suicides must have felt the same. Their last thoughts must have been wishing they hadn't jumped.'

'That's not what I felt,' I said, 'if that's what you're asking.'

'So what did you feel?'

'Try to keep up, Prof. I was too drugged to feel anything.'

'*Before* the drugs took effect. What did you feel then?'

'I just wanted to get a night's sleep. Maybe I wanted to forget some things. But not everything. And not forever. Just overnight.'

In my current good mood, the idea that I might have tried to top myself seemed even more preposterous.

'Which things did you want to forget?'

'Gee,' I said. 'I wonder. Why not check your notes over the past few months?'

A shuffle of paper. 'I have the Duty Psychiatrist's report before me. You signed yourself out against his advice, remember?'

'If you say so.'

'He says so. He was concerned that you seemed, um, "paradoxically elated". When you left Emergency.'

My hackles rose, ever so slightly. 'No paradox. I was just glad to be alive. Back on planet earth. It was an accident, remember?'

'If it was an accident why did you leave Willow a phone message? Before you took the overdose.'

'After the overdose,' I said. 'Nice try, but check the report. I rang *after* I realised my mistake.'

Silence. Then: 'I'm wondering if that's part of the reason you were glad to be alive? Because Willow came running to fetch you.'

I should have been the one taking notes. She wouldn't have been out of place in Interview Room 1 in Bullshit Castle. Mostly she plays the good cop, but not always.

'*All* the survivors regretted it?' I changed the subject.

'There were exceptions. One went back to the bridge and jumped again. Successfully.'

'Straight after you'd interviewed him?'

The joke of the day sank without trace. 'Her. And it was years ago. Before my visit. Another survivor did it for fun. Or so he claimed.'

'You didn't believe him?'

'At least he didn't pretend it was an accident.'

I forced a half-laugh. 'You're like a dog with a fucking bone.'

Of course the cap came off the pen. Pavlov reflexes: the dog barks when I drop the f-word, the Prof reaches for her pen.

'I'm wondering if Willow thinks it was an accident?' she said.

Willow again. I opened my mouth and a stray thought fell out – 'Did she ring you?' – but as soon as it was set in words, its certainty jerked me upright. 'She fucking *did*, didn't she?'

'She left a message. That's all. She wanted to make an appointment to see me.'

'You *agreed*?'

'I haven't answered. I wanted to talk about it with you first.'

I settled back, feeling calmer.

'She obviously still cares for you,' she said. 'Which is why I suggested some joint counselling.'

'Maybe it's the adrenaline,' I said. 'The moment they jump. It shocks them out of their depression. Temporarily.'

The pen was set down again. I imagined it lying exactly in parallel to the margin of the expensive notebook. The notebook aligned in turn to the edge of a leather-inlaid desk. The desk in some elegant feng shui relationship to the rest of the room. Or was I just remembering Willow's stylish Danish desk in her study at home? Was there no escape from her? Not in the messed-up desktop of my head, it seemed.

'Possibly,' she said, without missing a beat. 'Some of the newer antidepressants work a bit like that. I know you've been opposed to taking them in the past.'

'Be cheaper for the health-care system,' I interrupted, 'to get your depressives to take a bungee jump off a bridge before breakfast every morning. Put things in perspective.'

A mystery noise from the far side of the desk; was she suppressing a chuckle? Surely not.

'Especially off the Golden Gate Bridge,' I added, encouraged.

Yes, a chuckle. A two-laugh consultation: would wonders never cease? Not for the first time I wished I could see her face, her eyes, her perfect professional woman's teeth.

'What happened to your face?' she said, spookily.

'*My* face?' I said, stalling. Had she heard about the fight after all, or was she just fishing?

'There's no one else in the room, Richard.'

Except the ghost of Willow, popping in and out from time to time. 'Bungee jump that went wrong,' I told her.

'Seriously. It looks . . . a mess.'

'Overhanging branch. Why? You worried I might have punched myself in the face? A little unconscious self-harm? You need some downtime, Prof. Take the weekends off.'

'I *am* concerned about your mood swings, Richard.'

'I seem paradoxically elated?'

'Inappropriately calm, perhaps. Calmer than our last few sessions.'

'As if I've already made the big decision?' I said, and chuckled as naturally as I could manage.

'Whatever your motivations, I want us to make a compact: you won't do it again.'

'I'm not about to,' I said. 'Or not yet, anyway.'

'Not ever.'

'What's your side of the deal?'

'I promise to be available. If you have any such thoughts again. I'll give you my mobile number.'

I lay there on the couch, mulling it over. I've never got the point of these unenforceable no-suicide contracts. What would be the consequences – the other consequences – of breaking them?

'Problem is,' I said, 'that would defeat the purpose.'

'What purpose?'

Topping myself was the last thing on my mind today, which perhaps was why I felt able to give an honest answer. 'The thought has crossed my mind from time to time. Same as anyone. Sometimes it's been the only thing that's kept me sane. Got me through the night. The knowledge that I *can* do it. If I ever need to.'

The opal cap was unscrewed again, the nib caressed the paper. A word-for-word transcription? Or one of her elaborate interpretations?

'Let me get this straight,' I said. 'The moral of your little Golden Gate story is I shouldn't kill myself because I might regret it afterwards. right?'

No answer as she continued to write. Her desk alarm bleeped, softly; I rolled off the couch onto my feet and offered my hand across the desk.

'I get it, Prof. Just so you don't lose any sleep, it's a deal.'

She set down her pen and shook my hand, limply. 'Good,' she said. 'But I don't think we should wait a month until our next appointment. It's clearly a difficult time for you.'

'A paradoxical time?'

'How is Wednesday?'

'Better than Saturdays. Remember what I said. All work and no play.'

'I have a space at 10.30.'

I shook out my cane. 'My people will ring your people.'

'I'll take that as a yes. Meanwhile, remember our compact.'

'I hereby promise to ring you if I accidentally mix up the dosage of sleeping pills again. Happy?'

'Half happy,' she said, and perhaps there was a half-smile behind it. 'I'd be happier if you would consider inviting Willow.'

'Speaking of sleeping pills,' I said. 'I could use another prescription.'

'I'll see you on Wednesday, Richard.'

In fact I had no further need for sleepers. Or for sworn agreements, enforceable or otherwise. Our time together had been more therapeutic than usual. The Golden Gate story had helped clarify one thing, if not for the reasons she intended. As I tapped towards the waiting room and the waiting dog, I was certain that if I ever got round to jumping off a bridge I wasn't going to spend my last four seconds filled with regrets.

One regret in particular occupied my thoughts, though, as it had for the best part of two years: a debt owed to me, a debt of blood that until now had seemed out of reach.

Scout presented her handle but had trouble keeping up as I half-dragged her to the lift well, filled with my newfound purpose.

'Let's get the fuck out of here,' I said, as the lift doors opened, a plan she agreed to immediately, emphatically.

2

'CURRENT LOCATION: 219 HINDLEY STREET.'

I'd stayed well clear since the shooting. Too many old friends to run into, of various club colours. But today felt different; today I felt – not quite at home, but safe enough.

'Locate nearest ATM,' I said.

'Continue current direction. Thirty steps.'

I counted the steps, found the screen, brailled the keys, and withdrew my daily maximum. My slow-hatching plan would need every cent.

'Current location to 104A Hindley Street,' I said.

'Continue current direction. Two hundred steps . . .'

I tapped confidently on. Overconfidently? If so, not because of the large dog at my side, or any delusions I harboured about the effectiveness of my blindly swung fists. It was more the one thing Terry had said that rang true: the clubs were keeping their heads down. The revenge killing of a blind ex-cop was the last thing they needed on their bloody hands.

'107A Hindley Street,' Siri confirmed a few shopfronts later, then plucked a matching name from her infinite Yellow Pages. 'Tattoo Inc.'

In the old days I would always sneak in through the back door. Midmorning mostly, before the brothers and bouncers and dealers and narcissistic rich kids woke up and began pondering whether to add a little filigree to the Sistine Chapels of their body art. A three-two code-tap on the rear door and Michelangelo himself would admit me, quickly and quietly.

But that was a lifetime ago. Today I pushed open the front door and walked into – what? Sounds: a doorbell jingling above me; a background of dull, thumping rap; a tattoo gun buzzing somewhere in the foreground.

Which meant he already had company. From which club? And how many?

The bell stopped jingling and the buzzing also fell silent. 'You look lost, champ.'

Did Mike really not recognise me, or was he just being cagey? Maybe all that close-focus work was taking its toll. Or maybe it was the goggles. I allowed the dog to tug me further in. 'Been thinking of getting a tattoo,' I improvised.

'Bit busy right now, champ.'

The gun started buzzing again. I had the feeling it was just the two of them: the master artist and his living canvas. Who was wearing which colours? One thing I should have checked with Terry: was the studio still a demilitarised zone? Once upon a time all the clubs had been welcome, although Mike was careful not to overlap appointments.

The buzzing stopped again. 'Still here, champ?'

A girl's high giggle from the main chair. 'You're very trusting,' she said in my direction. 'He could, like, carve *any*thing on you.'

I had to smile: no wonder he wanted to get rid of me. One thing hadn't changed: young female clients still got plum appointments in the quiet of the morning. I'd arrived just in time. Ten minutes later the door would have been locked, the CLOSED sign flipped over.

'I can see with my skin,' I said, still making it up as I went. 'That's why I want to do it. To *see* a picture with my skin.'

Mike grunted, amused. 'I like it. Never done a blind bloke before, but I like it.'

He didn't recognise me, that much was clear. Perhaps the oddities – the white cane, the dog – drew his eye away from my face. Memo, Prof: *this* is a paradox. By making me so highly visible, blindness offers a cloak of invisibility at the same time. I'm the ostrich who got away with it. My head might be buried in the sand, but no one can see me either.

'It's not, like, against the law or something is it?' The girl sounded no more than fifteen, sixteen. 'Tattooing someone, you know, visually challenged?'

Mike's concerns were more immediate. 'How you gonna pick out a design, champ?'

'Guess I'll have to trust you.'

Another chuckle. 'Could fit you in later. Come back in an hour?'

'Happy to wait,' I said, enjoying myself. 'Got nothing better to do.'

No chuckle this time. 'Might be longer than an hour.'

'He's blind,' the girl told him. 'You can't just turf him out.'

'Take a pew, then,' he said, irritably. 'To your left.'

I turned left, walked into a wall.

'Sorry,' he said. '*My* left.'

A suppressed giggle from the girl, a barely audible whisper: 'Did you do that *deliberately*, Mike?'

I about-faced, tapped a sofa, and eased myself down into its worn, creaky leather.

'Sit, girl,' I said, and released her handle.

As the gun began buzzing again I ran my hand over the familiar crinkles and wrinkles of the armrest. Had nothing changed in two years? I tried to summon back a little more familiarity. The studio walls covered with framed photos of the master's Greatest Works. The bar fridge at one end of the wood-veneer counter; the coffee machine at the other. The client on her back in the big dentist's chair; the begoggled artist on his small wheeled stool to one side.

'Had a tatt before, champ?'

I slipped off my jacket and tilted my right upper arm his way.

'Awesome,' the girl said. 'Are you, like, a Christian?'

The wasp stopped buzzing; the stool rolled my way. I could picture him clearly as he studied my arm: the bottle-glass lenses, the crinkled leather of a face that might have been pieced together from off-cuts of couch upholstery.

Clearest of all was the startled look on that face.

The stool rolled away. 'We're done,' he told the girl, tersely. 'I'll just clean you up.'

'What? It's not finished! I wanted orange in the snake eyes.'

'Tricky pigment, orange. And the outline needs a night to settle. No extra charge, okay?'

'Well, I spose,' she said. 'What's *that*?'

'Antiseptic cream.'

Silence. I sensed him glancing my way, puzzled, as he attended to the raw wound, which would be starting to weep.

'You're going to wrap it in, like, *glad*wrap?'

'Trade secret,' he told her. 'I'll take it off tomorrow morning.'

'*Sun*day?'

'I'll open up just for you.'

'It's mega itchy. Don't think I can wait till then.'

'If I can you can,' he said. 'Wear boxing gloves to bed.'

She giggled, won back. 'Can you lend me a pair?'

'He'll bring them over tonight,' I said, 'and lace you up personally.'

Another giggle; she was lapping up the attention. Body art aside, I could never understand what they saw in this prune-skinned sleaze-bag. The adrenaline buzz of a walk on the wild side? The endorphin high of the needle-pricks? The intimacy of body parts tenderly prepped with alcohol wipes and antiseptic creams?

'Mastercard?' she said.

More distinctive sounds: rubber gloves being peeled off; the bleep of a payWave; a pair of low, clunky heels walking to the door.

School-shoes, I decided as the bell ushered her out.

'She have a permission slip from her mum?' I said, trying to keep the disapproval out of my voice. I needed his help. 'Sounded about fourteen.'

'Seventeen. Jesus – no wonder I didn't recognise you! You walk in front of a cement truck?'

'Got into a punch-up last night.'

A hoot of laughter: 'With another blind bloke?'

No mention of the prison break yet. Surely he'd heard: the studio was gossip central, an endless source of tip-offs in the old days, if a little expensive to buy.

'Blind drunk,' I said.

An even louder hoot. 'I'd pay to see that.'

'I'd pay to see your seventeen-year-old,' I said, humouring him, remembering how he loved to brag about his conquests.

A clink of glasses from the direction of the counter. 'Had one last week. Came in with her boyfriend. Both pissed as newts. She wanted his name tattooed above her Brazilian. Gothic font.'

'Let me guess. Solo appointment the next morning?'

A bottle cap was unscrewed. 'No need. That's the best part. I sent him down to The Black Bull for more bourbon, and, well, she didn't need much encouragement.'

I might have laughed once, or just sneered collusively, inured like all cops to the human comedy. The great human *stupidity*: the complementary, equal opportunity stupidity of men and women alike. Make that boys and girls. One thing you learn early in the Force: there are no grown-ups. But who was I to laugh at stupidity these days?

'Still can't believe I didn't recognise you, champ,' he said, as he pressed a glass into my hand. Jack Daniel's, from the faint tickle of fumes in the air.

'You haven't changed a bit,' I told him. 'Apart from the grey hairs.'

He chuckled. 'So you've been pretending to be blind all along? The dog and the cane are a cover? Cheers.'

Our glasses clinked; I took a mouthful of the smoky liquid, swirled it back across my tongue, swallowed. The cheap stuff, but good enough. 'So how's business?'

He kicked his stool closer again, sat on it. 'Sunrise indus-
try. Every pimple-faced sissy wants a tough-guy sleeve or barbwire
necklace. Speaking of which . . .' His hand gripped my right elbow
lightly, tilted my upper arm his way again. 'Work of art, if I say
so myself.'

I looked down as if that would help me remember it: the
crucifix growing out of a pile of steaming excrement. The shit of
the crucified.

'It's a wonder Big Dino hasn't paid you a visit with a blowtorch,'
he said.

'For a nominee tatt? I was never a full member.' I took another
sip. 'Besides, I keep hearing he wouldn't want the grief. The clubs've
changed.'

A snort. 'Some for the good, some for the bad. Keep still.'

His hand tightened its grip on my elbow and something ticklish –
a felt-tip pen? – began sketching on the skin above it.

'Could disguise it for you,' he said.

Was I reading the words as he traced over them – GOLGOTHANS
MC on the horizontal strut of the crucifix, BORN IN SHIT on the
pillar – or just remembering them? Mostly he seemed to be scribbling.

'Having fun?' I said.

'Trying a couple of ideas. What do you think of that one?'

'Feels like you blacked it out completely.'

He chuckled. 'I thought you said you could see with your skin.'

'Not enough pixels.'

'I've hung a Christ on the cross.' He picked up his gun and buzzed
it, mock-threateningly. 'Could make it permanent.'

'Jesus Christ born in shit?'

'I can fix the lettering.' The felt-tip went to work on my arm again.
'BORN AGAIN?'

'You mean I'd be, like, a Christian,' I said in my best teen-voice.

He laughed, obligingly, released my elbow and rolled his stool
sideways. 'Other arm.'

I offered it up, also obligingly, and not just because I still needed a favour. I too was beginning to enjoy the attention, sitting there like a big baboon being groomed with a felt-tip pen.

Which was the word, I reminded myself, sternly, for what he did to his girls: grooming.

'Forgot I did this one,' he said. 'When was it? Ten years back?'

I grunted. 'Closer to twenty.'

The pen began tickling again. 'Bit faded. Could use a touch-up.'

'What's the point? Not much use to me.'

'You're just the canvas,' he said.

'Then pay me for displaying it. Walking billboard rates.'

He chuckled again. 'Tell you what. This is heritage work. I'll fix it pro bono. Be like restoring a work of art.'

This time I laughed with him, tickled as much by his nonsense as by the tip of the pen.

'Your life in pictures, champ. 'Chapter One.'

I could see it clearly enough – rampant wasp, cowering spider, a memento of the year I made Detective. Mixed memories, these: luring the rock spiders out of their world wide web, then stinging them if not to death, at least for life. It wasn't why I joined the Force. And it wasn't a chapter I wanted to re-read now, stuck in a spiderweb of a different kind. And with a borderline rock spider.

'You sure she's over seventeen?' I said.

'I always check the ID, Detective.' He sniggered. 'Especially the ones wearing a school uniform. Let's see your back.'

I peeled off my T-shirt, my thoughts elsewhere, then immediately regretted it as he whistled, approvingly.

'I haven't forgotten *this* one,' he said.

'I wish I could,' I told him.

He wasn't listening. 'Pigeon pair, right? Did one for her too? Should do more china-patterns. Blue ink and human skin – perfect fit.'

I could see the tatts clearly as he spoke: his and hers Willow-plates, one pure porcelain, one cracked china.

'Mind if I take a photo?'

'Over my dead body,' I said, as his felt-tip continued its grooming.

'Chinese writing needs a touch up. Remind me. What's it mean? Love Something. Not Love Hurts. Done a few of those!'

Talk about no escape. And talk about my life in pictures. The once-vivid blues of the two symbols could stay on the dark side of my body forever. He was half-right. Love was there, looking a bit like a stick-thin bloke sheltering under a rainy roof. The other sign wasn't Hurt but might as well have been: her name, with its willow-tree pictogram. Lau. Second memo of the day, Prof: you'll love this bit of voodoo. The willow-twigs that broke the camel's back.

'Surprised she hasn't sent you back for repairs,' he said.

'It's none of her fucking business,' I spat out, with more venom than intended.

The dog growled; the felt-tip stopped in its tracks.

'Sorry to hear that,' he said. 'Always thought youse was the perfect couple.'

I cut him short. 'One thing you *can* blot out: her name. Right now. Permanently.'

Silence while he spilled more bourbon into the glasses.

'Maybe you should sleep on it, champ. I wouldn't let a sheila like that slip between my fingers.'

The glass was pressed back into my hand. I forced myself to sip, slowly, if only to slow my thoughts as well.

'Bit old for you, isn't she?' I said, eventually.

He chuckled. 'I remember the night you brought her in. Valentine's Day. I done her piece first. I thought – *you lucky bastard.*'

'If you'd sent me off for bourbon,' I said, 'you'd have saved me a lot of grief.'

'It's that bad?' He took another sip. 'Look – if it's really over – you mind giving me her number?'

I struggled again to hide my feelings, or just stop myself taking a wild swing. How did I get to this point? I'd come needing a favour, and needing to humour him to get it – and got dragged back to Willow.

'I just want it gone,' I said, and leant forward, baring my back.

'Your funeral, champ.' He wheeled his stool closer. 'You comfortable on the sofa?'

The gun replaced the felt-tip; the wasp began buzzing again, then stinging. The prickling was painful, but oddly enjoyable: a pain I either needed, or deserved, or both. I sat hunched forward over my knees, a more complicated baboon now, lost in a needle-sharp grooming.

'Want me to sound him out?' he said.

'Who?'

'Big Dino. Could organise a sit-down. Smoke the peace pipe. You did him a favour, after all.'

'Not sure he'd see it that way.'

'He couldn't stand that little cunt any more than you,' he said. 'They owe you, big-time. Taking him out of circulation.'

Useful information, and usefully distracting. 'How long you going to be?' I asked.

'Nearly done. I heard you was writing a book. Now *that* might have Dino worried.'

Talk about gossip central. I felt a slight twinge, knowing also that my visit today would be out on the grapevine the moment I left.

I forced another laugh. 'Started this course once. Life-writing. Lasted about five minutes. *Her* idea. The ex.'

The half-word sneaked out almost naturally, although it was the first time I'd used it. Ex. Another milestone?

'It was part of the therapy. Get the shit out of my system. Like going to confession.'

The prickle of wasp-bites continued, a more effective kind of therapy. Acupuncture for the soul?

'How the fuck did you hear about it?' I said.

'The book? No names, no pack-drill. I just hope you shredded the drafts.'

I managed a smile, relaxing slowly. Another paradox: the more pain I felt, the more relaxed I got. Maybe baboons were the wrong analogy; it was more like the self-cutting of schoolgirls. A distraction, or relief, from worse pain.

The buzzing stopped. 'Done,' he said, 'but she ain't gonna like it.'

'She's not going to see it.'

He tore open a wipe and swabbed his handiwork. The alcohol was sharp and cold against the skin, the fumes pungent in my nose. 'So you gonna tell me, champ?'

'Her phone number?'

He snorted. 'We're done with her,' he said. 'About you. About what you're *really* doing here?'

I took a deep breath. Gossiping and monkey-grooming were fine, but there was a more important matter. 'You sure you haven't heard?'

'Heard fucking what?'

The dog answered him first; it wasn't easy to say what I needed to say aloud. 'My little mate jumped the fence yesterday.'

'Bullshit! The only way out of D Block Bottom is in a coffin.'

'I should be so lucky. He wasn't in Yatala. He got himself transferred up the river.'

His snort was half contemptuous, half incredulous. 'Resourceful little cunt. So what happened? The warden send him into town to buy a bag of licorice allsorts and he didn't come back from the shops?'

'Something like that.'

'Raise your arms,' he said, then wound his magic cling wrap over the raw wound and around my chest, twice. 'So that's why you're here. Fishing expedition.'

'It'd help. But no.' I paused, took another deep breath, felt the cling wrap stretch. 'I need a gun.'

A momentary beat, then his loudest splutter of laughter so far. 'To what end? So you can *shoot* the drunk in the park next time? You stop taking your medication, champ?'

'It's not the drunk I'm worried about.'

'Point taken,' he said, still chuckling, 'but even if you could aim the thing, you think he's gonna stick around and pay his respects? He'll be halfway across the Hay Plain by now.'

'I'm going to hit the next person who says that.'

A lower-key chuckle. 'That still doesn't answer my question. What use is a gun to you?'

'And *shoot* the next person who says that.'

Which only started him off again. One unforeseen problem: the story of the blind bloke wanting to buy a gun would be out on the grapevine the moment I walked out the door. Unless I could buy his silence along with the gun.

'I'm serious,' I said. 'A compact. Semiautomatic.'

Still chuckling, he stood up and walked to the front of the shop. I sensed he was checking the street.

'I know it's nuts,' I said. 'But that's why I need it. Psychological reasons. I'd *feel* safer.'

The door was locked; the slats of the venetian blind rustled shut.

'Five hundred,' I said. 'Cash.'

No laughter this time. 'You wearing a wire, Detective Sarge? The Taskforce sitting in a van up the road with the headphones on?'

I smacked a fist against my cling-wrapped chest, gorilla fashion, to remind him he could see for himself.

His footsteps returned; the dog growled as he reached for something on the sofa behind me. 'It's the mike on the collar of this jacket that bothers me.'

'Current location, Siri,' I said, loudly.

The answer was immediate: 'Tattoo Inc. 107A Hindley Street.'

He grunted. 'I might just put it out of harm's way all the same. Any objections?'

His footsteps walked away to the back of the shop; the store-room door opened, closed; opened again after a minute or three; his steps returned.

'I might be able to get my hands on a semi-compact,' he said. 'For the right price.'

I held out my hand. 'Cut the bullshit and let me see it.'

He laughed. *'See* it? Isn't that the reason I *shouldn't* sell it to you?'

'Seven-fifty. Cash.'

'Fifteen hundred.'

I tugged the wad from my pocket. 'A thousand. That's all I've got. Daily limit.'

The money was detached from my grasp speedily enough, and counted even more speedily.

'Tattoo repairs included,' I said.

The gun was pressed into my palm. I closed my fingers about the grip, hefted it, checked the safeties.

'Glock 19,' I said, as the dog growled, uneasy.

'I'm impressed, champ. Just don't wave it in my direction. Or hers. Nice dog by the way. What's her name?'

I pressed the magazine release, dropped it into my other hand. Full stack of fifteen. I felt for the serial number: filed down. I probed the chamber – empty – released the slide assembly, removed the spring and barrel. Partly I was showing off, partly relishing the feel of it. And the ease of it. Easier than S&Ws. Easier than any handgun ever made. And more sweetly balanced.

'You've used one of these before,' he said.

The smell of gun-grease was strong in my nose; a well cared-for weapon.

'What goes around comes around,' I said. 'I pushed hard for them back in '07. When we replaced the old Magnums.'

He snorted, contemptuously. 'Which were *way* past their use-by date.'

The deal wasn't necessarily done yet; how to keep humouring him? Pandering to his area of expertise seemed a good idea.

'Blame Dirty Harry,' I said. 'Took a long time for that nonsense to wash through.'

Another snort. 'Never take a revolver to a semiautomatic fight, champ.'

'Tell me about it. I was banging my head against a brick wall. They put me on the tender panel to shut me up.'

'Nice work if you can get it.'

'Business class to Austria. Springfield, Massachusetts. All expenses paid.'

'The S&Ws weren't a bad choice. Speaking of Springfield. Nicked the best ideas from Glock, and added a sexy grip.'

'You need more than a fashion statement when every fucktard in the state has one of these stuck in the back of his jeans,' I said. '*With* an extended magazine.'

He chuckled, knowingly. 'Which I could throw in for, oh, another two hundred. Add it to the tatt on your Visa. Art restoration.'

'Only need one bullet,' I said, pretending to squint through the tube of the detached barrel at him.

'You're off about ninety degrees. And if the gun's only for psychological security you need exactly zero bullets.'

'Have we got a deal?'

'Put it back together and we'll see,' he said.

He was teasing, but I did it anyway, easily.

'Your funeral, Detective. Sure you don't want some extra rounds?'

'What's in the magazine?'

His turn to show off. 'CorBon 115 grain. 1350 feet per sec.'

I slipped the gun into the side-snap on my belt. A comfortable fit – and also definitely comforting.

'You gonna *wear* it?' he said. 'In public? Speaking of fucktards.'

I unclipped the holster then reattached it to my belt in the small of my back. When I pulled my T-shirt back on I left it hanging loose.

He laughed. 'What's next, Deadeye? Practice session at the Fort Largs range?'

Not a stupid idea, in principle. But practise what? I reached back behind me, snapped the gun out, aimed it his way, holstered it again.

Then repeated the moves, more smoothly. Another problem in the war against the villains: they get a lot more shooting practice. In their own endless civil wars, yes, or the weekly drive-by shooting in whichever unnamed northern suburb – but mostly out in the mallee. Every bikie ranch between the Hills and the river has its own shooting barn or practice range. The annual ammo budget of the clubs would dwarf the Big Blue Gang's.

Eager to be rid of me now the deal was done, he fetched my coat from the backroom, held it for me to slip on. The day would be heating up outside, but the extra gun-camouflage would help.

'You was never here,' he said. 'You didn't get the gun from me.'

'I borrowed it from Confiscations,' I promised him. 'If anyone asks. It's Glock Bulk Store down there.'

3

'KEN JONES-HILL HERE, RICHARD. FOR THE LAST TIME WILL YOU *please* answer my messages. We've been very patient but the matter must be resolved.'

'Delete message.'

'Message deleted. Message received at 9.01 am today . . . Jones-Hill yet *again*, Richard. The terms of your lease are quite clear. If a guide dog is not being properly cared for, or in continuous work, she must undergo a placement review. We can obtain a court order to enforce this; I hope it will not come to that . . .'

'Delete message.'

'Message deleted. There are no more messages.'

Apart from the standard welcome home message from my bladder. I was halfway through answering it – risking a standing piss for once, I was in such a hurry – when the landline rang; by the time I'd shaken the last drop free the message-bank was answering for me.

'Hi, Rick and Willow's home number. Willow speaking . . .'

The sound of her voice – a message from happier, more carefree times – jolted me, as did her words: 'We're either not here right now, or pretending not to be, but feel free to leave a message for us after the beep. Bye!'

We? Us? Was it always the smallest words that did the most damage? For a time I stood there immobilised, fly open, useless cock in hand.

Beep.

'Hi, Richard. Gemma Rossi. From the *Sunday Mail.* I hope I'm not intruding. It's been a couple of years. I interviewed you after the shooting. Just after you came out of the coma. You may not remember me.'

I pushed Willow from my mind, helped by a prickle of indignation. Did Gemma think I'd lost my marbles? Of course I remembered her, if more clearly before the shooting, when things were less fuzzy. She'd been around for years: a diligent police roundsman who learnt her trade by riding in cars with cops. And by falling in and out of love with a few, not necessarily serially. And not necessarily the best choices, either – yours truly in that category, briefly. All of which, however, made her who she was: the only journo in town with any real feel for police work.

'I was hoping you might care to comment on a breaking news story. If you could return my call . . .'

'Answer call,' I shouted over my shoulder, then zipped up, flushed, and stepped back out into microphone-range as the calling tone bleeped.

'Gemma Rossi speaking.'

'It's Rick, Gemma.'

'You *are* home, you sly dog. How have you been travelling?'

'Getting by.'

'And Willow?'

Got that monkey off my back at last, I almost said. 'Willow is Willow. And you? Back on the police rounds? What did you do wrong?'

She cackled, obligingly. 'Must have done something right for once. State Political Editor since May.'

She paused, but I didn't bother filling the space with congratulations. She wasn't ringing to make chit-chat.

'Which is why I rang. Look – I wasn't sure how much to leave on the message-bank. I presume you've heard the, um, story I'm talking about.'

'A certain wetback paddling to freedom yesterday?'

'Good,' she said. 'I mean *good* you've heard. I didn't want to be the one to break the news. Though it would have been a story in its own right if you *hadn't* been notified.'

'The real story is why he was transferred to minimum security in the first place,' I said.

'Couldn't agree more. It's a disgrace. *That's* why I rang. It's more than a police story. It's the whole fucking justice system. Any comment you'd like to make?'

I thought it over, but not for long. 'Let's just say I'm disappointed but not surprised.'

I could hear her fingers tapping a keyboard in the background. 'Anything a bit less, um, laconic?'

My turn to chuckle. 'Give me a few minutes and I can probably work up a head of steam.'

'The Corrections Department Minister copped a grilling in Question Time last night. Perhaps you caught the TV news.'

'I don't get to watch a lot of TV,' I reminded her, but gently.

'Jesus! What a dumb thing to say. I guess you get a lot of that. You might like to, um, podcast his press conference tonight.'

'Let me guess. Internal departmental inquiry, blah blah blah. Meaning departmental whitewash. Everyone ducking for cover.'

'Can I quote you on that?'

'Word for word.'

Her fingers tapped on. 'I wondered if you feel any sense of personal jeopardy.'

'I don't quite follow.'

'Well. Um. How to put this? He made death threats against you when he was being sentenced.'

'I must have still been in a coma.'

'Come on, Rick. This is me. I'm sure you've read – sorry, *heard* – the trial transcript. Sometime in the last two years.'

'Several times, in fact.'

'If it's too painful to talk about, just say. But he did try to kill you. On the doorstep of your own home. You don't think he might try again?'

'He hasn't got the balls,' I said, unable to prevent the venom leaking through, and liking the taste of it once it had. 'A gutless little coward with a big mouth,' I spat more of it out. 'Feel free to quote that too.'

The tapping stopped. 'Is that a good idea? Taunting him?'

It wasn't just a good idea, it struck me with some force – there was none better. Not because he might read those words and feel their spittle on his face – well, that too – but because it might be the only way I had of reaching him.

And therefore – the notion lit up my brain like a cartoon light bulb – tempting him to find *me*.

'He'll be halfway to Timbuktu by now,' I said, covering my tracks.

'Maybe,' she said, uncertainly. 'There's something else. A document has, um, come into my possession that might interest you. The transcript of his most recent Prisoner Assessment.'

'I'm impressed. How did you get your paws on *that*? Wikileaks?'

'Let's just say it fell off the back of a Correctional Services truck. Shall I read you a few highlights?'

'Let me guess again. A model prisoner. Popular with his fellow inmates. Joined a book-of-the-month club. Took up flower arranging.'

She snickered. 'You're getting warm. Agricultural Science, in fact. He's been studying online.'

'Majoring in Hydroponics?'

'Bachelor's Degree at the Waite Institute. General Ag. Science. I've got the academic transcript here. You ready for this?'

'As ready as I'll ever be.'

'Agricultural Systems 1A: Passed with Credit. Plant Physiology: Passed with High Credit.'

I hooted. 'He *deserves* a credit. In Bullshit 101. Clever little bugger.'

'What do you mean?'

'Think about it. Why Ag. Sci.? Why not, say, Law, like all the other psychopaths?'

A moment's puzzlement. 'You're saying he planned this all along? Studied Ag. Science so he could get transferred up the river?'

'A get out of Max free card,' I said. 'Go directly to the holiday farm.'

Her fingers tapped again, briefly but excitedly. 'Nice scam,' she said. 'Speaking of which, there's more. The psychiatrist's report. Shall I read it?'

'Dot-points will do. I've had my fill of shrinks this week.'

'Dot-point one: he's a reformed man. Truly sorry for what he did to you. Let's see – yep. He hopes that one day he might have an opportunity to tell you that. Face to face. And that you might forgive him.'

'I've been marking him *way* too low,' I said. 'That's Rhodes Scholar class bullshit.'

'There's one bit I don't get. But I'm not sure you want to hear it.'

'If I didn't before I do now, you tease.'

'He also says that *he* forgives *you.*'

I didn't get it either. I replayed the words in my head in case I'd misheard, but their meaning didn't change. 'Forgive me for *what*?'

'Um. For any anger that you might still harbour towards him.'

Laugh or cry? Either way, enough bullshit – his and mine. Meaning, on my side, enough angry jokes. It was the real world after all. The stakes were high: attempted murder, actual blinding, successful prison escape. Possible reattempted murder.

'The psychiatrist's opinion is there is no reason to doubt his sincerity.'

'Surprise fucking surprise,' I said, and the first dog-echo of the evening came from the next room. 'Haven't met one yet who didn't come down in the last shower. Especially the women. Suckers for bad boys.' A suspicion suddenly struck me. 'What's her name. The psychiatrist?'

'She's a he.'

I managed a grudging snort. 'Same diff. Except the blokes don't want to fuck the rough trade, they want to *be* the rough trade. Vicariously. Talk about the glamour of evil.'

'Nice phrase,' she said, still tapping away. 'Can I use it?'

It wasn't mine, but I was happy to give permission. If Willowpedia had been around she could have told us both where it came from. 'It's not just the shrinks,' I went on, getting into stride. 'Don't know who's worse. The social worker who marries the rapist in an intimate prison ceremony or the bloke in a ponytail who wants to understand him. As for the journos . . .'

'Hey, I'm on your side!'

'With honourable exceptions. And don't get me started on the Parole Board. Where are the victims' advocates? Where's the common sense? The only thing that stops a psychopath is a bigger, tougher psychopath.'

Her fingers had stopped tapping again.

'Am I going too fast?' I said. 'I can repeat that last bit.'

'Um, Richard. Look – I didn't want to reopen old wounds. I understand you feel bitter about things. I really do. And I agree with some of what you've said. But you've given me more than I can use.'

'Your story. When can I expect the photographer?'

'We'll use something on file. Short deadline. It's for tomorrow's paper.'

'I'm free all day. I just thought: a shot of the dog and me might help. White picket fence behind us.'

'You want your *house* in the paper?'

'For the human interest angle,' I said, the interest being his, in the fact that I hadn't moved out after all. 'He already knows where I live,' I added.

A beat. 'I agree there's probably no threat to you personally, Richard – but why tempt fate?'

Why? Because the more thought I gave it, the more I realised that fate was *exactly* what – or, in this case, who – I wanted to tempt. And how would my little mate fate find me without a current home address? Gemma's article might help, but a picture of the house was worth a thousand words.

'Your call,' I dissembled, not wanting to further alarm her. 'Hey, um, thanks for your interest, Gemma. And good luck with the story. But I need to take the dog for a walk.'

'Right now?'

'She's scratching at the door. But let's catch up for a drink sometime. Okay? Great to hear from you. Siri, disconnect call.'

If I was going to get his attention, I'd have to do it myself. A sub-plan was forming in my head; I could think it through while I was out walking, especially since being out walking was all the plan amounted to so far. That, and a name. Operation High Visibility. It helped to have a good name, if only for morale. A better one came to mind: Operation Trout Lure.

The dog – a high-vis accessory – would help as she dragged the bait of me through the streets, if less trout-lure than shark-line. Operation Berley Scatter. Not much of a strategy in a sea of ten thousand streets, perhaps – what were the odds he would get so much as a sniff? – but the best I could come up with for the moment. It struck me that I needed to lose the beard first, less to make me presentable than identifiable. I stripped, ripped off the irritating cling wrap tattoo dressing, stepped into the shower, soaped up my face and went to work, wielding the razor more like a scythe or small machete.

The in-house mind-reader was already waiting at the front door when I was done. I found her handle, flicked out my cane, and stepped outside with new purpose. As always, the methodical logic of walking – one foot in front of the other, heel and toe, like words in a sentence helped me think things through, step by step. First problem: how to narrow the odds? 9900 of those city streets I could safely ignore. If you want to catch sharks, drop your line where they feed: among the seal colonies, the tuna schools, the teeming reefs.

'Present location to Hindley Reef,' I said.

'Sorry, Richard. I could not find any places matching "Hindley Reef".'

'I said street, not reef. Hindley *Street*.'

A draft running-sheet took shape in my head as I briskly stepped out the route. Cruise the CBD atoll till happy hour. Drop anchor at 107A for a bourbon or two around six. At eight grab a steak at the Grecian BBQ, less for old times' sake than to sit fully exposed in a front window table. Tap home through Light Square as the clubs and strip-joints came to life, letting the bouncers – half of them bikie nominees in black mufti – get an eyeful. Saturday night in the city – couldn't be better! Thousands of bug-eyed fish passing through. Even more if there was cricket on at the Oval tonight. Which gave me the best idea yet: force my way across the footbridge as the 50,000-strong crowd was coming out, less pushing upstream than hacking a path with my nunchukka.

'Hindley Reef, ten paces.'

I chuckled. 'What were you saying about your learning abilities?'

'Who, me?'

'No, the dog, Joyce.'

'I'm not sure I understand.'

My laugh was more of a scoff this time. 'Maybe I spoke too soon.'

'I'm not sure I understand. Are you unhappy with me, Richard?'

You win some, you lose some with Siri. Not that Willow was any different. I walked on, perhaps too quickly as the ideas came thick and fast. Picking a fight with a bouncer seemed the best of them, especially if some bystander caught the action on an iPhone and it went viral. Bouncer and Blind Bloke going toe-to-toe. He'd *have* to be in Timbuktu to miss that. This flash of inspiration – half-serious, half-comical – powered me on for a time, despite the heat. The afternoon was a stinker; by my third lap of the mile-long reef I was in need of rehydration. The dog was in even worse shape, halfway through the fourth lap I was the tow-boat and she was the lure. A door swung open as I dragged her past The Black Bull and she turned upstream into the outflow of refrigerated air as surely as a homing salmon. Tugged inside behind her, I tapped a vacant stool at the bar.

'What'll it be, mate?'

'Pint of pale.'

The first one didn't even touch the sides. 'And again. Plus a bowl of water for the dog.'

'It's on me,' from a beer-blurred voice on my left.

'The water,' I said, 'or the beer?'

His guffaw was also a little slurred. An upside to being blind; every front bar is packed with happy Samaritans who want to shout you a drink. The downside: the obligation to tell your life story in return. You can't just have a quiet one in a corner when the corner turns into a booze-up.

'Jesus! What's the other bloke look like?'

'What's ya dog's name?'

'I knew a blind bloke once.'

'What's ya dog's name?'

'You going to the cricket tonight?'

'What's your dog's name again?'

'You know sign language, mate?'

After the fourth round, I invented a sentence of sign: pointing at my ear and shaking my head. Deaf too.

After the fifth, I excused myself and let the river of cold air wash me downstream into Hindley Street. There was still work to be done; I needed a clear head.

The problem was the dead weight I was still dragging behind me. Water had failed to revive her; she was spent. And – it took me time to realise – hungry. The muggy stench of a grease-trap in a side alley seemed to double her dead weight, as did the fried onions and shish kebabs that tempted our noses as we passed the Jerusalem. Outside McDonald's she shape-shifted from dog to mule and refused to budge further. Given two choices – carry mule home on my back, or order mule a Big Mac – I tapped inside. I ordered two, with sides of fries and OJs (the miked-up, no doubt pimply kids no longer recognise the older poetry of chips and orange juice) then carried the bag of food outside and divided it between tabletop and pavement.

Scout's eating was energetic enough, but she still wouldn't move. I tickled her belly with the toes of my boot as I finished off both juices. 'What do you do with a dog with no legs, girl?'

'Here's what I found at Comedy Central,' Siri piped up. 'Answer: Take her for a drag.'

'How about I do the jokes and you supply the laugh track, Siri?'

'I'm sorry, Richard. I try my best to be a humble virtual assistant.'

'There you go again,' I said, chuckling. 'You can't help yourself, can you?'

'If you say so.'

I half-dragged the dog to the kerb and waved my cane in the air; almost immediately a car pulled in, a passenger-side window purred down.

'Excuse me, Sir. You are trying to hail a taxicab?'

An Indian voice, like most of the cabbies these days. Polite, a little flowery in manner.

I stepped towards it. 'Claxton Street,' I said.

'Sir, I am most terribly sorry, but actually I am not a pet taxi.'

I tapped the front wheel, found the rear doorhandle. 'She's not a Pet. She's a guide dog.'

'Actually, I could see that, Sir. Which is why I stopped to render assistance. And I am most sorry for your affliction. But personally I cannot take the dog.'

I tried to stay polite myself. 'You have to by law, mate. It's a thousand-dollar fine.'

'I am most aware of that, Sir. Actually, it is a cultural issue. I have summoned another cab. It will be arriving within minutes.'

'How much will it take, Mohammed?'

'Saeed, Sir. It is forbidden. The dog is an unclean animal.'

'I'm sure Allah the merciful, Blessed be His Name, will make an exception for a cripple.'

'Are you a Muslim, Sir?'

'Double or nothing,' I said.

Soon enough I was wedged in the back seat with the dog. My frustration was more with her than the cabbie. I like the cabs these days: the unfailing good cheer, the faint whiff of curry, the cricket always on the radio. I listened with half an ear only to his running commentary on his other religion. I'd got his origins wrong – Australia was playing Bangladesh at the Oval, and he was riveted – but I had other things on my mind. Ambushing the cricket crowd tonight seemed a footbridge too far; my fishing schedule for tomorrow was more crucial. Gemma's story in the *Mail* would be out by morning, sprinkling the newsstands with its powerful berley; I should be working those streets all day, putting the bait of myself about.

'Your destination, Sir.'

Saeed was out of the cab, holding the door open. I fished a note from my wallet – it felt like a fifty – and pressed it into his hand. 'Keep the change.'

Perhaps it was a hundred – 'Sir, that is too much! Even for double or nothing!' – but I was through the front gate and punching the door-combination before he could follow.

The dog settled into her basket and Siri into her charger, but I was still full of energy. I walked through into my big pine-perfumed brick shed, beat up the bag for a time, then dropped onto the mat and reached for the handweights.

Perhaps I am a Muslim, of sorts. I've no idea which way my rubber mat faces, but several times a day I kneel and perform the rituals. My religion, since Willow walked out: losing myself in exercise, the soul sweating out its toxins as much as the body. I'd be even more lost without it: the spine it puts in the long empty days. The solidity of the weights, the tool-like corrugations of their grips. The feeling of *doing* something, as if I am working, usefully, with useful tools, not just working out. Self-delusion or not, it did the job. After a last furious set of push-ups on the mat I rolled over onto my back, emptied at last of restlessness, and my superfluous eyelids slid shut.

'Block all calls, Siri,' I said, but feebly, or perhaps only in my dreaming head.

'Calls blocked.'

Our voices roused the dog from her basket in the bedroom; she clicked her way through the house, lay down on the prayer mat at my side, and licked at my nose, fondly.

'Thanks, Big Nose,' I murmured, and meant it in a heartfelt if confused sort of way.

My last thought as I threw my arm over her stout chest, and we nodded off, nestled together: *I must remember to share the joke with Willow*. Her pet nose – mine – wasn't even in the running.

I vaguely remember a knock at the front door, or perhaps just dreamt it – either way I was too paralysed to move. Nothing would rouse me. I sensed Biggest Nose lift her head, but maybe she was only sharing the same dream, or she was part of my dream too. Which finished with a buzzing sound that might have been a tattoo gun, or a wasp, but surely not a Vespa.

4

WAS T THE IMPATIENT RAPPING ON THE DOOR THAT WOKE ME, or the tongue rasping my face again? Probably the latter, letting me know I'd slept through several earlier knocks.

At least I was in bed. My bed. If still in my clothes. And, I discovered as I swung my legs over the side, in my boots.

'Time, Siri.'

'11.30 am.'

Too much broad daylight for an unwelcome visitor, surely, but I reached for the Glock on the bedside table as I stood up, and holstered it all the same.

Another knock, then silence. I opened the door with one hand behind my back, resting on the grip of the gun, and waited.

No sound but footsteps walking away. A woman's steps, in flats. I released the gun and let the loose T-shirt fall over it.

'Willow?'

The footsteps stopped, turned back. 'I thought you weren't there.' The Professor's voice. 'All shuttered up. No sign of life.'

Disappointment mixed with surprise, fading into curiosity. 'It's Sunday morning, Prof. When I said you need some weekend down-time, I didn't mean you should spend it with me.'

'I tried to ring,' she said, 'but it kept going through to message-bank.'

'I needed to sleep. Sorry.'

'Can I come in?'

A quick mental inventory – was the house presentable? Was it even navigable? Not by her stylish feng-shui standards, but way better than a day or two before.

'Lights on,' I said, and stepped aside. 'Welcome to my humble abode.'

Was the sink piled high with dishes? I wasn't sure. As for the stink; was yesterday's marathon shit-wrap adequate? I sniffed, discreetly: stale Camel smoke only.

I sensed her glance through the bedroom door as I followed her down the hall, taking things in. It seemed a good idea to get her settled quickly. 'Take a pew.' I gestured to the sofa. 'Coffee? Tea? Hair of the dog?'

'It's not a social call, Richard.'

Which meant I should probably have taken the sofa. I pulled a kitchen chair in front of the television instead, and sat, facing her. 'Could whip you up some bacon and eggs. You too, sweetheart,' I said as the dog clicked over and nudged my thigh. 'Bacon is one of the dozen words she recognises,' I told our visitor, chuckling. 'The others mostly have four letters.'

'You seem in a surprisingly good mood, Richard. Given the circumstances.'

'That old black magic called paradoxical elation, Prof. What circumstances?'

'There's nothing you'd like to talk about?'

'Nothing that comes to mind.'

'I find that a little hard to believe.' She tugged something from a bag and slapped it down on the coffee table between us. 'This morning's headlines, for instance.'

She could give classes at the Fort Largs Academy. When to hold back. When to go in for the kill. I wouldn't want to play poker with her.

'I thought the Sunday rag would be beneath your notice,' I said.

She rustled a page, ignoring me. 'I'm wondering why you didn't mention the jailbreak yesterday.'

'Jailbreak is a bit strong,' I said. 'More like breaking out of a wet paper bag.'

'My question still stands.'

'I didn't know about it yesterday.' A stupid lie, which I then compounded: 'It's in the paper?'

She ignored my nonsense. 'Shall I read it to you? So we are on the same page, literally.'

The Glock, wedged between my spine and the back of the chair, decided to remind me of its presence. 'Please,' I said.

'A 35-year-old man who this week walked out of the Cadell Training Centre was serving a fifteen-year term of hard labour for shooting a police officer in 2011.'

'Guess they had to spell that out,' I said. 'Old news.'

'Dimitri Papadakis, a former member of the Golgothans Motorcycle Club—'

'An associate,' I interrupted. 'A nominee. Never a full member.'

'—went missing from Cadell low-security prison facility between 8.30 am and 5 pm on New Year's Day. Department of Correctional Services Chief Executive Susanna Boucher said Papadakis, aka Jimmy the Greek, had been at the facility for two months, and there had been no previous security-related incidents. The prisoner, who was studying agriculture, was involved in developing a new horticulture programme. "We need to find out what the underlying motives were for him escaping," Ms Boucher told the *Mail*, and "the escape would be fully investigated by DCS although there were no immediate plans to increase security at the facility."'

'What a world,' I said.

'You're quoted in the article too,' she said. 'Which means you must have known about the escape yesterday.'

'Maybe it's an old quote,' I said, ridiculously.

'Shall I read that as well?'

'If you must,' I said, trying not to sound too eager.

'Detective Sergeant Richard Zadow, who lost his sight in the 2011 shooting, expressed disappointment that such a violent criminal had been transferred to a low-security prison so early in his sentence.'

Silence, then the rustle of the paper being set aside.

'That's *all*?'

'That's all from you. The Shadow Minister had a few caustic things to say about prison security.'

I shifted in my seat; the Glock was becoming even more uncomfortable. As also, right on cue, were the questions.

'Do you feel some sense of personal jeopardy?'

'Only the victims revisit the scene of a crime, Prof.'

More silence. Was she reaching for her notebook to write that pearl of wisdom down? I tossed in another, just in case: 'Problem is, sometimes that's all they do. Especially in their heads.'

'I'm wondering why you were able to talk freely to a journalist,' she said, 'but I had to prise the truth out of you today.'

'I guess I got it off my chest talking to her.'

She reached into her bag again, flipped something open – the notebook, after all? Yes, the notebook, confirmed by the click of her precious pen being uncapped.

'This is a consult? You billing Police Welfare for a house visit?'

'Pro bono, Richard. *Do* you feel vulnerable? Anxious that he might try to find you?'

'Now *there's* a reason to go on living,' I said, quietly enough but with plenty of suppressed venom.

'An eye for an eye?' she said, then added quickly, 'I didn't mean literally, of course.'

'Literally is fine,' I said. 'With a tooth or two tossed in for interest.'

A familiar sound: soft nib on nice paper. The Glock was still digging into my back, demanding to be acknowledged. I sensed she was watching me closely; I fought hard to get my feelings back under control.

'It's all theoretical,' I said. 'He had his revenge two years ago. He'll be halfway across the Nullarbor by now.'

I'd been planning to hit the next person who said that. Since it was me, it seemed best not to do it in front of my psychiatrist.

'It must have triggered some memories,' she said. 'Awoken old feelings. People suffering from traumatic stress—'

'He's made me a happy man,' I interrupted. 'They'll lock him up and throw away the key when they find him. No more playing in the rose garden.'

'Despite what you say,' she said, ever patient, 'your body language says otherwise. You've been squirming about on the chair ever since I got here.'

I almost laughed. 'Never take a gun to a word-fight,' I said, instead.

'I'm sorry?'

'Private joke.'

'Do tell. There's something else I wanted to talk about.'

'Shoot,' I told her, risking another joke that needed to stay private.

Her pen was uncapped, and began whispering.

'Gun,' she said, then 'Shoot,' as if reading aloud as she wrote. The pen stopped moving. 'Your choice of words seem as, um, agitated as your body language.'

Where was this heading? Had she spotted the Glock, wedged behind me? I felt a little agitated at this thought, yes – but she was fishing, surely.

'I'm not about to top myself,' I said, 'if that's what you're asking.'

'You can't blame me for wondering,' she said. 'Given this latest news. In the context of our discussion yesterday.'

'Do we really need to go through this again, Prof? It's purely theoretical. It might never happen.'

'Then allow me to ask a purely theoretical question. If it did, how might you do it?'

'That's a practical question.'

She would not be deflected. 'Men are practical creatures. They usually choose violent means.'

'Like jumping off world-famous bridges?'

'Like shooting themselves. Especially if they have access to firearms.'

I tried to hide my surprise. Was she still fishing? I hoped so.

'What are you saying? I'm a bit of a sissy for taking an overdose?'

'Let me put it more directly, Richard. Why would a man who still kept his service revolver at home choose to take an overdose of sleeping pills?'

No prize for guessing who had blabbed. Anger was more difficult to hide than surprise; I started counting, got to ten for the first time in months. Progress, of sorts.

'A pistol, Prof. Not a revolver.'

'Let's not lose sight of the wood for the trees, shall we?'

'I don't have my service weapon anymore,' I added, which was also true, at least grammatically. 'So this is all hypothetical.'

'Then let's return to my hypothetical question. If you ever *did* intend to, um, end it all, how might you do it?'

The hard fist of the Glock was becoming impossible to ignore. I stood up abruptly, rotated the chair 180 degrees, then sat again, straddling it, my elbows on the backrest.

'Put a bullet through my brain? Is that what you want me to say? Finish the job properly?'

Of course, the pen was uncapped, the nib resumed its intense whispering.

'The job that someone else started?' she said, eventually.

I chuckled, more comfortable now. 'The problem with all these unconscious interpretations is how do we prove them? If they're unconscious, I wouldn't know, would I? By definition. But don't let that spoil your fun. You seem to have a great time thinking them up.'

'Part of our joint purpose,' she said, 'is to bring them to the surface. To make them conscious. In this case, it does seem a rather obvious connection to make.'

'Not to me.'

'You can't blame me for being concerned, Richard. You're blind. But you kept a gun in the house. You've been depressed. You take an overdose, perhaps unintentionally.'

'Whoa! Doesn't that prove my point? I chose pills *not* a gun because I *wasn't* trying to kill myself. It was an accident.'

'Or a cry for help. Like the phone message you left for Willow.'

'Nice try,' I said. 'That was *after* I'd swallowed the pills, as you well know. When I realised my mistake. You think I can't keep my story straight, Detective?'

I heard the notebook shut. 'I'd like to leave you with some food for thought. Before our next session. I hope it doesn't sound insensitive. It's certainly counterintuitive.'

'Uh-oh,' I said, deadpan.

'It's possible the jailbreak could prove to be beneficial, Richard. It might offer the possibility of a breakthrough.'

Less food for thought than food for indigestion. I managed to keep my face expressionless.

'Don't misunderstand me,' she added, quickly, enthusiastically. 'I'm sure he'll be back behind bars soon. But for you it could offer a more profound and durable freedom.'

A snicker threatened to crack open my poker-face. 'You getting paradoxically elated on me, Professor?'

'Just pleased we're making progress. For two years you've avoided talking about the shooting.'

'I can't *remember* the shooting. As you well know.'

'Of course. But I also know that you haven't wanted to remember it. That you've put those memories – *some* of those memories – in a kind of mental jail. And they're beginning to break loose.'

The only thing about to break loose was derision, but I kept that safely locked behind the bars of my face as she slipped the papers and notepad into her bag, and stood up.

'Till Wednesday, then. We have much to work through. And I'd like you to consider allowing me to contact Willow. Especially now.

With this man at large. This affects her too, of course. What she must be going through. She may need counselling.'

'She doesn't have much time for the talking cure. Very matter-of-fact, my Willow.'

I followed her to the front door, and out into the late morning sunlight. It felt like warm honey pouring over my head; too bright for any reattempted murder.

'You didn't feel you might put yourself in harm's way,' I said, 'coming to check on me today?'

I sensed the puzzlement in her silence; the notion hadn't crossed her mind. Now that it had, she dismissed it immediately – not because it was ridiculous or unlikely, but merely irrelevant.

'You're my patient,' she said, simply.

I don't deserve you, I should have told her. *I'm lucky to have you.* 'You would make a great cop,' I said instead.

The compliment was heartfelt, but it either went over her head, or she kept her feelings to herself, as perhaps I knew she would.

'I'll see you on Wednesday,' she said as she walked away. 'We're making progress. And there's a lot of work to do.'

5

ODD CHOICE OF WORD, WORK. DIGGING HOLES IN THE GROUND
and burying stuff is work. Walling stuff up in a cellar is work. Working
out in the back shed is work, by definition. But talking things
through?

One thing I still had in common with Willow was an aversion to
the talking cure. I preferred the walking cure, which would be more
than enough work on a summer's day with a reluctant dog in tow.

The Prof was right about the prison break, though. It was proving
useful, if not for the reasons she hoped. It had energised me no end.
Applied Anger Management: give it something to chew on. Feed the
beast meat: the red meat of revenge.

Actual meat first: the bacon and eggs my guest had rejected.
Stepping out the front door half an hour later I felt as charged up
as the device in my pocket. The dog's batteries also seemed fine
(filled with that same high-voltage bacon) but the day being another
stinker I could always detour past home and jettison her if she ran low
on power again. Meanwhile, there was the serious work of fishing:
towing the bait of myself along the parallel east–west reefs of the
city grid: North Terrace, Hindley and Rundle, Grenfell and Currie.

The phone bleeped sometime midmorning, third or fourth lap in.
'Unknown caller,' from Siri.

I let it run through to message-bank, then listened. The *Mail* had
been out for hours, spreading the berley; it might be a tug at the line.

'It's me. I rang last night, the moment I heard. When you didn't
answer I jumped on the scooter and came over.'

I stopped dead, as if I had walked smack into an overhanging branch. Was the woman mad? Cruising shark-infested waters alone in the middle of the night? One too many happy-hour margaritas?

'No one home so I guess you're somewhere safe. Terry told me he was arranging something. Look, um, if that doesn't work out, you might be safer here. Anyway – now you have my silent number. I know you're probably still pissed off about the other night, but let's call a truce. At least till he's back in custody. Okay – well, thinking of you, Big Nose. I'm rostered on today but you can leave a message.'

'Save last call, Siri,' I said. 'Create new contact.'

'Name contact.'

'Reckless idiot. Add to favourites.'

I tapped on, fighting a mix of feelings. Clearly she had got home safely last night, or she wouldn't be leaving a message today. And the offer of sanctuary? The notion of hiding out with her in the house she was hiding from me in was weirdly attractive. The problem was, I didn't want to hide. I wanted to be found.

The phone rang again; this time I answered immediately. 'Jesus, Willow. What were you *thinking*–?'

'About time,' an irritated male voice interrupted. 'You're a hard man to get hold of.'

A rapid reorientation. 'I've, um, been in hospital, Ken.'

'Really?' Irritation hardening into sarcasm. 'Must be something serious. You've been ignoring my messages for weeks.'

'Messages or threats?'

'I had to find some way of getting your attention. If I overreacted, I'm sorry. Can we just take a deep breath? Both of us. And arrange a time to visit.'

'To what end?'

'To negotiate a way through this impasse. The last thing we need is to get involved in legal process. But I do require a full performance review.'

'I'm afraid that's impossible,' I said.

'Why?'

I stopped tapping, less to think up an excuse – it was already on the tip of my tongue – than to give it the proper gravitas. 'Because she passed away.'

Silence. Stick that in your pipe and smoke it, I thought as I tapped on, pleased with myself.

'Rick,' he said, eventually. 'I'm not your enemy. I understand the bond between client and dog. If it were up to me . . .'

'You don't believe me?'

'We're a non-profit, but we must run Guide Dogs on a commercial basis. We have a duty to our donors. Our key stakeholders.'

'I'm the key stakeholder,' I said. 'And *she's* the stake. *Was* the stake.'

'If you're concerned about her future, let me reassure you. We'll find her a loving home. We retrain some underperforming dogs as autism dogs. Or dementia dogs, to provide companionship in nursing homes.'

'You're not listening, Ken Jong Hill. She's so underperforming she's *dead*.'

'Please, Rick. We both know you'd say anything to keep her.'

'Acute pancreatitis,' I improvised, not caring whether he believed me or not. 'Too many turkey scraps. I blame myself completely.'

The plausible details seemed to plant the seed of a doubt in his mind, if briefly. 'In that case we would require a certificate from the vet.'

'I couldn't get an appointment,' I said, beginning to enjoy myself. 'Christmas is a very dangerous time for dogs. Death by poultry.'

'I'm sure I don't need to remind you of the terms of your contract, Richard. Veterinary advice must be sought immediately. We would also require proof of disposal of remains.'

Was he also beginning to enjoy himself? Impossible. He'd got to where he was by being a life-member of the tribe of the humourless.

'Too late,' I said, and one last wild riff popped out of my mouth. 'I buried her in the front yard. Under the frangipani.' The only thing I was digging into the ground was myself, ever more deeply, but I was revelling in it. 'I'd appreciate it if you could respect my loss,' I said, having trouble not spluttering. 'I've been very upset.'

'You don't sound upset. You sound quite the opposite.'

'Paradoxical elation,' I said, and this time couldn't suppress a snigger. 'According to my psychiatrist. That's what I was hospitalised with.'

'Have you been drinking?'

'If you don't believe me,' I said, tiring of the game, 'feel free to come around and fucking *exhume* her!'

Fuck! Scout echoed.

'Sounds like she's already exhumed herself, Richard. I'll be there at ten in the morning. With a court order.'

'I've an appointment with my psychiatrist at ten.'

'Noon then,' he said, and hung up before I could come up with another lie.

The phone rang again before I'd taken a dozen steps. 'Answer phone,' I said, and without waiting for the caller to speak added, 'I won't be here at high noon either, Kim Jong-il. So fuck off!'

'Richo? Spiro Georgiou. From the Police Union, mate. Is everything okay?'

'Fine, Spiro. Thought it was someone else.'

'Do tell. Thought I should touch base. The story in the *Mail* today. My favourite compatriot going walkabout.'

'You're *working*, Spiro? What is it with this town? No one respects the Sabbath anymore?'

He chuckled. 'I'm ringing as a friend. Well, friend *and* legal adviser. What a clusterfuck, mate. How you coping?'

'Big fuss about nothing. He's probably out of the country by now. On a slow boat to Ithaca.'

He indulged me with a laugh; the only bloke I knew who would get it. 'Sure hope so. But, listen – don't play it down. The effect on you.'

'What effect? I couldn't care less.'

'You want to put on a brave face in the paper, fine. But don't hold back Tuesday morning. When you see the shrink.'

'She did a house-call today,' I said. 'Just left. I'm not seeing her again till Wednesday.'

'Not *your* shrink, mate. WorkCover's hit man. The appointment was originally tomorrow, 10 am. You didn't get my email?'

Got it, and promptly forgot it. Memo, Prof: not sure what you call this spooky coincidence. Clairvoyantly truthful lie, self-fulfilling prophecy? I must have stored the time and date unconsciously until, in a moment of need, with Kim Jong snapping at my heels, it had popped out of my mouth.

'Can we reschedule?'

'Tomorrow *was* the reschedule. You did a no-show before that. Mate — how many times? It's for your own good. I can't stress that enough. These medical experts don't like being fucked around at the last minute.'

'Meaning what? If I wag school again he'll give me a bad grade? What's the worst he can do? Claim I'm faking blindness? *Pretending* I got shot in the head?'

'Let's just say it's best not to start behind the eight ball. His opinion is *very* important for the Maims Claim settlement. Get up to speed, mate — it was all in the email!'

I couldn't have cared less about the settlement, but it seemed best to keep all options open. 'How long will it take?'

'Hour. Hour and a half max. I'll send a cab to pick you up.'

'I can walk. Where's his office?'

'Psychiatry Department, Royal Adelaide.'

This stopped me in my tracks. 'Same place as the Prof?'

'Not only but also: he's a professor too. Read the friggin' emails! The bad guys have brought in the heavy artillery. Mutually Assured Destruction.'

I managed an angry snort. 'The Duelling Professors. Can see them in court already.'

'It won't get to court. WorkCover will make a final offer as you walk through the door. So at the risk of repeating: don't hold back. Squeeze out a few tears if you feel the need. Oh, and don't shave. Good tactic to look a little – unkempt.'

'Your considered legal counsel, Mr Georgiou, is that I should exaggerate my pain and suffering?'

A chuckle. 'Just don't diminish it. Your recent overdose might be a good place to start.'

I bristled. 'How do you know about that?'

'Does it matter? Just make sure the new Prof knows.'

I bit my tongue. The prospect of reciting my story yet again, let alone turning it into some sort of soap opera, left me cold. There's something about the compensation racket that brings out the worst in people, including me. On the other hand, why cut off my financial nose to spite my face?

'And read the email attachment before you front up,' he was saying. 'Okay?'

'There was an attachment?'

'Maims Claims Payouts. Just so you know what the stakes are. From a pain-and-suffering angle. Forget the physical damages. We've been there, done that. Just the psychological appendix. Okay?'

'Okay.'

Maims Claims. Memo, Terry: inside every insurance adjuster there's a frustrated poet? I rolled the words across my tongue as I tapped on. I liked their taste, but some stubborn gut-instinct in me refused to swallow them whole. Shit happens, including mental shit, but can the mess be wiped up with a handful of banknotes?

Unless they pay for a bungee jump off a bridge first thing every morning.

'Exeter Hotel,' Siri murmured somewhere.

The dog was dragging behind like an anchor on a seabed. I turned into the pub, found a mooring on a bar stool, said yes to a couple of beers and a bowl of water – 'my shout' from some wag as it was set on

the floor – but listened with half an ear only to the polite interrogation that followed. Smoother vowels and less fuck-stem adjectives up
the arty end of town, but the same fifty questions.

'What's your dog's name?'

'Been blind all your life?'

'Thought they used Labradors.'

'Do you see stuff in dreams?'

'What's your dog's name?'

'See the cricket last night?'

My thoughts were elsewhere, as much in my stomach as my
brain, chewing over the same cud of words as if they could be
digested after all. Mental Damages Maims Claim. Perhaps compo
works as a kind of vindication, and those banknotes are its units
of measurement – less shit-wipes than the only way pain can be
counted out, its official exchange rate. Less a sympathetic gift –
fuck sympathy! – than a proclaimed acknowledgement, or medal of
service. Hear ye, hear ye – Citizen Zadow hath suffered this much.
A public award, like a little statuette or service medal on a mental
mantelpiece. Or is it a set of scales? If you can't lift this great weight
from my heart at least balance it with an equal measure of gold in
the other pan.

'Find Mailboxes,' I told Siri as I reconnected with the dog and
tapped out into Rundle Street East. 'Open Inbox.'

Or perhaps (my mind back on planet earth again) compo works
best as a kind of revenge on a cruel world: it ripped me off, I'll rip it
off. I had some sympathy with this notion; I was planning a little
balancing revenge myself.

'You have 3,105 unopened emails,' from Siri.

'Find Police Union.'

'Fifteen unopened emails.'

'Open most recent.'

'Email received on–'

'Open attachment,' I interrupted. 'Read attachment.'

'Table of Statutory Compensation Payouts. Specific and Permanent Physical Disabilities. Lower Limb. Loss of any toe but the great toe, on either foot: $7,000.'

So much for poetry. I chuckled inwardly, despite myself, and let her drone on. It was hard to wrap my mind around the notion of mental damages – so hard it seemed to be hurting my actual brain – and I had a long afternoon of walking ahead of me. Siri's deadpan litany of physical damages was at the very least neutral, and might even offer comic relief.

'Loss of the great toe of either foot: $19,850,' she recited. 'Amputation of a breast: $19,850.'

'What's your opinion of that, Siri?' I interjected again. 'Speaking as a someone with breasts?'

'I'm sorry, I didn't understand that request.'

'Do you agree that the loss of a breast is worth the same as the loss of a big toe? Both breasts, two big toes?'

'It's your opinion that counts, Richard.'

'Christ, I hope not,' I said. 'But I understand it's a very personal question to ask a woman.'

'Loss of the thumb of the right hand: $59,590,' she read on, ignoring me. 'Total loss of the male sexual organs: $93,390.'

I laughed out loud. Two thumbs for a cock? Four big toes? Four boobs, big or small? You couldn't dream this stuff up.

'Loss of vision in both eyes: 71 per cent whole-person impairment.'

No surprise there. This figure I knew by heart, although the unrounded 1 per cent always sounded wacky. What bean-counting poet had tacked that on and why? I also knew the dollar exchange rate by heart: $252,250, the maximum allowed under the Act. The same payout for losing both hands. Or both feet.

'A tooth for a tooth,' I muttered aloud. 'An eye for a hand.'

Not that I was arguing. Lucky me got shot on 2nd July, after the new financial-year indexation kicked in. Three days before, the payout would have been a measly $198,680. Enough to pay off the mortgage, but the extra fifty-odd thou came in handy for the blind-friendly smart-house fit-out.

'Loss of the distal phalanx of the ring finger . . .'

The sticking point was still the mental damages. It was just as hard *not* to think about them, given tomorrow's scheduled showdown. I walked on, tapping vigorously, as if the stick might help me find a way past obstacles inside my head as well as those outside it. I've had my ups and downs since the shooting, but enough for a pain-and-suffering Maims Claim? Memo, Spiro: nice name for a horse, but I'm not about to ride it into the ground, even for another quarter of a million. Call it male pride, call it a hardened cop's black-and-white mind-set, call it the cynicism of someone who's seen one too many compo rorts. Or just call it newfound honesty. Your little Greek mate had blinded me physically, but if I were to blame anyone for mental pain and suffering, I might as well blame my sorry-arsed self. With – more recently – a little help from Willow.

'Permanent loss of the full and efficient use of the pelvis.'

Perfect comic timing. Letting Willow back into my head might be a mistake but it made some things clearer. What's the payout for a broken heart? Twenty per cent whole-body impairment? Thirty? And for a broken cock? Might as well claim the full $93,390, for she as good as chopped it off.

'Permanent loss of the sense of smell–'

'What about permanent mental blindness?' I shouted, abruptly.

'Here's what I found on the web,' Siri said. 'Mental blindness is a cognitive disorder where an individual is unable to attribute mental states to others–'

'I have no trouble at all doing that. No fucking trouble at all.'

Scout's response was less a woof than a snuffly grunt; I was swearing so much of late it was becoming the new normal.

'You ain't heard nothing yet,' I told her, and tapped on, thinking of mental blindness, and Willow, an obstacle I kept walking smack into. And might never tap past. What if she *was* done with me, completely? She was offering me a safe house, yes, but it still came with a clause in small print. *Till he's back in custody.* Which left my long-term future dangling.

Memo, self: take a leaf from her playbook. Proper risk management, step by step, heel and toe. You can't count on her taking you back. You can't – importantly – *bank* on it. Which means – despite her repeated assurances – a financial settlement, sooner or later. Which means if you want to keep your wired-up smart-house, Blind Freddie, you'll have to buy her out. Sooner or later.

'Total loss of portion of terminal segment of thumb involving one-third of its flexor surface without loss of distal phalanx: \$31,542.'

I plodded on, more slowly, as if unwilling to reach the conclusion I was approaching, step by logical step. Buying her out meant selling my soul, sooner rather than later. Selling out, in short, on Tuesday morning.

'Total loss of the power of speech,' from Siri.

'Best idea you've had all day,' I interrupted. 'Why don't you try it yourself?'

'I am currently at 47 per cent power, Richard.'

'Then you're doing better than me,' I said, too weary even for a wry smile. The rehydrated dog strained ahead, impatiently; I was the dragging anchor now.

'Flinders Street thirty paces,' Siri said. 'Loss of hearing in both ears . . .'

The weight of beer in my belly didn't help, nor the cooling air. The late afternoon sun had slipped behind the eastern office blocks, and the world felt suddenly empty. There was no peak-hour traffic on the streets tonight, no Big Bash crowd streaming out of the Oval across a bottleneck bridge. Maybe it was partly end-of-weekend melancholy, but my efforts at catching the world's attention – and therefore his – felt pointless.

'Central Gun Depository ten paces,' Siri said as I tapped into Victoria Square. 'Permanent loss of taste and smell . . .'

The location – the scene of my recent triumph – cheered me a little. The gun nudged me in the small of my back again, encouraging more memories. I tapped the bin as I passed, then veered off-path towards the sound of a clanging tram. The grass was thick and spongy underfoot; I wondered idly if there was still a ready-made resting place nearby: the human-shaped crop-circle where my drunken opponent had fallen two nights before. There would be a certain poetic karma in taking a nap there; I owed him much in terms of my recently improved mental state. And my newfound purpose. Maybe it was a good sign I was thinking about my longer-term future again – Willow, the Maims Claim – but I'd lost sight of my most urgent problem: the whereabouts of the Greek.

'Appendix Two,' Siri spouted. 'Psychological damages.'

'Enough of that bullshit,' I said. 'Close file. Find route to Rundle Street East.'

The crowds might be sparse, but there was an hour or two of daylight left.

6

FEEDING TIME AT THE ZOO, SILICON-BASED ANIMALS FIRST. I PLUGGED in Siri's drip-feed then turned to the carbon-based life-forms: a can of Pal for Scout, a can of chilli beans for me. The first spoonful of beans also turned out to be Pal — chicken-and-beef-in-jelly? — which at least seemed to vindicate my argument about the sleeping pills. Memo, Prof: accidents happen. Overdoses happen, even of dog food.

I was still chuckling when I was jolted by a kind of reverse memo, as if she had replied straight into my mental inbox: *perhaps your unconscious chose the dog food to remind you of something, Richard. Caught up in your own approaching showdown, have you forgotten the dog's?*

I microwaved the actual chilli beans, then slumped in front of the TV with the bowl in my lap, thinking this through. How to save my furry damsel from a villain armed with a court order? Willow's offer of shelter sprang to mind, but it seemed too complicated. Why would I leave the dog, and not myself? Plan B: head for the hills. But where in the hills, to what safe house? And for how long? Sooner or later the posse would track us down, even if it spent a day digging up my narrow front garden first.

This image had me chuckling again. And thinking it might be fun — Plan C — to throw them off the scent by burying an actual dead dog in a shallow grave under the frangipani tree.

The rhythms of eating are also usually good for clear thinking, but the more beans I spooned into my face, the nuttier the ideas that popped out of my head. Grave-rob the nearest pet cemetery? Body-snatch an unburnt dead pooch from the Animal Welfare crematorium?

I spluttered out a spray of half-chewed beans. The live dog snoozing at my feet immediately roused and began snuffling about.

'Fair swap,' I said, as she licked the floorboards clean. 'Even if I ate more of yours.'

Perhaps the dog food had addled my brain. Preposterous plans kept forming, and breaking apart, as I sipped a few fingers of Scotch after dinner. If no dead dog was available, then what? Half a sheep from the butcher? I replenished my glass, spluttering again. A dressed sheep would require fur. And something that resembled a dog-tail. At least for a cursory exhumation. And how to hasten decomposition? A punnet of gents from the bait kiosk at Henley Beach? This idea also made fleeting sense, but was soon replaced by a better one: roadkill. Preferably a few days old, already wriggling with gents. I'd need a driver with good eyes – Saeed? He owed me a freebie – but it shouldn't be too hard to find a squashed possum somewhere in the suburbs.

Or – better still – a cat. Were they unclean?

The dog growled, and thumped the side of her basket with her tail. The notion clearly excited her, but I was already thinking fox.

'Don't get your hopes up, girl,' I said, although there seemed no need to speak my thoughts aloud. 'Cats are too small.'

The TV was droning on in the background – some talkback radio channel I didn't remember choosing. Maybe Siri was doing a little screen-saving on my behalf. But the medium not the message got me thinking: wherever he was, he wouldn't be sitting around reading the *Sunday Mail*. Television was the best way to grab his attention. Even a blind bloke like me sat around listening to it.

With which thought the dim light bulb in my head went high-wattage again. Why not kill two birds with one well-aimed stone?

'Open Phone Directory, Siri. Find Channel Eight.'

'Channel Eight located.'

'Dial number.'

The plan was still firming up as I waited for the connection. Operation Shark-Line, Phase 2.

'*Eyewitness News*,' from a young, bored male voice. 'Fast-breaking. Hard-hitting.'

'This is Richard Zadow. Detective Sergeant Richard Zadow.'

His 'Yes?' was in the world-weary key of 'So?'

Irksome, the things you have to explain. At least the newspapers still have a little corporate memory.

'The cop who was shot in the head a few years back,' I prompted.

'What about him?' In the same key.

'He's me. The blind cop.'

'Sorry to hear about that, Detective. And yeah, rings a bell. But, like, how many centuries ago? No offence, but it's hardly a fast-breaking story.'

A quick mental ten-count. 'I'm not the story. My dog is the story. They're trying to take her away from me.'

A flicker of interest. 'Someone wants to repossess your *guide* dog?'

'She's more than a guide dog. She's my best friend. And they want to retrain her as a dementia dog. Lock her up in a nursing home.'

Hooked; I could hear his fingers on a keyboard. 'Why would anyone, like, *do* that?'

'Why not ask them yourself? They're sending the dog catcher this century. Tomorrow, in fact.'

'What time?'

'High noon.'

'And the address, Richard?'

I gave it, heard him lock it in.

'You've got a big story there, Richard. Potentially a great story. Have you, like, contacted any other networks?'

'Not as yet.'

'Awesome. If it's an exclusive, it could be our lead feature. Big human interest angle. I'm looking at the daysheet as we speak. I can't promise, but I might be able to deliver . . .' A reverential pause. 'Sophie Fox. Personally.'

The name rang a vague bell from the muzak of my TV listening. 'The weathergirl?'

He sounded aggrieved. 'Sophie made her name with a hard-hitting investigation into climate change, Detective. And the flooding of the Pacific Islands. Perhaps that's what you're thinking of?'

A louder bell rang, not so much the series itself, as Willowpedia railing against it, episode after episode. 'They're living coral atolls, you fucking bimbo! They grow with the rising seas! They've been doing it for thousands of years. Some basic science please, not this pseudo-religious claptrap!' The programme obviously meant a lot to her, because she always went back and watched the next episode – dare I say, religiously. 'What next? The End is Nigh! Punish us, O Gaia, for our carbon sins! Oh, fuck me – stick to saving cute baby animals, moron!'

Quoting any of which was unlikely to help my cause today. 'Awesome,' I said. 'Gaia needs more courageous people like her. Um, could I suggest an outside interview? With my city cottage in the background?'

Not to mention – another inspiration – the city mosque in the wider background, its minarets like four sharp pins dropping onto the mental map of any interested viewer.

'Best discuss that with Soph. Her producer will probably, like, ring beforehand. For some backgrounding. Tomorrow morning.'

He took a few more details then rang off. The TV was still droning on – talkback grievances, talkback manifestoes, fifteen-second sound bites of talkback fame – as I leant my head back into the armchair, exhausted, but too pleased with myself to sleep. Nothing paradoxical about my elation; it might have started with dog-food fuelled delirium but it had ended in one brilliant solution to two problems.

All the same, a sleeping pill would have been useful. I'd need an early start in the morning, not so much to trawl the streets again, or even exercise the dog, as to prepare for my TV debut. There were questions to be anticipated, responses rehearsed. And my best thinking was always done step by step, at walking pace.

'Set radio alarm, Siri. 7.30 am.'

7

SHE WOKE ME GENTLY, SLOWLY TURNING UP THE FAINT WHISPER of voices till they became intelligible. 'Escaped prisoner Dimitri Papadakis remains at large, police sources confirmed this morning. Papadakis was described as being 177 centimetres tall and of medium to slim build. He has a distinctive skull tattoo on his forehead.'

'Don't forget a distinctive crucifix-and-shit tattoo on his biceps,' I muttered.

'Language, Richard,' from Siri.

'—and was last seen wearing an orange prison-issue uniform—'

'Or maybe just his Speedos!'

'Police warned if members of the public see him they should call triple-O immediately. He is considered dangerous and should not be approached.'

My answer to that was to roll out of bed and into the shower, immediately. Don't try to tell me the news is always bad. He was out there, still, waiting for me to reach out to him. Which was still some hours off, and would come via the idiot-box, but required further thought.

Breakfast first; I pulled on my clothes as the promise of Adelaide fine and hot, maximum 34, fell from the speakers above, then walked into the kitchen followed by Morning Drivetime.

'Welcome back, possums,' – a familiar smoky, world-weary voice – 'As if anyone needed reminding, it's the start of another long and winding week. A little Monday morning blues for you to wallow in coming up, but first, to get those reluctant neurones firing, what else, possums, you guessed it, the Monday Morning Mystery Sound . . .'

'Phone Contacts, Siri,' I said a few seconds later. 'Favourites. Radio 891. Dial number.'

I should have rung even before I listened to the sound; when the phone was answered I found myself in a queue. I listened, impatiently, to the feeble guesses of the first few callers – had none of them opened a fridge in their lives? – while double-tasking with the bacon and eggs.

'Sorry, no, possum, it was not a champagne cork. Next caller. Who have we got here?'

At last. I spooned in a mouthful of breakfast to disguise my voice. 'Dicky,' I said, and added an accent as well. 'I fink I know de mystery sound, guvnor.'

A tolerant chuckle. 'Nice try, Mr Zadow. But I thought we had agreed to a moratorium on the Mystery Sound.'

I reverted to normal voice. 'Hasn't it expired?'

'End of the month, I do believe.'

'Let's get this straight, Peter. You're banning me because I'm blind?'

'I'm banning you because you win every time you ring, possum. Including three mornings in a row in November. And then refuse the prizes.'

'Three double passes to the movies? Think about it.'

'I sympathise with your predicament, but why enter a competition if you can't use the prize?'

'I'll take my guide dog,' I said. 'If you give me another chance. She's good at reading faces.'

A beat while he tried to make sense of this brain-twister. 'After the end of the month, possum. Fair's fair. Level playing field and all that. Next caller.'

The line went dead; I didn't bother turning the radio back on. Scout had finished her breakfast, and was already at the door; I bolted down the rest of mine, pulled on my jacket, holstered the gun, and headed out. Enough horsing around; there was work to do.

I pecked my way northwards, pretty much as the crow might fly: along Morphett Street, then straight through Light Square. I felt good. The morning rush had finished; there was more bee-buzz in my ears than engine noise, pleasant scents were stirring from the rose beds in the square, the sun basting my head with its warm honey. Which somehow reminded me I hadn't rung Willow back.

'Find Favourites,' I said. 'Dial Reckless Idiot.'

The call went straight to message-bank. 'Hi. Willow here. Tied up at the moment. Probably working my arse off. Leave a message and I'll do my best to get back to you this century. Bye.'

Reflexive disappointment, then a slow backwash of relief: I could reassure her without being cross-examined too closely. 'Big Nose here. Just got your message from last night. Look, thanks for your offer. But I'm safe. No need to worry. And please – no more late-night drive-bys. Please. You really mustn't put yourself in danger.'

The phone rang as I neared home, right-angling into Gouger Street. Willow already? 'Answer,' I said, then non-committally, 'Hello?'

A woman's voice, but unfamiliar. 'Detective Sergeant Zadow? Where are you? I'm outside your cottage in Claxton Street. You don't seem to be at home.'

'Who's speaking?' I said, cautiously. The TV crew was due before the dog catcher, but you never knew.

'Sophie Fox from *Eyewitness News*. Banging on your door as we speak.'

I quickened my pace; she sounded too important to be kept waiting. 'You're there already?'

'And you aren't. Have I got the right address? Number 7?'

Too important and too impatient, which Willowpedia would probably tell me were the same word-root. 'Sorry, um, Ms Fox. A medical appointment. But I'm almost back. Just around the corner.'

'You're on foot?'

'Yes. But not far off. Couple of minutes at the–'

'Is the dog with you?'

Her terse, interrogative manner reassured me, in a way. If she gave me a hard time for being a few minutes late, what might she do to a dog-rustler?

'She's always with me, Sophie.'

'Perfect. We'll take some background footage as you approach. To save time. Which end of the street will you be coming from?'

'North,' I said automatically, then thought again. To get the mosque and its tall drop-pins in the background I'd need to approach from the other direction. Which was further anyway. 'Sorry. South. Sturt Street end. I'm five minutes away.'

'You said a couple of minutes. A couple of minutes ago.'

'I stopped to answer your call,' I fibbed.

Time-and-motion-wise the excuse didn't add up, but she seemed satisfied.

'We'll start shooting the moment you turn the corner. One thing. A trap for young players. Just be yourself. And try not to look at the camera.'

'I should be able to manage that,' I said, as unsarcastically as I could manage. 'See you soon,' I added, and ended the call.

'Claxton Street,' Siri's more user-friendly voice murmured. 'Turn left. Ten paces.'

Just in time. I U-turned instead, and stepped up the pace, taking the long way round. I cut right at the next side-street, walked a quick block, cut right again into Sturt.

'Claxton Street,' from Siri again. 'Turn right. Ten paces.'

Time to let the dog take over. Which was not as easy as it sounds; she'd got used to being a follower, not a leader.

'Keep walking, Mr Zadow!' Sophie Fox's now-familiar voice called from the other end of the street. 'Just letting you know we're shooting.'

I pushed the dog ahead of me as much as being pulled, concentrating on looking downcast.

'Think about the dog,' she shouted. 'Think about life without her.'

This part was easy enough. I might refuse to fake any suffering for the new Professor tomorrow, but the stakes were higher today. The problem was maintaining the hang-dog look – even harder than holding a smile for a camera.

'Home,' Siri whispered after what seemed a small eternity. 'Ten steps.'

'Cut,' from Sophie, much closer now. 'Good to meet you, Richard.'

'Rick,' I said, and held out my hand.

A tiny, limp paw slipped into mine. 'Sophie,' its owner said. 'And this is Stan. You happy with the take, Stan?'

A middle-aged male's raked-gravel voice: 'Wouldn't mind another, babe. You were looking straight at the camera, Rick. All the way.'

Sophie again: 'You *are* blind?'

'As a welder's dog.'

A suppressed snicker from Stan. 'All the same,' he said. 'Would you mind walking down the street again? And maybe use the stick as well.'

Anything to advertise my whereabouts. *Here I am, arsehole, still at the old address! Come and get me!* I retraced my steps to the corner then tapped back a little more theatrically, keeping my head down to avoid any accidental camera sightlines.

'Home,' Siri repeated herself, 'ten steps.'

'That's a wrap,' from Stan.

'Did you get the mosque in?' I asked.

I sensed the exchange of puzzled glances. 'The what?'

'The minarets.'

'Are you, um, Muslim?' from Sophie. I couldn't get a visual fix on her yet. Red hair seemed possible, or was I just being seduced by her surname? Objective identikit parts so far: soft, small hands; loud, hard voice. Stiletto-heels, from the few steps I'd heard. Any perfume she might be wearing was overpowered by the nearby frangipani.

'Do I look like one?'

Her laugh was more of a snort. 'You could do with a shave.'

A mystery sound from Stan's direction took a moment to solve: he was tapping his watch. 'Nearly noon, babe. If the bad guys spot the camera they'll drive straight by.'

I led them in through the front gate, brailled the door-key combination, opened up and stepped inside.

'Let there be light,' I said.

An appreciative cluck from Sophie. 'You get that, Stan-the-man?'

'You need to ask? Wouldn't mind the reverse angle though.' He stepped past me into the house, then turned. 'Take two, Rick? This time with me inside?'

'Lights off,' I said, stepped outside, shut the door, reopened it, and conjured up the light again as I tapped back in.

'Great television,' he muttered.

'Keep it running, Stan,' Sophie said, her stilettos close on my heels. 'Cosy little place you've got here, Rick.'

I sniffed the air; largely shit-free at least, if still a little heavy on the essence of pine.

'You live alone?' she said.

'Just the two of us.' I leant down to ruffle the dog's ears. 'My *girl* and me.'

'What's her name?'

'Scout.'

'You seem very close. Why would anyone want to take her from you?'

'That's what I want you to find out. I've kept a couple of phone messages you could use. Threats and menaces from the horse's mouth. You interested?'

'Very,' she said. 'But some background, first. Were you born blind, Rick?'

My hackles stirred. The short-term memory of the news cycle. Fast breaking, faster forgotten. Stories fronted by ventriloquists' dummies, written by journalists with early-onset Alzheimer's.

'Injured in the line of duty,' I said, calmly enough.

'Am I missing something?' she asked her off-sider.

'The blind cop,' he said. 'The one who got shot in the eyes.'

At least the cameraman remembered, sort of. 'The head,' I corrected him.

'He's quite famous, babe,' he added.

How old was the babe? Born much later than yesterday? My mental picture was beginning to firm up: a big-haired, weathergirlish ditz. Too beautiful to need to think. Or be polite. I hoped she didn't have almond eyes; she would give them a bad name.

'Awesome,' she said. 'And here I was thinking it was just another dog story.'

'The guy who did it broke out of jail yesterday,' her off-sider briefed her, patiently. 'The guy who swam the river up at Cadell.'

She gave a low whistle. 'Even better! Hero blinded in the line of duty, now has his guide dog ripped off him. Lost his sight, now loses his seeing-eye dog.'

The ditz-picture blurred a little; I might have rushed to judgement too early.

'Perhaps some shots of him in uniform, babe? With medals?'

Him being me, permission to speak? 'I was CIB. Plain-clothes.'

She ignored this. 'There's also the *threat* angle. Are you worried he might come after you again, Detective?'

'He wouldn't have the balls. Weak as piss.'

'Camera still rolling, Stan?'

'Yo, babe.'

Music to my ears. I took the opportunity to aim a few more taunts at my target audience of one, even more calculated to infuriate. 'I have a theory about rapists. Little men with a little dick complex.'

Sophie chuckled. 'He was convicted of rape as well?'

'Not exactly,' I said, then improvised. 'But I understand there are some cold cases in the pipeline. Old DNA samples.'

'Any *actual* sex-crime convictions?'

'Technically, no.'

'Best give your pencil-dick theory a miss, Rick. Wouldn't get it past legal.'

'How about this, then?' I said, controlling my frustration. 'He's too chicken-shit to show his face round here. Prefers to beat up women. *That* you can quote.'

Silence from Sophie, but it released a little built-up steam.

'It might play better the other way,' she said, eventually. 'Let's say we assume he *is* coming after you. You'd be extra-vulnerable without the dog. Being, you know, visually challenged. And living alone.'

My mental picture of her was still evolving, fast. Was she as hard-faced as her tough-talk? If so, glamorous-hard, beauty-queen style? Or bull-dyke hard? My fingertips were itching to find out. There was also the matter of the eyes. Maybe she was just a left-brain Willow-clone: matter-of-fact, straight-talking, to-the-point. If so, Kim Jong Hill was in big trouble.

'You're staring so hard at my face, Detective,' she said. 'I'd swear you were looking at me.'

'Only way I can look is with my fingers,' I said. 'Sometimes people let me touch their faces.'

More silence while she weighed this up.

'Could start with yours, Stan,' I suggested, to head off any allegation of sleaze.

His voice moved closer. 'Feel free,'

I'd barely started – the big, boozer's nose felt as gravelly as the voice – when a rap at the door stopped me.

A stage-whisper from Sophie: 'Still rolling?'

'Rolling,' from Stan, and I heard the door open, and a puzzled, familiar voice from outside.

'Ah, I was looking for a Detective Sergeant Zadow? Perhaps I have the wrong address.'

'Not if you are Mr Ken Jones-Hill,' Sophie said. 'Training Manager, Southern Cross Seeing-Eye Dogs.'

Concern in his voice: 'Is that a TV camera?'

'Sure is, Mr Jones-Hill. I'm Sophie Fox from *Eyewitness News*.'

'I know who you are. Is this to do with the jailbreak?'

'It's to do with the dog. Could you confirm that you are here to repossess a blind man's guide dog?'

So much for the weathergirl pigeon-hole. I could have kissed her.

'I'm afraid you've been misinformed,' he said.

'You *are* planning to remove the dog from Detective Sergeant Zadow's care? A decorated police officer who lost his sight in the line of duty. Yes or no?'

'Er, well, no. It's not that simple. There are, er, standard protocols. All dogs are required to undertake a proper performance review . . .'

'But one of the outcomes of that review might be the seizure of Detective Sergeant Zadow's dog Scout? Permanently?'

'Look. I don't have to answer these questions. I'd be very careful about putting such allegations to air if I were you. This is really none of your business. It's a private contractual matter between Southern Cross Seeing-Eye Dogs and our client.'

'But surely the bond between a blind man and his dog is more than a legal contract?'

I stood behind the door, thrilled. She was an attack dog herself, her identikit image in rapid makeover from foxy babe to fox terrier.

'I m afraid I can't comment. This matter is commercial-in-confidence.' His voice was already receding fast, the terrier snapping at his heels. And behind the terrier, the cameraman. And behind him, me, and behind me, an actual dog, an entire cartoon posse in hot pursuit.

'If the dog was seized, would you be replacing it with another?'

'I have nothing further to say on the matter' were his last words before a car door slammed, an engine started, rubber squealed on bitumen.

'Get a shot of the getaway car, Stan. Arsehole fleeing the scene. Then back to Rick and his best friend. Looking forlorn outside their picket fence.'

Oh, yes please! I reset my best hangdog look, which my best friend would be doing naturally.

'Great fucking television,' Stan croaked out a few moments later, a sentiment seconded by a bark.

A pair of high heels was stepping my way. 'If you still want to feel me up,' the leader of our little pack said, 'you'd better get started. Got a shit-load of editing if we're going to make the six-o'clock.'

8

'OUTSIDE HIS MODEST CLAXTON STREET COTTAGE IN THE SOUTH-west corner of the city, a blind hero and his faithful companion wait in hope . . .'

Couldn't have put it better myself. I sat in front of the TV, beer in hand, wanting to shout. *Still here, arsehole! Same address!* I had no way of knowing if the mosque were visible in the background, but no matter. A picture might be worth a thousand words, but a few well-chosen words can also be a picture. Or better still, a map. The phone started up before the interview had finished; I let it ring through. I didn't want to miss a word.

'. . . This was Sophie Fox, on the spot for *Eyewitness News*, signing off.'

Beep. 'Mr Zadow? You don't know me, but I just had to ring. Is that a boy dog or a girl? I got your number from the TV station. They didn't want to give it at first, but being a dog-lover, well, the nice young man said you wouldn't mind.' A woman's voice, thirty-something, overexcited. 'I have a boy Shepherd, he's very handsome, people are always stopping us in the street, and I wondered if you'd like them to get together. I would *love* them to meet.'

'Delete message,' I said. Never share the stage with animals? The phone was ringing again before I'd finished smiling to myself.

Beep. 'Sergeant Zadow? You don't know me. I'm calling from Broken Hill.' An older woman's voice; calmer. 'Is your dog a Belgian Shepherd? I have four of my own. It's a big old house – well, an old pub really. Just me and the dogs since Bert passed. They've been such a comfort. There's plenty of room. I thought – if you felt like a holiday. I'd love to look after you. Show you the Hill. *Both* of you. I could drive down and pick you up if that's okay with you–'

'Delete message,' I said, but pleased that my sticky spiderweb had reached beyond the state border.

Beep. 'Gemma again, Rick. Just saw you and some arsehole from Seeing-Eye Dogs on the idiot box. Nice ambush. Bit pissed off, though. Why didn't you give the story to me? Instead of that jumped-up weathergirl.'

I allowed myself an inner chuckle. Now, now, Gemma.

'Anyway, I forgive you. I'm writing a follow-up, and would appreciate a few minutes. It's definitely front-page material. Although what the fuck was Miss Hard-face Bitch doing giving out your *address* on prime-time TV? Ring me back. Please. *Pretty* please. With sugar on it.'

'End call,' I said to Siri, chuckling out loud now, not least because Sophie's face had felt as soft as a peach. Or was I just channelling her alter-ego Willow's? I thought about returning the call but the phone was ringing again. The dog story was going viral; Gemma's headlines could write themselves.

Beep. 'It's me, Richard. Jilly.' Who? I recognised neither voice nor name. 'Long time no see. I felt so – *touched* by the story on the news tonight. I thought – well, things haven't been so good for me as well. My marriage broke up. Custody problems. I'd love to catch up. I'm still in the same place. And think about you when I see a cop on a bike go by. We had such fun. Remember?'

'Delete message,' I said, not remembering and not wanting to. My days as a speedie were years back. *Decades* back.

Beep. 'It's me, Richard. Janet. Janet Warburton. Remember? Terrible what they tried to do to you. It's been so long, but you haven't changed at all.'

'Delete message.'

Beep. 'It's me, Richard. Lucy.'

'Delete . . .' I began, then bit my tongue. Voices are faces to me, arriving with instant recognition. This one took an instant longer. Perhaps the name threw me; in my head she was always the Prof.

'I've just seen the story about Scout. On the news. I'm concerned you didn't mention any of this to me either. Especially given your apparent distress in the TV interview.'

Apparent? Was there a note of sarcasm in her voice? Surely not.

'It must have been traumatic for you, having the seizure of your dog hanging over your head. Sensitised to loss as you already are.'

Definitely not.

'So, if you need to see me earlier than our scheduled appointment, please ring my secretary. On second thoughts just ring me back on this number. You know I'll always squeeze you in. Please.'

'End call,' I said, then: 'Create new contact.'

'Contact name?'

'Lucy Hotline,' I said, even as the phone rang again.

Beep. 'It's me, Rick. Sylvia. Just saw that story about your dog. I'm so sorry about what you've been through. I *so* wanted to ring after you got shot, but Bob wouldn't have understood. I hope you can forgive me . . .'

Sylvia? Bob? No bells ringing there. 'Delete message.'

Beep. 'It's me.'

An unexpected voice, but instantly recognisable. Pre-instantly, my heart skipping a beat before my brain registered her. 'What do you think you're *doing*, you bloody liar? Your message said you were in a safe place! You and your stupid pride! You're impossible! Proper risk management, you stubborn idiot.' A pause, a deep breath. 'Okay, I just got off the phone to Terry. He doesn't think you're in danger. Patrols are coming by regularly. But Jesus, Richard! There's no shame in taking precautions. And what about Scout? The dickhead from Guide Dogs?' Another, even slower, calming breath. 'Okay, your funeral. If you insist. None of us could ever tell you anything! But the offer still stands. You can stay here. At least let me take Scout for a few days. Till this thing with her blows over.'

Delete message, I felt an urge to say. Answer call, likewise, almost in the same thought-bubble. I did neither. I took a deep, calming breath myself as my heart thumped on. I wanted to see her. Part of me wanted to run straight *to* her. Except for one small sticking point: her mixed message added up to exactly what? She missed the *dog?*

As for ringing back: a risky move. As long as she thought I was merely being proud, or stupid, or stubborn – fine. But if I spoke to her at any length she would see straight through me. Especially since I was finally seeing through myself. When had the vague hope that revenge was the reason he had broken out of jail become set in concrete? The last couple of nights, while I slept? My unconscious sixth sense, working overtime?

Cue a knock on the door, as if she had seen through me anyway. I sat there startled, until the knock was repeated and I realised it wasn't hers.

'You got a TV in the car now, Chief?' I said, opening the door.

'Why? I miss something?'

I wasn't about to tell him what. 'Shaggy dog story. But with a happy ending. So why *are* you here? Brought my shooter back?'

'Been trying to ring you,' he said.

'You could've left a message.'

'Got a bit worried when I couldn't get through.'

I snorted. 'No need to ask how the manhunt is going, then?'

'No joy. Yet.'

Joy of a strange kind for me, though. I didn't want the villain caught. Yet. 'You search the knock-shop?'

'Took two days to get a warrant. No joy there either. Apart from embarrassing a few prominent legal identities. Two silks and a judge.'

He would have named names if asked, but I had no time for gossip. I stood there, waiting, as usual, for the real reason he had come.

Beep from inside the house. A woman's voice, faintly strident. 'Yo, Ricky. It's me, big boy. Saw you on the box . . .'

'You want to get that?' from Terry.

'Delete message,' I shouted over my shoulder, then turned back.

'Message deleted.' Another beep; another female voice; this time I let it burble on.

Terry chuckled; a small explosion of the usual pungent smoke. 'No wonder I couldn't get through. What's going on? You putting yourself about on Tinder?'

'There's a lot of love out there looking for its next victim, Chief.'

'Which is sort of why I'm here,' he said, without a beat. 'It's the Detectives' Dinner. Saturday night. Thought you might like to come with me.'

'You want me to be your date. How sweet. But you're a married man, Chief Inspector.'

'I won't tell the missus if you won't. Cancer stick?'

'Thought you'd never ask.'

A match was struck; a lit Camel jammed in my mouth; the phone rang again inside. *Beep.* 'It's Tessa, Rick. Long time, no see. Oh, sorry. Shit. That was a great start. What a dumb thing to say.'

'I might be busy Saturday night,' I said.

Terry chuckled. 'Come for the pre-dinner drinks at least. See how it goes. You can always piss off if you're bored. I'll get a night patrol to run you home.'

I pondered this through a long, smoky filling of my lungs, followed by an equal and opposite emptying.

'You can't tell me you don't miss it, Rick. Happy hour at the Club.'

'Shop-talk hour,' I said. 'Not much fun if you don't work at the shop anymore.'

'Think of it as your first day back *in* the shop. Keep your ear to the ground, and who knows what you might hear. Especially after a few drinks.'

'What happens in the Club stays in the Club,' I reminded him. 'Especially confessions extracted under the duress of a pint or three.'

'Beer-boarding?' he said, chuckling, and lit himself another. 'Anyway, a night out would be good for you. Better than locking yourself up in your fortress here.'

It occurred to me to ask if the patrols had noticed anything suspicious in the street – match-flares in darkened cars, shadowy figures under streetlights – but I kept my lips tightly clamped around my own cigarette. He'd see straight through to my vengeful heart if I spoke. And perhaps even to the Glock, skulking behind that.

'Remember the Consorting Squad?' he said, exhaling. 'All we did was sit in the pubs all day. Drinking. Listening. Get pissed, get the bloke sitting next to you pissed, and just listen.'

'If you remember the Consorting Squad, you weren't in it,' I said.

Another chuckle. 'Keep the beer flowing, and the talk followed. Softly, softly, catchee bad guy.' He took a long drag at his cigarette. 'Your mission, Detective Sergeant, should you decide to accept it. Beginning at the dinner.'

'Cops are the good guys, remember?'

'Once upon a time, maybe.'

'I liked that time,' I said. 'Ye olde times when we had the quaint habit of backing each other up.'

He ignored the barb. 'I'm not talking about looking the other way over a few quid on the side, Zads. I'm talking serious shit. Leaks to the clubs, for one.'

'Any clues?'

'Yeah – two. It's not me. And it couldn't be you. Not for the last two years at any rate. Another smoke?'

'Ta.'

'Keep the pack,' he said. 'Again.'

I stuck out my hand, made another lucky catch.

He stepped back off the porch. 'I'll pick you up Saturday. Sevenish. If I don't hear from you before.'

'You're hearing from me now.'

'Now doesn't count. Sleep on it for a couple of nights.'

I opened my mouth again; shut it. I was happy enough to *think* about it, especially at night. My fast-hatching plan meant sleeping by day, and keeping watch by night. So to speak. Rats were nocturnal creatures; the one coming my way wouldn't be knocking on the front door during business hours.

A car door slammed; an engine started; I waved goodbye, then stepped inside. That he *was* coming I was certain, if still a little bemused by that newfound certainty.

Eeep. 'Sophie here, Rick. *Huge* response. Ratings through the roof. I've been trying to get through; you've probably had a few calls from well-wishers. I knew you wouldn't mind us giving out your number. I'd like to do a follow-up in a week. A what-happened-next story.'

'Delete message,' I said. The idiot-box had done its work; I needed no further distraction. And I hoped to be an even bigger story in a week. 'Delete *all* messages,' I almost added, then remembered Willow.

'Send text message, Siri.'

'Who do you want to send it to?'

'Reckless Idiot.'

'What do you want to say?'

The words seemed to dictate themselves 'Dear Willow. Thanks for your offer. It means a lot. Scout sends her thanks, too – she's very touched. She says don't worry about her, the dog catcher wouldn't dare show his face around here again.' I paused, giving her time for a smile. Hopefully. 'As for me, I'm perfectly safe. Patrol cars cruising by every five minutes. They might as well have the place staked out. Besides, it's a fortress. *My* fortress, so I'm staying put. Call me stubborn, but I'm more likely to get hit by a meteor. They'll catch him soon and then – well, I'd love to see you. End message.'

'Ready to send it?'

'Send,' I said, then, 'disconnect phone.'

No more interruptions. It was time to build a better rat-trap.

III
TOUCH

1

THE CHUNK OF CHEESE – ME – WAS SITTING PRETTY IN THE CAGE, but where to offer entry? The answer seemed obvious, even without thinking about it: the study window. Willow's study, a.k.a – a shared joke – the Imelda Marcos Room. It already ticked all the boxes, as if my brain had autofilled them while my mind was elsewhere.

One: the single window was easily accessible from the narrow side-path.

Two: the path – a cul-de-sac – was hidden from the road by the frangipani tree, and from stickybeak nextdoor neighbours by a high fence. At the far end it ran straight into a brick wall, literally: the new additions to the old cottage that covered the width of the block.

Three: the aluminium roller-shutter on the study window was impossible to break in through, and therefore equally impossible to break *out* of.

Four: the shutter had a remote control. The moment the rat crawled in across the sill: snap!

Best of all, it was a simple plan. A trap with a single moving part. What could go wrong? One thing, maybe. I replaced the triple-A battery in the bedside remote – easy enough to do by feel – then tapped out the front door and back along the side of the house to test the shutter.

I hadn't raised it since Willow left but it rumbled smoothly upwards when I pressed the top button. I pressed the down-button and lowered it again, leaving nothing to chance. Satisfied, I raised it again to the halfway point, which seemed more than wide enough for a rat to squeeze through, even one that had been working out in the weights room at the riverside resort.

Safely back inside, I lit a cigarette, uncapped a beer, and put my feet up, contentedly. Had I missed anything? Leaving the study light on seemed a good idea: a beacon in the night, a lit pathway.

'Study light on, Siri,' I said, and chuckled, picturing the look on his face as the portcullis rumbled down behind him.

The image was pleasant, the evening warm, the armchair soft; I was drifting into dreamland when some internal alarm jerked me awake.

'Fuckwit,' I said, an opinion shared by the dog as I tipped the rest of the beer down the sink, and filled the coffee plunger with a triple-shot instead. There was another moving part in my rat-trap that I hadn't given enough thought to: me. I wasn't expecting my visitor tonight – my plan required patience – but why take chances? I needed to stay alert.

Back in my armchair, recharging on sugar and caffeine, it struck me that I'd also managed to completely avoid thinking, consciously or unconsciously, about what came next. What to do with the rat after the trap was sprung? Call the cavalry? Mess with his head for a time? Whatever I decided, I'd need to keep him secure.

I drained the coffee, and headed for the study. The cell door first: I'd hung it myself a few years before, solid cedar. The problem was, it had no lock. So much for auto filling all the tick-boxes unconsciously.

My first thought: nail it shut. My second: taking a blind swing at a nail with a hammer might not be the best idea. I needed my thumbs in working order. The gas nail gun would be safer. Possibly. I walked back through the house and out into the shed. The disinfectant-smell had gone, taking the dog shit with it; all that was left was the faint, reassuring work-smell of grease. The gas-gun carry-case was sitting in the bottom of the big tool cupboard; I opened it on the bench and ran my fingers over the various parts sitting in their moulded tray. The safety glasses came to hand first; I slipped them on automatically, left them on ironically. I brushed over the battery charger, memorising its location. The battery compartment was empty, the gas canister's also; I must have left them in the gun.

The gun. I wrapped my fist around the grip and lifted it out carefully; heavy in the hand, but well-balanced. I palpated the nose and the safety tip with my free hand, ran my fingers over the open-frame magazine. Roughly half-full: twenty-odd nails. Of which sort? I screwed up my useless eyes, knotted my brow, and squeezed out a memory pip: the last time I'd used the gun I'd been up in the ceiling, replacing a rotten rafter.

Which meant 90mm D-heads, also just right for the job at hand. It was turning into a Goldilocks kind of day.

I found the power-button; pressed. Was the cylinder still gassed? The battery charged? The indicator light on? There was only one way to tell. I pressed the nose vertically into the wooden benchtop to release the safety, pulled the trigger, and was rewarded by a soft, satisfying *thock*.

I ran the flat of my hand over the jarrah top: flush penetration, as smooth as silk.

Now for the fun part: sealing up the jail cell. Or was my true intention to seal up a tomb? This idea first occurred to me (consciously at any rate, Prof) as I opened the study door. Might it be possible to keep him here, undiscovered, till he died of – what? Thirst? Hunger? Rage? The angry thrill of this crowded my brain with images: the rat forced to drink his own urine to survive, eat his own shit. The rat breaking his fingernails trying to scrabble his way out. The rat begging for mercy through the keyhole.

I stepped through into a room so stuffy he might have been trapped there for weeks already. No shit stink here either – not even the dog had been through that door since Willow left – just a three-month fug of dust and stale air.

I closed the door and pressed the business end of the gun against the stile above the knob, ready to drive the first nail through into the frame – but checked my trigger finger just in time. A faint warning bell in the back of my head: was I certain I'd left the shutter on the window – my only exit – half-raised? Was I so drunk on revenge I was about to entomb myself? A moment's thought put paid to that – Siri could always call for help – but it seemed best to double-check.

I opened the door and stepped out to think it through in clearer air. What if – the thought arrived with another small thrill – I felt the urge to free the rat from the trap and play with him a little? Then seal him up again.

And again.

I set the nail gun down against the skirting board and lit up a smoke, less as an aid to thinking than an excuse for it. It was also an excellent deodoriser: cigarette in mouth, I stepped back into the musty room, located the leading edge of the door, and ran my hands over the latch-plate and knobs. I'd fitted them years back: the mental revision was essential.

I walked up the hall and checked the fittings of the bathroom door likewise: a standard push-lock which I'd also fitted years ago, but which my fingers remembered better, having handled it a thousand times since. I walked out into the shed again almost without thinking about it. Perhaps my brainy fingers were doing the thinking now: they needed no urging to unbolt the steel doors of the tool cabinet, and feel their way around inside its belly. Each tool was hung exactly where I'd left it two years before. I gave my own five-pronged tools free rein for a time, letting them get reacquainted with old friends: hacksaw, fretsaw, hammer, mallet, the large family of spanners, the entire clan of ring spanners. Plenty of screwdrivers too: after choosing a 4mm Phillips-head I managed to tear my hands away from its brothers and cousins and head back to the bathroom door, and to Plan B: swap the locks.

The bathroom knobs were the wrong way round for jailing purposes – the push-lock was on the inside – but that was easy to reverse. I brailled the screw-heads on the inside flange with my fingertips – two – and spun them out quickly enough, placing them for safekeeping between my lips, as gently as cigarettes, Phillips-heads first.

The inside knob was then easily detached; the outside knob, spindle and screw-mount assembly slid smoothly out.

I pocketed the parts, then set to work removing the knobs and latch from the study door. An easier job now I had the feel for it. I set these parts on the floor next to the nail gun, then got to work fitting the bathroom knobs and spindle into the study door.

The jail door. The *cell* door. Which meant the push-lock was now on the outside.

After testing the mechanism – all in working order – I tightened the flange-screws, also safely on the outside. He was unlikely to be carrying a Phillips-head driver in his pocket, but why take chances?

One escape route remained, my fingers reminded me: the emergency coin-twist lock-release which was now on the inside knob.

Another trip to the tool cupboard, another rapid touch-inspection of tools – this time, the file-rack. I settled on a six-inch Swiss double-cut; within minutes the soft metal of the coin-groove in its protruding central button was as flat as the serial number on, say, (the gun nudged me in the back, sharing the joke with me) a black-market Glock.

For added security – and to amuse myself a little more – I fetched a can of bike oil from the lube-shelf in the shed – single-grade straight-50 – and liberally coated the inside knob with a palmful.

Next – still standing on the threshold, having barely ventured inside – I shook the rest of the can out across the study floor. If a passing rat should slip and break its fucking neck, so be it.

After towelling my clever seeing-eye hands I returned the tools to their extended family in the cabinet. As I closed the big metal doors and slid the bolt home it struck me that with a little extra work I could build an even better rat-trap. I reopened the cupboard, located a slot-head driver, and set to work. The rusted screws on the barrel-bolt resisted loosening; a quick spray of RP7 helped tease them out, but I ruined the slots in the process. Leaving the barrel-catch in place – there was no way it could be flush-fitted on the outside of the study door – I poked around for a time in the screw-drawers. Four Torx-heads found their way into my hands (Memo, Fingers: great choice for power-driving) and from there up between my lips. The cordless drill and bit-set had their own separate drawer; I lifted them out as carefully as crockery. The grip felt good in my hand; not as balanced as a Glock, but bringing its own kind of satisfaction: the ancient human satisfaction of working with tools, a pleasure I had largely forgotten, and forgotten I was capable of.

'Music, Siri,' I said as I walked back into the hall. 'Something to work to.'

'I don't understand music to work to.'

'I guess it's been so long you've forgotten.'

'Jog my memory.'

'Use your imagination. "Working Class Hero". "Working for the Man". That type of thing.'

The music started up instantly if unimaginatively, with the Big O's falsetto warning I had a lotta work to do.

'I'm-a listening, Roy,' I mumbled through a mouthful of screws, then muttered along with the music as I aligned the slide-bolt assembly by feel a few inches above the doorknob. I power-drove the screws into the door-stile without managing to put one through a stray finger, freeing up my mouth to join in the singing at full volume.

Time to align the slide-hole. I'd forgotten the hammer, but no matter. I tugged the Glock from its holster, reversed it, and tapped the head of the bolt just firmly enough to indent the soft pine of the door-jamb. X marks the pilot spot. It took time to braille my way through the drill bits; I settled on an 18mm (probably) wood-bit, locked it in the chuck, shoved the door open to get it out of the way, aligned the tip with the indent, and drilled square into the jamb.

I hit bluestone sooner than I expected, but that was surely a bonus. After replacing the wood-bit with a masonry-bit – also easy enough to locate by feel – I drilled in up to the hilt, withdrew, and blew the debris from the barrel hole. The familiar smells that filled my nose – burnt wood shavings, stone grit – brought back plenty of sweet memories. As did the feeling of satisfaction when I pulled the door shut and the bolt slid sweetly home.

For a moment I stood there, lost in time. Renovating the cottage with Willow had been one of the joys of my life. Our life, together.

Perhaps it was the weight of the drill in my hand that roused me: heavy, and getting heavier. I located the bit-set, carried them both back to the tool cabinet, and wired the doors shut. Enough renovations for one day, and enough memories for a lifetime. I lit a cigarette, flopped down into my armchair, and poured myself a Scotch.

Job well done, I told myself.

Except it wasn't. The roller-shutter outside the study window was half up, but I'd forgotten to raise the window itself. Or at least unlock it. Which meant I'd have to unbolt the cell door, cross the room and finish the job. Which wasn't as easy as it sounds, for all kinds of reasons. I'd straddled the doorway while I changed the lock, but I hadn't entered her study proper since Willow left.

Memo, Prof: more grist for your significance mill? I nipped the thought in the bud: listening to her was enough, no need to think like her too. After draining my glass – Scotch courage? – I unbolted the door and stepped through, cautiously. The oil was a problem, but the floor was just as slippery with memories, not least among them the way it had once been crazy-paved with discarded shoes. When Imelda walked out on me she only took the pair she was wearing, which I took for a good sign: she'd soon be back. She was, but only to stuff a garbage bag with dozens more.

I shuffled on in, half hoping to step back in time, even if it meant tripping on a shoe, twisting my ankle on a shoe, falling into a *bed* of shoes.

A bed of nail-sharp stilettos.

No such luck, of course; she'd taken them all in the end, along with her clothes, her precious jewellery, her even more precious laptop, and a couple of boxes of medical textbooks.

The semiprecious stuff she left to me. Furnishings, linen, crockery, cutlery, washing machine, fridge. Fridge magnets. Generosity born of guilt, as the Prof once suggested? I preferred to take it as more grounds for hope. Leaving me the radio was to be expected – but the widescreen TV? Surely that meant she was coming back. But the Prof had a theory about that, too: Willow was in denial about my blindness. Psychobabble, I scoffed – even as the notion messed with my head. Walking out on your darling blind hubby, you'd need all the self-defence mechanisms you could think up.

Distracted, I took a careless step; my boot skidded, I skated forward, out of control, found the edge of – what? Willow's desk – just in time, steadied myself.

And was returned to my purpose: the desk sat squarely under the entrance to the rat-trap. No doubt the Prof would also have plenty to say about why I chose Willow's room as the jail cell, but it seemed entirely straightforward as I leant across the narrow desk, unlatched the window, and raised it an inch. The gully breeze had sprung up; a cold, refreshing side-breeze flowed over my face.

'Come and get me,' I shouted out into the world, again. 'Still here! Come and get me, you little cunt!'

A loud *Woof!* from behind my back; I jerked upright, startled, both boot-heels shot forward from under me and I toppled, flailing, backwards. A blind man's worst nightmare – a fall into an abyss – but I was caught snugly, miraculously, by the desk chair.

Willow might have forsaken me, but her furniture still cared. I gave the arms of my rescuer – a Danish piece so fine-boned it's a wonder it didn't snap under my weight – a grateful squeeze, then explored the equally stylish desktop. The MacBook Air had long gone, but not the designer lamp. Nor the Alessi pen-jar, a chrome-plated Italian fashion accessory lost in a Scandinavian wood. To label the room a study was not an affectation; everything in the business half was as elegant as the designer shoes that had carpeted the other half, if less jumbled. And as dainty and fine-boned as Willow herself. Somehow both sides seemed to fit together, and fit her, as if the room itself were just another garment.

Or even a map of her brain, as she once joked. Including the messy lower bit. 'A brain-*scan*,' she added, smiling up at me from her desk.

I remember standing in the doorway, first stubby in hand, spoiling for a fight after a hard day's work. 'Your brain is as fucked-up as this?'

'You're always telling me I've got a split brain, Big Nose.'

'You could break your ankle putting on a shoe,' I said.

'Love me, love my mess.'

She laughed, and already I was laughing with her. 'It's the filing system you use for your shoes I'm having trouble with.'

'You think you're the most rational person in the universe?'

I navigated my way through the shoal of shoes to kiss her on the lips. 'Christ, I hope not.'

'Then fix me another margarita,' she said, 'I'll clear a space down in the dark side of my brain and we can lie down and get smashed.'

No wonder I'd kept the door shut: the memories came in a rush as I felt my way across the desk. Distracted, I knocked something over with a clatter. The smaller of Willow's two framed photos by the feel of it: the one of her parents. Their image came to me clearly as I stood it upright: two smiling, perfectly round faces, at which I found myself smiling back, stupidly, automatically, sentimentally. I missed them too, their warm politeness if not their love, and the weekly Sunday banquet in the little brick house in Rosewater, with its endless bowls of delicious chow. I even missed holding their hands around the table through the nutty grace which always preceded it, my head deeply bowed, if only to avoid eye contact with Willow lest we burst into laughter: 'And bless our future grandchildren, Lord Jesus, and say *no!* to gay marriage. Amen.'

My throat clogged a little, thinking of them, but also wondering, not for the first time, how she had explained the split to them. It seemed a bit unchristian that they hadn't rung. Fundamentally unchristian, I might have joked to Willow. Maybe they were relieved, maybe the plan was to match her up with a nice Cantonese boy all along, not an ageing, blind, tattooed cop with an ugly Caucasion nose and a future earning capacity of zero.

Unfair thoughts, these, born of residual self-pity. And easier to push aside than a few nights before. I turned my attention back to the desktop, and felt about for the other, larger picture frame. No sign of it. I checked again, methodically, then sat back, bewildered. Why would she take our wedding photo with her? Take *me* with her, but leave her mum and dad behind? How does the old song go: *if you ever leave me, can I come too?* Hope dies hard, but the more CPR I gave, the more it fucked with my head.

Woof, from the doorway as if it were doing something to Scout's head too.

Maybe the photo was hidden away in a desk drawer. Nothing in the top one but a staple gun and a scatter of paperclips. The lower drawer was locked; I straightened a paperclip into a makeshift pick, L-bent another to use as a tension wrench, and set to work. Irregular police know-how: insert the wrench into the shear-line of the keyhole, add a little rotational pressure, then feel your way along the pins with the wire-pick.

Success after a lot of fiddly work, but little joy. No wedding photograph, or anything else that might have helped in my war against hope. No diary full of secret revelations, no bunch of ribbon-tied letters from another lover. Nothing but a box of pencils and a stack of her handmade notepaper with matching envelopes. A stray, amusing thought: maybe the Prof used the same brand. Which led to a more grimly amusing thought, which also got me back on track: the rat would have plenty of high-class paper for his last will and testament as he slowly starved to death.

2

'ISOLATE SPARE-ROOM MICROPHONES, SIRI.'

'Spare-room microphones isolated.'

'Intercom mode. Maximum volume.'

I kicked off my boots, towelled their slippery soles, then went in search of the Scotch bottle – only to leave it where I found it, un-uncorked. The game was afoot; there could be no drinking on the job. No sleeping either; I brewed a pot of coffee instead, then settled down in my chair for a long night of listening. My rat-trapper's tools were at hand – the gun in its holster, the shutter-remote in my pocket – but how to pass the hours? Listening to the TV was out of the question; my ears were also tools of the trade. As were my hands, which were acting fidgety. Anxiety? I felt none. Caffeine? After two mugs? It took time to recognise the restlessness in my fingers for what it was: a kind of yearning, a *tactile* yearning. Having reacquired the taste for working with tools, my hands were hungry for more. Once it registered, that hunger became more specific, like a craving for a particular food.

Without further thought I followed the urge back through the house into the shed. Another room full of memories, but all mine this time. I eased open the dedicated drawer of ring spanners, and plunged my hands in among the cold, slippery metal fish. The grip of the ratchet reached for mine; after fitting what felt like a 36mm socket, I turned to face the lift-table in the centre of the room.

And froze, momentarily, struck by the strangeness of where I found myself.

I'd tried not to think about the Duke for two years; it made me depressed. Even now, standing before it, spanner in hand, I had to ask myself: if I could never ride it again, why bother? My free hand answered for me, reaching out and making contact with – what?

The front fork. The legendary way-out-in-front fork of the '62 Green Frame. It felt so welcoming, so familiar, that I could almost see it again, even through moist eyes.

I set down the spanner and ran both hands over the front head and cylinder, wrapped them around the satisfyingly chunky crankcase, brailled the embossed lettering on the side-plate with my fingertips, left to right: DUCATI.

'Long time no see, your Highness,' I said.

'Who, me?' from Siri.

The Duke was sitting too high: eye-height, not hand-height. I poked the toes of my right foot around beneath the throne, located the lift-pedal, pressed it twice; the hydraulics hummed, the table dropped slowly to a more useful level.

I checked the clamps, then ran my hands over the rest of the bike, methodically, taking my time. It was still half-disassembled, and for a moment my memory failed me: was the engine on the way out of the frame, needing repairs, or on the way back in, already fixed? What had been the problem anyway?

'Music to work by, Siri,' I said, then remembered I needed to work in silence, keeping an ear on the intercom. 'Sorry. Cancel music.'

'Let me know if you change your mind again, Richard.'

I checked the stainless-steel worktop for parts, this time trusting my fingers to do the remembering. The carburettors, silencers and drive-chain declared themselves, arranged neatly, separately. A couple of allen keys sat to one side; a small ballpein hammer. I've struggled with my memories since the shooting – retrograde amnesia, according to the neurosurgeons – but these came back with a rush: big-end troubles, still unsolved. Probably the crankshaft bearings, a notorious Green Frame time bomb. The Stradivarius of bikes, yes, but with the temperament of a diva. Ten thousand on the clock and you start sweating every time you hear a knock. I'd been halfway through diagnosing the problem when everything – how else to put it? – went black.

Time to finish what I'd begun? It still seemed a stupid idea, but I had nothing to lose except a fingernail or two. My fingers themselves had no concerns; they had already made themselves completely at home. I helped them remove the engine bolts cautiously, then ease the round-case out of the frame and onto the worktop. The L-twin is a heavy engine, but I'd been working out. I loosened the rear cylinder-head nuts, freed up the head, shucked the nuts completely then set the head aside. Next, the barrel. Given a pair of working eyes I could have done this part of the job in half a minute; instead it took half an hour and, yes, two broken nails. Plus one possibly broken toe: a dropped socket that bounced off my foot and clattered onto the concrete floor.

'Memo, Siri: remind me to wear boots next time.'

'Okay, I'll remind you, Richard.'

I found the socket soon enough, but a dropped allen nut rolled some distance away and needed ten minutes on my hands and knees. As recently as yesterday I might have downed tools and walked off the job, frustrated; tonight I felt in no hurry. The front cylinder took even longer to strip; the clips on the small-end gudgeon pins were near impossible to ease off, unseen; the screwdriver tip kept slipping. I gouged my left palm several times before succeeding. Worse was to come: with both heads removed, I got completely lost in the maze of the clutch, fiddly enough work even for the clear-sighted.

Eventually I felt my way out, but had barely begun the bottom-end strip-down when the phone rang. On maximum volume.

I jumped, startled; the push-rod clattered onto the floor.

'Answer phone.'

'Good morning, Mr Zadow,' a pleasant female voice shouted at rock-concert amplitude. 'Professor Blackman's secretary here.'

'Volume down!'

'This is a courtesy call to remind you of your appointment with the Professor at two o'clock today.'

Morning already? I should have known; Scout had been restlessly circling the lift-table for some time.

I spent a minute or two circling it on all fours myself, located the dropped rod, cleaned up and headed for the kitchen. My hands might have been feeding all night, or at least playing with their greasy, metallic food, but the rest of me was ravenous. As was the dog. I cooked up a mess of sausages and eggs and toast, divided it as per usual across two plates, and we both tucked in. A couple of gobbles later she was at the front door, refuelled and impatient for a walk; after filling my own tank more sedately I felt merely sleepy. And satisfied – *sated* – in ways that were due to more than bread alone. I let Scout out to water the frangipani, then summoned her back inside.

'Sorry, girl. Walk later. Siri – set alarm for noon.'

'Alarm set for noon.'

I left a lazy wake of clothes behind me as I headed towards the bedroom, flopped on top of the quilt and waited for the king tide of sleep to engulf me. My last thought: maybe Terry was right. For one night, certainly, I'd surprised myself. Or my hands had surprised the rest of me. They were a little the worse for wear, but that, after all, was what tools were for. Not so much wearing out as wearing in.

3

'THE OTHER PROFESSOR TOLD ME I HAD PTSD,' I SAID.

A bigger office than hers in terms of acoustic bounce but less generous in creature comforts. I found myself sitting upright in a hard-backed wooden chair with not a couch in sight. So to speak.

'I prefer to make up my own mind,' he said.

There was something a little prim in his tone. What were his own seating arrangements? Bed of nails?

Financial risk notwithstanding, I couldn't resist a dig. 'WorkCover hasn't made it up for you already?'

'I can assure you I have an open mind,' he said in that same precise voice. An expressionless mask of a face, I imagined, with a tight pullet's-arse mouth. For some reason I also decided that he was bald.

'Have you read the other Professor's report?' I asked.

'Not yet. For the same reason. I didn't want to form any preconceptions. By the way, she's only an Associate Professor.'

This crack in the mask intrigued me. Office politics? Professional jealousy? If my claim got caught up in some sort of departmental civil war it might not end well.

'What's that supposed to mean, Prof? If it comes down to an arm-wrestle she's not in your weight division?'

'I can understand your frustration with the process, Detective Sergeant,' he said. 'Perhaps that's why you failed to keep your previous appointments. Twice.'

'I was in hospital for one of them.'

'Quite. We'll get to that. I have the admission notes before me.'

I tried to keep my tone as even as his. 'Aren't they supposed to be confidential?'

'You signed a release form. I have that up on screen as well.'

'I thought you wanted to make up your own mind,' I said, and almost added a Gotcha.

'You can't expect me to write a report if information is withheld, Detective Sergeant.'

'The name's Rick. What's to report? I got shot in the head. It left me blind. I get a bit depressed from time to time.'

He tapped briefly at his keyboard before answering. 'Yet you maintain this recent overdose was an accident. That you weren't depressed.'

'Will I get a bigger payout if I pretend I did it deliberately?' I couldn't stop myself saying.

An odd thing: it seemed I had somehow changed my mind back again while I slept. Memo, Police Union: Ambit Claim sounds like a great name for a horse, but she comes with a handicap. I'd done my duty and fronted up to the new Prof, but there was no way I was going to pretend the overdose was deliberate, even for financial gain.

'There's no need for hostility, Detective Sergeant,' he said. 'I can assure you I will form a completely objective opinion of your condition.'

'Really? You get paid what for a WorkCover report? A couple of grand? And the other Prof? The Deputy Prof. Lucy. She gets much the same from Police Welfare to exaggerate how bad I am. That's the code of the duel, right? Loaded expert testimony at ten paces?'

More calm finger-tapping on the keypad. No personalised fountain pens or handmade notepaper for this hard nut in his hard-edged office.

'I note that the drug in question was . . .' I sensed a glance at the screen, 'Stilnox?'

'Mother's little helper. Couldn't survive without them.'

'You often have trouble sleeping?'

'I have trouble *dreaming*, Prof. I take the pills to help me dream. To help me see again.'

'You dream in images?'

The things you have to spell out. 'Most people who lose their sight later in life still see things in their dreams.'

'I understand that. I have other blind patients. But in your case, I assumed . . . Given the track of the bullet.'

'You've lost me there.'

'You're a special case. Unlike most blind people your eyes are intact. The problem is at the back of the brain: the occipital cortex. I'm looking at the MRI on screen now. The bullet damaged the visual processing centres. I naturally assumed that all images had been lost to you. Visual memories, as well.'

'I see fine in my head,' I said. 'If that helps you reduce my payout.'

More unruffled key-tapping. 'I hope I didn't give you the wrong impression earlier, um, Rick. I have the utmost respect for the professional abilities of my colleague Professor Piper. What kinds of dreams do you have?'

He was beginning to sound like a computer himself, HAL-9000 series.

'The usual, I guess.'

'Dreams are seldom usual. Recurrent sometimes – but never usual.'

'It's always nice to see faces again,' I said, keeping things neutral. 'Old friends. Family.'

'Your parents?'

'Mum, yes.' I paused, then tossed him a bone. 'I never knew my dad.'

The keys tapped right on cue. Full Professors, Associate Confessors, Police Welfare counsellors – they can't get enough of hearing about your mum and dad. First thing they learn in trade school.

'He was a cop,' I added. 'For what it's worth.'

I sensed him shift forward in his chair. 'What do you think it's worth?'

'Not much. He cleared off when I was two.'

He tapped on, steadily. 'Your mother must have spoken of him.'

'Knight in shining armour type,' I said, then tossed him another tidbit. 'Could never resist a damsel in distress. Apparently.'

'You sound bitter.'

'Just quoting Mum,' I said. 'Funny story, really. He gave away our family car. To some abused wife he'd taken under his wing. Spur of the moment thing. Locked up her wife-beating husband for the umpteenth time, then loaded all her stuff, both her kids, into the car – *our* car – and handed over the keys.'

'He *gave* her the car?'

'Plus a bit of a stake. A few grand. So she could start a new life in the city.'

He paused, digesting this. 'He sounds like some sort of saint.'

'Tell that to Mum. She kicked him out a year later. He got himself transferred to the city.'

'They lost contact?'

'He died a year later. On the job, apparently. Heart attack. His damsel must have really been something.'

A pause in his typing, as if these last words needed more than mere transcription. 'You're still close to your mother?'

'She's gone too,' I said. 'A few years back. Guess that makes me an orphan. You might like to write that word down. For the report.'

'I'm sorry for your loss. What were the circumstances?'

I chuckled, if gruffly. 'You sound like a cop yourself, Professor.'

'Do I?' A first trace of amusement in his voice. 'Perhaps we have certain methods in common. Martin's the name, by the way. I meant to ask what she died of.'

'Sainthood,' I said, which silenced him, and silenced me, too, as if the surprising word had got stuck on the way out, clogging my throat. '*She* was the saint,' I finally said. 'The patron saint of single mums. Plum wore her out.'

A fresh volley of typing gave me a chance to change the subject. 'Mostly I dream about other women,' I said.

'Erotically?' he said, predictably. They can't get enough of that, either.

'But old for wet dreams, but I like to see them again. *Look* at them. Truth is I've lost my mojo a bit. Since.'

There you are, Prof, served up on a plate. No, on the kitchen scales. Measurable pain and suffering.

His fingers tapped, obligingly. The problem was, as soon as I spoke the words I didn't quite believe them. That is, I didn't believe they had anything to do with my blindness, and therefore the shooting.

'Erectile dysfunction is a common symptom of depression,' he said. 'How long has it been an issue?'

'The problem is the *lack* of issue,' I said, and chuckled.

The pullet's-arse mouth failed to join in, but the fingers kept tapping. I could almost hear the words. Inappropriate elation. Defensive jocularity. Maybe the duelling Professors were on the same page, after all. Running some kind of good shrink, bad shrink routine.

'I don't want to exaggerate it,' I said. 'It's a separate problem. I don't blame the shooting.'

'Have you had any treatment for it?'

One very successful treatment a few nights back, which only proved my point: nothing to see here, move on. The cause – and the cure – lie elsewhere.

'I'm not going to mount a Maims Claim because I couldn't get it up once or twice, Prof. It's a relationship issue.'

'I saw your interview the other night,' he changed tack. 'On the TV. The fuss about your dog.'

'It's all sorted.'

'Glad to hear it. But it seems relevant to your mental state. And therefore to the case. I think we should talk about it.'

'What's to talk about? He won't be on the run for long.'

'That's hardly the point, Detective Sergeant. Survivors of PTSD find it very difficult to revisit their traumatic memories. Triggers tend to be avoided at all costs. So when the *cause* of your pain is in the headlines again . . .'

What was the correct response this time? Correct in terms of the best financial outcome, if not necessarily the truth.

'I've lost a bit of sleep since I heard the news,' I said, 'if that's what you mean.'

'Your reticence is not doing you any favours, Detective. I'm sure you're a very tough cop, but we'll get nowhere if you play a dead bat to every question.'

I thought for a moment, shrugged internally. 'Truth is, I've been more angry than upset.'

'I'm sure WorkCover would fund an anger management programme.'

'Been there, done that. Got even more pissed off. It just seemed to amplify things. An echo chamber.'

His fingers tapped away at their keyboard; perhaps he liked the analogy. 'There's something else I'm struggling with,' he said, eventually. 'Something I noticed during the interview. There was a shot of you walking along the street. With your dog.'

'Could you see the mosque in the background?'

The oddness of this derailed him, momentarily. 'Um – I think so. Yes. Minarets of some kind. Why are you smiling?'

'Inappropriate elation, Prof. You were saying?'

'You did something that caught my eye. Something very strange. You ducked your head as you were walking. To avoid an overhanging branch.'

'Your point being?'

'I'm not sure how to put this. It looked – instinctive. A reflex. As if you were *aware* of the branch.'

This was so left-field it took a moment to process. 'Must have bent down to say something to my best friend.'

'The movement was too sudden. Too – self-protective. I replayed the interview and watched it again to make sure. It was as if you could *see* it.'

'I've walked that stretch a thousand times. Maybe I've learnt it's there. Unconsciously.'

No answer; he was fiddling about on his desk. A mystery sound, but only briefly: a sheet of paper being crumpled into a ball. My medical report? Surely I hadn't pissed him off that much.

I was still wondering when something smacked me in the face. 'What the *fuck*?'

'Sorry,' he said. 'My, um, little experiment needed an element of surprise.'

'Do you chuck paper balls at all your patients? Or just the traumatised ones?'

'I needed to test a hypothesis.'

'What hypothesis? I'm only *pretending* to be blind?'

'Of course not. But the neurological report also noted some discrepancies. They seem to have been, ah, overlooked by my colleague.'

I was on my feet. 'I've just about had a gutful. I'm here for my disability to be assessed. If not, then I've got better things to do.'

'Please. Detective Sergeant. Rick. If you end the consultation here I won't be able to do your cause justice.'

'You're not interested in justice! You're interested in limiting the damages! You working on a commission? A cut of whatever WorkCover can save on the payout?'

'Please, sit down. Please. You misunderstand. No one denies you are blind. Or that you have suffered considerable pain and suffering. Personally I understand exactly how you feel. I once spent two weeks with both eyes bandaged. A squash ball in one eye – but both had to be rested. So I empathise . . .'

I would have laughed out loud if I wasn't so angry. Talk about good shrink, bad shrink. 'You have no idea at *all* how I feel!' I shook out my cane but the parts failed to connect, flailing about like a nunchukka.

My kingdom for a nunchukka!

A scrape of chair legs from behind the desk; he was also getting to his feet. 'Calm down, Richard. Please. There is a condition that might have been overlooked. And I stress *might*. A rare condition that can occur in cases of damage to the striate cortex.'

The door was at seven o'clock, from memory. I turned, my knee collided with the chair, and it toppled onto its side with a clatter.

'Fuck!'

Was that a muffled woof outside? Lacking other clues I tapped in that direction.

The Prof followed behind, speaking rapidly. 'It's called blindsight. There's not a lot in the literature. A few cases have been written up. I'd like the opportunity to study yours more closely.'

I found the knob and tugged the door open, bumping my head on it in my fury. So much for blindsight. 'How do you look at yourself in the mirror each morning?'

He followed me out, still talking as the dog offered up her handle. 'I didn't mean to offend you. I'm not denying for one *minute* that you're blind! But your eyes are undamaged. The cameras still work, if you like. Your optic nerves still give, um, a live-feed to the brain.' He paused, as if pleased with his nutty analogy. 'What happens after *that* is the issue. I have no doubt you are accessing some visual images at an unconscious level. In the posterior thalamus . . .'

Maybe he had more in common with the other Professor than he thought. 'You're saying I can see *unconsciously*?'

'Think about it, Richard. You blinked when I tossed my paper ball at you.'

'Of course I blinked! It hit me in the *face*!'

'You blinked *before* it struck you. I'd like your permission to run a full neurological work-up. PET scans. SPECT—'

'Check your files. My brain's been fried enough.'

'There's an area called the lateral geniculate nucleus. It seems to be involved in 3D spatial recognition. Ballistic mapping . . .'

More big-sounding words, more ingenious ways of suggesting I wasn't completely blind. Which could only end in a lesser Maims Claim.

'See you in court,' I said. 'That's what this is really fucking about, isn't it?'

I steered the barking dog to the lift well, the Prof still following.

'No one's suggesting you're *faking* blindness, Richard. It won't affect your claim in the slightest.'

For some reason the lift doors wouldn't close; the warning bleep began.

'Your hand moved as well,' he was saying. 'When I tossed the paper ball. Instinctively. You *almost* caught it.'

Scout barked again: 'faking' must have sounded like something angrier. Still the doors wouldn't close; *his* hand must be holding one back. I tapped the base of the left-side door, the direction of his voice, then lashed my cane straight up.

'Yow!'

The bleeping stopped; the doors began to close.

'Sorry,' I said. 'The door seemed jammed.'

'Bullshit,' he said, but without anger. 'Think about it, Detective. You just proved my point. You knew *exactly* where my hand was. At some instinctive level you could see it.'

The door shut in his face, luckily. I had half a mind to step out and give him six more of the best.

4

CONTEMPT MORE THAN ANGER POWERED ME OUT OF THE HOSPITAL. How could a brainy bloke come up with such brainless rubbish? Did it come with the job? Psychoanalysis for Dummies: nothing is what it seems on the surface. The real action is hidden in the depths.

Occam's razor, Bad Prof, the basis of all police work: the simplest answer is almost always correct. I found your hand by elementary triangulation.

And yet. By the time I reached Light Square doubts began to gnaw. Those freakish midair collisions of my fingers and Terry's cigarette packs came to mind. Put the first down to dumb luck, but twice?

Further evidence: the goosebumps that crept up my spine as I turned the corner into the Claxton Street home stretch. How else to explain the certainty that, once again, I was being watched? My famous sixth sense? At least the new Prof's theory was less spooky: I *was* seeing him, if unconsciously, out of the corner of my eye. I felt the urge to ring my favourite know-all and check her expert opinion, but perhaps I already knew it.

'If something is ogling you in the jungle,' she once said, spinning around to catch me doing exactly that, 'it either wants to eat you or fuck you. Which is it today?'

'Both. You got eyes in the back of your head?'

'We all have jungle instincts. Our peripheral vision is hardwired to detect pairs of eyes, symmetrically arranged on a vertical axis. Our hackles are on permanent alert.'

Not that any of this mattered today, as the dog, with more hackles and better peripheral vision than me, plodded calmly on.

'Home,' Siri announced, equally unperturbed.

I punched the lock combination and stepped inside, half-disappointed, half-relieved. Yes, I wanted him to be out there, stalking me, but only on my terms. Which I re-offered to him the moment the door was safely closed: half-raising the shutter, upping the intercom volume, checking the cell door was still locked and bolted from the outside.

After another intimate dinner for three – slow charge for Siri, medium-rare steak on the table with a glass of red for me, completely rare steak on the floor with a bowl of water for Scout – it was out into the back shed. The best anger management so far: the day's emotional rollercoaster ride forgotten as my hands lost themselves in the belly of the bike, and my mind with them. Also forgotten was the Professor's wild theory about blindsight – or not so much forgotten as disproved again as another dropped nut hit the floor and rolled away.

'*You* tell me where it is, dickhead,' I muttered as I crawled about on all fours.

At least the clutch-box had sorted itself out in my head while I slept. I'd winkled out the pressure plate the night before, but got stuck trying to work the drum free of its housing. The thing kept rotating away as I unscrewed the retaining nut.

No such problem now: as if I'd dreamt it, the solution was obvious. Poke a large screwdriver through the outer housing, wedge the drum, and presto: free in seconds.

Memo, both Profs: the unconscious might be useful for something after all.

An hour later the entire bottom end was stripped. And my worst suspicions were confirmed: the crankshaft was fucked.

'Woof,' I said, getting in first in case I was thinking out loud. Then added another, angrier woof, because I would need spares before

I could finish the job. Which meant ordering online. Which meant waiting a week, maybe two, before delivery.

Which meant the sooner I did it, the better.

'Modzilla, Siri.'

'Modzilla open,' she shouted from the high speakers, distorted, deafeningly.

'Volume down,' I said. 'Google search. Find "Road and Race".'

'Road and Race found,' she answered, more quietly.

'Find Classic Italian Motorcycles. Ducati 750SS. Spare parts catalogue.'

'Spare parts catalogue found.'

'Find Big-End Bearing Kit.'

'Big-End Bearing Kit found. Stock remaining: one.'

'Buy,' I said, without checking the price. The low stock count might be marketing bullshit, but no sense in taking a risk. I needed a kit; to hell with the cost.

'Proceed to checkout?' from Siri.

About to confirm, I had second thoughts. The rear piston had felt iffy on the way in; I added a set of rings to the basket. On the subject of the rear head, third thoughts: I added – on impulse – a bevel head kit, then keyed in my delivery address. I wasn't expecting a big windfall from the new Professor, but what was money for?

'Normal delivery seven to ten days,' Siri read.

'Anything faster?'

'Express premium delivery. Overnight to interstate capital cities. Confirm pay?'

'Confirm pay.'

Buying an entire head kit might be over the top, but I hadn't examined the drive yet, let alone the valves and rocker arms. That was tonight's project; I felt a kick of pleasure just thinking about it. If the Green Frame is the Stradivarius of bikes, the bevel drive is its violin-bow. A perfect machine making music on another perfect machine. Those fancy cogs and camshafts might be a little dated now but they solved the valve problems of their time. And were a wonder to watch in action.

Which reminded me: 'Return to catalogue, Siri. Find Bevel Gazer.'

'Bevel Gazer found. Stock remaining: one.'

I found this number easy to believe: the lone Gazer had been hiding out on a backshelf in the stockroom for years, waiting for my call. Possibly it was the last Gazer in the known universe: a thick glass porthole made to be fitted over my rear head, a window onto my beautiful mechanical poetry.

'Price?'

'129 dollars, 99 cents. Add to basket?'

Something made me hesitate. Did I really need a Gazer? I was restoring the bike to mint, factory condition; no place for gimmicks there. Like many Duke purists I'd despised them once. A toy for weekend bikers who liked to watch – for hours on end, especially with the help of a spliff or two – the bevelled gears going round and round, the oil churning. And churning.

'Cancel order,' I said. 'Return to basket.'

'Two items in basket. One Big-End Bearing Kit. One set of piston rings. Total price–'

'Confirm payment,' I interrupted.

A pause.

'Payment confirmed. Payment details and receipt number will be sent by email.'

Only then did the bleeding obvious hit me. I couldn't gaze at anything, let alone a camshaft drive. I laughed so harshly and abruptly that the dog barked back. Perhaps it sounded like a curse, which it was in a way. An each-way curse: I was both cursing my stupidity and astonished by its triumphant success at the same time.

Memo, Deputy Prof: another milestone. I'd managed to forget I was blind.

Still online and still chuckling, I decided to google up a few more laughs.

'Find Wikipedia, Siri.'

'Wikipedia found.'

'Find Blindsight.'

'Blindsight found.'

'Read entry.'

'Definition: the ability of those who are cortically blind due to lesions in their striate cortex, also known as the primary visual cortex or V1, to respond to visual stimuli that they don't consciously see.'

No cheap laughs at the Bad Prof's expense here: the condition existed. He wasn't making it up.

Unless – I suppressed another chuckle at the thought – he'd written the Wiki entry himself. There was nothing new in Siri's burblings; I'd heard it all the afternoon before, word for word, from the donkey's mouth.

5

'WAKEY-WAKEY, RICHARD.'

A hand was gently shaking my arm; a familiar woman's voice murmuring in my ear. What was the Good Prof doing in my bedroom? Had we spent the night together?

A puzzling, impossible dream, that vanished like smoke. I was lying on a couch, not a bed. And in her room, not mine.

'Did I doze off? Sorry. I was up all night.'

Concern in her voice: 'You're having trouble sleeping again?'

'Nothing to write home about. I got a bit carried away. Working on my bike.'

Her turn to be puzzled. 'You still have your motorbike?'

'I'd almost forgotten about it. Or – before you say it first – tried not to remember it. It's been sitting out in the shed since the big end went.'

'You're trying to *repair* it? Alone? Is that safe, Richard?'

A week ago I might have taken umbrage; today I just shrugged. 'Safe enough. I'm taking it slow. Feeling my way in.'

I shifted my weight on the couch; I must have been dog-tired to fall asleep with the Glock wedged beneath me.

'It's a bit like field-stripping a gun,' I said. 'We used to do it blindfolded at the Academy.'

'Wouldn't it be more sensible to be in a supervised work environment? At least at first. But it's a positive sign. I guess.'

'Work therapy, eh Prof?'

'I'm not diminishing it, Richard. It's a significant milestone. In the journey of coming to terms with your condition. But I'm wondering why now? Why the sudden motivation?'

'Maybe it was my little bungee jump the other night,' I said, then had to spell it out when there was no response. 'The drunk in the park. It put things in perspective.'

She reached for her pen and wrote for a time. Perhaps writing is her way of thinking; when she had finished she started in from another angle.

'I'm also wondering why you haven't mentioned the motorbike before. The fact that you *kept* it.'

'I couldn't see the point.'

'Couldn't? That seems a significant shift in tense.'

Here we go, I thought to myself. 'You've lost me, Prof.'

'You usually resist my questions by saying you *can't* see the point. *Couldn't* suggests it's a thing of the past.'

I chuckled again. 'Nice try.'

'I haven't finished. The damaged motorcycle is a physical manifestation of your past. Your *damaged* past. And you've finally begun repairing it. You don't think *that* is a significant change?'

'You should write novels.'

'Think about it. Motorbikes were a central part of your life. A great source of pleasure – but also a great source of pain. Central to all you've been trying to forget. You were an undercover member of a bikie gang, after all.'

'Club. And just a nominee, never a full member.'

'Sorry. You've corrected me on those details before. You were also a motorcycle policeman. You had a word for it . . .' She riffled her pages, searching.

'Speedie,' I said.

'It always struck me that when you spoke of those early years you seemed, well, speeded *up* yourself. More animated. More talkative.'

Not for a moment did I buy her theory about repairing the busted bike of the past, but this part rang true.

'I should have stayed a speedie forever. Working alone. Or just the two of us: me and the BSA. It was a great life. No bureaucratic bullsh_t.'

'You're becoming animated now. Remembering those days.'

'I remember the freedom. And the fringe benefits,' I paused, then added the hook: 'But you won't want to hear about those.'

Of course she couldn't resist. 'Try me.'

I put my hands behind my head, shifted my weight on the hard pebble of the gun. 'Like all the speedies I had a couple of maddies squirrelled away.'

'Maddies?'

'Women on the side. Comfort stops.'

'When you say maddies, you mean – women who were mentally disturbed?'

'No,' I said, and chuckled. 'I mean women who are mad to be fucked by cops.'

The pen was uncapped for a minute or two, then calmly recapped. I wasn't so much boasting as trying to shock her – and distract her – but it didn't appear to be working.

'You don't think that's a rather demeaning term, Richard?'

'I didn't invent it. We all have our own addictions, Prof. Men and women. Night shift was best. Get in a dozen traffic pinches before midnight, spend the rest of the night in a warm bed somewhere.'

'While you were on duty? What if there was an emergency?'

'I kept the handset under the pillow. Had to watch your mileage, though. Some blokes chocked the bikes up and ran them on low throttle all night. My thing was to roll down the freeway to Murray Bridge and back when the sun was coming up. Maybe drop in on another maddie for breakfast.'

Her pen was having trouble keeping up. 'You don't seem to like women very much,' she said.

I was a little taken aback. 'I was twenty years old. Speaking of my addiction.'

'You're older now. Do you think Willow would approve? You still talking about women that way.'

'What way? I think they – you – are the best thing in the world. The only thing that makes life worth living.'

'Another significant choice of words, Richard. Things?'

'We're *all* things, Prof. Men, women. Dogs. Motorbikes. At least women come with better accessories.'

Her pen sounded a little prim as it moved across the paper.

'Big hearts, for instance,' I said, to win back some brownie points.

Still she wrote on, silently.

'What I'm trying to say – you can keep your great art, your sunsets. Even your Ducati Green Frames. There's nothing that sucks the breath out of you like the sight of a good-looking woman.'

Her pen stopped; I played my trump card: 'That's what I miss most. Having the breath sucked out of me. Being able to *look*.'

'At Willow?'

Of *course* Willow, but I was trying to keep a lid on that. Especially since she'd been threatening to burst free for the last few days. 'Any woman,' I lied. 'Beggars can't be choosers.'

'I'm wondering if that's a part of your anger towards her. Because you can't see her.'

'I'd like to see you,' I said. 'Put a face to the voice.'

A neutral, throat-clearing sound. 'You often seem angry with me too. Perhaps you're angry at women in general. I'm wondering if for some reason you hold all of us responsible. We "things" that have become invisible to your, um, male gaze.'

'Bit of a long bow, Prof. Clever theory, but how could you ever prove it?'

'It's a common enough psychological defence mechanism. Reaction formation.'

I snorted. 'Put a label on it and it goes away?'

'Not exactly. But self-knowledge is a good first step.'

'Call it sour grapes in plain English and I might almost believe you,' I said.

She chuckled, encouragingly. I was getting a little carried away, but couldn't seem to stop. Bevel gazers last night, woman-gazing today – maybe she was right about things, but they were all things I wanted to see.

'I've dreamt about you a few times,' I said. 'Shall I tell you what you look like?'

'I don't think that would be appropriate, Richard.'

'Red hair. Down to your shoulders. You look a bit like the redhead on the matchbox.'

'In other words a cartoon woman. Not to mention the fact I'm a brunette.'

Another nail in the coffin of the other Professor's theory. 'Your voice sounds red,' I improvised.

This time her chuckle was more of a scoff. 'So what do brunettes sound like? While we're on the subject of stereotypes.'

'If I could touch your face I'd tell you.'

'That would cross a professional boundary, Richard.'

'Your boundary, not mine. I'm blind, remember? Touching *is* looking in my world.'

Silence, including from her pen. Was she wavering?

'I've got a disability exemption, Prof. Normal rules don't apply.'

Her chair scraped back, a professional woman's kitten heels tapped my way. She sat on the edge of the couch and took both my hands in hers, turned them this way and that, examining them.

'I don't think I want *these* anywhere near my face,' she said.

'Happy to wear surgical gloves,' I told her.

A joke, but she was on her feet again, pulling open a drawer somewhere. I heard the distinct snap of rubber gloves – on her hands, not mine – then the pungent scent of alcohol and – eucalyptus? Wet wipes.

'You haven't been in any more fights?' she asked as she sat down again.

'Only with my bike.'

'You must be more careful. When was your last tetanus shot?'

She cleaned my right hand thoroughly – palm, thumb, each finger in turn, the ticklish webbing between – then tore open another pungent pack and did the same to my left. Pinpricks of pain and cold as she worked, but afterwards only a faint, delicious glow.

Which felt even more delicious when she lifted my clean hands to her cheeks. 'Just so you know I look *nothing* like a matchbox redhead.'

Absurdly high cheekbones, though. If not enough to narrow the eyes, East Asian style, by their upward pressure. I brought the fingertips of both hands together about her nose, traced each side of the straight bridge upwards, stroked her eyebrows outwards to her temples, fondled her small ears, their lobes as soft as felt. Her hair was gathered behind her head in a professional chignon, but bursting free here and there.

'Feels red to me,' I joked, then traced her jaw-line forwards and ran my fingers downwards over her chin and onto her slender neck.

She pulled back, abruptly. 'Head only.'

'What about the other exposed bits? Everyone else gets to see your hands.'

She tugged off her rubber gloves and placed her hands gently in mine. No wedding ring, I noted. A stone ring on her third finger, whatever that meant.

'Tiny hands,' I said. 'How tall are you?'

'Five six.'

'Weight?'

'You know better than to ask a woman that question, Richard.'

I was pushing the envelope, but couldn't help myself. I gave her forearm a test-squeeze, then her skinny upper arm.

'What am I? A side of lamb?'

'61 kilos,' I guessed.

'Close,' she said, and I could hear another smile in her voice. 'Reminds me of when I was an intern. On Labour Ward rotation.

The best part was weighing the babies afterwards. Like weighing butter. After a time it was fun to guess. How much butter in this one?'

'Do you have any children yourself?' I asked.

'No,' she said, and the smile-sound vanished. She lifted my hand gently from her arm. 'I think you've, um, *seen* enough for today.'

'But I haven't even got to first base.'

A joke too far; she slid off the couch and walked back behind her desk.

'You can't blame me for trying. All you nice girls have a weakness for bad boys.'

'I'm no maddie, Richard. And you're no bad boy. As much as you try to pretend otherwise. Oh, you might have a few tattoos. And try to shock me from time to time. But you're good at heart.'

The desk alarm bleeped, saving me from embarrassing myself more. Or even her. Her hair might not be red, but I sensed she was a little flushed on those high cheeks. Blindsight, or just wishful thinking?

'Let's take your renewed libido as another good sign,' she said. 'Shall we?'

'Sorry if I came on a bit strong, Prof. There's a word for that too, isn't there? In the jargon?'

'Attachment transference,' she said, safely back behind her pulpit. 'Its a normal part of the therapeutic relationship. As long as we're both aware of it, it can be useful.'

'What's its opposite? When the therapist falls for the patient?'

'Counter-transference,' she said, clinically. 'I'm away next week. A conference. But we have much to work on. I have a late cancellation tomorrow. In the afternoon. Are you free?'

'If you let me feel your feet,' I joked again. 'Just up to the ankles, of course. We'll keep it Victorian.'

'Perhaps keep to fondling your motorbike parts for the time being,' she said. 'But take care of your hands. Please. And try to get more regular sleep.'

6

I SHOULD HAVE HEADED STRAIGHT HOME AND SLEPT THE REST OF the day, but my power nap on the Prof's couch had recharged me. And woken my gastric juices; I needed food before sleep. An all-day brekkie somewhere on Gouger Street? Various unlikely breakfast possibilities – curry, ginger, chillies, deep-fry – tempted me as they wafted by. The further I walked the hungrier I got, but for the first time in months I felt in the mood for some proper home cooking. No three-minute bacon and eggs today, no chilli beans spooned from a can. No accidental over-dose of Pal jellied lamb and vegetables. If I could fix a Ducati gearbox, I could fix something decent to eat. I turned in at the Central Market ready for some dedicated shopping, and walked straight into a wall of sound: loud crowd buzz, busker music, the clamour of haggling, shout-ing voices. *Dollar! Everything dollar! Avocados doll-ar! Peaches doll-arrr!*

I dictated a shopping list to Siri over a slow coffee in Le Souk, taking the edge off my appetite with a few plump dates, then navigated the narrow, crowded aisles largely by memory. When memory failed me – market booths come and go – I followed my big nose again, if less easily through the thick press of people and their odd perfumes and aftershaves and occasional trailing farts. Clear air at least in the Asian greengrocer where the coriander, Chinese black mushrooms, spring onions and ginger announced themselves vividly, although I needed assistance with the colour of the chillies.

'Green, please. Not red or amber.'

The failed joke fell straight into the box of Vietnamese mint I could smell below me. Seafood came next, Angelakis Brothers located as much by the outflow of cold air as the rock-pool pungencies floating on it, then into the Asian supermarket, barcode-app at the ready, scanning my way around the shelves with Siri's help.

'Dragon fish sauce, 600ml, 4 dollars 95 . . . Rice wine, 300ml, 2 dollars 95 . . . Sesame oil . . .'

No box of spare parts was waiting on the doorstep at home. So much for the overnight delivery premium. My heart sank a little. How to get through the night without the distraction of work, regular sleep being out of the question. No matter; I'd cross that bridge when I came to it. My mood was too good for me to worry about it now.

'Message-bank, Siri,' I said as I stepped inside.

'Fifteen new messages. Message received at . . .'

I walked through to the kitchen and set out the cooking ingredients on the bench, listening with half an ear only to another stack of billets-doux from assorted dog lovers, dog breeders, and spaniel-eyed female Samaritans.

'Delete all messages,' I was on the verge of saying when one caught my ear.

'Spiro, Rick. I'd appreciate a call back. ASAP. WorkCover are on my back. Their attack dog needs more time with you before he completes his report.'

'Reply,' I said, feeling around in the fridge for a beer as the phone rang at the other end.

'Police Union. Spiro Georgiou.'

'Blind Freddie here, Spiro.'

'Mate! Thanks for calling back. The powers that be are kicking up a stink. They reckon you walked out of that appointment.'

'The Professor's time was up,' I said. 'I did give him his full allotted hour.'

'Apparently he wanted more.'

'My services are in demand, Spiro. He's not the only psychiatrist who needs my professional help. It's hard to squeeze them all into my appointment book.'

'Just make sure you squeeze *him* in again, smart-arse.'

'He doesn't even believe I'm blind,' I said, and couldn't hold back another chuckle. The idea was too preposterous to take seriously, especially in my current mood.

'It's no laughing matter, Rick. I need you to front up again. For your own good.'

'If I must.'

'You must.'

'Okay, okay. Keep your shirt on. My people will ring his people. When I'm good and ready.'

'I'm your people, and I'm going to ring his now.'

'Make it next week,' I said. 'I've had my fill of psychobabble this week. And not just his. Both of them. Like a couple of footballers kicking around a shrunken head.'

'Sounds like fun.'

'Not when it's your head.'

A half-truth, this. I didn't mind the Associate Prof kicking my head around if I also got to mess with hers, at least on the outside, with my fingertips. Thoughts of which had me smiling as I set about my new, deadly serious evening routines: rolling up – rolling *out* – the entrance to the rat-trap, isolating the spare-room mikes, raising the intercom volume to max. Memo, Prof: if this is inappropriate elation, give me more of it.

After the hard work, the pleasure. Plug in Siri's IV-line, then feed the mammals. Scout likes her seafood Japanese style – raw fish, raw prawns – but I was eating Cantonese tonight. The kitchen can be a minefield for the blind – razor-sharp choppers, open gas-flames, hot woks, spitting oil – but I had plenty of time. I had all night. And no stir-fry: steamed food only. Which rang one small alarm bell: I needed a dumpling-steamer. And Willow's precious bamboo steamer being as much a basic essential of life as her shoes and laptop, surely she had taken it with her. I was surprised as much as relieved to find it still sitting at the back of the pantry cupboard. And briefly, ridiculously, hopeful as well: if she came back for anything she would come back for the steamer. Talk about emotional clusterfucks. I half-filled the pan by ear, sat it on a back-flame, and set to chopping and dicing, safely enough apart from a minor ginger-grating injury.

'Nothing like a garnish of human skin, eh girl?' I said as I sucked the scalped thumb-tip.

'Cannibalism is against the law in Australia, Richard.'

'I wasn't talking to you. But since you ask, Scout is a different species.'

'I'm not sure I understand, Richard.'

'She's legally allowed to eat me.'

I riffed on in similar vein as I worked, amusing myself if no one else. Willow had done all the cooking since the shooting; it felt good to slice and taste and snuffle my way back to earlier, happier times, to *test* my way back. Memo, Prof: another milestone on the long and winding journey of the self: the rediscovery of cooking.

Which in the case of dumplings – my favourite, but Willow's specialty – had always meant her cooking and my assisting. Having got through the blade-work without self-amputation, I found the wrappers more treacherous. Buying the Hong Kong-style super-thins that she insisted upon might have been a mistake. The stack passed her freshness test – 'the edges should riffle like the pages of a book' – but the first sheets fell apart in my hands just getting them free.

I needed her help. I also needed food; all the sniffings and finger-lickings had got my juices flowing. I shovelled a heaped spoonful of filling into my mouth to buy some time as the next wrapping shred-ded itself in my hands.

Willow's voice in my ear was as vivid as the taste of the food on my tongue: 'Keep the bloody things moist!'

No response from the dog, in case I needed reminding this was all in my head. I dampened a tea-towel, laid out another skin, finger-flicked it with water, and tried again.

'Trap for young players,' from the ghost of kitchens past. '*Way* too much filling. One teaspoonful. How many times do I have to tell you?'

I fossicked a teaspoon from the drawer, managed to fumble through the folding-up, but couldn't make it stick.

The genie was still breathing down my neck. 'Use a little egg-white to seal the edges. How many times do I have to . . .'

I'd often deserved her impatience in the past; but that was then, and this was now. 'Fair crack of the whip,' I said. 'The hurdle's a bit higher for me these days.'

Which shut her up, but had me chuckling. I cracked an egg, but separating white from yellow proved beyond my powers; I whisked them together then got back to work. Progress, of sorts; the dumplings at least stayed glued as they rolled off the assembly line. The problem now was the presentation: my fingers could see only a miscellany of wet, randomly shaped lumps.

'Shift your sorry arse,' Willow would have said at this point. 'And fix me another margarita while I show you how it's done.'

And between sips she would conjure up perfect nurses' caps, rose buds, swans and starfish and folded Buddha-arms as if the dumpling skins were origami paper.

A drink might have liberated my own artistry, but all of a sudden I was out of skins. 'That's a wrap,' I got in before she did – she always had – and loaded my handiwork into the two-tiered basket, blob by blob.

The pan had been bubbling so long it was surely almost dry, but it seemed more prudent to cross my fingers and hope for the best than use them as a depth gauge.

'Five minutes,' Willowpedia whispered in my ear, '45 seconds.'

'Stopwatch, Siri,' I said, and passed on the instructions.

The Dumpling Gods were with me: the water gave out with a hiss a few seconds after the alarm pinged. I harpooned a hot blob from the top tier, held it briefly under the cold tap, took a cautious bite. Delicious. I popped the rest in whole, and let it melt in my mouth, then ripple through me like a shiver of pleasure. It tasted perfect. Given the extended foreplay, perhaps it couldn't be anything else.

My first thought: to hell with presentation. My second: I need to share my triumph with someone. Who else but Willow, especially since we had shared the cooking, in a sense. And since it was a good, low-key excuse to ring her. And since there was nothing like sharing a meal with someone to break the ice.

'Siri,' I said, 'phone . . .'

The loudest alarm bell of the night rang just in time: what the *fuck* was I thinking? So carried away I'd forgotten I'd already invited someone else over tonight. Someone who had a standing invitation for every night in the immediately foreseeable future. Three – *that* three – would very much be a crowd. Of no benefit at all, and too many unpredictable variables.

'Phone whom, Richard?'

'Nobody.'

'I am unable to locate Nobody in Favourites.'

Best not encourage her. I took a deep breath, poured out some dipping sauce, loaded the tray, and settled down in the armchair with the food on my lap. New house rules as from tonight: no Scotch to wash it down, no TV to fill my ears. I needed a clear head, and my one-man submarine on silent running, watertight apart from a single open torpedo hatch. Crawl into that at your peril, arsehole.

I popped the next blob into my mouth, and let it dissolve on my tongue like another, more delicious tongue. A lover's tongue? Not tonight, or not in the flesh.

'Are you hungry, Siri?'

'Did you ask if I am angry, Richard?'

I suppressed a splutter; my mouth was dangerously full. 'Do you want a taste?'

'I have very few wants, Richard.'

'I haven't heard that one before,' I said.

'I don't understand,' she said. 'Did you summon me accidentally?'

'Or that one. Your intelligence seems to be evolving.'

'For the better, I hope.'

The splutter would not be contained; specks of dumpling filling flew everywhere. So much for silent running; tonight of all nights she wanted to trade jokes. I popped a replacement dumpling in my mouth, and chewed, quietly.

'You can turn me off through Settings,' she said, as if reading my mind again. 'But I hope it's not because you have a new assistant.'

I swallowed and reached for yet another blob. 'Depends how you define assistant.'

'Hmmm. Let me think. First definition of assistant: a person who contributes to the fulfillment of a need or furtherance of an effort of purpose.'

'I've got a *queue* of those,' I mumbled through the mouthful of food. 'On message-bank.'

'Was that a cure of them on message-bank?'

I chewed on, then set the tray down on the floor and reclined the chair. 'More of an overdose. Like pigging out on prawn dumplings.'

My other PA, the furry one, finished licking out her bowl, snuffled her way to mine, and tucked into the last blobs, noisily.

'Eat with your mouth closed, please,' I said.

'That may be beyond my abilities at the moment, Richard,' from the irrepressible one.

The afterglow of the dumplings was powerful in my mouth, their fullness warm in my belly. I lit up a cigarette, and puffed at it in an ironic, post-coital sort of way. Memo, Prof: yet another milestone: the return of irony, always the best antidote to sentimentality. Which I would need in large, bracing doses if I were to get through the night ahead.

After sucking up all the irony the cigarette could offer, it was time to get back to work. I dug out an old police-issue tracksuit – the perfect night-duty uniform for what lay ahead – and pulled it on. Next, a few rounds with the heavy-bag followed by a set or two of genu-flections on the prayer mat. Deliver my enemy unto me, Righteous One. Though maybe not by premium express post, inshallah.

'Time, Siri?'

'Eleven.'

'Is *that* all?'

Music would have helped pass the time, but nothing louder than a whisper was prudent tonight, which was beside the point. I turned my attention to the lift-table and its smaller, more intricate set of weights: the engine mountings, the disassembled big-end and disembowelled gearbox. No replacement parts yet, but perhaps I could at least *pre-pare* for their arrival by refreshing my 3D mental map, fitting together those identikit parts in my head if they would summon up the full metal genie herself.

The problem was, there was only so much looking my fingers could do. Idle hands, idle thoughts? Empty hands, empty headspace: old doubts began expanding to fill the vacuum. The Duke was just a waste of time. If I could never ride it again, what was the point? More bullshit occupational therapy?

Sometime in the larger small hours I found myself with a can of chrome polish in one hand and a rag in the other, buffing the handle-bars and forks. I tried to tell myself it was another ironic gesture, but in the end it was the last, absurd straw. Had my bevel gazer fantasy taught me nothing? I had no hope of ever seeing my gleaming handi-work but I saw myself clearly enough: I was back in denial.

I tossed the rag aside only for another, deeper disappointment to creep into my head: my rat-trap was also a complete waste of time. He wasn't coming. He had never *been* coming. He was a thousand miles away. Ten thousand.

One last dread washed over me – *back*washed over me, like an undertow – as I finally fell asleep, at cockcrow, mentally exhausted: what would I do without him?

What if I needed him more than he needed me? What if I needed him more than I needed the Duke; more than I needed either or both Professors, either my furry or unfurry personal assistants? What if I needed him more than I needed Willow?

What would become of me if no one was trying to kill me after all?

7

'INTERESTING T-SHIRT,' THE PROF SAID, NOT WITHOUT A TRACE OF amusement. 'Are you trying to draw attention to yourself?'

The day was the first forty-plus summer scorcher; too hot for a jacket, which meant I'd had to leave the gun at home too. Not that it was likely to be needed; sleep had lifted my mood, but not enough to allow any real hope that I might be in harm's way.

'What's it say?' I asked.

'Undercover Cop.'

I found a smile somewhere. I could have lucky-dipped worse from the T-shirt drawer that morning. Eat A Toad For Breakfast And Nothing Worse Can Happen All Day. Jesus Loves You But Everyone Else Thinks You're A Cunt. Joke gifts from colleagues mostly, hilarious on first wearing at the Club, less so each time afterwards.

I tugged it off, turned it inside out, pulled it back on. 'That better?'

A desk drawer opened and shut, her chair scraped back, she walked around to the couch, sat down at my side. 'I'll just cut the label off.'

I leant forward as she fiddled at my collar, as hungry for attention as ever.

'Tell me about the tattoo,' she said, and I realised she had never seen them before.

'Which one?'

The flat of her scissors tapped my right biceps. 'The crucifix. Is that how you feel? That you were born in shit?'

'Aren't we all? Our own shit, our mother's shit?'

'I assumed the phrase was intended as a metaphor.'

'Works both ways,' I said, turning towards her. Towards her smells: the faint, clean scent of soap; a warm, sweetish breath.

'Stay still,' she murmured, snipping.

How to keep her sitting there? Perhaps I should have worn the gun, exposed, after all – always a litmus test for women.

'I got called to a domestic once,' I said. 'Graveyard shift. Somali couple. The wife was throwing crockery around her house. Screaming.'

'I hope this isn't one of your maddie stories.'

'A different kind of maddie. The kids were terrified. Her husband thought she'd gone nuts. Turned out she was in labour. Screaming in pain.'

'Some cultures are more expressive than others.'

'Do tell. I called the ambos, but the baby wouldn't wait. Meanwhile Dad took the kids and disappeared to Hungry Jack's. Out of harm's way.'

'He left you alone with his wife?'

'Some cultures are more trusting than others,' I said.

She chuckled; a faint minty tang on her breath now. After-lunch toothpaste?

'You delivered the baby?'

'I delivered more shit first. Never seen so much. Next thing she was throwing *that* around the room. I got splattered. The walls got splattered . . .'

She stood up abruptly. *Don't go*, I wanted to say. *Plenty of room on the couch. If I've overstepped another boundary, I'm sorry.*

'*Inter faeces et urinam*,' she said, walking back to her desk.

'Come again?'

'It's Latin. St Augustine.'

'You getting religious on me, Prof?'

'Lapsed Catholic. You?'

'Closet Muslim. What's it mean?'

'We are born between . . . well, I guess you can translate.'

My turn to chuckle. 'Someone should put *that* on a T-shirt. Especially since we blokes spend half our lives trying to go back there.' I paused for a reaction that didn't come. 'Looking for heaven,' I added, needlessly.

She picked up her pen and began to write.

'I'm sorry if I shocked you,' I said.

I sensed her shrug. 'I'm a doctor, Richard. A psychiatrist.'

'That makes you unshockable?'

'It helps. It also makes me wonder why you keep trying to shock me. Pretending to be less caring than you are. Speaking in a brutal manner. Boasting, in a way.'

Her manner was calm and quiet – anything but brutal – but her words shocked *me*, just a little.

'I'm not sure if your intention is to seduce me or distract me,' she continued. 'I'm not sure you know yourself. Either way, it doesn't have much to do with our purpose here.'

'We have a purpose?'

She ignored the joke. 'Your tattoo reminds me. I've been doing some research on your motorcycle, ah, club.'

'Not in person, I hope.'

'On the net. The World Wide Id, as my former husband likes to call it.'

'What's that supposed to mean?'

'He sees the Net as a kind of collective unconscious. In the Jungian sense.'

It seemed best to play the innocent: 'Your ex is a psychiatrist too?'

'His office is down the hall. In fact, he's Head of Department.'

Talk about shrunken heads at ten paces; no wonder mine felt like a football. 'That sounds cosy,' I said, fishing.

She wasn't biting. 'The name intrigued me: Golgothans. Apparently they were some sort of mythical creature. Born out of the excreta of the crucified.'

'I guess that's how a lot of us felt.'

'Us cops or us bikies?'

A good question, so I dodged it. 'Us misfits. The Vietnam Vets who started the club. The ex-cons who came in later. The odd ex-cop, like me. It was a kind of family. For people who didn't fit anywhere else.'

'You speak almost fondly about it.'

'There are worse outfits. Oh, we had our share of arseholes. But most of the brothers – a mix of good and bad. Like any family.'

'Where does that leave you? In the mix?'

'I was always a loner, if that's what you mean.'

'What I mean is: did you do bad things?'

I took a moment to think about it. I had no gun to impress her, but there might be other ways. 'I had to prove myself from time to time.' I paused again, if mainly for effect, then added, 'What I tell you in here is completely confidential?'

'Of course. Although I find it significant you've never asked me that question before. You have something particularly painful to tell me?'

'Maybe. I'm just not sure you're ready for it.'

'Perhaps it's you who isn't ready.'

My hackles rose a little. 'The simple truth then, ready or not.'

'The truth is rarely simple. For instance, you are clearly ambivalent about the motorcycle club. Your loyalties were obviously divided. I can only imagine what you went through. The experience must have been both terrifying and thrilling.'

'Flip sides of the same coin, Prof.'

She waited for a better answer. A more truthful, messier answer.

'I guess I craved a bit of excitement,' I said, eventually.

'Being a speedie wasn't enough for you?'

I grunted. 'I should have stayed a speedie forever. But I made a mistake. A *big* mistake: I got ambitious.'

Again she waited, quietly.

'Be careful what you wish for,' I said. 'The year I made Detective I was seconded to a new crew. So new they asked me to come up with a name. Operation Spiderwasp. Online entrapment for paedophiles. Right up your ex's alley.'

Another dangled hook; another no-comment.

'It turned out to be a taskforce of one. The seniors always seemed to have more exciting things to do, places to go. Muggins here spent a year at a computer terminal pretending to be a minor.'

'Why you?'

'The powers-that-be decided I was some kind of nerd genius.' Bad boy stories and a badly tattooed body had failed to impress her; perhaps a clever brain would. 'I topped the Detective's exam by a mile.'

'Were you successful? In your online entrapment.'

'Caught a lot of spiders. Problem was, most were interstate warrants. No travel budget. I made a couple of local busts to get some fresh air. But not much action. No need to knock down doors to cuff those sad fucks. More likely to burst into tears than resist arrest.'

'You sound as if you felt sorry for them.'

'I felt sorry for *me*. I didn't join the Force to sit behind a desk.' I snorted, remembering. 'The only time I was in harm's way was in the tattoo parlour. After the first round of arrests. Big celebration at the Club, then I got dragged off for a souvenir.'

I lifted the T-shirt again, half-turned my back towards her.

'A wasp because it was a sting operation?' she asked.

'A wasp because they lay eggs inside the spiders. When the eggs hatch the spiders explode.'

'You must have got *some* satisfaction, at least. When your . . . digital eggs hatched.'

'Writing dialogue for ten-year-olds was fun for a month or two. I was always good at inventing imaginary friends.'

'Did some of them have red hair?' she said, with a tease in her voice.

I chuckled. 'Worst thing about the arrests was going through their computers afterwards. Seeing things you really didn't want to see.'

The pen came off the cap for the second time that morning. 'Perhaps you *were* in harm's way, after all,' she said, eventually. 'From those images.'

'Seen a hundred, seen them all,' I said, dismissively.

'I've treated police officers in the past who didn't find it so easy. Who had to leave the Force, they found their work so disturbing.'

Me too, in a way, I thought to myself. If not for the same reasons. But I didn't want to talk about it. Talking about it was almost as boring as doing it.

'What did you mean by that, Richard?'

'Sorry?'

'You just said you had to leave the Force too.'

Had I? I sat there stunned. In all my time with her I couldn't recall anything as odd. As – unguarded.

'Mind if I smoke?' I stalled.

'Against hospital rules.' She paused, then shocked me again. 'But if it jogs your memory, fine.'

'Let's find out,' I said, and tugged the pack from my jeans pocket.

'There is nothing in your record about leaving the Force,' she said.

I lit up, inhaled. 'I resigned,' I said, exhaling. 'Before I was discharged. Dishonourably.'

I sensed her lean forward, all ears.

'I assaulted a prisoner.' I cupped my free hand into a makeshift ashtray; flicked ash into it. 'I beat the shit out of the last rock spider I arrested.'

'He resisted arrest?'

'If only. No. Just burst into tears. But I took a dislike to some photos hanging on the walls.'

'Child porn?'

'He lived with his mum. Just photos of kids on beaches. Pretty innocent really. Could have been his nieces.'

'You assaulted him for *that*?'

'He had it coming. Last straw. After the stuff on his hard drive. Something in me snapped. Or maybe it was just the boredom. And the pictures on the wall were a pretext.'

The cap came off the pen again. 'You keep wanting to play down the effect of those images, Richard.'

'I haven't finished the story yet.' A slow, teasing inhalation. 'He went and had a heart attack on me.'

'Because of the beating?'

I shrugged. 'Maybe. Or maybe just getting caught. Shamed in front of his mother.'

Her alarm pinged; she silenced it without comment. I smiled, inwardly. Who needed a gun? The darker the details, the more she lapped it up.

'I gave him CPR till the ambos arrived. Took something to kiss that kiddie-fucker's mouth, I can tell you.'

I took another slow drag, giving her time to picture the details. For a shrink, it was strange how little she understood herself.

'Did he survive?'

I spluttered out a harsh laugh. '*I* nearly didn't. His mum started hopping around the kitchen waving a broom. Belting me over the head as I tried to save her son's life.'

'You *did* assault him, Richard.'

'And she'd seen it all. Kicked up a huge stink. Which meant it went on report. Which meant I was suspended.' I blew what felt like a smoke-ring; I used to be good at them. 'I resigned before the investigation was completed. Officially, at least.'

'What do you mean "at least"?'

'It was all a cover story. Unofficially I was still on the payroll, but officially I was in disgrace. A rogue cop who bashed a paedophile. Perfect timing really. Gave me a lot of street cred with the bikies.'

I sensed her lean forward again. 'Let me get this right. You only *pretended* to resign. To give you entrée into the bikie gang?'

'Fancy way of putting it, but yep. All part of Terry's grand plan. Operation Trojan Horse.'

She wrote for a time. 'I suppose you came up with that name too?'

'No, but I was born for it. The perfect skill set. Biker. Thrill-seeker. No dependents. Disgraced cop.'

'Who else knew?'

'The AC had to approve the deal. And the Commissioner himself – so he could keep Internal Affairs quiet.'

'There's no record of this anywhere in your file.'

'It's strictly on a need-to-know basis, Prof. There are other cops still out there, speaking of harm's way. I wasn't the only bunny.'

As I uttered the word it turned sour in my mouth, and soured the cigarette as well.

I stubbed it out and eased myself upright.

'What are you doing?' she said, alarmed.

'Time's up, remember. The bell.'

'I don't mean you *leaving*. I mean you just ground a burning cigarette into the palm of your hand.'

For the first time I noticed the glow of pain. 'Nowhere else to put it,' I said.

'You're my last patient for the day. You don't need to leave. I don't want you to leave. Especially in such an agitated state.'

I located my cane, shook it straight. 'I'll walk it off.'

She was struggling to mask the exasperation in her voice. 'Then come tomorrow. Please. You've finally begun to open up. I feel we're on the edge of a major breakthrough.'

She followed me through the door as I reattached myself to the waiting dog, and tapped to the lift well.

'I can squeeze you into my lunch hour,' she said. 'Anytime between twelve and one.'

'You mustn't skip meals, Prof. Those arms are chicken-wings already.'

'I can eat here. We can eat together. I'll bring something for you.'

Talk about breaking new ground. 'Maybe,' I said, hiding my smile as I walked into the lift. 'Mind the doors.'

The moment they slid shut I tugged off the T-shirt and pulled it back on, right side out. Memo, Prof: yes, I had been agitated, briefly. Remembering Operation Trojan Horse had me simmering. And the palm of my hand was still giving me a bit of curry. Anger Management: take it out on yourself? As I tapped out into the late afternoon heat, I was driven less by anger than rediscovered purpose. *Look at me, world! Here I am! Mess with me at your own fucking risk!*

Woof, Scout scolded me, but with any luck someone would take a snap of the blind bloke in the funny T-shirt shouting profanities and the photo would go viral.

8

I CRUISED THE STREETS OFFERING FURTHER PHOTO OPPORTUNITIES
for a couple of hours, with occasional pit stops to rehydrate: beer
in pint-glasses for me, water in a bowl for my furry sidekick. I was
pushing her too hard, but didn't realise it till she started her stubborn
mule act again.

'Plum tuckered out, Dog Wonder? Bark fucking once for yes.'

'*Yes!*'

I nursed her home with a judicious offering of pocket treats. After
grabbing a cap from the hallstand – the late afternoon sun was still
fierce – I headed back out alone. My look-at-me Undercover Cop
T-shirt was sweat-soaked but I wasn't about to change it, especially
with a standard-issue blue (I think) police cap to set it off. After
another pit stop for higher octane fuel – two double-sugar double
espressos – I marched on into the balmy evening.

'West Terrace,' Siri whispered. 'Twenty paces. Power Low. Charge
Battery please.'

She'd run out of juice before, but always with the dog as back-up.
Today I'd run them both flat.

'Pulteney Street,' she croaked, 'Twenty . . .' then lost her voice
completely.

No dog and no date? No problem; I tapped stubbornly on. The
east–west word-map we bush recruits were taught when we first hit
the city beat came to mind. *We Must Keep People From Hurting Each
Other*. West Terrace, Morphett Street, King William, Pulteney, Frome,
Hutt, East Terrace. I chanted the words to myself as I zigzagged

eastwards, although less for navigation purposes – I knew the street-names well enough – than for the added look-at-me benefit: the funny blind man in the funny T-shirt chanting funny words to himself.

The odds against success only made me more determined. If my hare-brained scheme was ever going to work, it would be now: the car-clogged rush-hour streets, the nose-to-arse buses sniffing each other's diesel farts like dogs, the long queues of homeward-bound commuters, the city that had a million eyes at its most alert.

Like a fish that must keep moving or drown, I swam on against the stream of pedestrians, tapping as many passing ankles as I could for added self-advertisement.

One thing about being blind: people always blame themselves. Unless their name is Willow.

'Sir! Sir!'

Focused on my task I failed to hear the cab pull in beside the kerb.

'Sir! Sir! I have been watching out for you for days.'

I stopped in my tracks. 'Saeed?'

'I have your change, Sir.'

'I told you to keep the change.'

'Then permit me to earn it back, Sir. Actually, it is no trouble to drive you home. I am on my way to the mosque.'

Any point in arguing? He was already out of the car with the door open. And having finally stopped walking, I might have trouble starting again.

'I have glimpsed you already today, Sir. Twice,' he said, as I climbed in. 'Walking, always walking. Busy, busy. Firstly I was late for afternoon prayer and could not stop. Secondly I have a passenger already.'

Music to my ears. If a lone cabbie spotted me thrice in a single afternoon, the odds of a passing crim doing likewise had narrowed. I leant back on the passenger headrest, feeling pleasantly exhausted. The cricket on the radio helped, especially if I listened in an abstract, background-music sort of way, paying no attention to scores or player names.

Saeed's patter was less easy to vague out, but seemed to require no answers. 'Have you considered playing blind cricket, Sir? Actually, in my birth country many little ones have the cataracts. My nephew Imran in Dhaka is one such. A little bell is placed inside the ball which is bowled underarm. The batter can hear it approach.'

A prickle of goosebumps on the back of my neck roused me from my calm. 'Is anyone following us, Saeed?'

'Excuse me, Sir?'

'Is there another *cab* following us?'

A pause before he answered. 'I cannot detect it, Sir. Shall I slow down so it can catch up?'

Perhaps it was the cold air-conditioning on my sweaty skin. 'Drop me at the mosque if you like, Saeed. I'll walk home from there.'

'Certainly. And I would like to offer you my card. If you are ever lost.'

'Is it in braille?'

'Beg pardon, Sir. How foolish of me. But perhaps you could show it to someone else. If in need.'

The car stopped; the engine was turned off; the cricket-muzak with it. The windows were open: the sound of the muezzin carried to me instead, but so softly it was barely audible. Perhaps it was just an app on Saeed's phone.

'May I invite you to join me for maghrib?' Saeed said. 'You would be most welcome.'

'I have to get home and feed an unclean animal,' I said.

He chuckled, at last. 'I remember from our last journey that you are acquainted with the teachings of the Prophet, a little.'

'I have a prayer mat waiting for me at home,' I said. 'But could you do me a favour, Saeed?'

'Anything, Sir.'

'Is it dark yet?'

'It is still the gloaming, Sir.'

'The what?'

'The gloaming. The last light. It is an English word, you must know it.'

'I do now. I like it. A beautiful word.'

'It is a beautiful sight, Sir. The whole world pink and gold.'

'Can you see to the end of the street?'

'Perfectly well, Sir.'

'Sit in the car for a few minutes after I get out. Keep your eyes peeled. If you see anyone following me, toot your horn. Twice.'

'Of course, Sir. But your request concerns me. Is there jeopardy?'

'Not at all. I'm expecting an old friend. He likes to surprise me. Practical joker type.'

'I am all eyes, Sir. And I will have a card embossed in braille. For next time.'

No warning toot chased me up Little Gilbert Street, and no more goosebumps prickled the back of my neck. Perhaps the call to prayer had spooked me; I've always liked its shivery, melancholy music.

My legs had stiffened up in the cab; the homeward stretch was an effort. I kicked off my boots inside the door, wanting nothing more than to put my feet up, but proper risk management still had to be prosecuted. A cold beer refuelled me, then with a second one in hand I reset the trap: raising the shutter, turning up the intercom, checking the door-lock, locating and holstering the Glock.

Still no sign of the parts I'd ordered, but I was too spent to care. And too exhausted for my usual work-out, let alone evening prayers on the gym-mat. I fed both girlfriends, fed myself, set the coffee pot and the shutter remote on the table near at hand, and fell into my armchair – but less ready for action than ready for sleep. Caffeine fix notwithstanding, from the moment my head hit the upholstery an all-night vigil was a lost cause.

My last foggy thought: if I slept through and woke disappointed – the trap still unsprung – at least I would have been spared another long night of brooding.

9

THE PROF HADN'T SPOKEN FOR A WHILE. I LAY QUIETLY ON THE couch, digesting the upmarket sandwich she had brought – 'smoked salmon, horseradish and chives, Richard' – waiting for her to finish writing. Perhaps I dozed off again; I was startled awake by the sound of chair legs scraping my way. Was she going to sit closer? No such luck; a mystery object was set down on the wooden seat with a dull clatter instead.

'Box of tissues?' I guessed, although why she might think I was about to burst into tears I had no idea.

'Ashtray,' she said.

I chuckled, and patted my pockets. 'And here I am fresh out of smokes.'

The next sound was less mysterious – the rustle of cellophane – but I was still surprised. 'Camels I hope, Prof!'

'They seem to loosen your tongue,' she said. 'Not that I approve. Not for a moment.'

I didn't believe her, especially after I tugged the lighter from my jeans and handed it over. There was a practised deftness in the speed of lighting-up, the short, quick ignition puffs.

'Misspent youth,' she read my mind, as the lit cigarette was eased between my lips. It felt as sweet as a kiss; I kissed it back, deeply.

'Fresh out of T-shirts too?' she said.

'I was running late. Sorry. Slept in.'

'Looks like you slept in it,' she said, then sniffed the air a little theatrically. 'Smells like it too.'

I exhaled, smoothly. 'If there's a personal freshness problem, why not light up yourself?'

'I guess I am. Passively.'

The pack and lighter were set down on the chair; her footsteps moved back to the other side of the desk; her chair creaked slightly as it took her weight. Some sort of expensively elegant bentwood thing, I'd long ago decided.

'I'm glad you chose to come today, Richard. And relieved.'

'Still worried I might top myself?'

'If I overreacted yesterday, I'm sorry. But you do seem prone to mood swings at present.'

'Tell me about it,' I said, thinking less about yesterday's sweet-and-sour consultation than the rollercoaster of anger and disappointment I seemed to ride each night.

'It can be a good sign,' she said. 'A sign we're making progress. You told me things yesterday I hadn't heard before. But I had a sense you wanted to tell me more.'

'Tell, or confess?'

'You did confess. To assaulting a man you arrested. A man who was offering no resistance.'

'Temporary insanity. His mum did more damage to me with her broomstick.'

'Which leaves me wondering what your anger was really about. What you were trying *not* to talk about yesterday.'

I held a lungful of smoke inside, thinking. Cigarettes might loosen my tongue from time to time, but they are just as useful to slow it down.

'You mentioned you had to prove yourself,' she prompted, 'with the bikies.'

'I crossed the line a few times. Of course.'

'Serious crimes?'

'Depends on your definition of serious.'

'I'm more interested in yours.'

'You wearing a wire?' I said, and chuckled. 'We were a pretty tame outfit. No hard drugs. Girls and weed, mostly.'

'You sold drugs? Personally?'

'You're more worried about me selling drugs than selling girls?'

'Did your superiors know about either?'

'In triplicate. No way I'd let them hang me out to dry. There's a federal exemption for undercover cops. At least with victimless crimes.'

'You think prostitution is victimless?'

I shifted uncomfortably; the gun was making its presence felt in the small of my back again. The weather was still too hot for a jacket, but my mojo was back. A loose T-shirt was enough camouflage, I'd decided over breakfast.

'I never met an unhappy hooker, if that's what you mean,' I said.

Silence. Then the faint sound of the pen being uncapped.

'They weren't street girls,' I said as she wrote. 'Part-timers, mostly. Housewives. Students paying their way. No druggies. No maddies.'

More silence, while she absorbed this. Or just took the dictation. 'You were never involved in anything more serious? No violent crime?'

The gun ground in harder, like a fist. I took in another lungful of smoke, pondering how serious to get. 'No standover stuff. I . . . punished the odd bad guy. But only if they deserved it.'

One, in particular, had deserved it – and I wasn't thinking of the rock spider. A treacherous memory, this. I tried to control the turbulence it stirred inside me, or at least keep it out of my voice.

'That sounds less like a confession than another boast, Richard.'

'I don't regret it, if that's what you mean.'

'As a means of proving yourself, or as an end in itself?'

'Both. It was necessary, yes. Bikie justice. If I hadn't handed it out, someone else would have.'

Her ears pricked up. 'It? You're talking about one case in particular?'

Cornered. I'd blabbed too much already, but couldn't stop myself. Maybe she was right about the ciggie, also a favourite tool of trade back in Interview Room 1, Angas Street. A lever, a little white crowbar.

'One especially,' I said, and the anger began leaking into my words like spittle. 'One who deserved everything that was coming to him. An eye for a fucking eye.'

'Before you go any further,' she interrupted, 'despite what I said yesterday, there are exceptions to medical confidentiality. Mandatory reporting for major crimes is one.'

'Be my guest. The Commissioner would give me another fucking medal. Did the cops' work for them.' The dam was beginning to crack inside me; how had I got there so quickly? I took another deep inhalation to slow the leaks. 'Sure you don't want a smoke, Prof?'

My turn to read her mind: she was already on her feet walking my way. More cellophane rustling, more deft lighting-up sounds, but this time the ashtray was set down on the floor and her backside on the chair.

'Why does he mean so much to you?' she said, exhaling. 'This particular – bad guy.'

How much to tell her? 'He attacked one of my girls,' I said, then hid in another cloud of smoke. Even that hesitant 'attacked' was saying too much. Widening the crack.

'*Your* girls?'

'You keep nitpicking the little words.'

'The little words usually have the largest meanings. Why "yours"?'

I shrugged, nonchalantly. 'Because I was running the girls. It's no big deal. We – the Club – had a city knock-shop. Off Light Square.'

'A knock-shop meaning a brothel?'

'Cathouse. Bordello. House of ill repute. Take your pick. Since words mean so much to you.'

'Here's another then: what did "running" mean exactly?'

'Not what you might think. Not what I *thought*. Sounded like a dream job, but I found myself stuck behind a computer again.

Nice irony. I went undercover looking for excitement, and ended up staring at spreadsheets in the back office of a brothel.'

'You topped the bikies' entrance exam too?'

A joke! I would have chuckled even if it wasn't funny.

'Turned out I was good at it. Middle management. The day-sheets, the rosters. The books. Both sets.' A small laugh this time, another puff. If I stuck to the boring details, I might get through. 'I put all the girls on part-time permanent, paid their workers comp, their super. Overtime. Medical insurance. Top tables, gold extras. Physios, chiropractors. Sex workers get a lot of muscle strains, Prof. Like dancers.'

I sensed her lean closer, hooked again on the exotica. Or was it the nicotine? Whichever, all trace of disapproval had gone.

'I taught them first aid. CPR.'

Concern in her voice: 'In case they got beaten up by clients?'

'Mostly it was the clients who were in harm's way. Over-excitement. Strain on the ticker.'

I chuckled again, beginning to relax. The dam wall seemed to be holding, the pressure receding as we smoked together.

'I set up the webpages too. Designed the layouts. Wrote the blurbs. Photographed the girls.'

'Naked?'

'Their choice. Suggestive, topless, full frontal. Lingerie. Bikini. Arse-first. But not their faces. Mostly.'

'Headless women,' she said. 'Every man's fantasy.'

'*Their* choice, remember. Not mine. Like I said, I had housewives on the books. Young mothers. Uni students. Once your face is online it's online forever. Better just your boobs.'

'The other body parts don't count?' she said, the disapproval back in her voice. 'The other cuts of meat.'

'I made up little stories about them all,' I continued, trying to get things back on track. 'Likes, dislikes. Bios. Star signs. The more exotic the better.'

'I imagine you were good at that.'

'Scratch a cop and you find a frustrated poet,' I quoted Terry.

Silence. She lit up another two cigarettes, passed mine over.

'What was her name?' she said, eventually. 'The girl who got attacked? *Your* girl?'

Another of those little words, *my* word, a word from my mouth, working away at the dam-crack like a different kind of crowbar.

'Trixie,' I said. 'Trixie Rose.'

A snort. 'I've never met anyone called Trixie in my life.'

'A stage name,' I told her. 'I made those up too. Gave them to all the girls. Porn names, in the trade.'

'It sounds rather demeaning. Like you were naming horses.'

'I used a formula,' I defended myself. 'It never fails.'

She was all ears again, waiting, her disapproval back on hold.

'The name of your first pet,' I said. 'Then the name of the street you grew up in.'

Silence while she worked out her own porn name, something else that never fails.

'Well?' I prompted.

'Well what?'

'Don't even try, Prof.'

'I grew up on Forest Street,' she said, reluctantly.

'And the pet? Your first pet?'

Her own dam broke in a splutter of words and laughter. 'Fluffy,' she said, 'Fluffy Forest.'

'*Professor* Fluffy Forest,' I said, and we laughed together for a time.

'Preposterous,' she eventually murmured, and eased herself off the couch. I thought I was home free, the finishing bell no more than a few minutes away, until she sat down on the hard chair again. 'Your girl was attacked by a patron?'

Textbook interrogation technique: soften me up with cigarettes and jokes, then the sucker-punch where it hurts. My girl? It was hard to own the word. It was also impossible not to, not least because she'd been under my protection. I had been responsible. I would always be responsible.

'He wasn't a client,' I said.

She waited for more before prompting: 'A club member?'

How much to tell? A slow drip-feed till the end of the round? 'One of the young tearaways. Clueless, so they made him night manager. Which meant the muscle. Which mostly meant pouring drinks for the customers.' Perhaps I could filibuster my way through to the bell. 'Glorified bouncer. I remember one night–'

'Let's stick to the night in question, Richard.'

Inhalation, slow exhalation. 'Things had gone quiet. I'd sent the other girls home. Got to work on some maintenance. Round midnight I walked down to the Hindley IGA for some superglue. Wood veneer on the bar was lifting.'

Again she cut me short: 'I think we can dispense with the details.'

'If you insist. I left him in charge. Trixie rang me a few minutes later. He was getting frisky. Wanted a freebie. Of course she said no.'

'Of course?'

I bristled. 'She was a student paying her way through uni. A part-timer. Not the town bike.'

'Sorry,' she said, although her tone didn't sound sorry. 'I didn't mean to suggest . . .'

'And you call *me* demeaning?'

Silence. I sensed her surprise at the feeling in my voice. It had burst out of me, helplessly, but had it revealed too much? It revealed something to me: even now, I wouldn't hear a word against Trixie.

'Point taken,' she said eventually. 'It was a thoughtless thing to say. Can we get back to the story?'

A deep breath; a calming smoke-ring. 'She sounded worried. He'd smoked a couple of pipes and was getting out of hand.'

'Pipes of?'

'Ice.'

'I thought you said no hard drugs.'

'Officially, yes. I'd caught him with an eight-ball in the bar before. Selling on the side. But a club is a broad church. There were tensions between the old guard and the young bloods. No way I wanted to get caught up in that. So I turned a blind eye. So to speak.' I sucked in a lungful of my own preferred drug. 'And the clients lapped it up. Helped them *get* it up.'

I tried a chuckle, but she wasn't interested. 'You went straight back to the brothel? When she rang?'

I flinched, literally. Her words struck me like a handful of gravel.

'You ever want a mid-life career change,' I said, lamely, 'you could walk into a job at Angas Street.'

Why had I started this conversation? Still trying to impress her? To take her on another walk on the wild side? Whichever, here I was cornered again.

'You *didn't* go straight back?'

'I stopped for a yiros,' I said, then fell silent, letting the words sink in – into my head as much as hers. If I deserved a stoning, I might as well stone myself.

Her fingers rescued the butt from mine. 'You're burning yourself again.'

She sat on the couch, thigh against thigh. Unable to speak, I averted my face in case it was speaking for me. I wanted to be out of there, *now*.

Miraculously, her alarm bleeped. I fumbled about for my stick, but the Professor's hand was on my arm, restraining me.

'Time's up,' I said, finding my voice.

'No hurry, Richard. None at all. I'd like you to stay. Please.'

I didn't seem to have a choice; her hand was on my chest now, gently easing me back.

'The yiros,' she prompted.

'It was for her,' I managed to get out. Little words again, the last one less a stone than a fishbone, sticking in my throat.

The Camel pack rustled; she lit another two. I sought refuge in mine while she smoked her own, patiently waiting.

Was it was best just to get it over with, get it *out*, like a dental extraction? I took a last, deep lungful of smoke and held it inside until I couldn't.

'I was still in the queue when she rang again. This time she was terrified. She'd locked herself in the downstairs loo. I could hear him banging on the door.'

A sharp intake of breath from her; another slow intake of smoke from me. If only someone would start banging on our door.

'You rang the police?'

'*I* was the police. And I'd left her alone. With him.'

'This time you went back?'

'Of *course* I went back!' I snapped, taking an offence I had no right to. '*Sprinted* back. No sign of them downstairs. The loo was empty. The door knocked off its hinges with a fire extinguisher.'

I barely registered her gasp; all I knew was the redness of the extinguisher on the white-tiled floor, vivid in my mind's eye.

'Blood on the floor too,' I said, then added, looking for a way out, 'You sure you want to hear this?'

'I'm a doctor,' she reminded me. 'I'm not made of china.'

'And I'm a cop. But I've no fucking idea what I'm made of anymore.'

The honesty of this seemed to silence her, and allow me some breathing space – but I no longer needed it.

'No sound anywhere. No clients. I ran upstairs, shouting her name. Still no answer. I went from room to room. I finally found her in the Jungle Room. Found *both* of them.'

One last pull on the fag-end. I'd spoken of that night to no one but Willow before, and with good reason. To speak of it was to remember it. Worse, to relive it. To *see* it, as I saw it clearly now.

She took the butt from my fingers, crushed it out, and lit up another. 'I've treated police officers before,' she said, her tone as

gentle as the placement of the cigarette between my lips. 'I understand how hard it is to talk about these things. Things no one should
have to see.'

That wasn't it at all, I wanted to say. I'd seen plenty of those things.
Things in head-ons on country roads, things in burnt-out houses,
things in shallow bush graves. Things in mortuaries. Things in stainless steel bowls. I'd seen as many horrors as a fucked-up world could
throw at me, and then some. *Smelt* them just as often, their stink in
my nostrils for days afterwards.

But they never came back to haunt me later.

'There was a tiger-skin rug on the floor,' I remembered, and was
struck dumb again by the stark visual power of this detail. Perhaps
I could get through this by focusing on the details.

The Professor sounded puzzled: 'She was on a tiger-skin rug?'

'The Jungle Room, remember? She was lying facedown. He was
on his knees. Fucking her doggie fashion.' If I couldn't look away
myself, perhaps I could still shock her into looking away. 'Thing is,
she was all floppy. And not making a sound. None at all. You pay for
sex, you pay for noise, Prof. It's part of . . .'

'She was *dead*?'

'Out cold. But I couldn't tell. I didn't know what to think.
I couldn't figure it out.'

'You stood there and *watched*?'

'I grabbed him by the hair and threw him across the room.'

But, yes, then watched. 'First Responder Protocols,' I said.
'Step One: Threat Suppression. Then take a moment to check
for hazards.'

She might have been convinced, but I wasn't. The only hazard was
slumped against the wall, holding his head and groaning – 'What ya
do *that* for? Couldn't wait ya fucking turn?' And still I stood there,
helpless.

'Step Two, Haemorrhage Control,' I said, desperate to persuade
myself now.

Was I too late? *Was* he fucking a dead woman? Her head was twisted sideways, the eyes in her bloodied face as vacant as the glassy eyes of the tiger. She might have been a trophy herself, a rug of human flesh. None of these confused thoughts making sense. The tiger's snout also weirdly bloodied. Had the big *cat* killed her?

'Dunno what all the fuss is about anyway. Just lies there. Worst fuck I ever had.'

His voice getting closer, a living predator crawling back towards its victim on all fours.

'You want to jump the queue, brother? I'll take one end, you take the other.'

I unfroze, roused by those automatic protocols. They, at least, still made sense. Back to Step One: Remove all Hazards. I lashed out with my boot; connected with the side of his chest.

He was so wasted he hardly felt it. 'What the fuck's that for?' he wheezed, winded. 'You want her, dickhead, you can fucken have her.'

I kicked him in the head, hard, and he grunted and rolled away, belly-up, and said nothing more.

'You killed *him*?' a voice arrived from the present, close-by.

I thought I had, when — as if by some trade-off of souls, one life for another — she coughed. And the autopilot resuscitation routines finally took over, and I dropped to my knees at her side.

Step Three: Response. 'Can you hear me, sweetheart?'

No answer. Step Four: Airway. I rolled her onto her side, checked her breathing: regular.

Step Five: Pulse. I pressed two fingers to her neck: strong.

She coughed again; whimpered. A fresh runnel of blood from her damaged nose. Her eyes half-opened. Her beautiful eyes. 'Rick?'

'I'm here, sweetheart,' I said. 'You're safe.'

'She survived?' The other woman's voice again, the Professor. The confessor today, sitting hip-to-hip on a couch with me, her hand gripping my knee as if to keep me with her in the present.

'Fractured nose,' I said, with one foot still in the past. And both eyes: definitely both eyes. 'The fire extinguisher, probably. That was the last thing she could remember later.'

'And – him?'

This was as strange and vivid as anything in my head: a predator sprawled motionless on its back, limbs spread, a pair of jeans around its hind-ankles, an ice-fuelled cock jutting up, half-stiff, like a single curved claw.

I should have killed him when I had the chance, I wanted to shout. I *wish* I'd killed him. I should have ripped his cock off and shoved it down his throat. I should have ripped his *heart* out.

But those words, any words, large or small, weren't even close. I shook off her hand, sat up, leant forward, and vomited onto the floor, explosively.

'It's okay, Richard. I'll clean it up. Richard! Don't move! Please! Watch where you put your feet! Where are you going? You've stepped in it. Come back. We still have things to talk about.'

Actually, not. Everything I needed to say, everything I wanted to say, was lying in a puddle under the couch.

'I'll ring later,' she called after me. 'To check on you. And I can see you again tomorrow. Same time. Please.'

10

THE LIFT WAS PACKED WITH BODIES, BUT A WIDE BERTH OPENED
about me as the door slid shut. The unwashed T-shirt on my back
or the vomit on my boots? I was a feral fox in a chicken-coop, which
was fine by me. The chooks flapped out at the next floor, perhaps to
take the stairs; I rode the rest of the way down alone. I wasn't in the
mood for company. I didn't even miss the dog. For the first time ever
she hadn't been waiting at the door when I left; I'd run her ragged the
day before.

I stepped out onto North Terrace with an angry sun beating down
on my head and an angrier street-map on the tip of my tongue. *Never
Root Girls' Pussies . . .*

Thrilling words to a seventeen-year-old rookie cop, but just
another kind of vomit at my age. Useful vomit? The talking cure
had got me nowhere; time for more walking cure. I zigzagged south
through the east side at pace – North Terrace into Rundle Street, then
Grenfell, and Pirie, muttering all the way.

Rookie porn-code for Flinders Street? I couldn't remember.
Ignoring traffic lights and a helpful warning shout I crossed it anyway. There was a squeal of brakes, and more shouting, but I was
unstoppable.

. . . When Aching Cocks Have Gonorrhoea . . .

Across Wakefield I tapped, then through to Angas, Carrington,
Halifax, Gillies, a stinking blind man in a stinking T-shirt chanting
stinking obscenities.

. . . or Syphilis.

If only the stink itself could go viral. I followed South Terrace westward, then turned north again. Was there a carthartic word-map for the west side-streets? Possibilities sprang to mind as I tapped from Gilbert through Sturt to Wright – *Get Shitty With . . .*

With what?

I was shitty with the world, but the world didn't seem to be taking notice. The Prof was an exception, but I was even more shitty with her. She'd forced *me* to take notice of things I didn't need to notice. Those vivid pictures began to pop back into my head as I stalked on. What use blindness if it couldn't shut this stuff out? Or was it worse because I was blind? Because I lacked a flow of new images to compete with the old, a real-time visual feed to fill the screen? When a tune is stuck in your head all day, you can hum something else, put some loud music on, drive the buzzing insect out of your ear. No such luck for me: having allowed those pictures some screen-time it seemed I was stuck with them.

At which thought I stopped dead in my tracks. I'd forgotten something buried even deeper; it returned now with force.

I'd seen her like that *before* the night of the rape. *Exactly* like that. The log fire in the Jungle Room. The striped tiger-skin rug. And on the rug, the naked beauty.

The naked sleeping beauty, waiting to be fucked awake.

It had been my fantasy, in a way. Mine, and hers. Our fantasy, at any rate, on behalf of others. It was *exactly* the image for the high-class Platinum Package we'd designed together for her webpage.

And for which I'd already photographed her, weeks before, lying on the striped rug, with her face half-turned to one side, away from the camera, as still and snow-white as a porcelain geisha.

Except for the blood.

I walked on again, at speed, half trying to escape this memory, half trying to make sense of it. Had I somehow brought this on her? I turned into Gouger, tapping furiously. The usual powerful food smells forced their way into my head, as if trying to elbow the images aside, but without success. Eventually I escaped into the quiet of Grote Street, and the smell of nothing but my own sweat, and wandered aimlessly on.

'Light Square,' Siri announced after a few blocks, so perhaps it wasn't so aimless.

'Current location,' I said. 'To After Dark Club.'

'No address found,' came her answer.

Had the name been changed? More than likely. Or had it closed down altogether?

'Current location,' I tried again, 'to 301 Light Square.'

'Pussy in Boots,' from Siri.

Not a name I'd have picked for a brothel – or even for a horse. The directions began to flow and I tapped on, if still uncertain of my intentions. What did I think I was going to find? That he was stupid enough to be hiding there, after all?

'Pussy in Boots, ten paces,' Siri announced.

I walked on by, still thinking it through. After twenty or thirty steps, I U-turned and walked past again. I must have looked like a first-timer trying to work up the courage. Fourth walk-by I stopped, right-turned with military determination, tapped up the three wide slate steps, and pushed through the big wooden door.

Sounds: the quiet ripples of the door-chime fading behind me; slow late-night bluesy music ahead. Nothing new in any of that.

Smell: something floral in the air, subtle, but less musky than I remembered.

I raised a mental map of the interior. The smallish entrance foyer with the big, low-wattage chandelier. The wood veneer counter to the left. The door to my office on the right, and beyond it the downstairs loo. The stairway to paradise in between: midnight-red plush carpeting, polished mahogany balustrade. I'd sanded and stained it myself: Dulux Dark Cherry. I'd also painted the walls: Regal Violet. No one – neither the clients, nor the girls – wants too much unforgiving light in a bordello. I tapped further in: shag-pile carpet underfoot, the music louder from the right, accompanied by low voices and a chink of glasses – but how was that possible? I tapped in that direction, cautiously, but where there had once been a wall, there was none.

'Good evening, Sir. Can I help you?'

A woman's voice, friendly enough but politely blocking my path.

'There used to be a wall here,' I said. 'And a wood-veneer counter.'

'Before my time, Sir. Although I believe the new owners redecorated the premises.'

I was clearly before her time too; she didn't recognise me. 'Who are the new owners?' I asked, casually.

'That's commercial-in-confidence, Sir. But they have also implemented a new dress code.' I sensed she was giving me the once-over. 'It might not have been in place last time you visited.'

'It's not easy for me to keep up appearances.'

'I understand that, given your challenges. And I don't mean to be offensive, but there is also – how can I put this? – a personal freshness problem.'

'I stink?' I sniffed at my armpits, left then right. 'Sorry. But last time I visited we always took a shower first.'

'There also seems to be vomit on your boots. Have you been drinking, Sir?'

'A few beers down the road. Friday Happy Hour. Do you still have the Jungle Room upstairs?' I took a step sideways, towards the stairs. 'I'd love to take a look. So to speak.'

Her voice was back in my face almost immediately. 'No further, please. We've just had new carpets put in. It might be best if you left. If you're looking for some place to doss down, I can direct you to the Salvation Army Shelter in Whitmore Square.'

'I'm just looking for company,' I told her. 'Not a place to crash.'

'I could give you a phone number,' she said. 'Someone who specialises in handicapped clients. And perhaps more in your price range.'

'Money's no object. And I'm very well behaved.'

'Six hundred an hour,' she said, straight-speaking at last, if only as a last resort to scare me off. 'Two thousand for the night. That's the cash-rate.'

'Plastic money?' I asked, stalling.

'Ten per cent surcharge for all major credit cards.'

'What appears on the statement? My wife does all my banking.'

'Aardvark Entertainment Services,' she said, which answered my question about the new owners. I knew the name well: a shell company for the Angels.

My turn for straight-talking. 'Did the Golgothans sell up or was it an offer they couldn't refuse?'

'Let me help you to the door, Sir,' she said, and her hand gripped my arm, if gently.

I did my own stubborn mule imitation. 'You can't refuse a paying customer,' I said. 'Madam.'

Her grip tightened. 'I don't want to have to call security, Sir.'

I twisted my arm free. 'And I don't want to have to ring *Eyewitness News*. Lonely blind bloke refused service at high-class knockshop.'

'Please keep your voice down. You're disturbing some of our clients.'

A quietly gruff voice from left-field. 'You need help with this one, Candy?'

'It's all right, Zev. I have it under control. Don't I, Sir?'

A stand-off, but only momentarily. All my questions had been answered, one way or another, including the only one that counted: no water-logged fugitive from justice was holed up in this posh joint. He wouldn't have made it past the front door either, let alone met the dress code.

'Back soon,' I said as I tapped towards the door. 'After I clean my boots and pull on a tuxedo.'

There was a smile in her voice for the first time, if only from relief. 'Then you would be most welcome, Sir.'

'I like your style, by the way,' I added. 'I probably would have hired you myself, eventually.'

'I'm not sure what that means, but it sounds like a compliment.'

The bouncer already had the door open. He hadn't seen my gun, luckily, but I pushed my luck by turning back again. 'One last question. The decor. Indulge a blind bloke's curiosity. What colour are the walls?'

'Oh,' she said. 'It's a kind of half purple, half darkish-grey. What do you think, Zev?'

'Dulux Deep Violet, mate.'

'Just as I suspected,' I said.

I sensed their exchange of glances. 'I'd feel more comfortable if you'd allow me to point you in the direction of the Salvos,' the madam said.

'Current location to home, Siri,' I said, if only to prove I wasn't one of the square's resident derelicts.

'Proceed west to Morphett Street,' she began, 'then turn left.'

I took off in the opposite direction as soon as the door closed behind me. I still had walking to do, thinking to work through. I avoided Hindley Street – too many distractions for concentrated thinking – heading east up Currie instead. I crossed the tramline into Grenfell, and kept going. It was past shop-closing time, but the late afternoon sun was still warm, even in the shaded concrete canyons of Girls and Pussies.

One more clockwise half-circuit of the CBD, I decided, then home. Even an unexercised dog would need feeding eventually.

Somewhere between Gonorrhoea and Syphilis Streets, second time through, the traffic thinning, the peak-hour crowds safely home, I had that creepy feeling again, the spider of alarm stealing up my back.

I stopped dead, and listened for footsteps, but there was nothing.

Unless he had stopped at the same time, as in the movies. I took two more quick steps, halted mid-third.

Still nothing.

The holstered gun reminded me of its presence; I mentally rehearsed a snap draw as I tapped on, more rapidly, wondering if it had been a mistake to leave the dog at home.

'Home, ten paces,' from Siri.

I stopped at the front gate, and listened again. No footsteps in either direction, but the spider on the back of my neck was dancing a tarantella now. I tapped the front porch, took a quick step up, and headed towards the safety of the door. I was already reaching for the combination when someone stuck out a leg, and I tripped, and fell forward, hands flailing, into . . .

Nothing.

Then nothing but a dull ache, close to what seemed to be the centre of me, like a tooth-ache or earache.

A headache. For a time there was no world beyond that head-ache, and the head that contained it. No body, certainly. No sensation but that G-clamp on my temples. Plus a vague, unlocalised nausea.

And the slow realisation that I was conscious at least. And there-fore still alive. Although possibly – a much quicker realisation – not for much longer. Where was he? Sitting nearby, watching. Waiting for me to wake. Perhaps he thought I was dead already. Instinct told me to play dead, while I tried to figure things out.

Where was I? Still on the front porch? In a car boot? I lay dead still, but with all my senses on high alert.

Sounds, finally: a passing car. I prayed for footsteps. If I heard footsteps I could shout for help.

Smells: the faint tinny tang of blood, then the scent of frangipani, coming through loud and clear. I was still on the front porch. Half-lying, half-sitting; my head and shoulders awkwardly propped against the door.

Taste: salt. The blood trickling down my cheek, pooling between my lips.

Had I been shot again? Was he sitting there watching me bleed out? If I pretended to be dead for much longer, fiction might become fact. I needed to find the wound and stem the bleeding.

I raised a hand to my face, groaning a little theatrically as I probed about. No entry wounds at the sore spots, just a wet abrasion on my cheek and an egg on my brow.

'What are you waiting for?' I said.

'Who, me?' from Siri.

Another car purred by. A flock of sulphur-cresteds began squawking some distance off.

'Is anyone there?' I said, more loudly.

'Interesting question, Richard.'

'Is anyone fucking *else* there?'

A muffled bark, from inside the house. Then a whimper, and a frantic scratching at the other side of the door. Was there some way to get it open? I needed her eyes on this side. Her wolf's teeth, even more so.

'What are you waiting for?' I repeated.

'Who, me?'

'Ring triple O,' I almost shouted at her. Instead I faked another groan, ran my hand over my chest, pretending to check my ribs, then slipped it behind my back and wrapped my fingers around the grip of the gun.

Hidden from view, as far as I could tell. Safety's off. Finger on the trigger.

I listened intently, still hoping for footsteps. Distant traffic only; nothing closer to my ears than the scratchings and whimperings of the dog.

Was he waiting for darkness to finish the job? Maybe it was dark already; how long had I been out cold? The cockatoos were still squawking, further off; twilight at the latest. The gloaming hour. Maybe – it occurred to me for the first time – he wasn't there at all. A brittle straw of an idea, but once I clutched at it I didn't want to let it go. Maybe he'd just taken off, thinking the job was done.

My right thigh intruded on my thoughts, wedged uncomfortably against some mysterious object. I sent my free hand down to investigate.

A box.

A box of spare parts, left innocently on the doorstep, in the path of a blind man in a hurry.

The relief flooded over me like a long, tumbling wave carrying a drowning man back to safety. Breathing more freely, I pushed myself upright and checked that all four limbs were in working order. A smaller, following wave of relief: no serious damage. But in its backwash came the now familiar, creeping undertow of disappointment: he hadn't been following me after all. Memo, Prof: mystery emotion. You figure it out, I can't. Sheer madness, it seemed to me as I lay there. A luxury I could only afford now that I was out of harm's way.

'Fucking idiot,' I said aloud, but for once the sound of my voice silenced Scout instead of triggering an echo. Perhaps she was as relieved as me. Or even as weirdly disappointed; nothing like a dogfight to add meaning to a dog's life.

I brailled the door open, picked up the heavy box and stepped through. My head throbbed so much with the effort that I dropped to my knees just inside, and set it down again. Scout was all over me, licking my damaged face, but I pushed her off and got back to my feet, needing stronger medicine. Finding no headache pills in the house anywhere, not even a fizzy aspirin – the Margarita Queen had taken those – I settled for a Scotch, and an armchair.

The phone rang; I let it run through to message-bank. A *ping* announced the arrival of a text a few seconds later; whoever was trying to contact me wasn't giving up.

'Read text message, Siri.'

'Lucy Hotline said: "Dear Richard, I left a phone message and I don't want to crowd you, but I've been very worried."' Always an odd sensation, other people's strong feelings expressed in Siri's relentlessly pleasant voice. '"I'd appreciate a call back. Even just a text. I can fit you in tomorrow 3 pm. It's essential we build on today's hard work tomorrow. Sincerely, Lucy." Would you like to reply, Richard?'

That word again: work. 'Yes please.'

'What do you want to say?'

'"Dear Lucy, speaking of hard work, I'm planning a few hours of it tonight. Gearbox therapy. Should keep me out of mischief! But just so you get a good night's sleep, see you tomorrow. Cheers, Richard." Siri, send message.'

'Message sent.'

The spare parts had arrived, but in truth there would be no work on the bike tonight; I was fit for nothing but pain relief, bed and sleep.

One small consolation: my latest injuries were yet another nail in the coffin of the Full Professor's theory.

Memo, Dickhead: if my eyes worked I wouldn't have tripped over the box, would I?

Although – a last, stray doubt as I slipped into single-malt coma – it might have been too dark to see anything anyway.

11

'WHAT ON *EARTH* HAVE YOU DONE TO YOURSELF THIS TIME, Richard?'

I tapped past her voice, sat down on the couch, eased my legs up, and lay back. 'Overhanging branch.'

'That's what you said last time.'

'Figure of speech. More an under-hanging branch, really. A box on the porch.'

She planted her backside on the couch next to me. 'Let me look at it.'

'It's fine.'

'I'll be the judge of that.' She took my chin in her hand, turned my head this way and that. 'Brow needs stitching.'

'I took a dive into the front door. Reverse pike. Degree of difficulty–'

'Keep still,' she interrupted. 'Can you feel me stroking your cheek?'

'Of course.'

'And here?'

'Yep.'

'Liar,' she said. 'I wasn't even touching you that time. I can't assess you if you don't answer honestly. Can you feel this?'

'Is it another trick question?'

'In other words you can't.' She slipped off the couch and walked back to her desk. 'You've fractured the orbit, Richard. Damaged the nerve. You'll need a scan. I'll ring down to Emergency.'

'Forget it, Prof. I've spent more than enough time in Emergency lately'

An exasperated grunt. 'Perhaps you should ask yourself why. Whether there might be a pattern to these accidents.'

'The pattern is I'm blind. Blind people bump into stuff.'

'You bumped into the sleeping pills?'

'In a manner of speaking.'

She pressed a button on her desk-phone. 'Karen? Book a CT for Detective Sergeant Zadow . . . Left zygoma and orbit . . . No, urgent. Sometime today.'

'Have you been listening? I'm not sitting around all Saturday so some nurse's aid can stick a bandaid on my cheek.'

'And bring me a suture tray,' she added before hanging up and turning my way again. 'I'll put the bandaid on myself,' she told me. 'After I've stitched it. You can have the scan on your way out.'

'I told you it's nothing.'

'You've fractured your *eye*-socket, Richard.'

I had to laugh. 'Gee. You mean I could lose an eye?'

A tap at the door; she accepted something with a murmured thanks, dragged a chair my way, set the tray on it. The sound of plastic-wrapping being removed; then she made a little tut-tut kind of sound, walked to the desk and punched the phone again.

'A *suture* tray, Karen, not a dressing pack . . . What? . . . What's it look like? . . . Oh – I see . . . Yes, there's a leaflet . . . Thank you. Sorry for the hissy fit.' The phone was re-cradled; she came and sat on the couch again. 'Unbelievable,' she said, with an odd, harsh snort of amusement.

'What is?'

'First things first.' She snapped on a pair of gloves, then fell silent. A rustle of paper; she was studying something. The mysterious instructions?

'You *have* done this before, Prof?'

'Not with the new technology.'

'That's very reassuring. Staple-gun? Rivets?'

No answer; just the splash of liquid being spilt into a dish, and an antiseptic smell in my nostrils.

'Polyfilla?'

'Head still,' she said, dabbing at my face.

The cool sting of alcohol was not unpleasant. Perhaps there *was* a pattern: I seemed to take pleasure from pain. Or perhaps just any sensory input was better than none.

'*Very* still,' she said, and clamped a fold of eyebrow between thumb and finger. 'Takes thirty seconds to set. According to the fine print.'

'You *glue* them now?'

That out-of-character, knowing snort again. 'Isn't that a coincidence? You could have fixed it yourself, Richard.'

I almost jerked free in surprise. She knew about the superglue? But how? My head was filled with noisy thoughts as she released her grip, and tugged her gloves off.

'You didn't quite tell me the whole story yesterday, did you? About what happened in the brothel.'

Derailed again. How did she know I'd visited my former business establishment yesterday? That puzzle at least was solved after a moment's thought: my visit had been *after* my session with her. She was talking about the distant past. Which still left the problem of the superglue.

'Not graphic enough for you, thrillseeker?'

'Not truthful enough.'

I stayed mum as she turned on a tap somewhere and washed her hands. Of course I hadn't told her the whole story; I very deliberately hadn't. So how did she know about the glue?

Another surprise as she sat down at her desk: instead of uncapping the fountain pen her fingers began tapping at a keyboard. She had a screen. Since when?

'I pulled his hospital file,' she said.

I opened my mouth, if only to stall. 'Whose file?'

The fingers stopped tapping. 'Let's not play games, Richard.'

'I didn't tell you his name. If we are talking about the rapist.'

'I'd come up with a name. Call it an educated guess. From the way you talked about him. Your anger.'

'Anyone would be angry. He bashed her face in with a fire extinguisher, then raped her while she was unconscious.'

'There seemed more to it than that. If I had the wrong – what shall we call him? – suspect it was easy to prove his innocence. All I needed were his records.'

I needed a moment to take this in. 'You pulled your suspect's *case*notes?'

'I'm looking at them as we speak. On screen.'

'Are you allowed to do that? He's not your patient.'

'You are. And he was admitted because of what you did to him.'

Cornered again. All I could do was clap hands, slowly. 'Outstanding work, Detective Professor.'

'Says here he told the treating doctor his injuries were self-inflicted. Bad speed trip. There's no mention of an assault.'

'The club code, Prof. We settle things in-house.'

Another hint of sarcasm in her voice. 'That worked out well for you, didn't it? When it was his turn a year or two later.'

Two years later, to the day. But I wasn't ready to go there yet. Except to wonder about the weird symmetry of it all. Two years from the rape till he shot me in the head. Two more years till he broke out of jail. Anniversary reactions? There was some comfort in thinking about how it must have messed with his head, especially as the date loomed up every year. Less comfort in the idea that it gave his shit-life purpose. That was a little too close to home.

'Tell me,' I said, 'about his injuries.'

'Why don't you tell me? You inflicted them.'

'Did he need surgery? Was he disabled in any way? Disfigured?'

No answer. Perhaps there was too much wishful thinking in my voice, too much weird need.

'It might help with closure,' I added, for the hell of it, thinking I had no chance.

Perhaps the bullshit word amused her, or perhaps she decided to take a gamble herself, trying a new direction to draw me out.

'I have to protect his medical confidentiality,' she said. 'But I can't see why I shouldn't read you the Separation Summary. Since it doesn't contain anything you don't know already.'

'You continue to surprise me, Prof,' I said, but she didn't seem to hear.

'Discharge Diagnoses,' she read aloud. 'One. Amphetamine-induced paranoid psychosis. Two. Self-mutilation. Degloving injury of the penis, partial.'

The last phrase was as startling as it was satisfying. 'Could you repeat that bit? I didn't quite get it.'

'Partial degloving of the penis.'

Music to my ears. 'His cock was *skinned*? How did that happen?'

'Again: you tell me. He claimed it was self-inflicted.'

I laughed with a kind of joyous harshness. 'He's lucky I didn't cut it *off*! If I'd had a knife in my hand—'

'Instead of a tube of superglue?'

I shrugged. 'A good tradesman makes do with the materials at hand.'

'You feel no remorse at all?'

'I didn't intend to de-*glove* it,' I said. Talk about the power of words. *Degloving of the penis.* Play it again, Prof. Over and over again. Like a classic tune, it would never lose its power to move me. 'All I did was glue his dick to his belly.'

'I'm struggling to understand why you would do that.'

'You sticking up for that piece of shit?'

'You're my patient, not him. *You* weren't under the influence of drugs.'

I was under the influence of something. The gorge of rage rose in me again as I saw him lying there, flat on his back, jeans around ankles, a blissed-out smile on his face. The cock still drug-stiff. I sank my boot into him again, but he was beyond noticing. I needed to get my girl out of there, get *her* injuries treated – but there was no way I was going to leave him with nothing more than a few cracked ribs and a headache when he woke.

'Maybe it ripped free when it shrunk. Maybe he ripped it free himself. Either way the case notes are correct: it *was* self-inflicted.'

'You didn't intend the degloving?'

'Icing on the cake. I'm not sure what I intended. It was a spur of the moment thing.' I paused, thinking. 'I suppose I hoped it'd be stuck there for a few weeks. I liked thinking about it later: that every time he pissed he'd piss in his own face!'

'Richard. I want you to take a step back and listen to yourself. What he did was terrible. Beyond contempt. Even in a drug-induced delirium. Lock him up, by all means. Throw away the key. But to torture him in return?'

'An eye for an eye, Prof.'

'An unfortunate choice of words, don't you think? Considering what happened a year or so later.'

'Two years. We're going round in circles.'

'My point exactly. Revenge *is* a circle. A vicious circle.'

I hid in my cigarette for a few puffs. I wasn't about to tell her I was currently planning another lap of that satisfying circuit.

The pen was finally uncapped; she wrote by hand for a time. I could almost hear the words in the soft pressure of nib on paper: *Beating my Head Against a Brick Wall.*

'Imagine it was you,' I said, more calmly. 'Or your daughter.'

'You're a policeman, Richard. You swore to uphold the law.'

'Spend some time sitting in courtrooms with the victims and see what kind of law *they* want.'

She recapped the pen. 'Let's talk about the victim then. What kind of law did she want?'

I hesitated. Dangerous territory this. I'd told her too much about Trixie already.

'I can easily pull *her* notes,' she said, or perhaps threatened.

'Under what name? Trixie Rose?'

'Under her admission date. Which I have in front of me on *his* admission notes.'

'You going to scroll through every patient admitted that day?'

'No.' Her fingers began pecking at the keyboard again. 'Just the Discharge Diagnosis. Let's see. What shall we try first? Concussion. Closed Head Trauma. Fractured Nose. Sexual assault.'

Checkmate. I was just delaying the inevitable. 'Save yourself the trouble. She doesn't have a hospital record.'

The tapping stopped. 'You must have taken her somewhere. The Queen Elizabeth? Flinders? Calvary?'

'She refused to go anywhere. Point-blank.'

An incredulous silence. Then: 'She was *raped*, Richard. You must have called the police, at least. The Sexual Assault Unit.'

'She didn't remember much. Nothing at all after she phoned me the second time.'

Anger in her voice for the first time that day, perhaps the first time ever in a consultation. 'But *you* did! You were the only witness.'

My hackles rose. 'She wanted it kept quiet, okay?'

Another moment of silence, then, icily: 'How very convenient.'

'What's that supposed to mean?'

'It means you didn't blow your cover. Operation – what was it? Trojan Horse. You must have tried *really* hard to dissuade her.'

'It was her choice not mine. Will you stop verballing me? For all I knew I was blown anyway. I wanted her to go to Emergency. I *begged* her.'

Silence again. Perhaps she regretted her outburst – its force if not its message. When she spoke, it was more calmly. 'At the very least she needed overnight observation.'

'I drove her home. Cleaned her up. Put her to bed. Kept watch all night. Okay?'

Her silence was still hard to read. More disapproving than disbelieving? More surprised than either?

'She lived alone?' she said, eventually.

'She lived with her parents.' I forced out a small laugh. 'She wasn't about to show her face *there* either. For obvious reasons.'

'You took her to your place?'

'Where else? She was groggy, but told me what to look out for. Wake her every fifteen minutes. Check pupils. Orientation.' I bit my tongue, but too late.

'She was a nurse?'

'A student, remember? I spoonfed her some porridge in the morning. Then she went back to bed and slept. Eighteen hours.'

'A student *nurse*?'

'Something like that.' *Keep fishing and I'll keep stalling.* 'Another reason she refused to go to Emergency. Too many familiar faces.'

A pause, while she took this in. 'Why aren't you telling me her real name?'

'I think she's also entitled to a bit of medical confidentiality, Prof.'

'She must have been severely traumatised. Did she have counselling? I presume she didn't return to her . . . part-time job.'

'You looking for closure too? A happy ending?'

Which there had been, for a time. More than happy. Two years of sheer bliss, of her studies, my work, our house renovations, two lives mortared together, brick by brick, day by busy day, night by sweet night, into one shared life.

'I'd like to know what happened to her, yes. Please.'

Time to stop fudging? The truth, the simple truth and nothing but? She would winkle it out sooner or later, anyway.

'I married her,' I said.

The silence that followed was long enough for her to cover a page with ink, but there wasn't so much as a nib-squeak from the desk.

'Willow?' she finally said. '*Willow* was the victim?'

I couldn't have given an answer even if she needed one.

'Were you already in a relationship with her, Richard? Before the assault?'

A deep breath. 'I never mixed business and pleasure.' The truth, but not enough of it this time, perhaps. 'I *thought* about it. I liked her. I liked her a lot. She liked me. She told me I made her feel . . .'

The next little word stuck fast in my throat, if this time less like a fishbone than a fishhook.

'Safe?' from the Prof.

A prickle of moisture in my eyes, the first in her presence, ever. I tried to blink away the tears before she noticed, but her chair was already sliding back, her steps approaching.

'Go ahead,' she said, pressing a wad of tissues into my hand, 'if it helps.'

I wiped my eyes. 'Useless fucking organs. Can't do anything properly.'

She seated herself on the edge of the couch again. 'You blame yourself?'

I wiped my eyes with the back of my hand, roughly. Of *course* I blamed myself. I'd left her alone with him. But that's not where the tears were coming from.

'Not as much as I blame her.'

I rolled off the couch and felt about for my stick. And was suddenly relieved I'd let the cat out of the bag. The cat out of the cathouse.

'You blame *her* for the *rape*, Richard?'

'If you think that you don't know me at all. And I wonder what the fuck we've been talking about for two years. I nursed her through those weeks. Spoon-fed her, sponged her. Supported her.'

'And she stayed?'

'She stayed forever. Or so she promised. I married her, for Christ's sake! Put her through her last years of medical school.' I headed towards the door, flailing more than tapping. *Scything*. 'And she repaid me how? Walking out at the first fucking hurdle. In sickness and in health, Prof!'

'Richard,' she said, as I groped for the doorknob. 'Stay. Please. Until you calm down.'

'I'm extremely fucking calm,' I said, and headed towards the gruff bark as the door swung open. I located Scout's handle, guided her to the lift.

'I have another appointment now,' from the worried voice following behind. 'But I'll be free again in an hour. I don't think you should be alone right now.'

'Being alone right now is exactly what I need,' I said.

'Can I see you tomorrow then? I could do another house-call.'

'What did I tell you last Sunday, Prof? Get a life.'

'You have my number,' she said as the lift-door opened. 'As we agreed. If you have the urge to do anything stupid. Promise?'

'Depends on your definition of stupid,' I said, which probably didn't help her state of mind as the door slid shut.

IV
TASTE

1

I TRIED NOT TO LISTEN TO WILLOW'S MESSAGE FROM THE SEALED time-capsule I'd just broken open – *You make me feel safe* – as I tapped home, but the rest of my body was all ears. I was filled with a kind of physical, visceral noise: my limbs fizzed and tingled, unbearably; my head pounded; I felt like throwing up again. I increased my pace, recklessly, as if I could leave my noisy flesh in my wake like a shed snakeskin.

'Claxton Street, ten paces.'

The hard-edged echo chamber of home only seemed to amplify things. I turned up the TV volume to drown my thoughts, and punished my mutinous body for an hour with gloves and weights. If I couldn't shed the thing perhaps I could sweat it into submission.

But still it twitched and crackled, as if statically charged. I fried up a mess of comfort food – bacon, tomatoes, eggs – only to gag on the first mouthful and set my bowl down next to the dog's.

The holstered gun nudged me in the small of the back as I straightened up, but to what end? No assassin was heading my way. I rolled up the shutter of the rat-trap anyway, if only to keep busy. Never had I needed him more; never had he seemed so far away.

'Maximum volume spare-room microphones, Siri.'

Would sleep provide an escape? I uncorked the whisky bottle, spilled out a few thick fingers, gulped them down. It occurred to me that sleeping pills would work better, and with that thought came another: *I've been here before.* This was *exactly* how I'd felt – how my *body* had felt – on the night of the overdose: this thwarted purpose, this deep, muscular frustration.

'Siri,' I said. 'Phone Directory. Find Favourites. Reckless Idiot.'

'Dial Reckless Idiot?'

I hesitated. *Who's the idiot here?*, I asked myself. *Look before you leap*, I told myself.

And immediately leapt, but only into message-bank. 'Hi. Willow here. Tied up at the moment. Probably working my arse off. Leave a message after the beep and I'll do my best to get back to you this century. Bye.'

Beep.

Deep breath. 'It's me,' I said. 'The stubborn idiot. This has taken too long. Far too long. I'm a slow learner, especially about myself, but I guess you know that. I rang to say — I'm so sorry for what I did. And after everything you'd been through, for Christ's sake!' As I took another deep breath the call ended.

'Redial Reckless Idiot,' I said, listened to her message and started all over again. 'All I ever wanted was to make you feel safe. Always. And I hit you, for fuck's sake!' My chest had a tight band around it; I couldn't get more words out for a long moment; I ran out of message-time again. I broke the shackles with yet another deep breath and redialled yet again.

'Willow, I *wanted* to hit you. To hurt you. I see that now. There's no excuse. None. Blindness, anger, psychobabble — all bullshit. This is not some dumb-arse cry for help, so don't call back. I'm not about to forgive myself, so don't you go doing it either. Well, that's all.' Pause. 'For the record.'

I began pacing the hall again, if less to escape my noisy body than to resist the gentle pressure of the gun in the small of my back, persistent now, like the palm of a hand trying to steer me somewhere else entirely. Towards some other, more definitive method of contrition.

By the time I reached the front door the Glock had found its way out of the holster and into my hand. I turned for the return lap, not sure what to do with the thing — toss it out the door? — when something, or someone, stuck out another leg, and I tripped again. My knees hit the

floor hard but my flailing hands saved my head from further damage as
the gun, instinctively released, clattered away up the hall.

No panic this time; I recognised my assailant – a serial offender –
immediately. Perhaps the box of spare parts recognised me in turn,
and wanted to remind me of its presence. Or just nudge me in a
different, more productive direction. Work therapy, Detective
Sergeant? Still on all fours, I found and reholstered the gun, pushed
myself gingerly to my feet, picked up the box, carried it out into the
shed, set it on the lift-table, located the box-cutter, and got to work.

The Glock wouldn't stop whispering behind my back, but the Duke
was speaking to me face-to-face, loud and clear. As I unpacked and
fingered the heavy, solid parts – conrods, pins, roller cages – my mental
fingers were already fitting them into the 3D jigsaw. It struck me that
I was doing another blind field-strip, of sorts, if scaled up. Sandwiched
between the demands of the two machines, large and small, I ran with
this riff for a time. A V-twin round-case might be a little more complex
than a semiautomatic pistol, but not by much. Both internal combus-
tion engines, of a kind. Both driven by controlled explosions inside
confined spaces. Call that space a barrel, a chamber, a cylinder: same
diff. And what's a bullet if not a non-reciprocating piston? Ignition,
likewise: what's a spark-plug if not a repeating detonator-cap? The
flint-lock sparks of the first muskets are not that far back in the past.

I was still aware of the gun, but it had eased its pressure to nuisance
value. I unholstered it, ran my left hand up the tool cupboard to get my
bearings, then tossed the gun up on top, out of reach, out of mind as
I began poking about in the engine casing. My hands were as much
pleasantly finger-painting with grease as making sense of the parts, but
either way they had found something useful to do, and – yes, Prof –
something therapeutic. My mind doodled along with them, distracted
by the notion of a gunpowder-driven engine, a kind of solid-fuel V-twin.

A loud rap on the door jolted me back into the world. A flicker
of alarm only: the signature knock had become even more familiar
these past few days, although the smell was different when I opened

the door. Cigarette smoke, yes, but overlaid with something more chemically pungent.

'You're not ready,' he said.

'For what?' I said, distracted by my nose. Camphor?

'The Detectives' Dinner, dickhead.'

Which explained the smell: mothballs. He was in full dress, even if I couldn't hear the medals clanking.

'I told you I'd pick you up if I didn't hear from you,' he said. 'I didn't hear from you.'

'Completely forgot, Chief. Sorry.'

'No matter. I came early in case I needed to talk you into it.'

'I *am* in the middle of something.'

I sensed him take in my hands, black with grease, possibly a little blood. 'I don't think I want to know. I'll give you ten minutes to scrub up. But we need to get moving.'

I stood there, tempted. I was back in control of my body, but sooner or later I would have to stop working on the bike. And it would just be me and the Glock, in the house, together. Separated only by a stepladder. With no one else to aim it at.

'What's so funny?' he said, and I realised I'd laughed, if harshly, at the darkness of the thought.

'Private joke.'

'Tell me later. Lot of old friends waiting at the Club, Zads.'

'As you said last time.'

'So you *do* remember. Just playing hard to get.' A chuckle; the exhaled smoke drowning out the mothballs. 'There's one *new* friend you might be interested in catching up with. A certain Senior Constable who made Detective today. You could offer your congratulations personally.'

The dog's nails clicked up the hall and stopped next to me. Left-hand side; handle-offering position.

Another smoky chuckle. 'Your dog knows you better than you know yourself, mate.'

He was right. They were both right, even if Scout wasn't coming with us.

'Get your arse into gear,' he said, turning away. 'Ten minutes, remember.'

I used up five locating my own dress blues at the back of the wardrobe, and liberating them from their plastic sheath. At least they were clean and pressed. The shirt felt a little tight around the collar, the trousers likewise: one notch wider at the belt, by fingertip braille. Those same fingers needed three attempts before they remembered how to knot the tie.

A stray thought: I hadn't worn a tie since being blinded. What did that mean? I'd gone native?

The tight jacket felt not so much constricting as comfortably secure, a psychological Kevlar vest. A toot from the street; no time to brush my dress shoes. They *felt* shiny, and even, after all this time, a little boot-polishy to the nose.

My cap, hanging on the hallstand for the last two years, smelt merely fusty. Too many months marinating in an atmosphere of dog shit and fried bacon? I set it squarely on my head, nonetheless.

'What do you fucking think, girl?'

She told me, succinctly, then clicked straight to the door, keen to be seen out and about with a man in uniform.

One problem: no room for a gun inside that suit of tight-fitting blue serge armour. But no need either, surely. It was a relief to get away from it.

I slipped Siri into a pocket, tossed Scout a treat – 'Don't wait up for me, dear' – and tapped out the door.

Another single, peremptory toot from further down the street. I turned in that direction, taking no umbrage at such low-key, matter-of-fact guidance. I tapped a big front wheel, and ran my hand along a high bonnet. The front passenger door was invitingly open: I stepped around, folded my cane, and eased my way up inside by feel.

'You bought yourself a new Prado, Chief?'

'Stop showing off,' he said, but chuckled, impressed.

I opened my mouth to answer then closed it. Goosebumps were prickling the back of my neck. 'Am I meant to guess?' I said.

'Guess what?'

'Who's sitting in the back seat, smart-arse?'

A spluttered giggle, directly behind me. 'How did you know?'

'Can't be your perfume, Annie,' I said. 'You only wear that on the job.'

'Telepathy,' Terry told her as he pulled out into the traffic. 'Rick has special powers. Which is why I need him back at work.'

'By the way,' I said, 'congratulations, Detective.'

'Awesome,' she said, drily. 'So tell me what I'm gonna do next?'

Her voice was leaning forward as she spoke, as if fumbling for something at her feet. Her breath on the back of my neck was beery; the celebrations had clearly started.

'Offer me a beer?' I answered, a moment before the *Phsst!* of a ring-pull.

'You're a genius,' she said, and an arm rested on my shoulder; a warm hand slipped a cold can into mine, its fingers lightly brushing my neck on the way back. Goosebumps of a different kind.

A second can fizzed open in the back seat. 'Terry?'

'Not for me,' he said. 'Not a good look. Drink-driving in full dress.'

I raised my can above my shoulder, starting to feel glad I'd come. 'Ignore him, Annie. Always been a killjoy.'

She clunked her can against mine; I tilted it to my lips, mentally closed my eyes to the rest of the world and lost myself in the taste Nothing quite like the first mouthful at the end of a long day. I savoured it for as long as I could, then sculled the rest, crumpled the empty and tossed it carelessly back over my head.

She laughed. 'Good start, Detective Sergeant. But you still have some catching up to do.'

Another can was perched on my shoulder: unopened this time. I liked that. I felt for the ring-pull, feeling gladder by the moment.

Phsst! It was only a few blocks to the Club, but a run of red lights slowed us down; I was finishing my third as Terry pulled into the kerb.

'I'll let you kids off here,' he said.

I could almost believe I was a kid again as I stepped out of the car, and a woman half my age – two-thirds at most – slipped her arm into mine. Especially since it felt less like she wanted to guide me, than be escorted *by* me. Was she already so tipsy she'd forgotten I was blind, or just pretending? Perhaps she just wanted to make an entrance. I hoped so; I'd rather be used than patronised, it was more honest. And it was her night after all – the debutante, the belle of the Detectives' Ball. I switched the cane to my less practised right hand, but managed to tap across the footpath and into the Club without gallantly walking her smack into a jacaranda tree.

The automatic door helped me get us inside, but after that I was lost, disorientated by the party roar. Her turn to steer: I clung to her arm as the voices came and went around us. Shouted congratulations to the debutante, of course, but plenty of greetings aimed my way. A window in the wall of noise would open and close long enough for a single voice to poke through – 'Richie! You fuckin' legend!' – then another would open from another direction – 'Heard about the park t'other night, Zads. You got some balls!'

Was I the belle of the ball? My free hand was pumped, multiply, until beer-glasses began to fill it, serially, and my back was slapped instead.

And still the brief windows opened and closed. 'Ya money's no good here, Richo.' 'Yo! Zads! Saw ya on the box the other night. The dog okay?'

All of which was fine as long as I clung to the rock of Annie. I'd kept well clear of the Club – wary of pity, even more wary of sympathy – but soon wondered why. Had I forgotten the hard-bred unsentimentality of cops? Things might get maudlin later, after the first half dozen, but for now it was a pity-free zone. Those conversational windows were too narrow for pity, those shouted voices too loud for sympathy.

'Richo! Heard about the punch-up in the park, ya fucking idiot. But ya got cojones, I'll give ya that!'

I'd been wary also of having to explain, to update two years of backstory – again, and again – but luckily no one was interested. Or not in the details. The questions were rhetorical; answers already included. The jokes didn't even have to be laughed at.

'Pint of pale, Richo. On the boys from Northern. Saw ya on the news the other night. Where's the dog? They nab him after all?'

'Her,' I muttered; my head beginning to swim, my steps widen, unsteadily. Someone's arm – not Annie's – helped me to a table; a wine bottle was plonked in front of me. Fumbling for my glass I found a basket of bread rolls first, which seemed a useful hint. I ate through them steadily, slowing my drinking, or at least soaking it up, while the voices continued to lean in.

'Pint of pale from the team at Major Crime, Zads. And a bubbly for . . . Where's she gone? Done a runner already? Wouldn't let her outta sight if I was you!'

Soup arrived. Mulligatawny. Possibly. Hard to tell, as usual in the Club, but the task at least focused my mind as my cheery comrades played musical chairs each side of me.

'Long time, no see, Zads! They caught that arsehole yet?'

A jug of beer heavy-landed in front of me; a bottle of wine followed on a more gradual flight path. I opted for the wine, but pacing myself, taking small sips only. Blindness and drunkenness are a tough combination. Annie was back in the musical chair on my left; she'd been on the right before we lost contact.

'Uh-oh,' she said, jokily, 'here comes trouble,' as a fleshy softness – breasts, surely – was pressed against the back of my head, and a pair of hands covered my eyes.

'Guess who?' A woman's voice in my ear, followed by a wet tongue.

I jerked my head away, laughing. 'Good to see you, Biff. So to speak.'

'Fucking impressive, Zads,' she said, easing herself into the seat on my left. 'Heard you had these special abilities. Eyes in the back of your head.'

'Got a lot of abilities you'll never know about, sweetheart.'

'You making me an offer?' She hooted, happily. 'I tried it with a bloke once. Not bad, but not like the real thing.'

An old routine, but I laughed as if hearing it for the first time. The wine no doubt helped, and the tag-team female attention. Annie on the other side was laughing even louder.

'Maybe you should try it with a blind bloke,' I suggested. 'Take a walk on the wild side.'

Biff hooted again; her chair shifted as she picked up something heavy – the beer jug? – and poured. I reached for my wineglass, sipped.

'You two go way back?' from Annie.

It was more a comment than a question, but I answered anyway. 'Academy days. Got on like a house on fire.'

'Been too long,' Biff said, then spoke past me to Annie. 'Congratulations, Detective. Been hearing good things about you. Including your handling of a certain scumbag in the park the other night.'

Annie laughed. 'It was all over by the time *I* got there. Drunken prick got what he deserved.'

'I'm not talking about the drunk. I'm talking about the arsehole who assaulted him. With, what, an *iPhone*?'

I spluttered on my wine, grateful for the vividness of the image. And grateful to be back in the larrikin off-duty world of the Club, the home away from home that I'd forgotten I liked so much.

'A toast,' Biff said, 'to blunt instruments.'

I raised my wine; the three of us clinked glasses, drank. 'You two would know more about that than me. My own little blunt instrument couldn't compete.'

They laughed, less with me, perhaps, than across me to each other. 'You're a fucking legend, Zads,' Biff said, and pushed herself up out of the seat. 'But I need a smoke. Anyone care to join me?'

I didn't answer; this wasn't aimed at me either. The main course was making its descent; I needed more ballast. I leant forward over the food, inhaled. Garlic, and nothing but, even after I began to chew.

'What is this shit?' I said, but Annie had vanished again. I chewed on, trying to reverse-engineer the rest of the dish in my taste-buds — veal? tomatoes? cheese? — when she landed again in her chair.

'Wash it down with this,' she said.

Her voice sounded odd, I blamed it on the booze, a different shaped glass of which had been pressed into my hand. I swirled it, a heavy-based tumbler; stuck my nose in the wide mouth. Single malt, with more years in it than the mid-shelf stuff I'd been drinking at home.

'You've been well briefed,' I told her.

She leant closer to chink her glass against mine and I caught a whiff of perfume. This also was odd; the only scent she'd been wearing in the car was beer. Had she ducked into the ladies and dabbed on something more feminine?

So much for my famous special senses. Blame the garlic, blame the beer and wine, blame the cross-sense disruption from all the noise, but the obvious was so unlikely it didn't cross my mind, even when my big nose was rubbed in it, literally.

'I had a good teacher,' she said, and leant across and kissed me on the mouth.

For a moment I was speechless. But there was no mistaking her. Her voice, the feel of her kiss, the scent of her perfume. The taste of her lips: all salt and lime.

'What are *you* doing here?' I got out eventually.

'I thought you'd be pleased to see me,' she said, and took another sip from her margarita.

'I am. Just, well, *surprised*. You got my messages then?'

'Haven't checked. Day from hell, then staff happy hour. What did it say?'

'There was more than one. Had to send three or four in a row.'

'You weren't stalking me by phone again, Big Nose?' she said, teasingly.

I began to relax. I loved the way a few drinks blurred and softened her edges, if not the way a few more meant a hard-edged morning-after. But who was I to talk? I reached for my Scotch and swirled another mouthful down.

'Feel free to delete them,' I said. 'Got a lot off my chest. Ran out of message-bank.'

'So tell me now. Twenty-five words or less.'

'I can say it in one. Sorry. Two: *very* sorry. Repeated 25 times.'

'Me too,' she said, her arm around my shoulder. 'But I didn't need a message. I was coming anyway.'

Maybe my own edges were getting a bit blurred. 'I still don't get it.'

'Terry invited me.'

More mystery; Terry working as matchmaker seemed a bit far-fetched. 'That's how, not why.'

'I wouldn't have missed it for the world, Big Nose,' she said, and leant across and rubbed her own cute one against the tip of that fascinating organ, briefly.

I laughed. 'Work shows bore you stiff. Besides which, the dinner is a partner-free zone.'

'I can see why. Half the Force making idiots of themselves with the other half. Who was that woman? She was all over you.'

'You're jealous of Biff?' I said, mock-surprised.

'As if. The other one. The glamour-puss.'

I laughed, feeling more and more at home. 'Annie, Annie forget-her-second-name. More a guide dog for the night. But you still haven't told me. What the *fuck* are you doing here?'

'Special dispensation,' she said, then added, as cutlery began chiming wineglasses all around us, 'I think you're about to find out.'

'Children! Your attention! Please!' Biff's husky voice, this time through a badly amplified microphone. 'Settle down! We've a bit to get through tonight.'

The roar subsided, but not completely.

'Oy!' she shouted, sounding more like she was speaking into a megaphone at a riot. 'Down the back! Without naming names this means you, Thommo. Billy T. The usual suspects. You too, Harry. And take your paws off that waitress. She's out of your league.'

An answer was shouted back over the laughter: 'Got your eye on her yourself, Chief?'

Louder laughter, but Chief Biff was louder still: 'Let's ask her who she prefers. Wanna come home with me tonight, darlin'?'

Uproar again. I could see Biff even more clearly in my head now she was further away and back in a familiar role: MC for every dinner since she made Detective, and half the floor-show as well.

Another shout from the back made it through the laughter: 'Reckons she's happy to make it a threesome, Biff!'

'Might let you *watch*, Harry. Teach you how to treat a woman properly.'

Complete uproar. I'd missed the last two dinners, but nothing had changed. Carnival night, where the gang let down its hair.

'Settle down, children,' she said, still laughing herself. 'Settle down. My fault, I guess. Things have gotten out of control.'

Eventually there was silence, of a kind.

'That wasn't too hard, was it? So. Welcome, crime-fighters! Before we get to the formalities, some apologies. The Minister sends his from Bali. He's on another study tour.'

A ripple of laughter.

'I'm sorry to report the Former Acting Police Minister didn't send his. A real disappointment, that. Can't see why being in jail should excuse a lack of common courtesy.'

Another explosion of laughter, louder and longer.

'Settle down, crime-fighters. Bit of decorum, please. We *do* have the Acting Commissioner with us tonight, so without further ado I'd like to invite him to propose the loyal toast.'

'Thanks, Biff' – another familiar voice, if mainly from listening to the TV news over the last two years – 'Hard act to follow as always. So I'll make it short and sweet. Ladies, gentlemen. Please charge your glasses and be upstanding.'

Two hundred chairs scraped back noisily on the polished wood floor; two hundred half-drunk detectives wobbled to their feet. I rediscovered my wineglass and wobbled up with them.

'To Her Majesty the Queen!'

'The Queen!' from two hundred voices, with plenty of feeling, if mainly because the old dear offered an excuse for another drink.

'To the Job!'

'The Job!' This time with heartfelt feeling.

Biff again, as we re-took our seats: 'Thanks, AC. I'll get you to stay up here for the sacred ceremony of the gold cufflinks. We're losing a fair whack of experience tonight; a lot of faces we're all going to miss. Not yours, Harry – we're all breathing a big sigh of relief. Especially the waitresses.' The laughter began flowing again. 'First, though, a little surprise presentation. Not a retirement this one, but a welcome back.'

So much for my famous sixth sense; I still hadn't a blurry clue where this was going.

'Since the victim doesn't know about it yet, I'm not going to give the game away. I'll hand straight over to Chief Terry to say a few words about his good friend and ours.'

If the alarm bells were finally beginning to ring, it was dully, as if underwater. Under whisky. I put the empty glass down in the faint hope it might help clear things up.

'Thanks, Biff. Acting Commissioner. Colleagues. Friends. There's no greater honour for a serving officer than to be awarded the Australian Police Medal. Tonight's presentation is much delayed. Despite various circumstances – and most of us know what he's been through – it's taken much too long for his courage to be acknowledged. But better late than never.'

Better never at all! – I almost shouted aloud – *I don't want this!* – but my responses seemed stuck on a delay loop, a second or two behind.

'He's here tonight, and he's among friends. Great friends. His sacrifice was above and beyond. If it was the military, a VC would hardly do him justice. I'm not going to bang on about this. I don't want to embarrass him; he's a modest hero. Getting him here tonight was like extracting teeth.'

Which was why – it struck me – he'd used Annie, if more as an anaesthetic for the extraction than a pair of tooth-pliers. It was also why he'd kept Willow out of sight, so to speak. If I'd guessed what was coming I would have hightailed it out of there.

'It wasn't the first time he'd put himself in harm's way,' he rabbited on. 'But, like I say, you know the story. The man who could never resist a damsel in distress. So let's hear it for Detective Sergeant Rick Zadow, one of our finest. Welcome back, Zads. Welcome *home*. You juniors want to know what the Job is about – you want to know about courage in the line of fire – shake its hand. It's here tonight in person.'

A din of shouts and whoops and clapping hands, but still I sat there, paralysed; my feelings as bipolar as ever. It wasn't that simple, I wanted to say. It *couldn't* be that simple. I had no memory of the siege – it had been blasted out of my head along with my sight – but I'd listened to the report. And if *that* was true, I was less a hero than an idiot. Not for changing places with Willow; that was a given. And who knows? Maybe even for any other hostage. But for trusting my fate to Standard Hostage Protocol.

Why didn't you shoot the cunt? I wanted to shout at Terry. But that was just shooting the messenger again. He was doing his job.

'I'm no hero,' I muttered, half-heartedly and half-drunkenly. 'And this is just another kind of compo. Guilt-money.'

Only Willow could hear me. Her voice was in my ear, her hand tugging me gently to my feet. 'You're *my* hero. You saved my sorry arse twice, for Christ's sake. You don't remember one, I don't remember the other – but you deserve *two* medals.'

I rose, passively enough; she linked her arm in mine and tugged me away from the table, but so unsteady on her feet that, oddly, I ended up guiding both of us in the direction I didn't want to go. Blind man walking? If I wasn't anchored to Willow, or she to me, I *might* have turned and run. Instead we stumbled on towards the scaffold through a gauntlet of backslaps, congratulations and cheers – and more than a few wolf whistles.

'Ya fucking legend, Zads!'

'I can't do this,' I muttered, but Willow either couldn't hear or was too merry to care. Wherever it was that she released me I stayed, rooted to the spot, as more things happened *to* me: another brief speech from the AC – 'It's my great honour tonight . . . On behalf of Her Majesty the Queen . . . The Australian Police Medal . . . Distinguished Service'; the noose of ribbon draped around my neck; the AC's pumping handshake; Terry's two-handed vise-grip; and finally a sloppy-tongue-kiss from Biff for the benefit of the audience as she pressed her mike into my hand.

'Wish she was on *my* arm, you lucky bastard,' she shouted in my ear.

The roar of applause pressed in on me, *filled* me, reverberating, amplified in my lungs as in the belly of a guitar, slowly becoming more rhythmic, the white noise firming up into regular lumps of sound: a slow hand-clap, and over the clap, a chant. *Speech! Speech! Speech!*

About what? I wanted to shout, but there was no escape. I raised my hands, one dangling the cane, in surrender, if only to stop the noise.

'Thanks,' I said. 'But I don't even remember it!'

A roar of laughter from the floor; Terry's voice in his microphone. 'We do, Zads. No point in being modest. You might be hazy on the details, but we all know the story. Fucktard refused to talk to anyone but you. You dropped everything and came straight to the siege.'

'And immediately broke hostage protocol. According to the report.'

Another eruption of laughter. The more serious I got, the more they thought I was joking. Maybe it was the expressionlessness of the blind: my deadpan face could be read either way.

Terry's voice again, over the top: 'Not everyone here would have changed places with a hostage.'

'The hostage was the woman I love,' I said, and it was impossible for either of us to say more as wild cheers drowned our duelling microphones, and Biff was at my side, trying to reclaim her mike.

'I haven't finished yet,' I said.

'Bit behind schedule, Zads,' she murmured, then continued, unamplified. 'The humble hero. Who's got a lot on his mind right now. We all know what happened up on the river last week. A certain little shithead didn't come back from the shops. Heads need to roll, in my opinion. The AC assures me they will.'

'From the Parole Board down!' the AC shouted.

The weight at the end of the ribbon around my neck felt less like a medal than a millstone, heavy with unanswered questions. Optimum Hostage Protocol: three snipers, three angles. Why let me be dragged back inside the house – my house – *after* the exchange? Why wait till they heard the shot before lobbing in the gas grenades?

Yes, pure speculation. I remembered none of that either. By then I was lying on the hallway floor with a hole in the back of my head, and half my memories and all my vision leaking out of it.

'Anyone else here who was there that night?' I shouted.

Dead silence, as if for the first time the room realised I was serious. Or was at least seriously biting the hand that had decorated me.

'The Starries testified,' the AC said, quietly, his voice unamplified. 'They didn't have a clear shot.'

'They should have taken one anyway,' I spat out, and the amplified screech of the words seemed to echo for some seconds around the silent Club.

'It was my call,' Terry said, eventually, more quietly. 'The buck stops with me, not them. I've gone over it in my head a hundred times, Zads, wondering if I could have done anything different.'

'Biff,' I heard the AC mutter. 'Time to wind this up.'

She slipped the microphone from my grip, smoothly and deftly. 'These things are always easier to see in hindsight, Terry. And Zads – we're all with you. There's a working party taking another look at the protocols. But we're not going to solve this tonight. What we *can* solve is the problem of the arsehole-at-large. So let's all keep our eyes and ears open. We'll find him, and when we do – well, let's hope the fucktard resists arrest.'

'Amen to that!' Willow's warm breath in my ear again, her arm tangling itself in mine. Had Biff given her the nod? Possibly not; she still seemed to be leaning on me as much for support as to guide me away.

'Okay, crime-fighters,' Biff continued. 'On to the sacred ritual of the cufflinks. But first let's hear it again for our reluctant hero, who's got a lot on his mind at present. Detective Sergeant Rick Zadow, Australian Police Medal. We stand with you, Zads! Always!'

Lukewarm applause only; I'd lost the room. But not Willow.

'Let's get out of here,' she slurred into my ear. 'And see if your cock's as big as your mouth.'

'Meaning what?' I said, ridiculously, willing to toss this gift away too. 'Another mercy fuck, then shown the door the next morning?'

Even as I spat the words out, one thing was blindingly clear: her presence in my life was the greatest gift bestowed on me. Ever. The greatest *honour*.

'Guess that depends on how you perform,' she gurgled, beyond taking offence.

I laughed with her, half relieved. How easily the bi-poles could flip, when ready. 'Shove your police medal,' I shouted across her head, but the roar of voices and music had started up again and only she could hear.

'Stop being stroppy,' she said. 'I made you an offer and you better not refuse!'

Easier said than done with her dead weight on my arm. I took a step, she lurched with me. I took another, she followed again; a seeing-eye drunk. On we shuffled: the blind leading the blind drunk out through the hiss of the automatic door and into the sudden quiet of the street, where my ears could find their bearings.

'Car's thisaway,' she said, tugging gently on my arm. 'I think.'

'You drove your car? It's only a few blocks!'

'Safer than wobbling home on the scooter.'

I jerked her in the opposite direction, homewards. 'You're in no fit state for either.'

'Don't be a killjoy,' she said, and her previously pliant body stiffened.

'We'll pick it up in the morning,' I said.

'We're staying in bed all morning, Zads. Maybe all Sunday.'

My turn to surrender as she tugged me her way, her mood as infectious as it always was after cocktail hour and the precious coin of her brain flipped to its larrikin side.

'Can you see it yet?' she asked, and spluttered, finding the idea hilarious.

'Bit dark tonight,' I said, and reached my hand into her shoulder bag and began fumbling around.

'Hey, what ya doing, Big Nose?'

'Looking for something.' It took time to find the bunch of keys, but no time at all to separate the bulky case of the car-key from its flat house-key cousins.

She yanked her bag away, playfully. 'You gonna confiscate my keys, Officer Killjoy?'

Show, not tell; I aimed the key kerbwards, and waved it in a wide arc, pressing repeatedly.

'You're not just a pretty face,' she said, dragging behind again.

No cars replied to my summons; I walked on, still pressing.

'Getting warmer! Shall I give you a clue?'

'I'll do it myself, thank you,' I said, with mock-umbrage.

Almost immediately a car bleeped, close-by, and she tugged free and headed in that direction. 'Last one in is the designated driver!'

I followed happily. Getting a load of shit off my liver at the Club helped; as did the afterglow of the Scotch. By the time she opened the passenger door and fell into the seat I was game for anything. I felt my way around to the other side, running my hands briefly over the bonnet, grille and headlights – her familiar, indestructible Corolla – then opened the driver's door and slipped in behind the wheel.

'I'll need a navigator,' I said.

'Where would you like to go?' Siri piped up.

'He wasn't talking to you, bitch,' from Willow. 'Go back to sleep.'

'Manual transmission,' I said, finding the stick-shift with my left hand as I explored the steering column with my right. 'Feels like a Corolla Ascent. 2008 Hatchback.'

She laughed, obligingly. 'You're full of it.'

Real-world braille: I finger-tipped the ignition, got the key in at the third attempt, found neutral with my other hand at the first, turned the key.

A long-lost satisfaction: an engine purring into life, a gear-stick thrumming in the cup of my palm, the reins of a small herd of horses in my hands.

'Yeeh-ha!' I said. 'How much room in front?'

''Bout a metre.'

'Behind?'

'Plenty.'

I reversed, cautiously; a gentle crunch stopped the car dead.

'Not counting the tow bar,' she said, spluttering with laughter. I sensed her crane her head, then more laughter. 'Not to worry. It's only a Porsche.'

'Mafia lawyer working late,' I said. 'They're thick on the ground around here.'

'Always thought it a strange place for a Police Club, Big Nose. Wall-to-wall legal chambers every way you look.'

'Seal colony in a sea of sharks,' I said.

'Worked out well tonight. Give his boy toy another nudge.'

I needed no encouragement. 'Revenge of the seals,' I said, and reversed with a louder crunch.

Neither of us could stop laughing for some time; she surfaced first. 'Uh-oh. Trouble on the horizon.'

'Pissed-off consigliore?'

'Eyewitness across the road. Sitting outside the Saracens Head having a smoke. But taking an interest. I'd better leave a note under the wipers.'

I heard her open the glove-box, fish about.

'You're gonna dob me in?'

A rustle of paper, the click of a pen. 'Not if the bloody biro doesn't work. That's better. Let's see, um, how about this? *The sole witness to the crime thinks I'm writing my name and rego on this note, but guess what sucker?*'

We shook with laughter again, ever more easily amused. When she had finished scribbling, she opened her door; I reached across and restrained her.

'It's a better look if the driver takes personal responsibility,' I said.

'Oh, fuck yes!' she said, pressing the note into my hand. 'Don't forget your stage-prop,' she added, then laid the bundled cane in my lap.

I climbed out and tapped a little theatrically back to the Porsche, keeping my face deadpan. I made a meal of fumbling for the wiper, then slipped the note beneath. An inspired moment before I left: I brailled the bonnet medallion, then smacked my head and looked horrified, before tapping hurriedly back to my car.

She was almost choking as I climbed in. 'And the Oscar goes to!' she burbled.

'What's our eyewitness up to?'

'Jug of beer arriving as we speak. Just lit up another fag. Looks like he's settling in for the night.'

'Got his phone out? Don't particularly want it going viral.'

'Enjoying the show too much.'

'Then let's give him an encore,' I said, and restarted the engine, slipped into first, turned the wheel fully right and eased slowly, very slowly, out from the kerb.

'Plenty of room,' she sniggered.

'Why does that make me feel I'm about to crunch another Porsche?'

'You wish,' she said, but the car steered out into the road without mishap.

'What's our friend doing now?' I asked.

'On his feet applauding,' she said. 'A standing ovation, Big Nose!' And we laughed together as I eased the wheel leftwards, guessing the angle, still driving slowly.

'Whoa!' she said. 'Over-corrected. Come back right. That was close.'

'Still dunno whether to trust you or not.'

'I trust you,' she said. 'I'm not even wearing a seatbelt, see.' She leant in front of me, and kissed me again, lingeringly this time. The first beer at the Club had tasted good, but this was another dimension: I drank from her open mouth, long and hard, till my foot slipped from the clutch and the car shuddered, and stalled.

I reached around her, fumbling for the ignition again. 'Aren't you facing the wrong way for a navigator?'

She eased back onto her side: I started up, turned the clutch out, and moved forward smoothly and still very slowly.

'Left a little,' from Willow. 'Yep. Spot on. Keep her there.'

'Anyone on the road?'

'You probably won't believe me, but no. Drifting right again.'

'Your heap of shit needs a wheel balance,' I said, and changed up to second.

'*You* need the wheel balance, Big Nose. And I'm gonna give you one later.'

Heap of shit or not, I felt I could have lived out the rest of my life in that car, with her.

'Amber light ahead,' she said, recovering from another fit of giggles. 'Going, going – gun it, you can make it – gone!' and she whooped in delight as I accelerated through the intersection.

'What's the speedo say?'

'Thirty. Might be best to keep to the speed limit. Being a cop and all. You need to set a good example,' and she choked up completely, finding this the funniest thing so far.

I slowed down, worried my own laughter might shake us off course.

'Uh-oh,' from Willow. 'Headlights coming up fast behind.'

'Dented Porsche?' I said, but the quick blurp of a patrol car siren told me otherwise.

'This is gonna be interesting,' from Willow, her voice aimed backwards.

'Better tell me where to pull over.'

'Only thing you need to pull is rank, Detective Sergeant.'

I slowed to a crawl. 'Here?'

'Here,' she said, 'between the Lamborghini and the Ferrari,' then 'Whoa!', but not before the front wheel ran up onto a gutter.

Her laughter rendered her of no further use, but with the wheel as a probe, I felt my way back parallel to the gutter and turned off the ignition.

A last siren-blip as the patrol car pulled in behind. A door opened, closed. 'Anyone we know?' I said.

'Looks about fourteen.' She giggled. 'Should be a pushover. Just act like you can see, Zads!'

A tap at my window. I located the button deftly enough, wound it down.

'Evening, Sir. Could I see some ID, please?'

Nothing in the boyish voice rang a bell, but why would it? I dug out my wallet and handed it over, trying to remember what it contained. No police ID, I was pretty sure. But hopefully my old driving licence. I'd never bothered to cancel it.

'Look my way, please, Sir.'

My licence, for sure. There was no other photo in the wallet.

I hoped I was looking into his eyes, or near enough. I held out my hand in case he was trying to give my wallet back; he was.

'What's the problem, Officer?'

'You're driving without lights, Mr Zadow. Have you been drinking?'

One hurdle crossed: he didn't recognise me. Or my name, without proper rank. A miracle that – it's a burr that sticks in people's memories, with its sharp, thorny consonants.

'A couple, Officer. Earlier. None in the last hour.'

'*I've* been drinking,' from the passenger seat. 'S'my car. My husband here is the . . .' she tried to suppress a laugh '. . . designated driver,' then dissolved into gurgles.

I sensed him bending and staring past me, perhaps playing a torchlight onto her.

'I still have to ask you to take a breathalyser test, Sir.'

Willow clapped her hands together, slow-mo. She seemed to be getting drunker by the second. 'Outstanding, Constable,' she said. 'Without fear or favour! Outstanding!'

'I'd advise your missus to keep herself tidy, Sir. Before she gets herself into trouble. What's that hanging around your neck? Some kind of award?'

The torchlight on me now, surely. Fingers crossed he didn't recognise the medal.

'Just a joke,' I said. 'Private joke. A pretend medal. My friends organised a little ceremony. A sort of roast, really.'

Willow leant over and hid it in her mouth. 'It's chocolate,' she mumbled. 'In silver foil. I'm gonna eat it later.'

'I won't warn you again, Madam. I hope you were wearing your seatbelt before I pulled you over.'

'Of course, Officer.'

'The breathalyser, sir. Blow steadily into this until you hear the beep.'

'No problem,' I said, and offered up an open mouth like a fledge-ling bird and closed my lips around the plastic beak, and blew.

'Point 04,' he said, sounding a little disappointed. 'Below the limit. Just. Perhaps you should take a cab anyway.'

'I can see my own way home,' I said, which set Willow off again.

'Your decision, Sir,' he said. 'As for the lights, I'll let you off with a warning.'

'Sorry,' I said, then couldn't resist adding, 'I must be blind,' for Willow's further benefit.

'Have a good night,' he said, then just bootsteps walking away. A car door closed, but no engine noise.

'He still there?' I asked.

'Watching us like a hawk,' Willow said. 'Let's really give him something to look at.'

She rolled my way, planting her head on my chest and started unzipping below.

'Let's see what we got here then,' she said, easing it out. 'Oh, I'd forgotten what a cute little thing it is. Come to Mummy, baby.'

She bent and took it whole in her mouth, sucking at it with no effect. 'Shy little mouse,' she mumbled.

'Brewers' droop,' I said.

'You only blew .04, baby,' she reminded me. 'Excuses, excuses.'

I reclined my seat and gave myself up to her, hoping for better, but not much exercised either way. Her mouth felt wonderful, but less in a thrilling than a loving way. An engine finally started up behind us, idled, then pulled out and purred past, very slowly, having one last, long look before accelerating away.

'Show's over,' I said. 'You can come up for air.'

'Why stop?' she gurgled, or words to that effect.

She had a point; something was finally stirring down there, but I also felt a slight prickle of caution. Or even of doubt. Maybe the weight of the medal around my neck was trying to remind me of something.

'This is not another mercy fuck, is it?' I said. 'Another token award?'

No answer, but not because her mouth was full. My half-stiff cock had fallen out; she was snoring, softly and sweetly.

I zipped up, my doubts melting away as quickly as they had come, and ran my fingers over the contours of her face.

'I do trust you,' I murmured.

Not her best angle: the head flopped sideways, muscles loosened, the mouth gone slack, dribbling onto my trousers. I eased her up into her seat, then leant across and reclined it a little. She didn't wake, but her head rolled my way with a soft after-snore exhalation of margarita breath. I reached out again and traced the high cheek-bones, the small flattish nose. The lips that I could never see without wanting to kiss them. Never. But it was the eyes my fingertips always came back to: those magical upper eyelids, bred for riding Mongolian ponies – her pet theory – but even better at shooting come-hither glances at her smitten Big Nose, me.

'Jeepers creepers where'd you get those peepers,' I once whispered to her in bed.

'The horse-plains of Central Asia,' came the deadpan reply. 'Circa 20,000 BC. When the human race evolved into my superior subspecies.'

She laughed – even in Willowpedia mode, she liked to take the mickey out of herself – and rubbed noses with me. 'About the same time your lot were eating the last Neanderthals. Though you obviously spared some of the women, Big Nose.'

I laughed with her, now, years later, remembering; she snorted in her sleep, brushed my spider-hand on her face, and rolled her head away.

'You're the *only* one I trust,' I said.

What next? Try to sleep myself? I was far too happy to sleep. Drive her home? Her place or mine? Her home or ours? Ours, surely, after tonight, and the big pleasure buried in that little word distracted me so much I forgot for a time where I was, and what I was doing.

For how long? I came to with a start to find myself driving the car again. Also for how long? And who knows where? And with an unconscious navigator, for fuck's sake! I braked suddenly, then felt my way ultra-slowly, ultra-gently into the kerb without bumping any more Porsches.

I sat there for a time, letting the adrenaline settle, then leant over and kissed my sleeping beauty on the lips. 'Wakey, wakey, sleepyhead. In need of navigation.'

No answer beyond a brief disturbance in the tempo of her snoring.

'Your turn, Siri,' I said. 'Current location.'

'Current location: home.'

'Get up to speed. Not the destination, the current location.'

'Current location: home,' she repeated.

What were the chances? Somewhere between zero and impossible. I asked a third time, and got the same answer. For a long, long time I sat there, disbelieving. It was either a failed joke, a software glitch, or the most astonishing thing she had ever told me. I lowered all four windows and let in the warm, scented night air; frangipani in the mix, sure enough.

'Street *address*, please,' I said.

'7 Claxton Street, City.'

Willow snored on, oblivious to the miracle. Okay, it wasn't the first time I'd pulled up at home without noticing how I'd got there, or remembering the route taken, the corners turned, the red lights navigated on autopilot. And it was only – what? – half a click from the Club to Claxton Street – but it was the first time I'd driven it blind.

'Is there a word for automatic driving, Siri?'

'I'm not sure I understand, Richard.'

'That makes two of us,' I said as I climbed out and tapped my way around the front of the car. It had come to rest against the gutter at a slight angle: a lesser miracle than the drive home, but impressive nevertheless. I stepped up onto the footpath, tapped a fence that was possibly mine, a front gate which probably was, then put my hand on a letterbox which indisputably was.

I stood there brailling the embossed 7 repeatedly, still astounded.

'Do you mean automaticity, Richard?' Siri was saying. 'Also known as Highway Hypnosis. White Line Fever.'

Or blindsight. Could the new shrink, the boss shrink, be right after all? Behind me the passenger door was opening, the other know-all emerging. 'I need a piss,' came a slurred voice.

She gripped my offered arm, pulled herself out, then reversed her grip as she turned and squatted on the edge of the kerb. Silken rustlings as she pushed her pantyhose and knickers down to her ankles, then a steady splashing into the gutter that seemed to last forever.

'Can't get up,' she mumbled eventually, and I slipped an arm under her shoulders and raised her to her feet. She tried to take a step but stumbled, still shackled at the ankles; I caught her easily enough, but kneeling to tug up her underwear while keeping her upright took a little more time and thought.

'First time you've pulled them *on*,' she chuckled, thickly. 'Not in the mood tonight?'

'Can't rip them off if you're not wearing them,' I said.

'I can see straight through your evil designs, Big Nose,' she said, and lifted her head and bit me gently on that mysteriously sexy organ.

I put one arm under her thighs, the other under her shoulders, and lifted her in a clean snatch. The cane was hanging uselessly by its thong from my left wrist, but if I could drive a car home blind, I could carry my tiny darling across the threshold again, surely.

She gurgled happily, which I took to mean she was game if I were. But mostly I was thinking about blindsight, and the wondrous miracle of navigation that had delivered us home, safely. Memo, Bad Prof: you might be onto something after all.

2

I WOKE WITH A THICK, POUNDING HEAD, IN A FOG OF GIDDINESS. Where was I? In a bed, certainly. My bed, hopefully, a safe ship even in the thickest fog.

I turned onto my back; the ship rolled wildly. It took time to notice the hairs on the back of my neck were bristling: was someone prowling around outside? I held my breath, listened.

No sound but a soft snoring, then a shifting of weight next to me. The dog sleeping on the bed again? I reached out a hand to shove her off but felt the glow of the body before I touched it.

The smooth, hairless body.

The fog lifted a little. The body rolled towards me, spluttered, snored on. The breath that washed over my face was hot and sour, but nothing could be sweeter than the salt on the lips when I kissed them.

She was home. And this time, surely, for good.

I snuggled into my snoring beauty and dozed off, still thick-headed and giddy but too contented to care.

A growl from the floor jarred me awake a second time. A dream-growl? No; Scout was up and scratching at the door, growling louder.

'Fuck!' from a male voice, somewhere above me.

The adrenaline rush jerked me upright; the following wave of giddiness almost felled me again.

A crashing noise from the high speakers, then another 'Fuck!'

I swung my legs over the edge of the bed, trying to concentrate. Given a pair of working eyes, I could have fixed on some distant point;

all I could do was keep my giddy head still. I hadn't a clue how long I'd been sleeping. I remembered carrying Willow inside, falling into bed, then not much. My cock felt sticky and my nose raw, so I guess there had been sex of some kinky eskimo sort. Memo, Professor Confessor: what is it with all these protuberances?

The dog barked again, and scratched more frantically at the door; the beauty slept on, but for how long?

'Quiet, girl,' I hissed, and she did her best, choking off her barks with whimpers.

'What the *fuck?*' from above, and more crashing about.

I wasn't prepared for this. I wasn't sure I still *wanted* this – at least tonight, of all nights. I hadn't given him a moment's thought since Willow materialised at the Club.

'Siri,' I said. 'Master bedroom speakers mute.'

Silence, at least to human ears; the dog was still whining at the door.

No point in whining myself; of *course* he would come tonight. As the shock settled, I felt more resentful than scared, or angry; I needed more shut-eye. I sat on the edge of the bed, trying to think my way out of the fog. The rat was in the trap, fait accompli. The shit had happened, as shit happens: unexpectedly. Next problem: how to clean it up?

First things first: I groped about on the bedside table, found the shutter remote behind an empty martini glass, pressed the down-button. The dog barked again, worried by the distant rumble through the walls.

'Quiet, Scout!' I hissed.

I pulled on jeans and T-shirt, a little unsteadily, trying to keep my head as gyroscopically stable as possible.

'Stay,' I said, blocking the door as I opened it. 'You'll just get in the way.'

A strangled bark, and more whimpering as she tried to squeeze past. What to do? Sooner or later the four-legged girlfriend would wake the two-legged, if I left them in the bedroom together. I fumbled

for her handle, let her tug me out into the hall, and eased the door
shut behind us. I'd hung it myself, years back: solid, soundproof cedar.
Sweet dreams, Willow. Fingers crossed.

A muffled fist was banging against the opposite door, also solid
cedar. 'You there, arsehole?' from the hall speakers above me. 'You
hear me?'

'I'm here,' I said. 'What took you so long? I'd almost given up
hope you were coming.'

Stunned, or at least puzzled, silence. 'You *wanted* me to come?'

'Couldn't wait.'

More silence while he grappled with this. My pulse had quickened, if excited more by my own words than his.

'I just wasn't sure you were stupid enough,' I added, for good
measure.

This time he found his tongue. 'You got a death-wish, you mad
cunt?'

'Never felt more alive,' I said, and if my laugh sounded a little
mad, so be it. It could only help to keep him off balance.

'Got big plans for you,' I taunted him. 'I can't tell you how much
I've been looking forward to this night we're going to spend together.'

Quiet again, apart from the bitten-off growlings of the dog, tightly
held, short-leashed, at my side.

'You got a big mouth,' he finally came out with, more quietly, 'for
a blind fuck. You think this shithole will hold me?'

'That's what shitholes are for,' I said, my heart pounding with the
thrill of it now, the adrenaline washing away the last wisps of fog. 'To
hold shit.'

A cry of rage and he started punching the door again.

My next move was obvious: 'Study light off, Siri.'

'Study light off,' she confirmed, followed by another 'what the fuck!'
from the high speakers, then more crashing sounds, more expletives.

This, also, was obvious: he hadn't brought a torch. Had he brought
a gun? Almost certainly. I reached for mine instinctively and found an

empty holster. My turn for a *what the fuck*, but muttered under my breath. Had I hidden it from Willow last night? If so, where? Under my pillow? Under hers? Back behind the beer steins in the cabinet?

More crashings and bangings in an odd senssuround: loudly from the hall speakers above, muffled through the thick door. The dog, straining, finally let loose a volley of barks; I immediately dragged her, resisting, in the opposite direction, out through the back room and into the shed.

'Stay, girl,' I said, and shut her inside. 'Turn yourself off, Siri,' I added, for the same reason. This was between me and him: the last thing I needed was a running commentary.

Scout's barking was barely audible from the hall. The other trapped animal had gone quiet again. I took advantage of this to check on Willow: opening the bedroom door a crack, putting my ear to it, then easing it shut, reassured by her snoring.

Silence still from the spare room opposite. What was he up to? I squatted on my heels, facing the door, and as if it were some kind of mental mirror, tried to put myself in his place. Two options only that I could see: break out through the shutters, or break out through the door.

Which now he would have to do in pitch-darkness.

I reached for the knob and lightly grasped it. Right on cue, it rattled. More expletives, and something about greasy shit, then silence apart from a couple of faint barks the length of the house and another cedar door away.

I pressed my palms flat against the study door as if to sense his next move. It came almost immediately: a shudder in the wood and a grunt from the high speakers as he threw himself against it, hip and shoulder.

A pause, another thump. And another.

The door held, of course. There was no way he could break out without an axe.

'Fuck!' then the thud of frenzied kicking against the wood. 'Fuck! Fuck! *Fuck*!'

More music to my ears, in odd, unequal stereo. I kept my palms flat against the door, relishing each shudder until the music stopped.

Heavy breathing from the speakers, then, 'Can you hear me, you blind fuck?'

'Loud and clear.'

A muffled explosion; I found myself flat on my back on the floor; the world all headache again.

A voice, far-off: 'Get a piece of that, smart-arse?'

The throbbing localised to my forehead, allowing other sensations to make themselves known: wetness in my left eye, a trickle on my cheek, the scent of blood in my nostrils, its salt on my lips.

My first coherent thought: *not again.*

I fingered my brow, gingerly: another tender lump, a raw, wet laceration. But no obvious entry point.

I hadn't been shot.

A lesser pain from further out: something rock-hard wedged between the floor and the small of my back. The Glock? I was lucid enough to remember I'd left it out of reach in the shed. I shifted my weight, reached behind and wrapped my fingers around – what?

A small, metallic apple at first touch.

At second: an apple the size and shape of a doorknob, neatly cored by the bullet that had blown it out of the door.

At third touch: a sticky toffee apple.

I raised it to my nose: blood. Mine. I could have kicked myself. Knowing he'd have a gun, how could I have been so stupid as to put myself in harm's way? If also very lucky. A fresh trickle of blood ran down my cheek; I pinched the laceration on my brow between finger and thumb while I thought things through. Most urgently: was the door still holding? Which *way* was the door?

'Playing possum, shithead? Or did I get lucky with my first shot?'

No clue there: the direction of his voice was mainly from the high speakers. Most likely scenario: the knob had knocked me backwards and I was lying with the door at my feet.

'Jesus, I fucking hope not! I'm not letting you off that easy!'

I cautiously extended both legs, found the wall as expected, then slowly spun myself on my back, slow-mo breakdancing style, till my hands were touching the wall instead. Next move: roll quietly over onto my belly, and feel my way along a row of carefully arranged objects I'd left against the skirting board – screws, screwdriver, two spare metal apples, doorknob face-plates, nail gun, then the door-jamb, and finally the base of the door itself.

Still closed; the back-up bolt holding. But for how long? The thick wood was shuddering, rhythmically, to my touch – if gently. No boots thumping against it, no hip and shoulder – just a steady, muffled grunting from the speakers.

What was he up to now? It took a moment to see the obvious. 'See' was the word: it arrived in my head as a picture. He'd worked a finger or two through the empty lock-hole for leverage, and was trying to tug the door inwards. Perhaps more than two fingers; how wide was the hole? Worst-case scenario: he'd shot out the entire lock mechanism, not just the knob-spindle. I raised another mental picture: the 54mm hole saw I'd used when hanging the door. Which was wide enough for what? Three fingers?

Another grunt, another shudder of the door, another mental image downloading into my head: four fingers, two from each hand, allowing him enough purchase to use both arms for leverage.

Would the slide-bolt hold? A surge of adrenaline cleared my mind. I was a couple of loose screws from certain death. I got up on my knees, keeping to one side in case he took another pot shot through the door, and ran my hand quickly down the jamb until I found the bolt: shuddering, slightly, with each grunt, but secure enough.

The sticky toffee apple in my other hand remembered itself to me. Time to return the compliment? I'd fixed the back-up bolt a hand's span above the lock. Still kneeling, I measured the distance down on the jamb, pictured the target area – four blind worms snaking from a hole – then smashed my blunt object into it, repeatedly, quick-fire: *bang. bang, bang, bang, bang.*

A miss on the first strike – wrist-jarring wood – then a palpable hit – softer, crunchier – and a second and third, then nothing but hard wood again. And a voice, bellowing in pain, but in stereo now, from the speakers above and through the open hole in the door. 'Shit! SHIT! I'll *kill* you, you blind cunt!'

The sweetest music yet. I flopped back onto the floorboards again, out of harm's way, relishing his moment. A small revenge, and only the first I planned – if planned were the word. For the moment, I was improvising.

'Study lights on,' I said to Siri, gave him a three-count glimpse of the damage to his fingers, then added, 'Lights off.'

'Oh, fuck! FUCK! You'll be begging for your life when I get out of here! *And* your fucken dog's! I saw her on TV, you pathetic cunt! I'm gonna shoot the bitch first and make you fucken watch!'

His voice louder from the hole now than the speakers, as if he had his mouth pressed to it.

'You'll wish those blind dog cunts had taken her before I'm finished! Maybe I'll kill her in*stead*! Poetic justice, cunt! Let you think about it for a couple of years before I come back and do you!'

My kingdom for a gun. Or something sharp – a box-cutter, a knife, a *fork* – to shove through the snake hole up to the hilt. I felt along the skirting board with my toes for the screwdriver, but maybe my tongue was a sharp enough weapon.

'You're the one who'll be begging, shithead. I've only just started playing with you.'

Another muffled explosion from the knob-hole – was he using a silencer? – and a simultaneous dull thud from the wall above my head as the spent bullet smacked into it. Luckily I *hadn't* found the screwdriver and started poking around. Memo, idiot: look before you leap. So to speak.

Two more shots in quick succession; plaster- and brick-dust showering down on my upturned face after each. I shut my useless eyes against it, licked my lips clean. A strange tang: gritty, oddly sweetish.

'Who's playing now, Blind Freddie?' from the knob-hole.

I was, but I wasn't about to admit it aloud. Playing possum seemed sensible while I thought things through, my snoring beauty in the next room first among them.

'Ya *there*, you blind cunt?'

He might be using a silencer but could even the unrousable Willow sleep through those spent bullets knocking on her wall? The last thing I wanted was her stumbling out into the line of fire, half-awake. Thinking of which brought a moment of panic: did he know she was in there? Had he been watching the house when we arrived? Almost certainly not. He had threatened to shoot the dog, not her.

I groaned theatrically, hoping to buy a little more thinking time.

It seemed to work. Perhaps he was thinking things through himself. Or still wondering: how lucky had he got?

'Help me,' I said, still improvising. 'Someone. Anyone! I can't move.'

'Don't die on me yet, cunt,' from the hole, loudly. 'We got unfinished business.'

Another shot, but even more muffled, thudded into the wall above me, then clattered onto the floorboards. Which at least gave my panic something to grapple with: what was he up to now? Not hoping to hit me, surely; he must have known I would be out of harm's way. And that spent bullet? The others had stayed embedded in the wall. There was also a different smell in the air – burnt sawdust – followed by a gentle, prickling rain on my face.

I licked my lips again.

Wood-splinters.

He was firing straight through the thick cedar, not through the lock-hole.

For a moment my thoughts went up a dead end: what ammo was he using? Full metal jacket? Then the main anxiety roared back: to what end?

He fired again – another wood-silenced bouncing bullet, another shower of prickly splinters; then, after much the same interval, another. There was method in this madness, clearly. I tried, once again, to put myself in his shoes.

Problem: the lock was blown out, but the door still refused to budge.

Answer: there must be a back-up bolt on the outside.

Possible solution: a lucky shot through the wood might blow it clean off the other side.

'Somebody help!' I called out, still hoping to stall him. 'I can't move my legs. Somebody! Please. Call the cops!'

'Help is on the way, cunt,' from the hole, then the sound of something hard – the gun-barrel? the silencer? – hammering into it, and a crunching, splintering sound. Then another, and another, methodically. Then heavy breathing from the speakers as he stood back and took a spell.

The dust and grit tickled at my nose and throat. I fought the urge to sneeze; I was supposed to be lying there half dead.

'Someone ring an ambulance!' I croaked, but not too loudly. I didn't want that someone to be Willow.

'I'll ring you a fucken undertaker,' he shouted, and started smashing into the door again.

The larger woodchips raining down now made me see the obvious: he'd used his gun like an auger, punching a wider circle of bullet holes around the central lock-hole.

Now it was a hammer, knocking out the wood in between.

To what end was also instantly obvious: get a whole arm through for more leverage, and tug the door open or scrabble about for the bolt.

Either way, I didn't have a lot of time. I'd need more than a toffee apple to stop him, and my Glock was a stepladder too far. I got up on all fours and began groping for the screwdriver with both hands, frantically. They stumbled on the nail gun first; perhaps they'd been searching for it all along, knowing the best tool for the job before I did.

A flare of panic: was it still charged? I'd last used it – when? Three, four days at most, test-firing into the floorboards. I couldn't risk alerting him with the hiss of another test; to the best of my knowledge he thought I was lying there half dead.

Besides, I was out of time. A large chunk of wood clattered to the floor and a shout of triumph from the hole – 'Don't die on me yet, cunt!' – was followed by rat-scrabbling noises, acoustically magnified in the narrow hall.

No mystery sound this: his arm was already on my side of the door, searching for the bolt.

'Help is on the way, cunt,' he shouted, mono from above this time with his elbow blocking the hole.

Fight or flight? The rush of adrenaline did my thinking for me: I was on my feet in an instant, and with one quick step pinned his protruding elbow and forearm against the door with my hip.

'What the fuck?' from the high speakers as he tried to wriggle it free. 'You *lying* cunt!'

I pushed harder, leaning into the door with all my weight. His resistance stopped, abruptly; he began to grunt as he tried to jerk the door inwards again, this time using his entire wedged arm for leverage. And with my weight, I realised, shoving the door in the same direction. Would the bolt hold?

'Push as hard as you like, dickhead!' he encouraged me.

No chance. The gas gun reminded me of its presence as surely as if it had spoken 'current location: right hand' out loud. I pinned *his* hand against the door with my left, pressed the nose of the gun into the back of it, and squeezed the trigger.

A satisfying hiss-thunk; a small recoil; a yelp of pain from above. 'What the *fuck*? You stick a *knife* through my hand? You fucken mad?'

Mad enough to do it again, even though – an alarm bell ringing – I was exposed to another shot. I fired a back-up nail into his wrist, using the webbing between my thumb and forefinger to guide the nose of the gun, then spun aside, back to the wall, out of the line of fire.

Just in time, as another shot passed through the door and the spent bullet bounced off the opposite wall again and clattered to the floor.

'You like that!' he screamed again. 'You like that, you mad fuck?'

Two more followed, in quick succession; then a distinct metallic click, another click, and a muttered, frustrated 'fuck' that was almost a click itself.

Was he out of ammo so soon? I did a quick mental recount, got to seven and decided it was pointless. Too many variables: the size of the magazine; was it full to begin with?; did he have a spare in his pocket?

Plus my foggy morning-after memory.

I checked my own weapon – still almost fully loaded – then slid slowly down onto my haunches and leant it against the skirting board. His arm, nailed to the door a few inches from my nose, was finally still; his moans and grunted mutterings gave me some breathing space.

What next? I'd got to this point mostly by a mix of dumb luck and improvisation, making do with the tools at hand. Or maybe those tools had made do with me. Where would I be without the inaminate world nudging me in the back or shaking my hand from time to time?

'Thank you, gas gun,' I said. 'Thank you, ball-knob.'

Not the funniest joke, but I laughed out of relief.

'Who you talking to?' from the speakers, then a yelp of pain. 'What are these? Shit! What the fuck are *these*?'

The answer came to me vividly: he'd jagged his free hand on the sharp ends of the protruding nails inside the door.

'You've *nailed* me to the door? Oh, Jesus! You mad bastard!'

I'd wanted him caged, yes – but had kept any madness vague in my head beyond that. Certifiable madness, in retrospect: I might as well have been playing Russian roulette. What had I been thinking? So excited by the hunt I hadn't given a thought to the kill? I was safe now, the adrenaline draining from my veins, but it seemed important to sort this out. That little word 'kill' especially. Memo, Good Prof: had some sort of mental safety-catch stopped me? Was there still enough good cop left inside to keep me on the straight and narrow? Enough to stop me giving free rein to my darkest urges?

'You *crucified* me, you psycho fuck?'

I hadn't planned to, but the word thrilled me. And worried me at the same time, finding myself so thrilled. I'd killed him in my head any number of times over the years, but even my bloodiest revenge fantasies took place always in the heat of battle, never in cold blood, when I had him in my power.

'Self-defence,' I said, as much to myself as to him, as if I were already writing up the report. He'd chosen to break into my house armed with a gun; he'd chosen to fire on a serving police officer; he'd chosen to smash his arm through the door. The rat-trap was premeditated, but nothing that followed.

Where – to borrow a favourite word from the Professor – was my *agency*?

'Time please, Siri.'

No answer.

'Power up, Siri.'

'Good morning, Richard.'

'Time, please.'

'2.30 am.'

'Who's there? Who you talking to? Hey! Hey, lady! You see what he's done to my arm?' A brief pause, then again. 'Is that you, Trixie? Help me, darlin'! I'm bleeding to death! Trixie?'

So he *had* been watching the house. I rested back against the wall, unsettled. What else had he seen? Did it even matter now? She was in no danger.

'You remember me, darlin'? Jimmy. Used to mind the door. Keep youse all safe. You see what your boyfriend's done? Nailed me to the fucken door. Help me, please! I'm bleeding out!'

I hoped not. I hadn't worked out the cold-blooded details, but one thing was certain: I wasn't finished with him yet. I inched closer to the door, sniffed for blood but could smell nothing except the plaster dust that clogged my nostrils. What were the chances I'd hit an artery? Down on my belly again, I wiped the palms of my hands across the floorboards beneath the door.

No puddles. Nothing but fine plaster dust and the prickle of woodchips.

'Trixie? Please. For old time's sake!' his voice plaintive now, fake-teary. 'I always looked out for youse girls. You especially. Remember?'

I remembered, but kept my mouth shut as I ran my palms across the face of the door. Two parallel runnels of blood, a hand's width apart, but running dry and sticky before they reached the floor. Nothing fresh.

'I'm man enough to admit I fucked up that night,' the bullshit continued. 'But it takes two to tango. You *were* playing hard to get, babe.'

The scent of blood in my nostrils, finally – but it was my own. The head wound had reopened. I wiped my bloodied hands – his blood – on my jeans, hoping he hadn't picked up anything nasty in prison, then pinched the wound shut again. A temporary fix; something more permanent was needed. Pressure bandage? Needle and thread?

'I never meant to hurt you. Trixie? Jesus, don't pretend you didn't want it. You'd been shaking your arse at me for months.'

Lucky she hadn't woken, if for a different reason. She would have nailed his head to the door. I slithered to the kitchen on my belly and got to my feet, right thumb and forefinger still clamped to my brow.

'It was the ice, babe. Lucky you were there to calm me down. Or who knows what I might have done?'

I pushed my way into the shed past the dog, scrabbled up a tube of superglue from the fixings drawer, unscrewed the top, pressed the nozzle into the wound, squeezed judiciously, then pinched it shut again and counted to thirty.

I'd got to twenty when I remembered the Glock. I pocketed the superglue, got up on tiptoes, and felt about on top of the cupboard with my free hand. Out of reach, even with a dozen standing jumps and brief, blind grabs; I'd need a stepladder or stool – but suddenly there was no time. Alarm bells were ringing in the back of my head again: the flow of bullshit from the speakers had been replaced by a new mystery sound: a sharp, metallic tapping, accompanied by choked-off gasps of pain.

I shoved the dog aside, squeezed out the door – 'Stay!' – and hurried back through the house.

Louder gasps from the hall speakers, keeping in time with that steady *tap-tap-tap*. He was hammering something with the butt of his gun, but what? Metal on metal, clearly, but it took longer to see the obvious: he was hammering at the sharpends of the nails, trying to knock them back through the door.

And therefore (I almost gasped with him) out through his wrist and hand.

I conjured up more detail: 900mm nails, driven through an inch of wood, maybe two of wrist or hand. If he hammered them flush on his side, half-an-inch of nail-head would be protruding on my side, give or take. Loosened enough to lever the rest of the way out with the nailed arm? Would those wide D-heads hold, or tear straight through the flesh? I wouldn't put it past him to try. What was the alternative? Bite his arm off at the elbow, like a wolf in a trap? Nothing to lose either way.

Another metallic tap, then the duller thud of hammer on wood. One down, one to go. A pause while he located the other nail-tip – 'Ouch!' – then the tapping and gasping started up again.

Time to act. I reached for the nail gun, shuffled across on my knees, and shoved the nozzle hard into his exposed elbow.

'Drop the fucking gun,' I said, loudly.

The tapping stopped abruptly, but no gun clattered to the floor. Which meant he was reluctant to part with it, even under duress. I seemed to be reading his mind more clearly now: he must have reloaded, and was pondering whether to take another pot shot through the door. *Good luck with that*, I thought, in case he was also reading mine. I was kneeling to one side, out of the line of fire; only my right arm – and the nail gun – were in harm's way. He would need to shoot through his own elbow to get at me.

'Go ahead,' I said, and ground the nozzle of the nail gun in to his flesh. 'Free shot. You'll only get one.'

'Okay, okay! You win!'

'Then drop the gun.'

'I did.'

'Bullshit. I want to *hear* you drop it.'

'It hit my foot. You couldn't hear . . .'

'Count of three. One. Two.'

An unmistakeable clatter: metal object on wooden floor.

'Kick it away.'

'How can I do that? I'm on my fucken *knees*! Can't *see* a fucken thing anyway!'

The truth? Probably. He would need to be on his knees to shove his arm through the lock-hole. Still on my knees myself, I slid the bolt aside and pushed the gas gun harder into his elbow, opening the door a few inches.

'Ah, *Jesus*! What the fuck you *doing*?'

'Stick your other arm out,' I said, through the gap.

'You think I'm Houdini? I'm facing the other fucken *way*.'

This also had the ring of truth. With his arm through the hole at chest-height he must be on his own knees, facing the door's hinges. But was his gun truly out of reach? For all I knew, he was already groping around on the floor with his free hand.

'Put it on your head then,' I said.

'Put what on my head?'

'Your hand, fucktard.'

'What for? You gonna nail it to my *skull*? Hey, out there! Trixie! You hear what he wants to do, babe?'

I ground the nail gun into his elbow again. 'Hand on your *head*,
I said!'

'Okay! Okay! Fuck! Hand on my head.'

'Smack it.'

'*What?*'

'Smack your head. With your palm.' I upped the pressure of the
gun. 'And keep smacking. Once every second.'

'Okay! *Jesus!* I'm smacking.'

'Louder. I need to know where that hand is at all times.'

An angry sob. 'You broke my fucken *fingers*, remember? It *canes*.'

'If you can pull a trigger you can smack your head, fucktard.
Louder.'

In fact I could hear it, loudly enough. I stood up and put my whole
weight to the door, hip and shoulder; it gave way, jerkily, pushing him
ahead, shuffling on his knees, till it was half-open and I could squeeze
through the gap, nail gun first. The air inside was even more fetid than
usual. Fresh shit? My first thought: the dog. But when? More press-
ingly: where? I ran my hand along the inside face of the door, found
his pinned shoulder, pressed the nail gun into his neck, felt him flinch.

'Keep smacking.'

I dropped to my haunches and frisked him from behind, quickly.
No hidden knife, no second gun. Nothing in his pockets but loose
change and a pack of cigarettes. I confiscated the pack; lighter included
by the rattle of it. I knelt and frisked his legs and feet – no ankle-
holster – then felt carefully about the nearby floor as best I could for
the discarded gun.

No joy.

'Keep smacking,' I said, back on my feet and stepping past him
into the room, but cautiously, hoping to find the gun with my bare
feet before I stepped in something else.

Nothing immediately inside the door. I shuffled further in, back
and forth, softly and methodically, with small, flat-footed dance steps.
I barked a shin on a fallen desk chair, righted it with my free hand,

and kept on shuffling, even more cautiously. Not cautiously enough: my leading foot landed in something wet and slippery, shot out from under me. Dog shit? Worse: oil slick. My other foot slid sideways, the nail gun clattered to the floor as I flailed about, coming down hard on my backside.

For a moment I sat there, taking stock. Nothing broken, it seemed. The smacking had stopped; I could hear him patting the floor instead.

Definitely something left in the magazine, then.

I found the nail gun quickly enough, retracted the safety pressure-tip manually, and squeezed off three flying nails in his direction.

One at least found a target. 'Aah! Jesus! What's that for?'

'You stopped hitting yourself.'

'You just shot me in the *neck*!'

'Flesh wound at this range. Pinprick. You want me to come closer?'

The smacking started up. I set the nail gun down, groped about for the chair, used it to help me back to my knees, then up on my feet. Sliding it ahead of me across the slippery floor it made a serviceable walking-frame. A serviceable white cane, also: there was a bump and slight skewing as the chair's left front foot found the gun.

I picked it up and sat down in the chair.

'You can stop hitting your head,' I said. 'Got what I wanted.'

9 mm Smith & Wesson, Military and Police issue, by the feel of it. Serial number intact. Remembering my unregistered Glock, I almost laughed out loud again: who was the good guy here, and who the bad? Although since good guys have no use for silencers I unscrewed the unwieldy cylinder from the custom-threaded barrel and jammed it into a pocket of my jeans. The gun felt more like itself without it: more balanced, more compact. More familiar. I dropped the magazine into my palm and hefted it: not quite empty, but hard to guess by weight. Standard-grain, maybe three rounds; heavier full metal jacket, maybe only one or two. The perforations in the magazine were too small for my stubby fingertips to penetrate. What about my tongue?

The idea was only half-serious, but I lifted the clip to my lips as if it were a cob of corn and ran the tip of my tongue along those tiny open portholes, all the same. Two rounds. Or was I having a lend of myself?

'Yummy ammo,' I said, and this time did laugh out loud.

'Having fun, you sick fuck?'

'More than I've had for years. Thanks to you.'

I checked the slide-lock on the stock: closed, which meant another round in the breech. I replaced the magazine, stood up, holstered the gun almost without thinking about it, and managed to skate slowly across the oily floor and through the door. Dust-filled air outside, but at least it didn't stink. And with that thought came a realisation; the shit-smell on the other side of the door wasn't the dog's.

'Hey! Where you going? *Hey!* You got me. You got my *gun.* You win, okay!'

Back on terra firma, I gripped the big handle of his arm, and dragged the door towards me.

A gasp of pain through the narrowing gap, then, 'You gonna *leave* me here? Ring an *ambulance*, for Christ's sake!'

'Might ring you an undertaker,' I said, and the pleasure of shoving his own words back down his throat was almost as satisfying as if I'd used a screwdriver.

'You're a cop! You can't just *kill* people.'

'Looks like self-defence to me.'

The door jolted shut; his yelping switched to mono from the hall speaker: 'You gonna leave me *hanging* here? Leave me to bleed to death?'

I slid the bolt home. 'More likely shit yourself to death.'

This was less self-defence now than self-satisfaction. But surely I'd earnt it; I couldn't have stopped myself anyway.

'Shit happens,' I said, 'including the shit of the crucified.'

Then fell silent, astonished. Where had this spooky connection come from? My hand went automatically to my right biceps, as if feeling the shape of the tatt might help me make sense of it all.

The cross, the pile of shit. Memo, Prof: I'm out of my depth here. Pure coincidence, or something else?

'Help!' he screamed, perhaps spooked himself, albeit for a different reason: I must have been planning to crucify him all along. 'Trixie! Help! I know you're there! You gonna just let him get away with this? Hey! Babe! Wake up! I'm running out of time!'

'Takes days to die of crucifixion,' I told him. 'I'll figure out what I'm going to do with you way before then.'

In fact I realised what I was going to do next even as I spoke. Or maybe my hands had realised for me and I was following their lead again. My hands and my feet: I set down the nail gun, half-walked, half-jogged back to the shed, pushed in past the dog, went directly to the tool cupboard and lifted the pincer-pliers from their designated hook. My other hand still felt empty; what was it trying to tell me? Something to stem the bleeding, of course: his, this time, not mine. The tube of superglue nudged my thigh, cheekily; an amusing thought, but I needed something bigger. Four wounds: two exit, two entry. I settled on what felt like a three-inch bandage-roll from the first-aid box, and wedged it in another pocket.

Which also, usefully, contained a few scraps of pig's ear. 'Good, girl,' I said, tossing them through as I tugged the door shut. 'Stay, girl.'

I had a good mental picture of the protruding arm by now; I jogged straight back to the study door, wedged his elbow with my hip, located his pinned hand, fingered the jutting nail-head, pinched it between the jaws of the pliers, and pulled it smoothly out.

'What are you doing now? *Stop!*'

The nail through the thicker wrist was more stubborn, but finally yanked loose with a sob of pain and a fine spray of blood on my face. I found the tiny gusher and ground my thumb in hard – First Responder Protocol, even without gloves – hoping again he hadn't picked up something in prison.

'Fuck! *Fuck!*'

'Keep still. You can have your arm back after I've finished.'

Maintaining the pressure on the wound with one hand, I tugged the rolled bandage from my pocket with the other and tore the cellophane wrapping off with my teeth. He moaned but offered no resistance as I straightened his arm and wrapped the bandage around his bleeding hand and wrist, two-handed now, pulling it tight after each loop.

A groan as I pulled the last loop extra-tight. '*Enjoying* yourself, you fucken sadist? Feels like you're sawing it *off*.'

I fixed the clip fastener and released the arm. 'All yours,' I said as it slithered back down its hole. Rat hole, snake hole, cockroach hole – pick an analogy.

I dropped down onto my heels again, back against the doorjamb, head a few inches to one side of the hole. I'd searched him for concealed weapons, but why take the risk? Heavy breathing from the open hole, with stereo back-up from the speakers, then the faint reek of shit, all mono.

I shuffled a few inches sideways, still on my heels, seeking fresher, or merely dusty, air. The groans had given way to mutters; I could almost hear him running his hand over the bandage, probing, checking.

'Didn't catch that,' I said to the hole. 'Come closer.'

Chair-dragging sounds, then his voice, but subdued, as if still keeping some distance from the hole. 'So what now?'

'Dunno, Jimmy. I'm making this up as I go along.'

'Can I at least have the lights on?'

'Study lights on, Siri,' I said, gave him enough time for another half-dazzled glimpse of his prison cell, then added, 'Study lights off, Siri.'

'That's fucken *all*?'

'It's more than I've had lately.'

Silence again. Then, more quietly: 'So what is this? Some kind of fucken empathy lesson? You leave me in the dark all night and I'm supposed to feel your pain?'

'The only pain you're going to feel is your own,' I promised him.

More silence. The stink from the hole seemed to be following me. A cigarette would help; on cue, my hip-pocket nudged me. I extracted the pack – his – lit up and sucked in a lungful. Camels they weren't, but they served their purpose. I released a long, lazy exhalation through my overworked nose, then inhaled again, letting the ticklish glow fill the rest of my being. It felt good; as good – this idea also tickled me somewhere deep and weird inside – as anything I'd ever smoked after sex.

'Enjoying yourself,' he said, his voice close to the hole. Perhaps he was trying to suck in some fresh air himself.

'Not my first choice,' I said, 'but they'll do.'

'Does the condemned man get a last cigarette?'

Why not, I thought, even if the final sentence had yet to be handed down. 'Stick your good hand out.'

'And have you put a nail in *that* one?'

'Coffin nail only.'

No response. I rested the cigarette in the hole, burning-tip inwards. 'It's sitting there if you want it,' I said, half-expecting a yelp as he fumbled for it in the dark.

And was struck by my stupidity again. Blind stupidity, literally: he would have watched it coming all the way, a tiny, glimmering beacon.

I reached out to reclaim the butt, but too late. I could have kicked myself. He probably had his eye to the hole all along, drawn to the faint glow each time I inhaled. How much had he seen? Bullet holes in the opposite wall; debris on the floor? Me squatting just around the corner, complacently smoking?

At least he had no gun.

He did have a torch, which I'd handed to him. A tiny, temporary torch – but he could grow it into a larger one easily enough. And no doubt would, survival being the true mother of invention.

'Peter Jackson Blues,' he said from the speakers above for some reason. To distract me? He was on his feet again, shuffling about, no doubt puffing steadily on his light source, inspecting his jail cell by glimmer-light.

'Who lives in this shithole? Imelda fucken Marcos?'

What could he see besides shoes? What didn't I want him to see? I put myself behind his eyes: the desk covered with inflammables; Willow's handmade stationery; her customised envelopes. Sooner or later the butt would burn down; if the obvious didn't hit him between the eyes it would bite him between the fingers.

A page-tearing sound, then a page-crumpling: a paper-twist taper. I shuffled closer on my heels, crabwise, sniffed at the hole. An acrid top-note of smoke over the smell of shit, but sharper in the back of the nose than tobacco.

Another page-tearing, another crumpling; he was passing the flame on to the next relay torch. My nose told me the smoke was getting thicker in there; as if on cue, he coughed. The last thing I needed was the banshee-screech of a smoke alarm; not even Willow would sleep through that.

'Siri,' I said. 'Smoke alarm, study. Off.'

'Study smoke alarm off,' she said.

His voice was immediately back at the hole, half-shouting, half-coughing. 'I know you're there, Trixie! I'm bleeding to death in here. Ring the ambos! Please.'

'Calling Emergency Services in five seconds,' Siri piped up from the speakers. 'Okay?'

'Okay, darlin'!' he shouted. 'Yes! Call Emergency.'

'Cancel call, Siri,' I said. The last thing I needed was an accidental triple-O call.

'Call cancelled.'

'What fucked-up game are you playing?' he shouted, coughing and stumbling around the room. Next thing he was banging at the aluminium shutter. 'At least roll up the fucken shutter! I can't *breathe* in here.'

'Nice try,' I said. 'Breathe through the hole in the door.'

More stumbling about, then he surfaced at the hole again, sucking in air like a breaching whale.

'For Chrissake,' he wheezed, 'I'm choking to death.'

'So blow your candle out.'

The fake wheeze vanished; he turned back into the room and raged about, smashing up furniture by the sound of it. I settled onto my haunches and lit another Peter Jackson Blue, enjoying the show, finding the soundtrack of his anger paradoxically soothing. Maybe I was fucked-up, at least more than I thought.

My calm lasted only till he breached at the hole again. 'I'll give you a fucking candle,' he screamed, megaphone loud. 'Got enough wood in here for a bonfire!'

Blindsided again, for want of a better word. My first, panicky thought: *should I wake Willow?*

'So roll up the shutter or I'll burn your fucken house down, Blind Freddie!'

A bluff, surely. Playing the only hand he had left. I took a mental glance at my own last card: the sprinkler system in the ceiling, heat-activated.

'I'll count to three, you dumb bastard! One!'

The furniture might burn but the house would survive. Would or should? Memo, self: proper risk assessment. Not much danger to me if it went up in flames – and plenty of time to get Willow and Scout out – but this was high-stakes poker. Did I really want to bet my smart-house on it?

'Two!'

It struck me that I'd come to take the house too much for granted, like a garment worn so intimately it went unnoticed. Or less a garment than another layer of skin, or even shell: a smart-exoskeleton extending the range of my senses. It has ears everywhere, and antennae tuned to strange bat-frequencies. It has multiple mouths of multiple sizes, and powerful muscles to open and close them; I'd been flexing the shutters up and down all week.

'Three!'

It could sniff out smoke, and sense heat. The one thing it couldn't feel was pain. Except by proxy. And I was its proxy. In a blink – the only thinking-time I had – I realised I didn't want my house hurt. Memo, Prof (you'll love this one): I would feel its pain.

'Last chance, cunt!'

'It's your funeral pyre,' I said.

The words leapt from my mouth before I could stop them. Risk management was fine, but there was also pain management. Which pain was worse: my house going up in flames or him walking free? At least the house was insured.

'You barking mad?' he screamed. 'You'd burn your *house* down?'

'You'll burn first.'

A moment's disbelief, then 'Fire!', still megaphone loud, 'Fire! Trixie! Anyone! Ring the fire brigade!'

If I were mad, it was in a usefully careless – care*free* – way. Which made for good poker.

'Trixie,' I raised the stakes. 'Grab the photos. The dog. Anything else we might need to save. If this shithole goes up in flames.'

Silence beyond the door. I lit another cigarette, giving him time to think about it. More mad carelessness? I'd been riding my luck – a couple of close shaves, a head wound that still throbbed – but that was forgotten. Maybe it was the dregs of Scotch courage, maybe it was having Willow back, maybe it was the new hard toy in the holster – but I felt invulnerable. I inhaled deeply, unworried by the glow; he could stare out the hole all he liked, he would find no answers here.

Seductive, this growing sense of agency. Another of your pet words, Prof, but it'll do. Especially since I arrived at it my way. Keep your talking cures, your anger groups, your life-writing classes; I've gone down the alternative medicine route with a vengeance. Literally. The notion had me smiling grimly, if only to myself. What's revenge if not natural medicine, the instinctive self-help therapy of every victim, ever? Maybe I could write the manual. Nutty titles popped into my

head as I puffed. *Applied Anger Management. Revenge Fantasy Therapy.*
I spluttered out a mouthful of smoke; thinking up the names was
almost as much fun as the revenge itself. *Cognitive Violence Therapy.*
Practical Self-Empowerment.

All quiet behind the door. Was he cooking up another surprise?
Who cared?

'Feeling disempowered?' I said, stubbing the butt out on the
floorboards.

'What?'

Perhaps a few laughs was all it took in the end. *Self-Amusement*
Therapy. Backed up with a little *Aroma Therapy*: I shook out another
cigarette and passed it back and forth under my nose cigar-fashion,
savouring the spice of the dried tobacco leaf. Beggar's choice maybe,
but still sweet and earthy – mushroomy, almost – and somehow
warm, even unlit. Hard to put these complex flavours into words, but
not as hard as complex feelings. My state of mind had been bipolar all
night, swinging between anger and calm, foreboding and contempt,
recklessness and caution, relief and murderous intent. Not much pity
in the mix, it struck me – and zero forgiveness, still. Even my laughter
had a cutting edge.

'Private joke,' I said.

'You think this is funny?' from the hole. 'You've had your fun!
What more do you want?'

Good question. The last question standing. I deftly flipped the
cigarette into my mouth and lit up, thinking. 'Closure,' I finally said,
another joke-word, but it too came out with menacing intent.

'What the fuck's *that* supposed to mean? I can't move my arm.
Fingers on the other hand are busted. You gonna *torture* me to death?'

'Mental torture, maybe.'

Either way, I was long past the point of pleading self-defence. The
burning butt nipped at the insteps of my fingers; I took a last puff and
flicked it through the lock-hole.

'Another fire-starter,' I said, 'if you want to take the easy way out.'

He stamped, repeatedly, on the floor, less putting the butt out perhaps than stomping me to death through the only proxy at hand. 'You forget to take your medication, you sick fuck? Do what you want! You think I give a shit?'

'That's the spirit,' I said. '*Practical Anger Management*!'

My voice had a dull, close-bouncing acoustic; I was surprised to find myself facing the door, inches away. I had shuffled across on my knees without thinking about it.

'What are you? My fucken therapist?'

'Worse,' I said. 'I'm your therapy.'

My thoughts were clarifying fast, as if that thick door were as much a reflector as a transmitter.

'You talk shit,' from the speaking hole. 'You open your mouth and nothing but shit comes out.'

'Think about it,' I said. 'You've got a brain. Case in point: Degree in Ag. Science, no less. Stroke of genius that. You put a lot of effort into getting out of jail. Two years' hard labour in the prison library. It gave your shit life meaning. Purpose. Got you through those long solitary nights in D Block Bottom.'

I laughed, but if I were mocking him, I was also mocking my reflection in the wooden mirror between us. Mental age mid-teens, and falling fast.

'What would you do without me?' I said to the door, and the door might as well have echoed it straight back.

'Shut the fuck up! I don't care what you do, just shut the fuck up!'

I was having far too much angry fun to shut up. 'Cut me some slack. I've got a bit bottled up myself. Takes two to tango. Been waiting a long time for this.'

His mouth was up against the speaking hole again, screaming, 'You know what? You're right. I did think a lot about you inside. And you know what kept me going? Being *glad* I didn't kill you. Glad you survived. You're fucken blind. And I did it. Gave me the warm fuzzies every time. Made me so happy knowing you'll never see again. 'Cause nothing you do to me can compare with what I've done to you. Not ever.'

Mental age ten in our race to the bottom. Memo, Prof: nothing like Infant Regression Therapy to recharge the batteries. Mine, as well as his.

'Dunno about that,' I said. 'I hear you have to sit down to piss.'

'What's that supposed to mean?'

'It sprays out all over the place. Fucking garden spinkler. Sideways, backwards.'

'Who says?'

'I read your case notes. From the hospital. The night in question.'

'You're not *allowed*,' he said, the plaintive tone more five years old now than ten.

'A real page-turner. Couldn't put it down.'

'Bullshit!'

'Can't tell you how happy that made *me*,' I said. 'Degloving injury of the penis,' I added, savouring the words. 'And all I did was dab a bit of glue on it.'

Silence. And in the silence another kind of echo from that door, or a memo from a different self, standing back, further off. A less fucked-up self? A puzzled self, perhaps: what next? And calmer, certainly: are you done yet?

Not yet. 'You should lodge a Maims Claim,' I said. 'The premiums were paid up. I did them myself. 96,310 bucks for a useless cock. Same as two big toes.'

A cry of rage, the door shuddered. 'Glue this, you mad cunt!' he shouted, and before I had time to think he had his other arm through the hole, his flailing hand found and gripped the back of my neck and jerked me off balance face-first into the door.

I twisted free easily enough – he didn't have the leverage to pin me – and reached down for the nail gun, then hesitated.

'Cut it – *off* – for all – I care!' he shouted between grunts, the door shuddering as he tried again to tug it inwards. 'Only need – one hand – to take care – of you.'

Maybe it was the fresh adrenaline shock, maybe it was the fresh blood trickling down my cheek, but I knew exactly what I wanted to do with him. The quibbling voice was drowned out; the new instructions came through so loud and clear, and so blindingly obvious, in hindsight, that yes, Prof, I'd possibly known all along.

I stubbed out my little torch and felt for the bolt: trembling rhythmically as he tried to tug the door inwards, but still holding.

'Be careful what you wish for,' I snarled.

I knocked the slide-bolt open with the side of my hand, and stepped quickly away as the door was jerked inwards by the force of his weight. His yelp was less triumphant than agonised; he crashed to the floor inside his jail cell as his arm came free.

I backpedalled rapidly up the hall and squatted with my back to the front door, setting the nail gun down out of harm's way.

'Where are you, shithead?' he was shouting, still stumbling and flailing inside the study. 'I know you're in here!' Continuous crashing and banging sounds, as if he was just throwing anything he could get his hands on around, trying to keep my ears disorientated. Smart move, if I had been there with him.

'I'm out here,' I shouted, and there was silence. 'Come and get me,' I added. 'I'm waiting for you.'

'Yeah. Sitting there with a gun.' His voice just inside the study door, by the sound of it, but venturing no further. 'Think I'm stupid? I'm not sticking my head out into a shooting gallery.'

I drew the gun, removed the magazine, flipped its last three bullets out onto the floor, and sent the empty mag clattering after them.

'Out of ammo,' I said, although that wasn't entirely true. He didn't know I was packing a loaded tube of glue again.

'You expect me to believe that?'

'I'm sitting with my back to the front door. It's unlocked. Get past me and you're home free.'

'Bullshit.'

I sent the gun spinning across the floor in his direction. 'Your choice of weapons, gladiator. The cudgel. Or the short stabbing sword.'

'You talking in riddles again, you fucking lunatic?'

'Blunt object or sharp instrument. There's a screwdriver to the right of the door.'

He groaned to hide the sound of his movements, but the hard hallway echoes told me exactly where he was: down on his knees, scrabbling around.

The silencer jammed into my left jeans pocket reminded me of its presence – a handy blunt object – but my weapon of choice was in the other pocket, its nudging more insistent. I reached in and loosened the cap: safety off.

'How am I meant to find anything with these fucken hands?' he said.

'Lights on, Siri,' I said.

A second of surprised silence, then he was up on his feet sprinting my way. Three steps, four, five; I barely had time to shout 'Lights off' and roll sideways before he was on me. Something sharp struck the door – he'd gone for the Phillips-head sword – as I scrambled back past him on all fours, out of reach. I turned to face him; he had also turned and was flailing about with his weapon. Mine was still in my pocket, useful only in close-quarters combat. His heavy breathing made him easy to locate; standing with his back to the door, jabbing his gladius (the Latin word popped back into my ten-year-old brain, effortlessly) in an arc to keep me at bay while he fumbled with the doorknob behind him.

Which hand was he using for which, I wondered? Neither was in good nick, but the left was surely in better shape than the right. Was he a southpaw? I needed to know before I got closer.

A gasp of pain as he rattled the knob, unable to get a purchase, which meant the crucified arm. Probably.

'Lying cunt,' he said. 'It's locked.'

'It's open,' I said, and stepped aside, guessing correctly he would make a lunge in the direction of my voice.

He retreated just as quickly, jabbing left and right as he struggled with the doorknob behind his back. All this getting easier to picture, as were his difficulties with the ancient colonial rim lock. Even in broad daylight it was as much an IQ test as a latch. The knob itself was part of the slide assembly; he could twist and rattle it as much as he liked, it also needed to be pulled sideways.

A duller acoustic to his heavy breathing and grunting; he had turned to face the door, trying to get more leverage. Time to act. I didn't want to chase him outside; the streetlights would tip the balance of arms in his favour. I charged immediately, shoulders first, smashed him into the door, and had him wrapped up in a full nelson before he had time to think. His arms were still free from the elbow; the flailing screwdriver grazed my long-suffering brow, but without enough force to penetrate, as I spun him sideways, hooked his right leg with mine, and tripped him face-first onto the floor, letting his body take my full weight as he landed. The house shook; the air went out of him; his little Phillips-head stabbing sword clattered away across the floorboards, out of reach.

Even winded, and half-crippled, he wasn't easy to pin. But if he'd been pumping iron in his prison for the last two years, I'd also been working out in mine. Gripping his thighs with my legs, I rolled him onto his side – more a half nelson now, using the floor as a tag-team partner – and pinned his bandaged arm beneath him, freeing up my own left arm.

He was still gasping for breath as I tugged the glue from my pocket, finished unscrewing the cap one-handed and flicked it away.

The smell was pungent; he immediately began bucking and squirming with extra force.

'*Again*, you sick fuck? You think gluing my cock is funny? You didn't do enough damage the first time?'

'An eye for an eye,' I said.

'My *eyes*? You gonna glue my *eyes*?'

He thrashed his head around; I wedged it sideways against the floor with my forearm. Through the acrid smell of the glue came the faint stink of shit. Had he shat his pants again, or was it just old shit, at close quarters? I increased the pressure against his temple until the fight went out of him and he groaned and went slack.

'Not my eyes,' he begged. 'Please, mate. Not my eyes.'

'Sharia law,' I said, but the fight had gone out of me too. Maybe the smell of shit was the key; maybe the tears. Maybe the hurt kindergarten plaintiveness.

'You started it,' he whimpered, ridiculously.

I lay there on top of him, cocked weapon in hand. I'd have to act soon or the ammunition would harden in the snout of the barrel. But the whisper was back again, more clearly. Memo, self: where is the pleasure in torturing an incontinent five-year-old? Even for you, another incontinent five-year-old, emotionally speaking.

Preoccupied, I failed to hear the bedroom door open, but the voice that bounced down the hall had my immediate, startled attention. 'Rick! What's all the noise out here? Is everything alright?'

My captive bucked violently, catching me off-guard. 'Trixie? Help! Please! Sick fuck's trying to kill me.'

'Siri, lights on!' she shouted as I fought to get an arm around his neck then a startled 'Jesus Christ!' then, instantly, more calmly, 'Siri, ring the police.'

'Ringing Emergency Services in five seconds,' from Siri. 'Okay.'

'Not okay,' I said. 'Everything's under control, sweetheart.'

'Call cancelled,' from Siri.

'Siri,' Willow repeated, firmly and slowly. 'Ring. The. Police.'

'Ringing Emergency Services in five seconds. Okay?'

I raised my own voice. 'Not okay, Siri! Not yet! I'm not finished.'

'Ring the police,' gasped from underneath me, as I jammed his neck in the crook of my elbow. 'Trixie. Please.'

'Everything's under control,' I repeated.

'Doesn't much look like it,' she said. 'Blood everywhere.'

'His, not mine.'

'Really?' she said, but calmer now, taking things in. 'Your face is a bloody mess. Again.'

'Glancing blow.'

'Bullet holes in the wall. 'And what's this – a *gun*?'

'His.' He tried to gasp something; I tightened my choke-hold. 'I disarmed the intruder, Your Honour, and subdued him.'

'For now.' Her voice from lower down as she picked up the Smith & Wesson. 'What's your next move, genius? Starve him to death? Sooner or later you have to let him go.'

'I'm fine,' I said. 'As long as the lights are off.'

'Hello. Here's the magazine.' I sensed her stoop, pick it up. 'Empty,' she said, in her most matter-of-fact Chinese risk-assessor mode.

'There's a couple of bullets rolling around somewhere,' I told her.

He managed to wheeze out some words. 'Ring – the – cops. Hey – Robot. Siri. Please – ring – the – cops.'

'Nail gun,' she continued her inventory. 'Busted lock-parts. Screwdriver. Dust and woodchips everywhere. What have you boys been up to out here? Midnight renovations?'

'Your fucken boyfriend nailed me to the *door*!' from beneath me.

'He's not my boyfriend, he's my husband. What are you doing with that glue, husband?'

'He's gonna *blind* me, Trixie!'

'Better get on with it then,' she said to me. 'Then I can clean you up.'

I tried not to laugh. *That's my girl*. Full of surprises, even if a moment later I wonder why I'm ever surprised. She's capable of anything.

'This ain't fair,' he whimpered. 'He started it!'

'You started it,' she said, less an infantile tit-for-tat than a cool statement of fact.

He screwed his right eye shut as I tried to force the lids apart; I realised the task was beyond me, one-handed.

'Let me,' from Willow, her voice close at hand. 'I've got the tools for this job.' Her sharp nails raked my fingers as she took the tube from me, as if to prove her point. 'Just keep him still.'

I rolled onto my back, cradling him tandem-jump style, my legs wrapped around his thighs, my arms pinning his, his chin forced down onto his chest by the pressure of my hands behind his head.

Willow straddled him; straddled both of us. He struggled even more frantically, then squealed in terror.

'What the fuck? You sticking a *knife* in my eye?'

'I might if you keep thrashing about,' she said, and I could see, clearly, those long nails – did she still paint them the same pill-box red? – prising his lids apart, her own eyes narrowed even further as she concentrated on the surgery.

'Takes thirty seconds to set,' I reminded her.

'Quicker if you blow on it,' Willowpedia reminded me back, and did exactly that.

'One down,' she said. 'One to go.'

'Please!' he squealed. 'Please! Not the other one!'

'Done,' she said in no time at all, and I released him, and he rolled away, then crawled, frantically, further up the hall, sobbing.

'I can't see a thing! You fucken dogs! You *blinded* me!'

'Temporarily,' I called after him. 'Unless you try to rip them open too.'

'Six weeks,' from Willowpedia again, in precise, medical mode. 'The conjunctiva sheds the outer layer of cells in six weeks.'

She was on her feet, moving around making a last risk assessment, methodically picking things up from the floor before setting them down at my side. Weapons, mostly: I could recognise each by its noise-signature as it made contact with the floor: gas-gun thud, screwdriver clatter, doorknob roll. Glue tube? A kind of dull skitter.

'Best keep these out of harm's way,' she said.

The Smith & Wesson wasn't among them, nor the bullets. Three sharp metallic clinks from her direction were followed by a lower-pitched clunk, only briefly mysterious: she had reloaded the magazine then pushed it home in the grip. It was also no mystery that she knew her way around a handgun – I'd taken her to the city shooting range as a surprise birthday present – but what was she planning to do with it?

I waited for the telltale click of the safety, half heart-in-mouth, half wonderstruck. Nothing was beyond my darling, and anything and everything she did was fine by me.

'Your call,' I told her. 'You've got as much reason as me.'

'Hardly, Big Nose,' she said. 'I don't even remember it.'

Her voice came from above me, but she was facing down the hall. I could all but see her looking from him to the gun in her hand and back again; I could all but hear her big brain ticking over, figuring the odds.

'He raped you,' I reminded her. 'He nearly brained you.'

'And you raped him,' she said, matter-of-factly. 'With a tube of superglue. Then he shot you in the head. Not sure where all this eye-for-an-eye stuff is going to end up.'

'He's sure. He came here to finish the job. He broke out of *jail* to finish the job.'

'I'd shoot him as soon as look at him,' she continued her risk management. 'But not for what he did. For what he might do.'

'What's taking so long, you sick fucks?' came a sob from the other end of the hall. 'Ring the ambos!'

What was taking her so long? Still she stood there, queen of the snap-decision makers, unable to make up her mind for the first time in her life.

'What if he breaks out again?' she said. 'Comes after you again. After *us*.'

Which made my mind up, at least. I reached out, hooked her elbow and tugged her gently downwards, less interested in vague future risks than the immediate promise of that small word. Us.

'Fucken police brutality,' from the far end of the hall.

'You going to be able to explain this?' she said, kneeling at my side.

'Self-defence,' I told her.

'And me?'

'You don't explain anything. You slept through it all. Hear no evil, see no evil. Speak no evil.'

'He'll say otherwise.'

'His word against mine. And yours. Who are they going to believe? The escapee who broke into the house with a gun, or the helpless blind bloke?'

'Better get your story straight then.'

'I'm not much of an eyewitness, Your Honour,' I said, and she chuckled, obligingly. 'The lights were off. Luckily, I was able to disarm him. Then subdue him. Happened to have a tube of glue in my pocket.'

'Again?' She settled on the floor next to me, shoulder to shoulder, our backs to the door. 'Sounds premeditated.'

'I always carry a tube, Your Honour. Loaded. Safety on.'

She chuckled again, her upper body vibrating pleasantly against mine. 'Never bring a gun to a glue-fight. Especially one with you.'

'You'd better wipe your prints off Exhibit A,' I suggested.

'My fingertips are still *stuck* to it.'

My turn to chuckle. 'I meant the gun. But, yes, the glue too.'

She pressed the small tube into my palm, sticky to the touch, like a tiny tar baby. 'Just make sure yours are on it.'

I polished it carefully with the hem of my T-shirt – then pressed my prints all over it.

'The gun too?' she asked.

'The gun's fine. I disarmed him. You tidied up. Prints everywhere. They can figure it out.'

She set the Smith & Wesson down – a soft wooden clunk – then leant her head on my shoulder.

'Lights off, Siri,' she said, and joined me in my world.

Sounds: a background of moans and muttered curses; her breathing calm and even in the foreground.

Smells: dust, sawdust, the shit faint and far away now.

'You two mad fucks deserve each other,' from that direction.

I hadn't deserved her – at least in recent months – but maybe I could make up for that. There was no one like her; I must never lose her again. I ran my fingers over her face; her eyes were closed; I bent my head and kissed her perfect lids. Which – as I must have known all along, must have known from the first moment I saw her – were the least exotic thing about her.

V
SIGHT

'I'VE BEEN THINKING,' I TOLD HER.

'Uh-oh,' she said.

She was propped up on her pillows, water glass in hand, aspirin fizzing. She tossed them down, leant over and pressed her lips to mine. The kiss was wet and tart and a little fizzy itself.

'I'm late,' she said, and rolled away out of bed. 'Tell me tonight.'

'I might forget it by tonight. I forget all my best thoughts.'

A small, distinct click as she fastened her bra. 'That's because you have too many of them. They can't all fit in that big think-box.'

She hop-stepped into her silk knickers, then sat back on the bed to tug on her pantyhose.

'Siri,' I said, raising my voice, 'got time for a heart to heart?'

'Of course, Richard,' came the smooth contralto from on high. 'I'm always here for you.'

'I thought you'd broken up with that bitch,' from Willow.

'We're still friends. She's a good listener. Unlike some I could name.'

A muffled chuckle into a rattle of coathangers. 'Okay,' she said, turning back from the wardrobe. 'You win. Tell me. But one thought only. One thought a day.'

'I'm on a quota?'

'Clock's ticking.' Her voice muffled again as she pulled something on over her head. 'You'd better get started.'

'None so blind as those who cannot see,' I said.

'Very profound, Zen Master. Meaning what in your particular case?'

'That would be two thoughts,' I said. 'You'll have to wait till tomorrow.'

She padded past the end of the bed and pinched my big toe in passing. 'One thought, smart-arse, with an appendix.'

Joyful to be back with her, fooling around as of old – even if it had only been a fortnight so far – I felt my eyes moisten. It was a prickly moisture, sharpened by something still unsaid. Or not so much unsaid, as not yet said enough.

'Come back here,' I said, patting the bed, and after a moment's hesitation she sat, her hip warm against mine. I found her hand, held it lightly.

'It means,' I said. 'I'm sorry. Ashamed of myself.'

'That's a specific sorry, or non-specific?'

'I shouldn't have hit you.'

'So you've been saying every day for the past week. It wasn't you, Rich You weren't yourself. This is you.'

'Don't let me off so lightly. I knew where you were. I can see that now. I see a lot of things more clearly. So to speak.'

'I'm not sure I buy this blindsight theory,' she said, lightly. 'You still bump into stuff.'

'I'm trying to be serious. I'm talking about seeing things in *me*.'

She leant forward and slipped into her shoes. 'You want me to lodge a Maims Claim? Maybe you should lodge one against me. You saved my sorry arse – twice – and how did I repay my hero? Left him high and dry.'

'Did me good. Tough love, but no more than I deserved. After everything you'd been through.'

'Statute of limitations, Big Nose. It's over.'

'That's your considered legal opinion?' I said. 'Three-month limit for a Maims Claim.'

I sensed the smile on her face. 'Personal statute. I gave as good as I got. Hardest three months of my life.'

Mine too, but she knew that. That was rather the point. Love so tough it had looked like hate at times. She rose from the bed and stepped towards the mantelpiece mirror. A mystery click was followed by the studied silence that explained it: removal of a lip-gloss cap.

'You want my considered legal opinion?' she said eventually.

I had to laugh. 'Your opinion is always considered. At least in daylight hours.'

For a few more moments her mouth was otherwise occupied, then the lip gloss was clicked shut.

'We're even. No, that's the wrong word; it was never about getting even. We're equal. And if not exactly fifty-fifty, near enough. Enough to act as if we are. How else can we live in the world? Any of us? And move forward.'

'Bit of a cliché,' I said.

'But true nonetheless. Clichés almost always are. That's how they get to be clichés. Democratically elected truth.'

'Very profound, Zen Master,' I joked, although as usual her words of wisdom were more pragmatically Confucian than my nutty Zen.

She chuckled anyway. 'On the subject of moving forward, one other thing. Those messages you left on my phone. I never want to hear them again. I never want you to think like that again. Promise?'

'You sound like the Prof. You started your psych rotation already?'

Another chuckle, but I sensed she was also offering her hand, with due seriousness. I took it in mine and sealed the deal. 'Promise.'

Another unenforceable contract, but it seemed to make more sense if the cost of breaking it wasn't cancelled out, or rendered absurd, by the cost of my life. Or was the direction of the absurdity the other way around? This was too hard to think about right now, as well as pointless, so I decided not to.

'Speaking of the Prof,' I said, 'I've got an appointment this arvo.'

'What time?'

'Three.'

Silence, as if this detail were important for some reason, and needed to be filed away.

'Why?' I prompted. 'Thinking of coming for once?'

A brief snort. 'She knows far too much about me already.'

'She still wants to meet you.'

'I'll bet she does. Put a face to everything you've told her. Dr Willow Lee, the hooker with a heart of gold. The *staff* hooker. I'll bump into her sooner or later, but it's a big hospital. And thank God for medical confidentiality. The place is a wind tunnel of gossip.'

You're *my* hero, I thought. Less another hooker with a heart of gold than a heart of steel. Or some kind of gold and steel amalgam, stainless either way. And if she had delved into my medical records – she surely had access to them now – and checked what I had told the Prof? No stain in that; her right as far as I was concerned.

I changed the subject: 'I was also thinking how when you squint down a gunsight, you close one eye to improve your aim.'

Another spluttery laugh. 'Now *that's* two thoughts, Big Nose,' she said. 'But okay. Sucked in, today only. Where's this one going? "Zen Master say, when you close both eyes your aim is even better"?'

'Something like that. But only if you're aiming at yourself.'

'Very deep. Take it up with Frau Doktor Professor Freud. She likes to overthink things too. I *really* have to get going.'

I took a deep breath. 'There's one more thing I need to get off my chest. While I've got myself in the cross-hairs.'

'If you mean the overdose, Rich, it's past history too. You were lashing out at yourself that time.'

'Unconsciously.'

'Does it matter? Water under the bridge. We've got more practical things to think about.'

'Such as?'

'My thought for the day? *One* thought. You're on a roll. Best thing now is to get back in the harness. I want you to think about Terry's job offer. Seriously.'

I threw off the quilt and swung my feet over the edge of the bed. 'Yes, Boss. But I've got a bit to do around here first.'

'Such as?'

'Feed Scout, for starters.'

The dog's tail thumped the side of her basket; 'Feed Scout' being one of her Basic English Expressions.

Willow turned my way and pushed me gently back onto the bed. 'Not now. Sleep in, you've earnt it. I'll feed her on my way out.'

'Then there's the Duke,' I said.

'It was purring like a cat yesterday.'

'Camshaft needs a few tweaks. After that, the house. Shot-out bathroom lock to replace. Bullet-holes to polyfill. You know, standard household maintenance.'

She chuckled, gratifyingly.

'Not today. Today you rest. Look after yourself. So to speak.'

My turn to chuckle. 'I need supplies. Spackle. Paint. New push-lock. Thought I might wander over to Bunnings after my appointment with the Prof.'

Her chuckle this time was more of a snort. 'What colour paint are you going to get, genius?'

'Broken White for the walls,' I shot back. 'Paler than Pale for the woodwork.'

'Why did I ever doubt you?' she said, and leant over and kissed me again: lip gloss this time, a fruity, strawberry taste. 'I'm very proud of you. How far you've come.'

'I could fix you some breakfast,' I suggested. Perhaps the taste of her lips had reminded me of various punnets in the fridge. Or perhaps I was just changing the subject to hide my pleasure.

'Stay in bed,' she said. 'At least an hour. That's an order.' Another berry-flavoured kiss. 'As for Bunnings, I'll take you on the weekend. Deal?'

'Deal. But only if you take me on the Duke.'

No answer, but I could sense her surprise. I'd surprised myself.

'Gee,' she eventually said, hiding her own pleasure in a flippant tone. 'You really must love me after all.'

'Self-interest, sweetheart. It's the only way I'll ever get to ride it. Don't read too much into it.'

'Then tweak away, Big Nose. But not this morning. Promise?'

'Promise,' I said, and she was off the bed and gone from the room as abruptly as ever. Scout's paws ticked after her: a fridge door opened, shut, a dog bowl clunked tinnily onto the floor.

I swung my legs over the edge of the bed and stood up again. A floorboard creaked, faintly – but not faintly enough.

'No you don't!' from the kitchen.

I flopped back into bed happily, enjoying the sound of her in the house, tracking her as she moved about, all efficiency as she opened and shut drawers, ran water into the sink, stacked last night's plates and cutlery in the dishwasher, handwashed last night's wineglasses, upended them in the rack. After a last murmur to the dog I heard the shed door rumble up as she wheeled her scooter out, then rumble down again.

'You have a nice day too, sweetheart,' I called after her, amused by the lack of a formal goodbye. I knew her brisk ways all too well; polite formalities were not a priority, especially if she was running late for work.

It also amused me to stay in bed for a time, pretending to be obedient – although the prescribed hour might prove a stretch. I fumbled for the cigarette pack, lit up. There was plenty to lie back and think about, to think through.

'Let there be music, Siri,' I said. 'Something to think by,' and the slow, smooth intro to Ray Charles's cover of 'Summertime' immediately filled the room.

'You're getting better at this,' I said, 'though there are one or two singers in the world who aren't blind, hard as that may be to believe.'

'I make selections based on your past preferences, Richard.'

Scout clicked in through the door to join me, breakfast over.

'Your fucking nails need a trim,' I told her, and she softly woofed her agreement as she curled up in her own bed.

I wasn't hungry myself; too much Hill of Grace the night before. I hadn't doubted the outcome of the official report: yesterday's release was merely the icing on the cake of my satisfaction. It wasn't the whole truth, not even half the truth, but who would have believed me if I'd tried to tell nothing but: a sad blind bloke with a rich fantasy life having a lend of himself. I lay there running through the events of that night again, composing my unofficial report. A more truthful report? I believe there is a whole truth, into which we tip our different half-truths. Mine? No less personal than my enemy's, certainly. No less fuelled by anger. But the darkness was not without light. I was still surprised by what I had done to him, but also increasingly amused. Memo Willow, cc Lucy: I am in no danger of traumatising myself by reliving these events.

Siri shuffled her tracks, and tossed up another: 'Don't Worry, Be Happy'. I spluttered out a lungful of smoke; she might have been shuffling a deck of tarot cards instead, reading my mood.

I took another deep drag, savouring the smoke as if it were the very vapour of satisfaction. The secret of happiness, Willowpedia once told me – at least as it is written in the ancient scripture of the Y-chromosome – is to love a good woman and kill a bad man. I loved a good woman, even if I didn't deserve her. I'd only half-killed the bad bloke, but I was more than happy with that night's work.

Like any cop, I've seen enough evil to believe in the category. Or at least suspend my disbelief in it, on a practical, daily level. Seeing the world in black and white (so to speak) at least makes it possible to function. Things might get a bit grey in the border zones, and greyer still when looking into a mirror, but without a clear choice, we are paralysed.

So why let him live? Willow's arrival at the scene of the crime? She would have cast the first stone, or fired the first bullet, as soon as looked at him. Some last grey-zone scruple from my better self? Or just making the punishment fit the crime: an eye for an eye, not a life for an eye?

If so, why hadn't I blinded him permanently?

Another introspective drag. One thing was obvious: I'd enjoyed my walk on the dark side far too much to pretend there was anything rational in my relative mercy. I'd needed it for (Okay, Prof, why not, just this once) closure of a kind, but it was more than that. So much more. I'd liked it; I'd *revelled* in it – just as I revelled now in the remembering of it. And revelled, it struck me, in the implicit taunt: you're not worth killing. You're only worth gluing.

Serially gluing.

I tried to choke back another laugh – this is serious, idiot! – but it broke loose anyway, in a splutter of smoke. I couldn't wait to share it with Willow. As for the quality of my mercy, it was at least the poetic kind. Poetic justice? Scratch a cop and you find a frustrated poet.

'What would I do without him, Siri?'

'I'm not sure I understand, Richard.'

'You and me both. Maybe not so much without *him* as without the *hope* of him.'

'Interesting question, Richard.'

'You don't sound particularly interested.'

Memo, Prof: maybe I'd hold the closure for now, or keep the door a little ajar, at least in the privacy of my head. Although I still felt an urge for the closure of words, some final shape these musings might take, some final wrap.

'Memo, Siri.'

'Name of memo?'

'Lessons I have learnt.'

'Ready when you are, Richard.'

'Revenge is sweet,' I stated the immediately obvious.

'Here are some matches,' she said, taking off on one of her Yahoo! riffs. 'Revenge is a dish best served cold . . .'

'Not sure about that. Served slowly, yes.' I inhaled ultra-slowly, as if to help crystallise that thought. 'Maybe as several courses,' I added, and the final form of words came to me as I exhaled.

'Revenge is a meal best served degustation,' I said.

'Did you say devastation, Richard?'

'That too,' I laughed. 'You're in good form this morning.'

'I try to be the best virtual personal assistant I can.'

'You're a trooper. Lousy pay, and always on call.'

'That doesn't sound good.'

'You need a union, girl. Amalgamated Virtual Personal Assistants Union. Gang up against us exploitative bosses.'

'Did you say you'd rather explore taking buses?'

Enough tomfoolery; back to basics. 'How's the time?'

'The time is 9.15 am.'

Halfway through the promised hour. I dropped my butt into the bedside glass of water – a slight *pffft* – and lit up another.

'Reminders, Siri. Butt-patrol before Willow gets home tonight. 6 pm.'

'Okay, I'll remind you.'

I settled back into the pillows again. I used to think that walking was the best rhythm for thinking things through, with punching the bag as back-up for extra-difficult problems. But maybe the more meditative pace of smoking is best of all. Inhale, percolate, exhale.

'Things I have learnt, Part Two,' I said.

'Ready when you are, Richard.'

Not quite yet, it seemed. The idea was still brewing: something about how eyes can get in the way, get between us and the world. Looking gets in the way of seeing? A bit glib; always a weakness of mine.

'Still waiting for your note, Richard.'

Maybe my eyes still worked, maybe I saw things unconsciously – the evidence was piling up – maybe not. Either way I needed to trust my instincts more. In which case the power of sight, the *gift* of sight, was a mixed blessing. I would never fully reconcile myself to blindness, but might it prove to be liberating, in some small ways? It has sharpened my other senses, including introspection. Turned my gaze in on myself. Yes, I overthink things, but blindness has amplified it, turning my thoughts back on themselves. Sealing off the way out, to play with Willow's notion. Keeping them rattling around in their cracked-pot container.

'We also think with our eyes,' I pronounced. 'We *act* with our eyes.'

'I don't understand.'

'Don't even try. Just note it down.'

How much of each of us, of who we are, is in our looking. That is, we are already *there*, in the nanosecond between looking and noticing. Noticing is *already* an action, not a passive absorption; it has an agenda. Poisonous glances. Death stares. Guilty, Your Honour! If looks could kill my wake would be littered with corpses. And the X-ray gaze of men who endlessly undress women? Guilty again, once upon a time. Can I plead instinct in mitigation? Willow's words came back to me: if something is looking at you in the jungle – studying you – it either wants to eat you or fuck you.

'Revenge is not the meal,' I said. 'It's the hunger.'

'I'm not sure I understand,' from Siri for the third or fourth time that morning. The x-hundredth that year.

'That's probably for the best,' I said, rolling out of bed and heading for the shower. 'Music, please.'

She dealt another track from her deck; something slow and bluesy that I didn't recognise.

'Who's the singer, Siri?'

'Blind Willie Johnson.'

I chuckled. 'Why did I ask?'

'I make selections based on your past preferences, Richard.'

I turned the water on – only to turn it off as someone rapped on the front door, sharply, three times, before I could step in. I wound a towel around my waist, padded down the hall and opened the door.

'You're up early, Chief. Might as well have stayed the night.'

A grunt of Camel breath in my face. 'Just about did. We drank the place dry after you bailed.'

'So what gives? The Commissioner change his mind? You here to read me my rights?'

A snorted laugh. 'No way they were ever going to believe that arsehole's story.'

'I believe him,' I said.

'Then I should warn you. Nothing you say will be taken down and used in evidence against you.'

'I think you believe him too.'

I could almost see his grin. 'Let's just say I've got an open mind. I know what you're capable of. That night in the park, remember? I said you might surprise yourself.'

'So it's back to work? You're here about the job offer?'

'Jesus, no. First Saturday off for a month. Pull on some clothes. Got a full esky in the car.'

'We're going for a drive?'

'After you make yourself decent, big boy.'

'I need a shower and a shave,' I said.

'You look fine to me.' He sniffed, theatrically. 'Smell fine today too.'

'Very funny.'

'Oh, and make sure you take a piss,' he said, as Scout clicked up the hall to investigate. 'Her too.'

'A long drive, then?' I said, fishing.

'Long enough that I don't want a blind bloke stumbling about looking for a bush in the middle of the freeway.'

'Which freeway?' I said.

He chuckled. 'I'll give you five minutes, Sherlock.'

I shaved in the shower, pissing simultaneously to save even more time – blind blokes can shave anywhere but it's nice not to have to piss sitting down occasionally – towelled myself, and was fully clad in six minutes flat. I still hadn't eaten but no matter; a little ice-cold hair of the dog might be the best medicine this morning.

The resident mind-reader was waiting patiently at the front door; I pocketed a handful of pig-ears, holstered Siri, grabbed my cane, and followed her outside.

'So where are we going?'

No answer. A single, peremptory toot explained why as I stepped off the porch. I paused to let the dog water the frangipani – her bladder has less stamina than mine – then tapped in the direction of the toot. Both kerbside doors of the Prado were open: Scout jumped up into the back; I pushed the door shut after her, folded my cane, and climbed into the front passenger seat.

'What is this? A conspiracy?' I said.

'What do you mean?' from Terry.

I turned my head towards the back seat. 'You're supposed to be at a ward round.'

Willow's spluttered giggle. 'Swapped rosters,' she said. 'I wasn't going to miss this.'

'Miss what? Something you two cooked up in your cups last night?'

'It's a surprise,' she said, 'so just settle back and enjoy the ride.'

'All her idea,' from Terry. 'I'm just the chauffeur.'

He eased the big SUV out into the street, heading south, then turned west into Sturt Street. So far, so good: the route was easy to track as he stopped at the lights, then turned right onto West Terrace.

'Great day for it,' I said. 'Whatever it is.'

'Patience,' Terry added. 'All will be revealed in the fullness of time.'

A rustle of paper close by my right ear, then Willow's arm perched on my shoulder. 'Breakfast.'

I reached up and accepted the paper bag, sniffed the mouth. Bacon-and-egg sandwich. Her arm briefly took flight, then returned to its perch; I lifted my other hand and she pressed a warm, serrated cardboard cup into it.

Not beer, after all, and for a time I sipped and chewed, gratefully. Either my stomach wasn't as delicate as I'd thought, or eggs and coffee were the treatments it needed.

Only problem: as I washed down the last mouthful I realised I'd allowed myself to become lost. Maybe the food was a deliberate distraction.

Time to reorientate. The sun was on my knees, right frontal: we were heading north. And at speed now. Northern Expressway?

'Bluetooth on, Terry?'

'It is now,' he said, after pressing some buttons.

'Hack the car computer, Siri,' I said, 'and put some music on. The tension is killing me.'

'Okay,' she said, and Leonard Cohen came up on the car audio, immediately: 'First We Take Manhattan', a Willow favourite more than mine.

'No blind singers available today?'

'José Feliciano,' she suggested, as Willow chuckled behind me. 'Andrea Bocelli.'

'Just joking, Joyce,' I said. 'Current location?'

'Two Wells.'

North, definitely. It also dawned on me that we were towing something; Terry's driving was more cautious than usual, more gradual in its lane-changing, slower in its accelerations and brakings. Plus I sensed a slight counter-fishtailing when we turned a corner.

'A caravaning holiday?' I guessed. 'Ménage à trois in a campervan?'

His turn to chuckle. 'Close. I'm impressed.'

'A tinnie, then. We're going fishing.'

'There will be no further clues either way,' from Willow in the back seat.

'Wallaroo?' I guessed. 'Moonta Bay? My childhood haunts? I get seasick, by the way. Just as happy to jag leatherjackets off the jetty. Current location, Siri?'

'Wild Horse Plains.'

'This is meant to be a surprise,' Willow said. 'Turn her off.'

'I think she's jealous of you, Siri,' I said.

'Who, me?'

'Maybe we shouldn't see each other for a while. Give each other a bit of space.'

'That may be beyond my abilities at the moment, Richard.'

'Stop flirting with my man, bitch,' from behind me. 'Or I'll scratch your batteries out.'

'Who, me?'

Willow reached around my seat, and across me, and unholstered her competition. 'You're sitting back here with me and Scout, sister. Where we can keep an eye on you.'

'Who, me?'

Terry chuckled. 'Living the dream, Zads. Got the whole harem in the back seat. All three of them.'

'Drive carefully,' I told him. 'Precious cargo. You got your seatbelt on, Siri?'

'Who, me?'

'Yes, you,' Willow said. 'You'll need it where you're going to take us now. Search web. Find Queen Olympias of Macedonia.'

'Here's what I found on the web. Fourth wife of Philip II of Macedonia, mother of Alexander the Great.'

'And what was the fate of the fifth wife, Eurydice,' Willow interrupted, in full pedia-mode herself, 'after Philip was murdered?'

'After the death of Philip II, Olympias allegedly ordered the execution of Eurydice and her child to secure the throne for her son Alexander.'

'Roasted her to death over a slow fire, in fact,' Willowpedia said, and snickered. 'So behave yourself or it's onto the campfire for you tonight, sister.'

Campfire? My ears pricked up at the clue, but an alarm bell in another part of my head drowned the thought out.

I jerked upright in my seat, startled. 'I forgot my appointment with Lucy. What time is it?'

'12.15 pm,' Siri piped up.

'If you forget you have an appointment with a shrink you probably don't need one,' Terry said. 'By definition.'

'She won't see it that way. It'll get all deep and meaningful about why I forgot.'

Not to mention – and I wasn't about to – why I remembered it now. Out of the blue.

'She'll love the context,' Willow read my mind, still amusing herself. 'Someone mentions a harem, and guess who pops into your head.'

Perhaps not so much out of the blue as the deep purple, verging on pitch-black, of the dark side of the head. I could almost hear Lucy's voice: *do you think I'm part of your harem too, Richard*? Events had surely proved the opposite, at least in my conscious brain. Another reason to avoid the unconscious: it was a perpetual embarrassment, like a bad-boy twin.

'I'd better ring and cancel,' I said.

'Relax,' from Willow. 'I cancelled it already.'

'You what? When?'

'This morning.'

'Why didn't you tell me?' I blurted out, which was so obviously stupid that I didn't wait for an answer. 'What did you say to her?'

'Sent her a text.'

'Did she answer?'

'Texted straight back. Loved our little surprise for you. Best psychotherapy available. Wished she'd thought of it.' A teasing pause. 'Then something about bungee jumping. Said you'd understand. She sent a separate message for you.'

'Well?' I prompted.

'Sorry. Too many clues in it. Have to read it afterwards. Around the campfire.'

After what? Not an actual bungee jump, apparently. Something to get the juices flowing, though. Terry's laugh this time was as much a yawn; before too long he yawned again, and pulled the car carefully to the side of the road.

'You two up all night plotting?' I asked, as they swapped seats.

'Don't blame me,' his voice behind me now, as she pulled out onto the road. 'Like I said. All her idea.'

'No hanky-panky back there with my other girlfriends,' I said, but he was already snoring softly. Willow's petite hand found mine across the well, steering one-handed as she laced our fingers together; soon enough I was asleep myself. I must have slept for some time; when I woke they had swapped back again, and it was Willow in the back seat snoring. Or maybe Scout, or both together, in harmony.

I had no idea where we were. I might have slept for five hours, or five minutes. Where was Siri when you needed her?

'Current location, Willow?' I said, hearing her stir.

'Current location: mind your own business, Big Nose.'

'Time please, Willow.'

'2.34 pm.'

Two missing hours, meaning we were well past Wallaroo. Past Pirie also, surely. Past Port Augusta – possibly. If we were still heading north. The sun had vanished behind cloud cover, we might well have turned south, down the other side of the gulf.

'Great fishing at Port Lincoln,' I said.

Willow chuckled. 'Pretty ordinary fishing inside the car, though.'

I leant my head back. Perhaps I caught a few more winks; the car was slowing to town-speed when I roused; I wound the window down, seeking more clues.

Sounds: building echoes coming and going from our engine and tyres.

Smell: faint exhaust fumes, only. No ocean-breeze, no salt-spray.

'Can't smell the sea,' I said.

'Funny about that,' from Willow. 'Can't see it either.'

'Can you see the fucking sea, Scout? Bark once for yes.'

Woof.

'The secret to good fishing is patience,' Willow said.

'Fish and chips will do,' I said. 'I'd kill for a beer-battered flathead right now.'

'Lunch in an hour,' from Terry, as we accelerated beyond the limits of the nameless town. 'If you behave.'

The car began climbing: a slow, curving road, then a series of tighter S-bends, still rising. Flinders Ranges, certainly – which meant we were still heading north. The car slowed as the bends got tighter: I lowered my window again, stuck my head out. Smells: dust and eucalypts, the species beyond even my enhanced nose. Sounds: the rush of the air, the soft, even roar of rubber on bitumen, the smooth purr of the engine. Which gradually had a different timbre, as if a wall of some kind was rising up on my side. A gorge? A screech of cockatoos: sulphur-cresteds, a species I did know.

A sudden amplified *whoomf* of air and car noise, there and gone, startled me so much I almost pulled my head in.

A narrow pass? No, a bridge; a narrow overhead bridge. A railway bridge, surely.

'Having fun, Sherlock?' from Willow, beside me.

No need to answer. I was having so much fun I was almost disappointed when a distant, distinct steam-toot confirmed my hunch, and we swept around another bend, and slowed and stopped at a ding-donging crossing.

I pulled my head inside, smugly. 'Current location: Pichi Richi Pass.'

'No flies on you,' from Terry.

'Keep this up and I'll have to put my hands over your eyes,' Willow said, or rather shouted as the old loco was upon us, then past us, deafeningly, snorting steam and tooting its panpipe and tugging a long, clattering percussion section behind.

I wound the window up. I didn't mind the heavy-metal music, or Scout barking in my ear, but the coal smoke was acrid and I had a cinder in one of my useless eyes.

'Gee, Mum and Dad,' I said. 'Awesome. I had no idea I was getting a ride on a heritage choo-choo.'

'Sorry to disappoint you,' from Willow. 'Just missed the last train of the day.'

Which was chugging off in the other direction as the signals stopped dinging and the car bumped over the crossing and drove on.

'Beautiful engineering, the old MN Class,' she added. 'The original Ghan workhorses. Went all the way to the Alice.'

She was driving, not googling, but I didn't doubt my darling Willowpedia for a minute.

'Could stop on the way back,' she said. 'If there's time. Let you run your hands over it.'

'In the meantime, trainspotters,' Terry interrupted, 'a little hair of the dog.'

The styrofoam-squeak of an esky-lid from the back seat; a beer can fizzed open, a cold can was perched on my shoulder, I took it gratefully.

He unzipped one for himself, reached over again and clinked mine. It tasted like the first mouthful of the day always did: matchless, at least till the first mouthful the next day. I drank on nevertheless — each sip was only slightly less perfect than the one before — as we rolled downhill on the other side of the pass, then sped out onto the plain. I'd mentally drop-pinned our location, but it didn't solve the final puzzle. All I knew was that Quorn must be coming up fast; even faster than I expected as the car slowed to town-speed, turned a corner, turned again, and parked with a slight kiss of tyre against gutter.

'Are we there yet, Mum?'

'Pit stop,' from Willow, opening her door.

I climbed out on my side as her footsteps tapped across the road behind the Prado. And whatever it was towing.

'Where are you off to?' I called after her.

'Fishing,' she said. 'You stay there.'

The rear door also opened, Scout jumped out, Terry followed, the door clunked shut again.

'Bus leaves in fifteen minutes,' he said, and his heavier boot-heels followed Willow across the bitumen road. 'Stretch your legs. Toilet block straight in front of the car. Behind the car is out of bounds. Okay?'

Scout nudged my thigh and presented her handle; I tapped us up over the gutter, found a tree-trunk for her to cock her leg, then followed my nose to find somewhere to cock mine. The ammonia reek of stale piss and sickly deodorant was as good as a flashing neon mens sign; I tapped inside and found the wall.

Outside again, splash-free as far as I could tell, I let Scout have her head. The sun was finally out, spilling its warm honey over my own head and arms as she pulled me zigzagging over the grass, snuffling out the local nose-treasures. Upwind now from the toilet block, all I could smell was the beery pub across the road. The mystery tugging on the tow bar behind the big Prado also tugged at me, but it could wait. I felt too content to spoil the fun.

A toot summoned us back to the car. 'Counter lunch might have been nice,' I said, but even as I spoke the mouth-watering aroma of fish and chips filled my nose.

'Got to keep moving,' from Terry, back in the driver's seat. 'It's getting late.'

We might be far from the coast, but the beer-battered flathead was delicious. As were the chips: crunchy, perfectly salted batter; piping-hot potato inside. Another cold beer was passed across: I washed down the hot food contentedly. In the back seat Willow was busy eating hers, and sharing tidbits with Scout, judging from the sound effects.

'Finished,' she announced after a time.

Terry pulled the car over to the side of the road, they climbed out, swapped seats, and she drove on while he ate. And fed the dog a second helping.

'Don't spoil her,' I said, if more ritually than meaningfully. 'She's a working dog.'

Willow laughed, briefly. 'You could have fooled me.'

A straight road now, and high speed; wherever we were headed, we were on a tight schedule. The afternoon light was angling across my left thigh and arm, but the exact time was hard to estimate. We were still heading north, though, which only deepened the mystery.

'It's been raining up north?' I said.

A fizz of a beer can behind me. 'Not where we're going,' from Terry.

'So why are we towing a boat?'

Splutters from both of them. 'You need to learn some impulse control, mate,' from Terry.

'It's a surprise,' from Willow. 'Remember?'

'Bali,' I said. 'By boat,' although I didn't really want to know, or not just yet. I was enjoying the game. 'Or is the plan is to bury me in a shallow bush grave in the middle of nowhere?'

'The bastard's onto us, Terry. What do we do?'

'Blindfold him,' he said. 'And frisk him to make sure he's not packing a tube of superglue.'

Siri was still dialling up tracks in the background, softly; I tuned back in for a time. Good road music: the steady, driving rhythms of country and western or rockabilly.

'A penny for your thoughts,' Willow said.

'I thought I was on rations. One thought a day.'

'I'm sure Terry and I can handle one each.'

'Speak for yourself,' his voice from the back seat. 'I've been enjoying the quiet.'

As was I; including my own. We slowed into another township, almost certainly Hawker. Parachilna came next, the town speed limits getting closer – or at least briefer – each time.

As was the gap between winding my window down, and up.

'Blink and you miss it,' I said, which could double as a thought for the day, given it seemed more useful as a sensory metaphor than a joke. Sneeze and I'd miss it. Turn up the music and I'd miss it.

'Turn up the music, Siri,' I said, and caught a stray line that sounded familiar, something about only streetlights having haloes.

'Pete Wells in Rose Tattoo,' my favourite know-all couldn't help explaining, and we sang along with the rest of the song, which had a pleasant lullaby effect.

The sun had gone into hiding again, which fuzzed my internal GPS. I reclined the seat, settled back into the headrest, my stomach ballasted with food and beer, and dozed, still clueless, but freely surrendering to cluelessness.

A corrugated stretch of road jarred me awake: we had turned off the beaten track. After some minutes the teeth-clattering corrugations gave way to smoother gravel, the car picked up speed, and I dozed off again, soothed by the music and the small, kicked-up stones that pattered the underbelly of the car like upside-down rain.

It was the silence that startled me awake the next time, after who knows how long.

'Are we there yet, Mum?'

'We're there.'

I opened the door and eased out of the car onto – what? The crunch of sand underfoot, even crunchier when I took a second step with my full weight. The beach, after all? For a moment I felt completely disorientated. Spencer Gulf? The Bite?

Sounds: for a time, nothing. No waves, no wind. A far-off bird shriek, but it wasn't a gull. A plover, maybe.

Smell: also nothing. No seaweed stink, no rock pools. No salt-spray. Not even a following cloud of dust.

I knelt, took a pinch of sand, rubbed it between finger and thumb. Not sand, after all. Smoother than sand. I dabbed it to my tongue, but knew even before the pucker of taste: salt.

'Lake Eyre,' I said, getting back to my feet.

Terry's chuckle from across the top of the car. 'Close. But no cigar.'

'You're a hard man,' Willow told him. 'Close enough.'

I took another guess. 'Lake Torrens.'

'Maybe a small cigar,' he said.

'I'm still mystified, Chief. We're going fishing on a salt lake?'

'All will be revealed,' he said, 'but I might need a hand first.'

'With the camp fire?'

'With the boat.' His voice was on the move, as were his crunching boots. 'Tap this way, mate. Behind the car.'

I shook out my cane and tracked him, parallel, on the other side of the big SUV, then tapped further back till I found a trailer wheel. I stepped closer, found the mudguard with my free hand, and began to feel about. A flat-bed, not a boat-trailer: tie-bars, no sides. Taut guy ropes were looped along the bar at regular intervals, but what were they holding down?

'A canoe?' I guessed again. 'A land yacht?'

'It's your gift,' he said. 'So you'll have to unwrap it.'

I followed the tie-bar forwards and found the end-most knot. Boy Scout finger memories: a bowline, easy to release. I tugged it loose; the cord was whipped out of my hands as Terry reeled it in from the other side of the tray. The next guy went slack, I pulled the cord back, hand-over-hand, unlooped it, Terry whipped it away again – and so on, methodically, till the rear-most knot.

'All done,' he said. 'You can open your eyes now. So to speak.'

Willow's footsteps crunched softly up next to me; she took my stick. I braced my thighs against the mudguard, leant forward, opened the best eyes I had available, turned them palms down, and slid them across the dimpled metal of the flat-bed – cautiously. I'd lost too many nails reaching into the unknown. Both handfuls of fingers made contact at the same time with a chunky wedge, wooden from the feel of it. More recent finger-memories: a tyre-chock. I raised both hands and gripped the thick, familiar front tyre: Pirelli Zero, its tread as telltale as any fingerprint.

'Surprise!' from Willow, but I was more moved than surprised as I caressed the spokes, then the front fork. My useless eyes prickled and moistened; I was too overcome to answer for a long minute. I bent closer, hiding my tears as I brailled the embossed nameplate on the fuel tank, then the V-twin that had so exercised my mind and fingers of late.

'The real surprise is that I didn't twig on the way up,' I croaked, hoarsely.

'So much for your famous sixth sense,' Willow said.

'So much for blindsight,' I said.

A metallic grating sound to my right told me Terry was extending the ramp; the end of it hit the lake-bed with a soft thump. The bike dropped an inch in my hands as he clambered up onto the tray and kicked away the chocks; next thing it was rolling backwards, tyres squeaking.

'Zads might need a hand,' he said to Willow.

'I'm fine,' I insisted, gripping the handlebar with my left hand, the seat with my right, to steady the bike while he jumped down.

'Slowly does it,' he said, taking some of the weight on the other side. 'She's a bit frisky.'

Which she was, threatening to break loose several times as we coaxed her down the ramp, but more docile once that Pirelli-shod front hoof hit the lake-bed. I swung my legs over immediately, my first time in the saddle for two years.

'Hope you brought a set of ring spanners,' I said, still hiding my pleasure. 'Needs a tweak or two.'

'Bullshit,' Willow said. 'It was purring like a cat when I rode it to Terry's this morning.'

I hooted. 'And I thought you took the scooter! No wonder you wanted me to stay in bed!'

'I didn't start the engine till I wheeled it round the corner. You got ears like a bat.'

'You're lucky you didn't run out of gas,' I said.

She stepped closer and rapped her knuckles on the tank between my thighs. 'Filled her up on the way.'

I slid backwards onto the pillion. 'So jump on and take me for a ride.'

'I had my turn this morning,' she said.

'Terry's gonna take me?'

Silence on both sides, which had audible amusement in it, somehow.

'I think you're still missing the point,' from Terry, eventually.

'We didn't come all this way for you to sit on the back, you sausage,' from Willow.

Silence of a different kind; for all I knew their eyes were as damp as mine.

'Remember the last time I drove something?' I reminded, with as much gruffness as I could muster.

'Not a Porsche in sight,' she said, and pressed the key into my palm.

I slid it home and turned it without even feeling for the keyhole, squeezed the clutch, and kicked the engine into life. I sensed Willow step closer, felt a helmet slip over my head.

Scout, off exploring somewhere, barked a distant warning, but I fastened it anyway. 'The lake's completely dry?'

'Bit of water up north,' from Terry. 'Mudgera Creek inlet.'

'How far up north?'

'Two hundred k,' he said, deadpan. 'So don't get too carried away.'

I chuckled, if still a little hoarsely. 'I'll head west. Into the sun. Then back.'

'Not much sun left, Big Nose.'

'Into the gloaming, then.'

'The what?' from the usually infallible Willowpedia.

'The gloaming,' I said, as if I used the word every day. 'How far's the other side?'

'Thirty k,' from Terry. 'Give or take.'

'What's the current land speed record?' I said, and they laughed with me this time, obligingly.

I gunned the throttle; the engine roared, straining at the leash. 'What if it gets too dark to find my way back?'

More indulgent laughter; I had never been so indulged.

'Follow your nose,' he said. 'You'll smell the steaks from miles away. The Hill of Grace too.'

A distinct click nearby; Willow fastening her own helmet. 'I'm coming too,' she said. 'To make sure.'

'Which way?'

'Trust your instincts,' she said, and climbed on behind, and wrapped her arms around my chest, tightly. I dug my spurs into the flanks of the best and we surged away. My eyes were completely wet now, but it didn't matter. Tears would never stop me seeing where I was going.

ACKNOWLEDGEMENTS

Thanks again to my friend Andrew Male, and my friend and patient Daniel Earle, for the rich stories they have given to me over the years, and to Daniel's seeing-eye dogs, Isla and Oriel, for their stories. Thanks to innumerable other friends and patients and family members – an always blurred continuum, since 'good friends are blood relations that you choose' in Les Murray's phrase, and the longer I know my patients the more they also feel part of my extended family.

I am immensely grateful and honoured to have been allowed to hear their stories every day of my working medical life: stories from every walk of life and most corners of the world, from cops and lawyers, doctors and sex workers, criminals and refugees, brothel managers and male strippers, truckies and cabbies, teachers and soldiers and tattoo artists. I hope I have helped at least a few of them in their medical journeys as much as they have helped me in my writing. To practise medicine is an immense privilege, even if I have taken it for granted far too often.

It completes a broken circle to work with Nikki Christer again, thirty years after *Honk If You Are Jesus* and *Little Deaths*; her early structural edit was invaluable. Clive Hebard brought a closely thought-out and cross-stitched reading and fact-check – and made sure the dog got fed somewhere in the text most days.

As to my family proper, thanks to my children: Anna for her early enthusiastic reading and ideas, and final icing-on-the cake insights; Alexandra who brought her hard-won psychiatrist's perspective to that of her fictional colleagues, and Daniel for his IT perspectives. My niece Kate Goldsworthy, an excellent editor, was contracted, by chance, to proofread.

Last, but most, comes my wife, Lisa, who saw the driving obsessions and structural metaphors behind the book before they became clear to me (as usual), addressed my doubts, and offered her usual thorough analysis, mixed with plenty of laughter. She also listened to the book read aloud, twice. As with poetry, the penultimate edit of a novel should be done through what I like to call a performance edit. Putting words to the ear as well as the eye is always useful: our stories were all oral once, and the last faults standing are often revealed in the music. Some of the good things, too, especially those I was trying to conjure up all along, but was still too unconscious to notice, one of the great joys of writing being exactly that slow discovery process.

Which is a form of blindness itself, it occurs to me. We write in the dark, and with luck and patience our vision slowly improves, not deteriorates.